P9-BZQ-425

THEY HAD
ONE CHANCE IN A MILLION
TO SURVIVE THE KILLER STORM

Within the airplane the roar of engines and the flailing scream of propellers mixed with the rush of the wind, the groan of metal, the sounds of rocking impact, the shuddering of the huge structure.

It was a demonic symphony, a fitting orchestration to the madness of where they were and what they were trying to do . . .

They had to punch into the air . . . climb fast enough to clear the ridges that were consumed in snow and darkness all around them. They were squeezing, praying, pulling . . . If they could make that left turn . . . A sudden shock turned them white . . .

WINGBORN
BY MARTIN CAIDIN

Bantam Books by Martin Caidin
Ask your bookseller for the books you have missed

AQUARIUS MISSION
SAMURAI! (with Saburo Sakai and Fred Saito)
WHIP
WINGBORN

WINGBORN

MARTIN CAIDIN

WINGBORN
A Bantam Book / February 1979

Cover art copyright © 1979 by Bantam Books

All rights reserved.
Copyright © 1979 by Martin Caidin.
This book may not be reproduced in whole or in part, by
mimeograph or any other means, without permission.
For information address: Bantam Books, Inc.

ISBN 0-553-10937-5

Published simultaneously in the United States and Canada

Bantam Books are published by Bantam Books, Inc. Its trade-
mark, consisting of the words "Bantam Books" and the por-
trayal of a bantam, is Registered in U.S. Patent and Trademark
Office and in other countries. Marca Registrada. Bantam
Books, Inc., 666 Fifth Avenue, New York, New York 10019.

PRINTED IN THE UNITED STATES OF AMERICA

For long hours through our nights, for always being there when she was needed, for love. This book is for DeeDee.

WINGBORN

1

He saw the flash of yellow first. With every passing second the winged shape took on clearer definition, and now he could see the big floatplane sliding expertly down just above the carpeting forest of the mountainside. A smile tugged the corner of his mouth. For a moment, sun and light had played their trick on him; he had seen a great yellow butterfly reaching for the ground. From across the lake rolled gentle thunder. He liked that; the pilot wasted no energy, easing with delicate grace down the gravity hill.

Harold Archer sighed. His fingers tingled with sensory memories of caressing throttle and yoke. Too long ago, really. The stiffening of joints during the years between—well, never mind. At least he understood the sensations going on within the approaching machine. Silvered floats kissed water and sprayed white plumes to each side. The aircraft came closer to dockside, the pilot playing wind and machinery and momentum to a smooth rubbing of metal to wood.

The propeller ground to a halt, and the sound of small waves against floats and dock emerged again. The cabin door opened and the pilot came into view, a slender and attractive woman, dark-haired, with high cheekbones—thirty-three years old, he knew. A flashing smile and a fawnlike grace.

"Hi!" she called.

He smiled and waved back.

In moments the floatplane was secured to the dock. She stood on one float, not moving. He had the feeling that she was waiting for earthly time to dispel the last sensations of her flight.

"Miss Brandon?" he called.

She waved again. She would have been astonished if

she'd had any idea of how much he knew about her. He had come a long way to see Kate Brandon, and he had spent a long time learning about her. But she knew none of this, and he carried on according to his own well-laid plans. He moved forward slowly to greet her. She took his hand with a gentle but surprising strength.

"My name is Harold Archer. I'm very pleased to meet you." He gestured to a car at the top of a rise behind them. "My wife is with me."

She nodded to the white-haired man. "What can I do for you, Mr. Archer?"

They walked slowly along the wooden surface of the dock, and he welcomed the warming sun. His slightly stooped walk, his unhurried movement concealed sharp eyes and the careful study he was making. "I understand you hire out as a guide, Miss—"

"Kate will do fine, Mr. Archer."

"Kate it is, then." He hesitated. "You, ah, do hire out, from what I understand?"

"Yes, sir," she told him. "Tell me what you have in mind."

He smiled. "Your assistance. And your advice," he added quickly. "In fact, Miss—sorry, Kate—in fact, Kate, we'd like to place ourselves completely in your hands. My wife and I would like a trip for several days where we could simply relax and fish a little. Some out-of-the-way place, you understand."

He chuckled and gestured at his own body. "The bones aren't what they used to be, Kate. Roughing it is not what we'd like. But some place we could reach easily enough by your airplane. A campsite that's in the wild, with as many amenities as you feel could be accommodated." He stopped and looked directly at her. "It would be entirely up to you."

"There's an island about ninety miles from here, Mr. Archer. East-southeast. It's part of the Chugach National Forest. The area is mostly islands in Prince William Sound. They have one island with campsites and, well, I do recommend the amenities."

His smile came easily. "I felt we would be in good hands. But, you said there were campsites. Plural, I mean. I'd hoped we could be—"

"You won't see another human being, Mr. Archer. Except maybe in a plane going overhead or in a boat. But there are cabins, and they'll do better than tenting gear."

He understood she was reckoning his age and that of his wife. And their experience. He nodded slowly.

She seemed almost to read his mind. "Going off into any remote area in Alaska without experience, or extensive equipment, isn't wise, Mr. Archer."

"Yes, I can see that. Can you arrange for the fishing gear, whatever else we might require?"

"I can take care of it all and work out a single price for everything."

"Thank you. That would relieve us greatly." He touched her arm. "If I may say so, Kate, you appear to have made a quick decision about myself and Mrs. Archer. You seem to be very cautious. For us, I mean."

Her laughter was pleasant. "If you have experience, Mr. Archer, you have your own equipment. You've come to trust it. If you're renting—" She shrugged, and his chuckle followed her gesture.

She took his arm as they climbed the short hillside to an office that overlooked the lake. "Would you and your wife like some coffee? You may as well relax while I ask you the rest of the questions."

"More?"

"Yes, sir."

He brought Mrs. Archer in from the car. They were pleased and impressed with the young woman's meticulous attention to detail. She noted anything that might develop into a serious medical problem while they were away from doctors. "This will go on file with a central communications office," she explained. "I want to be certain you also have any medication you might require. And that you're not allergic to anything that might do you more harm than good." Finally, she put aside her notebook. "You would like to catch your own dinner?"

Evelyn Archer smiled. "My dear, I may be old, but I'm still a whiz with trout over an open fire."

"Good," Kate Brandon told them, "because I've just become your first customer, Mrs. Archer."

She explained everything she did, and the elderly couple delighted in her running commentary. Kate let the breeze carry them slowly from the dock before bringing in power to the floatplane. As she went through her checklist prior to takeoff, she called out each step—why she moved the controls a certain way, the reason for checking magnetos independently, why she pulled full carburetor heat, why they turned into the wind as her hand went smoothly forward and thunder rolled back from the engine, now under full throttle. The Howard floatplane rocked gently, and spray hissed to each side as they picked up speed. She held back pressure to the yoke, then eased forward, and they were "on the step"—racing swiftly over the light ripples of the lake. Only the sudden end to the trembling of metal floats against the water told them they were airborne. Kate eased the Howard to eight hundred feet and reduced power as she leveled off.

"Enjoy the ride," she told them. "It's quite beautiful from here."

It was. Islands everywhere, almost all thickly covered with trees. Several times Evelyn Archer exclaimed aloud at the sight of bear or moose along shorelines. A bright red biplane came into sight, passed to their right, and Kate rocked her wings. The Archers waved as the other aircraft did the same.

Then they were sliding down from the smooth morning sky. The Howard sailed to the dock of the island Kate had picked for their three days "in the wild."

She set them up in a comfortable cabin; helped bring firewood; assured that their meals were plentiful, their dress adequate; and fussed over Evelyn Archer's required medication twice daily. They shared their meals, although Kate insisted they have the cabin to themselves, and she slept in a small tent nearby. They rose at first light each day to enjoy the fishing. The Archers refused to have a thing to do with hunting. "There's no need, child," the older woman reassured her. "We've never been people to kill animals without reason. And here," she gestured to the lush woodlands, "there's neither need nor reason."

The rifle remained with Kate's gear in the tent. Until

their third and final night on the island, when her sharp senses picked up crackling undergrowth and a snuffling sound that brought her instantly alert. Silently, she came slowly from the tent, her powerful rifle held before her. In the night gloom she waited, listening. Then she saw the thick shape, a large bear pushing its immense paw against the cabin door.

If the animal, no doubt more curious than dangerous, were to enter the cabin, the Archers would face a terrifying sight on awakening. Panic would be their most likely reaction. Panic, and screams. Enough to transform a curious animal into a frightened beast that would strike blindly.

Kate ran forward, shouting, hoping to distract the bear. A huge head turned to stare at her, then moved slightly in response to new sounds from within the cabin.

My God, thought Kate, they're awake. They'll be moving in a moment. She brought up the rifle, fired a shot into the air. The beast swung away from the door, facing her. It reared to its full height, menacing, an engine of destruction. Kate held the rifle steady. If she had to fire again it would be for keeps. And against an animal of that size, she would need the full clip.

The bear stared at her; she stood her ground, the rifle aimed, unmoving. She knew these creatures and she knew their way. Every animal, unless crazed or cornered, prefers the path of least resistance. And if this one knew the smell of man and the sound of a rifle, it would—

The huge body lowered, the bear gave a final grunt and shambled off into the darkness. Kate wiped the perspiration from her upper lip, trembling slightly. A lamp came on in the cabin and she saw the Archers standing by the open door.

"Kate! Are you all right, child?"

Kate Brandon smiled. God bless that lovely old woman.

"I'm fine," she called back.

Morning came with a fine cool breeze blowing across the water. Evelyn Archer panfried the trout caught by her husband only the hour before.

But it was an angry young woman who shared their breakfast. "The engine," she said, holding her coffee mug in both hands. "I think it's a broken fuel line. It may take me a while."

"Can I help?"

She nodded to Harold Archer. "I can use it. It takes quite a balancing act to get to that engine from the floats. An extra hand for the tools would be neat."

He grinned at her. "Neat it is. Whenever you're ready."

Three hours later they sliced their spray furrow along the waters of the sound and lifted easily into the air. Kate gave them the scenic route on the way back, cutting along the western edge of Montague Island, then flying a long sweep past Seward and a breathless treetop run through the valleys by Moose Pass. She went slowly for altitude by Arctic Valley, and the flaps came down as she turned into the wind to land on Strenite Lake where she berthed her floatplanes.

"It's been like a dream," Evelyn Archer sighed.

Her husband nodded, squeezing Kate's hand. "We've been wanting to do this for twenty years. You've made it come true for us. We both thank you."

The Archers spent an extra day with her. "You're a fascinating young woman," Harold Archer told her. "And we, well, we've nothing to rush back to Kansas for. Would you mind showing us how your airline works?"

"It's not really an airline, Mr. Archer. We do a great deal of charter flying, air taxi, some specialized runs, that sort of thing."

"If you could spare the time, we'd very much appreciate it."

"I'd be delighted."

There was no question of her pride. Nor of her skills, or what she had accomplished. Both her parents, Vance and Emily Brandon, had been killed a few years ago. "One of those accidents that, well, no matter how good you are or what you're flying, sometimes the world just catches up with you." She took a deep breath. "They were two very beautiful people and they lived a full, wonderful life."

Kate gestured to take in the view from her office. They were several miles outside Chugach. Anchorage and Spenard lay farther west. Outside the window stretched a runway seven thousand feet in length. Chugach Airport years before had been a military base; now military activity centered on Elmendorf Air Force Base, just outside Anchorage. "They left me Brandon Airways, along with fourteen planes and some very good customers."

"I still can't get over it," said Evelyn Archer, looking at the hangars and airplanes. "I mean, a woman your age, running this whole business, and flying all those complicated machines. In my day, Kate, all this would have been impossible. And the thought, the very thought, of handling those monsters out there—" She shook her head and shuddered.

"If it's got wings, Mrs. Archer," Kate laughed, "I'll fly it."

2

Harold Archer scribbled quickly in a notebook, tapped his pen several times against the page, then nodded to himself, as if arriving at a decision, and activated a small tape recorder. He spoke steadily into the microphone, completed his thoughts, switched off the recorder. Just as he turned to his wife they were jolted mildly by turbulence shaking the big jetliner.

"I've completed my notes. Full preliminary report. I'll have enough time to dictate the final report and have it typed up for the meeting." He slid the tape recorder and notebook into his attaché case.

"Would you like a drink?" he asked his wife.

"Vodka martini. I could use a double."

He pressed the stewardess call button. His wife took his hand. "You know, she really is a remarkable young woman."

His chuckle came quietly. "I can hardly remember back to the time when thirty-three wasn't young."

"It's been young for a long time, Harold."

"Yes," he admitted, "it has. And what you said is true. Kate Brandon is remarkable."

"I don't know whether I was more impressed by her flying skill or the way she stood up to that animal." Evelyn Archer sighed. "And to think she was protecting us."

"It all goes into the report," her husband reminded her.

"As it should." They paused as their drinks were brought. The elderly couple had slipped into a professional role that Kate Brandon would never have recognized.

"Harold, do you think she had any idea about your being a pilot?"

He shook his head. "No. I managed to fumble quite well." He laughed and held up his drink in toast to years past. "Although a few times I wanted to ask her to let me take the controls. That country, Evelyn. It makes the blood run faster. I had this—this tremendous urge to take that plane right down, below the trees, and—"

She rested her hand on his arm. "Easy does it, Harold."

He sighed, leaned back. "Twelve thousand hours, and a heart muscle twitched, and they pulled my ticket."

"It still makes you an excellent judge."

"Of course, of course. And that girl—that woman, if you like—is beautiful. My dear, some pilots fly; others, like Kate Brandon, wear their airplanes like birds wear feathers."

They sipped their drinks quietly until the jetliner eased into its long descent for Kennedy International Airport. Picking up their last words, Harold Archer turned to his wife. "I don't think there's any question. She's the one."

"I don't know about you, you old fogy, but she's been my choice right along."

They smiled at one another. They had been an investigative team for years, and they always delivered.

In New York, they checked into a suite in the Americana Hotel, shook off the mildly upsetting effects of jet lag, and went to work. Evelyn Archer took film to a lab that would do immediate processing and printing work and deliver the finished product to the hotel. Harold Archer worked steadily with two bonded secretaries, keeping close survey of his report as the final sheets were typed and collated. On the third day of their return, precisely at 10:00 A.M., they walked into Suite 1213 of 666 Fifth Avenue and announced their presence to the receptionist of Markham Mining and Industrial Corporation. With the Archers were their reports, a series of eight-by-ten glossy photographs, a number of color slides, and several hundred feet of film. They waited several minutes and then were guided

to a large conference room. A slide projector and a film
projector were ready and waiting, as were several secretaries.

Several minutes later, another secretary came into
the room. "Mrs. Markham appreciates your punctual-
ity, Mr. and Mrs. Archer. It will be a few minutes before the group will be ready for your presentation.
Would you please come with me? We have coffee if
you'd like."

"Thank you, miss."

Harold Archer and his wife followed the secretary
to the lounge. They both knew the move was a ploy.
When they returned to the conference room, where
they'd left their reports and film, twelve seats would be
occupied. By twelve women. Of whom only one would
have anything to do with the Markham Mining and
Industrial Corporation. That would be Sarah Markham
herself.

The office was a convenient blind for completely
private business meetings of the American Congress
Party. And the ACP was determined to bring women
into the forefront of national politics.

Harold Archer knew people well enough, as a professional observer and investigator, to recognize the
characteristics of the women Sarah Markham had chosen to work with: strength, intelligence, drive, money
—and a sobering ability and willingness to function as
a team. With those elements and a goal clearly in mind,
they were already a power to be reckoned with.

Harold Archer didn't know the details. But he knew
a great deal about Sarah Markham, for it was she who
had retained him and his wife to do a thorough inves-
tigation of Sarah Markham. A clever move, he had
learned. He hadn't thought so at first - because it all
seemed so stupid, but it made more sense as time went
along. The Archers were experts. Sweet white-haired
Evelyn Archer had behind her fifteen years of dangerous espionage work. They found out things about Sarah
Markham and about her senator husband that paled
Mrs. Markham's face and thinned her lips. But what
they did report to the woman also permitted her to

start closing doors and putting her business and political house in order.

That had been the first step. Protect their own enclave by hiring professionals to penetrate. Behind all this was their goal, of course. Women in the political mainstream. More specifically, a definite goal that demanded financing, planning, leadership, and, when necessary, some old-fashioned backroom clout.

Their plan insisted on meticulous preparation and control of groups, forces, and events that contributed to political life in the country.

If they were successful, they would see a woman on the political slate for vice-president of the United States in the 1980 elections.

The long-sought goal. A reachable goal.

The country wasn't ready for a woman in command at the White House. Not yet. Too many opinions had to be molded, changed, even created. But the number two position would do well for now.

The problem, strangely enough, lay more with female constituents than with male. Reality proved—once tabulated into counted votes—that women at the polls did not pursue what they shouted at meetings and conventions. Because what many men did not accept was itself taken as a guideline by their women.

Sarah Markham understood all this in exquisite detail. No single event would bring about the enormous shift in attitude that was necessary. For the seat of vice-president to be made available as an accepted goal by women the nation over, Sarah Markham's party must create an air of acceptance for women in many areas where public opinion remained dominantly masculine oriented.

Harold and Evelyn Archer had already proved their loyalty to Sarah Markham, and their effectiveness in their assignments would lie in direct proportion to their own understanding of what was needed. As such, they became privy to the innermost thoughts of Mrs. Markham—who personally disdained being called Ms. She was an impressive, even a stunning woman. A large woman who retained enviable proportion and grace to her body. Her mind, to the Archers, was a mixture of woman, steel trap, and computer, and she possessed an intrinsic appreciation of the factors that motivate human thinking and decision making.

"We've got to follow a broadband approach to reach a singular objective," she had explained some time before to the Archers. "We need to bring before the public, with careful exposure, a number of women actually performing roles that right now women believe only men can do. It's a fine line, Mr. and Mrs. Archer, and it's vital for you to understand it. Your job will be to search for a certain woman."

Harold Archer's questions were brief, quiet, to the point. "The category?"

"A woman who can fly an airliner. No, that's not enough. A woman who can fly an airplane the size of a commercial airliner, who qualifies to fly that machine, and," Sarah Markham paused for emphasis, "who will fit into our program. If we—you two—can find that woman for us, we will make certain she has the opportunity to break the sex barrier in the airlines."

The Archers appreciated what Sarah Markham had indicated so clearly. They did not simply want a woman as an airlines captain—they wanted a woman who could earn her way into the seat.

"I would have thought you would want something like a female astronaut," Evelyn Archer said quietly.

Sarah Markham smiled. "That was our first reaction, Mrs. Archer. But it's a false attraction. Esoteric, but not realistic. There has already been a woman astronaut. Valentina Tereshkova, the Russian who flew in space in one of their Vostoks. It was an admirable feat, but it was also self-defeating. Valentina was a factory worker and a skydiving enthusiast. She was young and she was healthy and she was excellent material for Pavlovian training. It wasn't necessary for her to do a thing during her space flight. Most of the controls were automatic or operated from the ground. I'm not detracting from her training or her courage, but the conclusions are not confidence-building.

"Do you understand the point? No one else risked

a thing on her flight. *No one depended on the outcome
of her performance.* And that was, and remains, the
crucial issue. Orbiting the earth in a space-going boiler
is hardly conducive to polling votes, and that is what
we must always keep in mind."

Harold Archer nodded. "You're talking about a
woman qualified as an ATP."

"Explain that, please."

Archer coughed to clear his throat. "The old term,
Mrs. Markham, was ATR. It stands for Airline Transport Rating. They changed it to Airline Transport Pilot, but it still means the same thing. The, ah, kicker
you're looking for, I believe."

"Do go on, please."

"Well, you've made it very clear that it's not the
exotic or the esoteric you're looking for." Sarah Markham sat quietly, her hands clasped on the table before
her. For a moment, he thought of the exquisite taste
in her jewelry as it reflected light points; then he continued. "The captain of an airliner is someone to whom
innocent people entrust their lives, the lives of their
children, the lives of their loved ones. It is total trust,
and it takes place on an everyday basis."

Sarah Markham's eyes widened slightly. "My dear
Mr. Archer," she said slowly, "I could not possibly
have said it better. I compliment you." Before Harold
Archer could comment she turned to her desk telephone and pressed a button. Her orders to her secretary were crisp and explicit. She rattled off several
names. "They are to be here in two hours. At three
o'clock this afternoon." She switched off.

Two hours later, the Archers were back in Sarah
Markham's office, updating their conversation for four
women who listened intently. Finally, Sarah Markham
swung about to face her associates.

"Do you understand the import of his words? *Total
trust—on an everyday basis.*" Mrs. Markham was almost fierce in her verbal thrust. "We are planning certain women to be moved into various industries and
professions and public positions. This one is absolutely
essential. It is almost critical, I would add."

Her eyes flicked from the four women to the Archers

and back. "Understanding what you have just heard," she announced, "we cannot settle for less than a woman who is a fully rated airline pilot in the left seat, in command of a commercial airliner."

"It won't be easy," came a warning. "There are women copilots, and we could—"

"I will not settle for a copilot. The woman must *command* the aircraft. It is that simple."

"Getting it done won't be so simple," came another voice.

"Of course it won't," Mrs. Markham said quickly. "It will be less simple because we aren't going to have any playacting here. The woman must qualify. The problem that any woman faces right now is that, even if she does qualify, she can't get the chance to prove it."

Susan Bartlett, whom Harold Archer would come to know better in the future, gestured for attention. "There are twenty-two women copilots and flight engineers now flying on major airlines in this country."

Sarah Markham's eyes seemed to flash. "Precisely the point. Second string, every one of them. Ladies," she addressed the group, "we're going to make every move carefully. I have already decided that we won't meet the opposition head on. The airlines, they—what is the official term, Mr. Archer?"

"The major carriers, Mrs. Markham, include the larger lines with passenger-carrying scheduled commercial service. These include such lines as American, Eastern, TWA, United—"

"Thank you." She turned back to the women. "Mr. Archer and I have already discussed the most viable alternative. Considering all factors, including our gaining voting control of stock, there is one line that meets our needs. Alaskair." She turned her head. "If you would, Mr. Archer?"

He shifted in his seat. He knew the need to keep it simple. "Alaskair is one of the larger lines serving Alaska. The complete territory—although they prefer to call it a state now. But Alaskair operates the length and breadth of Alaska, as well as running flights to and from the continental United States." He paused.

"The major airlines I just described operate on fixed schedules and routes. Alaskair, like Saturn Airways, is what we call a supplemental airline. They fly some schedules, but they fly far more airplanes to meet special needs. They carry everything—because of the unusual nature of where they operate—and that everything includes pipelines, bulldozers, women and children, sled dogs. If it can fit into an airplane, they'll carry it, and they'll do so in and out of some of the most terrible fields and in the worst weather you can imagine. They fly in everything from single-engine airplanes to the biggest jetliners. Their main aircraft, however, is known as the Hercules. It's a four-engined machine with turboprops." He thought for a moment. "It has jet engines turning propellers. This enables it to operate from fields much shorter and rougher than an all-jet airplane could handle."

He looked at Sarah Markham, who nodded, and said, "Susan? Can we get control?"

Susan Bartlett rubbed a perfectly formed lip. "We can. It will involve a great deal of money."

"We have that. And it's not as if we're spending it. We *can* increase the value of the purchase. Please keep that in mind. Now, some details that require immediate action—"

That had been several weeks ago. Now the conference room would hold twelve women. He knew they would be scanning the reports he and Evelyn had brought back from Alaska, and—

"Mr. and Mrs. Archer, if you please. Mrs. Markham is ready for you now."

Twelve women around the conference table turned to greet them. The secretaries blended into the background, unobtrusive, recording every detail. Harold Archer led his wife to her seat, waited until she was comfortable, then eased slowly into his own chair. He waited. Sarah Markham nodded to him and then turned to her associates.

"You've only had the opportunity to scan the report of Mr. and Mrs. Archer regarding Kate Brandon. I want you to take your copy with you and study it. If this report is on a level with their previous work, there will be no unanswered questions. Then, after today's presentation and your study, if we decide on Kate Brandon, we will commit fully to that course of action. I want this young woman to have her chance to earn the left seat, the captain's seat, of a commercial airliner. Make no mistake about it, there will be no favors. We will not—"

Alice Whittaker gestured. "Let me be certain on that issue. Will the Brandon girl know anything about us?"

Sarah Markham shook her head with a sudden sharp gesture. *"No.* She is to know nothing. I have already said there will be no favors. We don't intend to squeeze anyone, except in one area. Kate Brandon must be permitted to compete on an equal basis for the captain's seat. Harold Archer is convinced she has the skill and the capability to do so. Our control of Alaskair is to assure her that chance, but no more. What I wish to avoid is inequity."

She turned back to the Archers and the sharpness left her face. She had become genuinely fond of these two people. "Now," she said with a nod, "I suggest we all learn just who and what our Miss Brandon really is."

Harold Archer stood. "Kate Brandon began flying when she was only eight years old—"

3

"You in nice and snug, honey?"

Kate looked up at her father. Through goggles much too big for an eight year old, her eyes were shining brightly.

"Yes, Daddy!"

He grinned at his daughter in the rear seat of the old Waco, propped up on thick pillows beneath and behind her, wrapped in a heavy jacket, leather gloves fitted proudly to those little hands. Vance Brandon inspected the seat belt running across his daughter's lap as well as the extra belt he had rigged to snug her in by the waist. Satisfied she couldn't come loose or even extricate herself from the webbing, Vance stepped forward on the wing to climb into the front cockpit. He strapped himself in, went through a quick mental checklist, and brought the biplane to trembling life. Through the wide-angle mirror he looked back to see his daughter's delighted grin. She saw his glance and waved to him.

Emily Brandon watched from the front porch of their Nebraska farmhouse. Whatever fears she had concerning her daughter's safety came and went. She had flown too long with her husband to question either his skill or his concern for Kate.

The tall grass behind the airplane flattened from the propeller blast. It was not strange to Emily Brandon that the blatting thunder of the Waco should be pounding along the porch and into the front rooms of their house. Flight had never really been any farther away than their front steps.

The Waco, ah, that was Vance's private love, gleaming along its fabric surface from layer on layer of wax, hand-rubbed to achieve an eye-stabbing reflection of the sun. The leathered cockpits were saddle-soaped to a warm texture. She knew what had gone into that machine—when it had been reduced to parts spread all across the barn floor, and every part examined, brought up to perfection, placed back in the airplane with no margin for error. Every screw, nut, bolt; every cable, torsion bar; the rigging, all of it brought to better-than-new condition. Even the engine was chromed, and the gear legs, and the bracing wire—well, no matter what else Vance might do in the air, this machine was a remarkable reflection of himself.

The engine snarled, throaty and powerful, and the Waco bumped gently along the grass. Emily had always marveled at how an airplane came alive under Vance's hands and feet, and this moment was no different. The biplane rolled forward, the tail came up as Vance eased forward on the stick, and there was almost no time for it to race over the soft grass on the main gear because he had judged the wind just so. The miracle was happening once more, invisible to the eye. The air rushed above and below the wings, and it was shaped to a physical force. Pressures changed, a thousand unseen hands pressed upward beneath the wings, and the earth fell away gently.

It was a blending of man and machine and nature, shaping those wings and their movement to the elemental forces of the thick air blanket covering the planet. Vance's feet touched gently on the brake pedals; spinning wheels and tires rubbed gently to a stop. As altitude and speed increased, carrying the Waco skyward, his left hand came back first on the throttle, to baby his engine, and then on the propeller control. Sharp blades shifted in their sockets and changed the path through which they clawed greedily at air. It was all a matter of gentling the machine, of permitting flight without flailing engine parts. The man who took care of his engine would not be the one to cope one day with its failure.

To Vance—and he was already teaching this to his child through words and demonstration—there was no need to gouge the air and whipsaw the engine to gain the flight you wanted. It was all balance, it was all fitting the many parts into their proper places. If he could impart this, at this early time in her life, then she would be born of wings just as surely as she had known birth from her mother.

Vance took the gleaming biplane to two thousand feet and leveled off, trimming the ship so that the many forces acting on its flight would achieve a new balance. He waited until their airspeed settled down; he tightened the friction knob to the throttle and the propeller; and he leaned the mixture to change the proportions of fuel and air hissing through the carburetor system. When it was all done it felt right, and it was, and he eased his feet back from the rudder pedals, took his hand from the stick, and held up his arms so Kate would see what he had done.

He almost laughed aloud when he glanced in the rearview mirror. The little girl's arms were held as high as she could reach in the air tearing across and over the curving windscreens before each cockpit.

They flew like this for several moments, satisfying one another that the Waco was perfectly balanced, trimmed for hands-off flight. Then his feet were resting easy on the rudder pedals, and the stick was caressed by his right hand, and he moved hand and feet to bring up the nose in a steady climbing turn until the sound of the wind lessened and the wings hung at a precarious angle to the horizon. Just before that lowering speed would trouble the wings with burbling airflow, he let the nose come down and slide around to the side, and the Waco sighed through the blue sky as though it were a yellow and orange dragonfly out for an afternoon's drifting hover over God's domain.

He flew like this for several minutes, knowing that Kate would be gaining comfort with the sensations of flight. "How you doing, honey?"

"Oh, boy!" Her voice came to him from the small microphone in the cloth helmet Emily had sewn; they heard each other through earphones in the helmets they wore. He didn't want the child distracted by transmit buttons or a microphone. With the way he and Emily had rigged up the airplane, they could talk on an open intercom with one another. Sometimes they flew without helmets, the wind whirling and tugging at their faces and hair, but today he wanted to be able to speak to Kate whenever the moment came.

"Daddy, can we do a roll? Please?"

He laughed, delighted with that little-girl voice. "Okay, baby. You want to follow through with me on the controls?"

In the mirror he saw her head shake. "Not this time, daddy. I just want to feel it this time."

"All right. I'll call them out. Maybe we can come out of the roll into a loop."

"Neat!"

"All right, we'll start off with forward pressure on the stick, Kate." His right hand eased the control column forward; at once the sound of wind increased and the Waco's nose slipped below the horizon, accelerating earthward. Down they went until the speed was exactly where he wanted it; he called out every move to the child in the cockpit behind him.

"Okay, now we start coming back on the stick. Right here we bring in the power, the nose is coming up above the horizon, we keep it coming up until we're thirty degrees up, and, nice and easy does it, the stick all the way over to the left and we bring in left rudder—"

The biplane swooped upward, rolling smoothly over on her back. The maneuver was a wide and easy roll around the inside confines of a great invisible barrel in the sky. Even when they went inverted, the way Vance kept the Waco in the roll there was no change in the pressure on their bodies. If their eyes had been closed, they wouldn't have been able to tell that the Waco was rolling through the horizon.

"We're inverted now, and we keep the rudder in, and hold the stick well over, and be sure we keep the stick back—"

Upside down now, the nose coming down, and then they were diving, continuing to roll.

"There we are. We ease off on the power, start coming back on the stick. Okay, we bring the controls to neutral so the wings are level with the horizon, and we're coming out of the dive, and let's hold it in the dive to get some speed, and we'll make a sharper pull-up this time——"

"Can I help?"

"Sure you can. You on the controls, baby?"

"Got 'em, daddy."

He felt the mild pressure as her right hand took the stick and her feet went firmly to the pedals. He wanted to laugh with the mental picture of Kate propped up on those pillows, strapped in, still barely able to reach the stick, her tiny feet reaching the rudder pedals only because of the long extensions he had built for her. She would follow him through, keeping the same pressures he applied to the controls, and this way she would learn.

"Okay, Kate, we've got the speed we want. You come back on the stick. That's it; steady pressure, a little harder there, honey, suck it in, that's my girl——"

The nose came up, higher and higher, reaching past the white cloud puffs and aiming for the deeper blue sky directly above them, and Vance brought in power. Kate was just a bit easy on the stick.

"We want firm back pressure, honey." He came back with his own powerful hand, helping her. "That's it, full back pressure, hold it there as we go over the top."

The Waco slid through its high arc, upside down, the speed bleeding off, and Vance let it hang, let Kate take it through. He said no more now. Even if the biplane fell through, there was plenty of room and all the time they needed to make the recovery, and coming out of a situation was more important than knowing how to get into something. But Kate knew what to do, and she had gravity to help. The Waco sailed through the top of the loop, and the nose began to fall, and she was holding just enough pressure as speed picked up swiftly and they started rushing toward the green and brown patterns of the flat earth beneath them.

"You can come back on the power now, daddy!" Her voice was a squeal and a shout and breathless excitement as she called it out to him.

"Okay, Kate, coming back on the power, now." He came back gently, no abrupt motions here, on the throttle.

"Can I use both hands on the stick? It's pretty hard to do—"

"Both hands are fine, baby."

He could feel her straining, and he offered no help. They were pulling some stiff pressure, about two times normal weight now, and he knew just how tough it was for that little body behind him, and he heard her labored breathing as she fought her own doubled weight and the strain of coming back on the stick.

"Ease it out now, Kate."

"*Whew!* That was tough, daddy!"

"You were beautiful. I've got it for a moment."

His daughter relinquished the controls, and he went to three thousand feet where the air was cooler. That was enough strain for Kate right now. He wanted her excitement level down, wanted her to observe more carefully. He didn't want to teach, not yet. He had to build within the child an absorption level so that, as she grew older, her knowledge of flight and flying would become and remain a matter of osmosis.

He waited five minutes, glanced at her as she stared at the clouds and the wings, the earth, the sky, the fractional movement of controls, a bird flashing past as if it had been propelled from some great invisible gun. Time now.

"All right, honey. You want to fly?"

Her answer was another delighted squeal.

"You've got it, baby." He held aloft his hands so that she could see them.

As he expected, her first moments were overcontrolling the sensitive biplane. Yet he could honestly marvel at her feel with the Waco. Eight years old—awkward, childish, overeager, yet she had that same budding grace up here that he saw when she ran the tall grass, a child then of earth and wind, her dog racing along by her side.

He smiled. She had the feel now, and she was testing herself, moving the controls a bit more each time, banking the wings in gentle turns, and frowning at the stick because the nose had a tendency to dip at first and then to rise more than she expected or wanted it to do. But it was all a matter of feel and practice, and finally you knew what to do because you could anticipate, and that's when a person, child or adult, began truly to fly. You didn't fly for the maneuver you were doing that very moment, but for the moments ahead.

Childish laughter sounded in his headset as she skidded and slipped, and the sun seemed warmer and brighter than before.

Emily Brandon shaded her eyes from the Nebraska sun. She knew that exact moment when her child had gone to the controls. She knew just what Vance was doing, and how, and why. She watched the tentative responses of the biplane to the child's hands and feet. Kate was her father's daughter, certainly.

Emily ran her thoughts back through the years. Kate had been conceived in her body just before Vance left for war-torn Europe and the sleek fighter planes awaiting him. Emily dreaded every day. She thought of Vance in the cockpit of the swift Mustang fighter he loved so much; and she read with fear, pride, and understanding what lay behind his words when he wrote her of the great clashes in the cold sky above the battlements. His words came in breathless rushes—how he had flashed and swirled through icy air to bring his guns against a skilled adversary, and, in the next line, without hesitation, he told her of his love for her and his thoughts of their child to come. She laughed and wept and worried, emotions rushing through her like a great surf breaking on jagged rocks. She knew he was an expert pilot, but she knew that other men in black-crossed airplanes also were professionals at their job of fighting and killing.

Vance came home when Kate was six months old, and the gulf between the world of hammering dogfights and flaming metal over Berlin and the world of this child of theirs seemed wider than the span of light-years across a galaxy. Was this warm and loving man who held his daughter with such pride, and embraced his wife with tears unashamedly in his eyes, the same killer who had swept fourteen enemy planes from the sky?

Vance took her and the child into the sky for the first time. It was a gentle flight in a small airplane with a comfortable cabin. She didn't know how high they flew, but it was high enough to see forever across Nebraska and to see fields and rivers and hills as she had never known them. He touched clouds with the wings, and he soared and rose and fell gently, and all the time he said not a word.

Later that night, on the porch, he spoke of it. "Flight is beautiful, Emily, and the winged creatures we fly give us a miracle every time we leave the ground. The war taught me something: it's a bloody shame, a crime, to use airplanes to kill people."

Emily began to understand that flying wasn't something Vance merely pursued. It wasn't simply a part of his life: for him, it was *living*. The Brandons became a flying family, to whom airplanes were as common as tractors or trucks might be for any farmer.

Vance planned to work their sprawling farmland, but the plodding pace dragged on him, clouded and befuddled his senses. He was all for work, but not for tedium. He had tasted too much of the wine of life.

The answer lay within the reach of his hands. Their own spread demanded crop-dusting, and Vance did his own spraying, keeping two dusters on the farm. Then came a request from a neighbor. Could Vance dust his fields? He'd be glad to pay. And so would another man, and another, and Vance realized suddenly he had it all in the palms of his hands. He traded off dusting for attention to his own farmland and charged a fair but worthy rate for his neighbors. The demand for his services spread, and Vance Brandon became a full-time crop duster, spending his days in small planes—snarling across fields, pounding low over furrows, swooping upward to avoid trees and power lines. It was hot, dusty, sweaty, stinking work, and it was dangerous, for an engine that coughs at a wrong moment, or a wind gust that stabs capriciously at a wing tip, is enough to send a man into a tree or a power line or a slope.

He loved it, and the farmyard expanded into two

grass airstrips, and the demand for his services grew until he had eight planes and pilots working for him.

Young Kate's world was filled with the coughing roar of winged craft that rumbled into the air any day the weather permitted. She saw more of airplanes close up than she did of cars, trucks, or tractors; and engines and flashing propellers were the stuff of which her world was made.

She became, inimitable and enthusiastic youngster that she was, a favorite of the pilots—their mascot, as it were. She carried water and iced tea and lemonade and sandwiches to the men from the house. She asked a thousand questions and she got a thousand answers and more for her nose-freckled curiosity. Most of the pilots were ex-military, and they had come to the crop dusters from sleek fighters and massive bombers and lumbering transports, and the rainy days and the nights were filled with the yarns of men who knew what it was to brave death in the skies.

Young Kate's life was flying. By the time she was twelve years old she was an excellent fledgling pilot. Now tall and gangly, the rudder pedals no longer beyond her reach, she had developed levels of maturity in the air that would never be gained by pilots far older in years and experience. Other budding teenagers eased into their world of hot rods; Kate soared on wings. She knew aeronautical theory and navigation and maintenance; she had the pilot's view toward weather; she was comfortable with radio equipment. Without undue or even direct effort, she continued to gain competence and skill.

It was not a life without tragedy. Mitch Tomlinson died before her very eyes on a spraying run. The Pawnee under his hands was sweeping high and sharp through a turn when it seemed to stumble into an invisible wall in the sky. The engine screamed like a wounded animal, and she saw the control surfaces moving rapidly as Mitch clawed wildly for control. But something was wrong with the lift and balance, and the Pawnee gave it all up and fell straight in, twisting once, until it smashed into the ground. There was no fire because Mitch had cut the switches, but he was very dead of a broken skull.

Vance Brandon set his jaw, and he made Kate go with him to the wreckage. His daughter threw up when they removed the mangled body from the crumpled metal. "I want you to see it, Kate. I want you to *understand* it. This sort of thing is always waiting, it can always happen, *and there's always a reason.*"

She looked up with dumb, pained eyes. "Can I go back to the house, dad? Please?"

"No."

Her eyes showed no understanding.

"Not until you know why and how this happened. Because then it won't ever happen to you. I'm sorry, baby, but you've got to do it."

They went back over the records. The Pawnee was in good shape. No problems there. They checked the quantity of chemical he had taken into the hopper. "He took more than usual, Kate. How much more?"

She worked it out at fifty-three pounds.

"He had full tanks. All the fuel he could carry. How much was it?"

She added it up and put it into a column of figures. "Mitch weighed 220 pounds. Add it on."

The numbers grew.

"What was the temperature today, Kate?"

The answer was eighty-four degrees.

"What was the density altitude?"

The higher the temperature, the thinner the air. And the less lift available to the wings.

"What runway did he use?"

It seemed that the wind was light and Mitch took off downwind. Only three miles an hour, but the numbers were critical long before that.

"We'll never know at what speed he lifted off, Kate. He had enough to get into the air. You know what ground cushion does. It buoys up the plane when it's low over the ground, right? But Mitch was overloaded, the density altitude was high, he took off downwind, he came back on the stick before the airplane was ready. He climbed out of ground effect, and then he banked steeply. He was too heavy, it was too hot, and he was too slow."

Vance took a deep breath. "That was no accident, baby. Mitch killed himself through stupidity. Don't ever forget it."

4

Vance glanced up from his newspaper. He cocked an ear to the south wall of the house. Muted thunder drifted into the living room. He looked at his wife.

"That's the Stearman. Who's flying?"

Emily shrugged. "You tell me what's in my oven, and I'll tell you who's flying." She smiled. "Without looking, of course."

"Roast beef, woman." The paper dropped to the floor and he showed his annoyance. "No one's scheduled to go up." He ticked off a list of names in his head, then looked sharply about the room. "Where's Kate?" he demanded.

Emily's expression froze. "Vance, you don't think—"

"Goddamn it." He came out of his chair running for the door, nearly tearing through the screen. Down the stairs in one jump and running to the back of the house. Emily was behind him.

Just in time to see the red Stearman racing smoothly over the grass. In the front cockpit, hair flying in the wind, was Kate.

"Vance! Oh, my God!"

The wheels came off the ground and the Stearman climbed out straight ahead.

"Vance, she's only—she's only fourteen years old! How *could* you!"

He swung about, angry, arm gesturing. "You think I knew anything about this?" He turned again, watching the red biplane. "If I know the girl, she'll stay in the pattern. She'll —"

"Is that all you can think of? She's *alone* up there. Do something!"

He didn't turn back to Emily. "If you're going to wring your hands, woman, do it in silence."

She started to reply but closed her mouth before any more words came out. What was wrong with her? What could Vance do?

If nothing else, he was flying the airplane with Kate. His fists clenched and unclenched, his lips moving, he was in the cockpit as the red wings banked around the far end of the field. Emily looked from the airplane to her husband's face. The alarm was gone, he was grim but calm, and with that single glance Emily knew her daughter was flying the airplane well enough to satisfy her father.

Instantly her mood changed. She went closer to Vance, holding his arm. "She is flying it well, isn't she?"

Her words jerked him from his trance. "What? Oh, uh, yes, of course she is. What did you expect, Emily? The girl's been flying for years, hasn't she?"

The biplane eased out of another turn and flew downwind, parallel to the grass strip.

Emily's hand stroked her husband's arm. "I mean, you looked so angry, Vance. After all, Kate's—"

"Only fourteen. I know, I know." He shifted mood, his mind back in the cockpit, at the controls with his daughter.

"You're not worried about her, are you?"

"What? Uh, no, no. She's flying that thing like a veteran." In the same breath, "When I get my hands on her, I'll—"

"Is she, I mean, shouldn't she be turning on base leg now, Vance?"

"No, no, no. Not yet. See? She's holding downwind just right, setting up the wind. It'll be just about now—"

The Stearman banked into another turn, the nose lowering. The engine sound died away to a pleasant rumble as Kate came back on power. She was in the groove now, coming around on base leg perfectly, at exactly the right height, the right speed, the right rate of descent.

"That's it, baby, hold it right there—" Vance's hands closed around an imaginary throttle and stick . . .

Kate rolled onto her final leg, gliding as serenely as a butterfly returning to earth. The nose came up and

she held back pressure, flaring exactly, and the plane
three-pointed perfectly, the two main wheels and tail
wheel touching ground exactly at the same moment.

Emily Brandon let out her breath in a long sigh.
Vance gritted his teeth and started forward, but his
wife clutched his arm. "Wait—she'll come to us."

His concern for Kate's safety gone, Vance was building to a fine, heated anger. "Wait? That girl took that
airplane up alone! Alone, you hear me! Why, she
could have been—"

The engine roar drowned out his words as the Stearman swung from the grass strip and stopped only yards
away. The propeller jerked to a stop and Kate climbed
from the cockpit, her face flushed, the smile dazzling.
She ran to her parents.

"I did it! My first solo! And—"

Her voice faltered as her feet slowed. Her father's
cheek muscles twitched. Several times he started to say
something, each time he ground his teeth. His arms
rose and fell with his frustration.

"Daddy?" She had her head cocked to one side in
unconscious imitation of him. She came forward, puzzled.

"You're not angry, are you, dad?"

He spluttered, his neck muscles straining, and his
arms waved again.

"You could have killed yourself up there!" His voice
bellowed across the field. "You damned-fool girl, you
—you—"

"I—" Her voice quavered. "I thought—I thought
you'd be proud." She scuffed one toe into the ground.

Vance's voice grew louder, even as he struggled for
words, but he was torn between his pride and the reali-
zation that she had really flown the airplane solo. Fourteen years old. My God . . .

"You—you're grounded!" he roared.

Emily held her daughter close as they watched Vance
stalk away like an angry bear. Kate chewed her
knuckle. "Oh, mom—"

"It's all right, baby. It's just killing him not to tell
you how proud he is."

She looked up, her face brightening. "You really think so, mom?" Kate hugged her mother tightly.

"But dad, it's been *three weeks!*"

Vance looked up from his steak. "You know I don't like arguments at the dinner table."

"I'm not arguing." Kate leaned forward, intense. "I'm asking."

"When you ask and I say no, and you keep asking, isn't that an argument?"

"Well, no, not really. I mean, I know you grounded me for a month, but—"

A forkful of meat stabbed in her direction. "And like you said it's been three weeks. That's one week short of a month, the way I figure it."

"But you grounded me from *flying*. Mr. Senstad's doing the flying." Her face screwed up in a grimace. "I won't be flying. I'll be going along for the ride. I'll be sitting."

"Now, look, Kate, I said that—"

"She has a good argument, Vance." Emily stepped quietly into the conversation.

Vance looked from daughter to wife. "She just said she wasn't arguing. You tell me what a good argument she has. Why don't you two get together before the fight?"

"Because I'm not fighting! Dad, please? It'll be good for me. I'll do the navigation, and you always tell me experience is the best teacher, and—"

He gestured for her to be silent. "Where's Ken flying?"

She took a deep breath, flashed her mother a quick glance, and returned her attention to her father. "Wichita. About three hundred miles."

"How far?"

"Two hundred ninety-eight miles."

"That's better. When's he leaving?"

"He said he'd pick me up at seven. Right here."

"At seven, huh?"

"Only if it's all right with you, of course." A long pause. *"Please?"*

"You, ah, are only going to navigate?"

"That, and some radio work. Mr. Senstad's flying his Aztec, and it'll be night work, and——"

"Okay."

"You mean it?"

"It's 6:30 now. That means you'll have time to help your mother clean up the kitchen—and to let me finish my dinner in peace."

She nearly strangled him with her impulsive hug. Two dishes crashed to the floor as she started carrying things into the kitchen.

"Thanks a lot," Emily said dryly.

"Well, you always said you needed a new set."

"You surprised me. I didn't think you'd let her go with Ken."

"She did have a good argument. Everything she said made sense."

Emily laughed. "But you wouldn't admit it to her, would you?"

"She's already too much like her mother in getting around me, Mrs. Brandon."

"That was a *beautiful* landing, Mr. Senstad. I mean, really beautiful the way you brought her in at Wichita." Kate turned to the elderly pilot of the twin-engine Aztec. He leaned back in his seat, a pipe held comfortably between his teeth.

"It's nice of you to say so, Kate." He looked around the cabin. "Of course, this iron bird and I have been making landings together a long time. In fact, sometimes I wonder if I'm just along for the ride."

Kate shook her head. "Oh, no. I mean, sure it's important the way the airplane flies, but you've got that magic touch." She caressed the control yoke. "Only a week to go and dad will let me fly again. You knew he grounded me, didn't you?"

"Grounded you? What on earth for?"

She grinned impishly. "I soloed. In the Stearman."

"You soloed." The words were an echo. He started suddenly. "And Vance didn't like that."

"He was pretty mad, Mr. Senstad."

"You're how old?"

"Fourteen."

Senstad shook his head and chuckled. "I'd have been pretty mad, too."

"I think he was proud of me. Sort of, anyway."

Laughter met her words. "I'll bet he was." He took on a more serious look. "Aren't you a bit late for your ground speed check?"

"Oh! I'm sorry. I guess I forgot how fast the time was going up here. You know, it's so beautiful, and you just forget what's happening, and—"

The pipe stabbed at her chart, which was bathed in red light. "Go to work, Kate."

"Yes, sir." She bent to the chart and a note pad. Chewing the end of her pencil, she twisted dials on the navigation instruments before her. She wrote steadily, checked her stopwatch, and looked outside. The look was pure reflex. A dull red light from the rotating beacon flashed off the metal wing. Beyond that spread a velvet blackness studded brilliantly with stars. The Milky Way was a glowing stream, and the brighter stars were almost like beacons themselves. She stared for several moments at Orion's belt, looked at the big W that was Cassiopeia. There was Jupiter, so bright as to seem unreal.

They seemed suspended in air. She looked from the beckoning heavens to the instrument panel. The needles barely quivered. Everything was rock steady. The night air at 8,500 feet was so still that—without seeing lights moving by the wing—she could hardly have known their height or that they were speeding northward.

"Worked it out yet, Kate?"

"Oh, yes sir. We've got a ground speed of 215. I figure we've got a tail wind of 12 miles an hour. That's pretty neat."

"Yes." Orange light flared in the cabin as he relit his pipe. "I can remember many a time, Kate, when we were praying for a tail wind like we have right now. Any kind of tail wind. Even still air would have done. Anything was better than those head winds we used to have over the North Atlantic."

"Dad said you were a ferry pilot. In the Second World War."

"Uh huh. We ferried planes from Canada to England. All kinds, any kind. In those days, Kate, we didn't have the weather services we have now. Half the time we flew it was guesswork. We always kept an eye open for an emergency landing into Greenland or Iceland, but they were fogged in a lot of the time, so we just kept going." Senstad laughed. "Here we are, just taking it easy, and there's a small electronic brain doing all our work for us, holding altitude and course and keeping us right where we want to go. In those days we——"

"Didn't you have autopilots?"

Senstad nodded. "Sometimes. But they were so anxious to get those planes over there that most of the time the fancy equipment wasn't working. You see, we didn't have many bombers in England, and we needed every plane we could get."

"Gosh."

Her eyes lingered on the panel. All those beautiful round gauges, and the automatic pilot, really a computer—and you could even change course just by twisting a small knob.

"Mr. Senstad, did you ever have to make a blind landing in those days?"

He didn't answer right away. He must be thinking back to what it was like in the old times, mused Kate. I can't blame him. What memories he must——

"Mr. Senstad?"

He sat without moving, staring off into the distance, the pipe in his right hand resting on his lap.

She spoke to him a third time. "Mr. Senstad? Is anything wrong?" She touched his arm.

He didn't move. Alarmed, she pushed against his arm. "Mr. Senstad!"

His body fell softly away from her, his left shoulder against the cabin wall, his head unmoving against the window. The pipe fell to the floor.

"Mr. Senstad! Answer me!"

He was unconscious. Or dead, or something. My God . . . she pulled away, biting a knuckle to control herself. It must be a heart attack. It must be. Maybe he's only passed out. They just don't die when they have an attack, I mean, they can faint or something . . .

Several minutes later she was forcing herself to be calm. She had been gasping for air, trying to bring a sign of life to the slumped body beside her. Nothing. She placed her hand over his chest. He was alive. At least . . . at least she thought she felt something beating. But with the engine roar and the vibration, she couldn't be sure, and . . .

Oh, daddy, I wish you were here with me now—

The thought of her father brought a calming effect. How many times had he said one phrase over and over again? Accidents don't happen, Kate. They're made, and almost always by the man who's flying the airplane. And he'd said something else, too, something about panic being the worst enemy any pilot could ever have in the air.

That's the time to *think,* baby. That's the time to use your head. You don't let the situation get away from you.

She was terrified. The cold lump in her chest kept pushing up into her throat. It was real. Oh, God, here they were so high and flying more than two hundred miles an hour and she didn't even know what to do, and . . .

That's the time to think, baby.

Her father's words sounded in her head. She forced herself to be calm.

Fly the airplane.

She began to think. Step by step. Her breath slowed and the fright receded. The airplane . . . it was still flying. She stared at the instruments. *Of course! The autopilot!* It was maintaining their heading, holding the wings level, as it had been doing since Mr. Senstad had turned it on.

She sagged in her seat. All this time she'd never even thought about flying the airplane. And if the autopilot hadn't been operating, it might have been too late to—

She sat up straight. *Think, Kate, think,* she told herself. She knew she could leave the airplane alone for a few minutes more. Nothing would change. Another plane might appear in the sky, but let the other pilot worry about that. They had flashing lights and . . .

Her thoughts tumbled one over the other. Was Mr. Senstad still alive? Wait, there was another way. She reached for her purse on the seat behind her, fumbled for a mirror. She held the mirror directly beneath the unconscious man's nose. She needed more light. The switch, directly above her. She moved it, filled the cabin with light.

The mirror was fogging. That meant he was alive, breathing! Even if he stayed unconscious. She checked his body. If he slumped forward on the controls she might not be able to do anything. She loosened her own seat belt, half knelt until she reached the seat release to her left. She struggled, bracing against the panel. There, his seat had gone all the way back. She used all her strength to lean him backwards, head against the rest. She cinched his belt tighter. He would stay that way now.

Checklist. The word popped into her mind. Of course, when you're not sure of what's happening, and everything's calmed down, use your checklist. She went through the gauges before her. She looked at the fuel indicators. More than half full on the mains. The auxiliary tanks were full. She decided against switching the tanks.

Where were they?

The charts. She had done their ground speed check not too long ago. The checkpoints. She studied the lines Mr. Senstad had drawn with her before they took off. They left Wichita on a heading just east of north. "We'll fly to Manhattan, here, in Kansas," the old man had explained, "then up to Beatrice in Nebraska. We want to return to Ericson Field, right next to your farm, but we can't go directly, Kate. There's some weather reported in this area," his finger tapped the chart, "so we'll play it safe and swing a long curve around to the east. See here? From Beatrice we'll fly to Lincoln, and then, when the weather is behind us, cut back to the northwest and home."

She studied the charts. That meant Lincoln was dead ahead, maybe seventy or eighty miles. She looked again at the charts. She wanted the people in the air traffic center. She had to talk to them, let them know what was happening. For that instant she realized she would have to fly this airplane down, *and land it, at night.*

Oh, God. It was one thing to fly the Stearman and the Waco from the grass strip right outside your front door, but this was so different! She thought of the Aztec—the twin engines, constant-speed propellers, flaps, the gear she would have to lower, the mixture, all the things—

Kate clamped a trap on her mind. Do it by the numbers. First things first. She wasn't sure of the radio frequency. There, Lincoln Radio. She knew she could talk to them and receive on a certain frequency. No, wait. There was always the emergency frequency. It wouldn't have any voice traffic. But what if they weren't listening!

She had to send and receive on the same frequency. The one they used for emergencies was, uh, there—121.5. Make sure the cabin speakers are up in volume. She twisted that knob. She picked the microphone from its cradle, held it in shaking hands close to her lips, and began talking.

She didn't complete the first sentence. She was talking into a dead mike. She forced calm on herself. This time she depressed the transmit switch.

"Lincoln Radio, Lincoln Radio, this is Aztec Five Six One Niner Able. Mayday, Mayday, Mayday. Lincoln Radio from Aztec Five Six One Niner Able. Mayday, Mayday, Mayday. Do you hear me, Lincoln? Do you hear me? Does anybody down there hear me? Lincoln Radio, Mayday, Mayday—"

Shut up, girl! They're trying to talk to you!

"I say again, Lincoln Radio on 121.5 to Aztec Five Six One Niner Able. We read you loud and clear, One Niner Able. Come in, please. Over."

They had her! She stammered, "Uh, Lincoln Radio, from, uh, One Niner Able, I'm in trouble up here, and—"

They broke in. "One Niner Able, do you have your aircraft under control? Do you need assistance with your aircraft? Over."

"Uh, no, Lincoln, I'm on automatic pilot. Uh, over."

"Okay, One Niner Able. Leave everything just the

way it is. Can you read off your instruments to us? Just take your time. We want to be sure of your position and the nature of your emergency."

"Uh, yes sir, Lincoln. Uh, our true airspeed is, uh, 205 miles an hour, and we're, uh, at 8,500 feet, and—"

"That's fine, One Niner Able. Give us your heading if you can."

"Oh, okay, sure, I think we're, uh, maybe forty, that's four zero miles from Lincoln, and uh, my heading is twenty degrees. That's, uh, zero two zero degrees, and the autopilot is holding everything."

The air traffic team in Lincoln Center had already come full alert. The Mayday call, the labored breathing of the woman on the radio—they recognized all the signs. They were trying to keep the woman calm, get all available information, do everything they could to help. Then they felt the roof come down on them.

"One Niner Able, can you describe the nature of your emergency to us? Over."

"Uh, yes, Lincoln. The pilot, that's Mr. Senstad, he's had a heart attack, I think. He's unconscious. He's pretty old, and a little while ago, he just slumped over. I know he's alive because I held a mirror under his nose and it had fog on it. I moved his seat all the way back so he can't fall on the controls. But he's real sick."

"You're doing fine, One Niner Able. What was the pilot's name again?"

"Senstad. That's Mr. Ken Senstad, and we took off from Wichita, and—"

Another controller was already picking up a hot line. They started checking the aircraft number, the pilot's name, whether a flight plan had been filed, what the destination might be, the passengers on board—everything.

Jack Weathersby, on the mike, felt he was keeping all the loose pieces tied together. "One Niner Able, how many people are on board, please?"

"There's, uh, just Mr. Senstad and myself."

"Would you give us your name, please?"

"Uh, sure, it's Kate. Kate Brandon."

A sudden sliver of alarm wedged into Weathersby's mind. The voice—a woman under stress, high-pitched, obviously. But the hunch came to him. He glanced at the others with him and took a deep breath.

"Kate, Lincoln Radio here. How old are you, please?"

"Uh, I'm fourteen, sir."

Jack Weathersby turned pale. A girl only fourteen years old! Someone behind him voiced it for the group. "Oh, my God." The men had some more work to do. Instructions snapped out in the room.

"Notify SAC headquarters *and* Offutt radar of this situation. Clear all air traffic out of this area. Get me airport conditions at Offutt and anywhere else we might have to bring her down. You getting confirmation on Senstad? Good, stay with it. Jack, get some more information from the kid—"

"Kate, where is your home, please?"

"Ericson. That's Ericson, Nebraska."

"Very good. You're doing very well, Kate. Do you have your telephone number, please?"

"Are you going to call my folks? I guess that would be a good idea, but mom worries a lot. I—"

"Could you give us the number, please, Kate?"

She gave them the number, and one man placed the call to the Brandon home immediately. In the meantime Weathersby stayed on the radio. The Aztec was almost over Lincoln, and their best bet was to keep it from wandering away from their immediate control. At better than two hundred miles an hour an airplane gets away pretty damned fast.

"Kate, I want you to take a close look at the autopilot control box. Can you see it clearly from where you are?"

"Yes, sir."

"All right. Before I say anything else, Kate, I don't want you to worry about any other airplanes up there. We have you on radar and we're steering everybody away from you. So there's nothing to worry about."

"Yes, sir."

That was the first thing you did and always kept do-

ing. Keep the people calm. Jack Weathersby was nearly overwhelmed the way this kid was responding. She
was just beautiful.

"Is there a control marked Altitude Hold, Kate?"

"Uh, yes, there is. I can see it."

"Is it switched to the On position, Kate?"

"Yes."

"Have you ever used that autopilot before?"

"Uh, no, not really."

Weathersby talked to her, explaining the autopilot
and the control dial for adjusting course without dis-
engaging the mechanism. He directed Kate to disengage
the heading lock, to turn the course adjuster slightly to
the left, and to leave it there.

"All right, Kate, you're doing just great. Your airplane will now hold a gentle turn to the left and keep
you in our area. Every now and then I want you to
look at the airspeed and the altitude. You know how
to read them? Good. If there are any sudden changes
let me know right away. Now, let's talk a bit about
Mr. Senstad . . ."

Tom Engle motioned Weathersby from the microphone. "We've got a bit of luck. I spoke a little while
ago to the kid's father, in Ericson. He's on his way here
right now, and—"

"What the hell good will that do?" Weathersby broke
in. "The last thing I need is a hysterical parent on my
hands!"

"You don't understand, Jack." Engle knew that
Weathersby was under a tremendous strain. "Her father is flying here in his own 310. He's an old fighter
pilot and runs a crop-dusting outfit." He squeezed
Weathersby's arm. "Jack, the kid knows how to fly."

Weathersby looked up, startled. "Say that again?"

"She can fly. Her father told me. Wacos, Stearmans,
the lot."

"She's only fourteen!"

"And she's got a couple hundred hours. Now, listen.
Brandon said his kid can fly, but she hasn't got much
multi time. Certainly not in landing an Aztec at night
from the right seat. But she's a cool kid—"

"You can say that again. God bless her."

"—and he's going to talk her down from the 310."

"Christ—it could work."

"It's got to work. It's the best possible chance we could have!"

"What about the old man in the plane?" Weathersby asked. "Can we, I mean, is there a chance—"

Engle shook his head. "We contacted his doctor. He's afraid it's a massive seizure."

"When does Brandon get here?"

"He took off right away. It's a thirty-minute flight. Another ten minutes or so. We're in contact with him already."

"Stay with him. I'll tell the kid."

Vance Brandon picked up the flashing beacons of the Aztec. Lincoln Radio told him his daughter had used the autopilot to keep the Aztec in a wide, sweeping circle.

"Okay, Lincoln. I'll keep a receiver on your frequency, and I'm switching to 121.5 for the Aztec. You can monitor us all the way."

"Roger that, Seven Two Whiskey."

"Lincoln, is the wind holding on runway two seven?"

"That's affirmative. Twelve knots and right down the center line."

"Okay, Lincoln. I'll take it from here."

"Good luck, Brandon. That's quite a girl you've got there."

"Seven Two Whiskey out."

Vance Brandon took up formation with the Aztec, staying well off to one side so as not to startle his daughter. He dialed in the Mayday frequency.

"Kate, do you read me? This is—"

"Daddy!" Her voice burst from his speakers.

"Take it easy, baby. I hear you loud and clear."

He heard her voice choke from tension and sudden relief. "Daddy, I—"

"Honey, I want you to relax. Just breathe a few times. Long, slow breaths, okay?"

She still had the mike button down and he heard her breath shuddering. Several moments passed. In

Lincoln Center, Weathersby and the others looked at one another, held up crossed fingers. The sky was completely clear for the two planes.

"I—I'm okay now, dad."

"Good girl. Now, we're going to get you down nice and neat, Kate. We'll do it in formation. All you have to do is fly the airplane the way I tell you. I'll be with you all the way, talking to you, understand?"

Her voice quavered just a bit. "Y—Yes."

"Okay. Now let's do this like any training flight, baby. What do the fuel gauges read?"

"Uh, we're on the main tanks and they read, uh, a quarter full."

"Great. Leave them where they are. Now, when I tell you to, use the autopilot knob to roll out of the turn so you're flying straight and level. Got it?"

"I'm ready—"

Vance's original plan was to have Kate fly the airplane almost to the runway using the autopilot. He decided against that when he realized she'd need all the time she could get to accustom herself to the feel of the Aztec. It was a spirited airplane and responded immediately to control movements. He talked to her for several minutes, making sure she understood where all the controls were. He would have Kate handle all the critical functions of the airplane while they still had plenty of altitude.

"Now remember, Kate, that airplane likes to fly. It will move just as fast as you move the controls, so I want you to do everything slowly and gently. Don't bother answering me unless you have a question. Move your seat forward as far as it will go so you can reach the rudder pedals easily. You can tell me when you've done that."

He waited. "I moved the seat up." A pause. "Daddy, I'm scared."

"You can make it, honey. Now, I'm going to move in just a bit closer. Don't worry about me. Just fly the airplane like I've taught you. Okay, with your right hand on the yoke, I want you to move the autopilot control to Disengage. That's that handle with the knob on the end of it."

Almost at once the Aztec went into a climb. "Easy does it, Kate. You've got too much back pressure on the yoke. Just ease it forward. Slowly. That's it, you're doing fine. Don't worry about the instruments, baby. I'll take care of that."

"O—okay. What's next?"

He wanted to shout for joy with her question. She was thinking, *flying.*

"There are three sets of controls on the quadrant, Kate. The ones on the far left are the throttles. I want you to bring them back very slowly. Go ahead. I'll tell you when to stop."

She came back slowly on the power and the Aztec gentled its way into a long descent. Little by little Vance brought her closer to the ground. First the power reduction to start her down a few hundred feet a minute. Then he had her bank left and right, pull the nose up, put it down, to get the feel of the controls so she'd know what to expect closer to the ground. By the time they descended through four thousand feet, she was building confidence and flying better than he'd hoped.

He had her bring the mixtures to full rich and come back more on the power. When he held formation with her, he told her to adjust the trim with the overhead crank handle. The next critical step was the gear, because that would bring about a shift in trim. But she was ready for it, she stayed with it as his voice kept up an unbroken stream of instruction and correction, and by three thousand feet the gear was down and locked, the propellers were in flat pitch for immediate power response, and she had brought in twenty degrees of flaps.

He had kept them in a wide circle, the lights of Lincoln always in view, so that she would have a constant horizon reference and there wouldn't be the terror of having to use instruments for balance. They were descending at three hundred feet a minute, and he was working it out so that she wouldn't descend any faster. He knew that extending her time in the air carried its own peril, but the Aztec could dip its nose in a move faster than she would expect if he went to a faster descent.

If it all worked out, they would hold their formation until the final turn. Kate had made enough night landings to be competent in the flying, but with a hot airplane, flying from the right seat, and the tension of the past hour . . . well, there was no other way.

"All right, Kate, we're making our final turn. We're at eight hundred feet, and you can see the runway directly ahead of us. Okay, level the wings now and fly straight for the runway lights. I'll take care of our speed and altitude. Bring in just a bit more power, that's right, the throttles are all the way to the left. Remember to use your rudder pedals to correct for drift. Use your feet just the way I taught you. That's good. We're doing fine, baby. I'm right with you. Just keep flying her in the way you are right now. That's fine, we're about a mile out and we're in the groove. You're doing great, honey, just great. Look at the runway. Keep looking well ahead of you. Don't worry about the lights or anything else. Just stay lined up. That's it, baby. We're coming up to a half mile now. Hold that power right where it is, we're coming right down the groove, we'll be over the numbers in a few moments. Perfect, Kate. Keep flying just the way you are. There's no crosswind down there. Keep going, that's it—"

Lights sped beneath the wings. "Okay, baby, come back very easy on the power. Back, back, very good, Kate, leave the power where it is, look well down the runway, come back *gently* very gently on the yoke, hold it right there, you're almost down, use just a bit of left rudder, that's it, you're about to touch, chop the power, Kate, chop the power, *all the way back on those throttles,* that's it, hold it right there—"

"I landed!" she screamed, but no one heard her because both hands were on the yoke and she was yelling and crying suddenly, and her father's voice kept talking to her. "The brakes, press down with your toes, gentle pressure, you've got lots of room, all the room in the world, that's it, straight ahead, now, the red handles are the mixture controls, pull them all the way back to kill the engines, that's great, you're coming to a stop right now—"

She heard a sudden roar as Vance threw power to the 310 and flew overhead. His lights flashed in her eyes as he landed in front of the Aztec. She saw the red flashing lights of the crash trucks and the ambulance and the—there, her father's plane, turning, the landing light throwing a dazzling swath on the runway as he taxied back and came to a stop nearby, and she saw him open his door and come quickly around, running to the plane, and she didn't know why but she just couldn't stop crying.

5

"Fortunately, word had gotten to local news media,"
explained Harold Archer, "and they had cameramen
waiting. They managed to get some excellent footage
of the two airplanes landing, and, well, excuse me
while I run the projector, and I can provide commentary as we go along." Archer nodded to a secretary who
lowered the lights. The twelve women at the conference table turned toward the far end of the room.

"The aircraft on the left side of the screen is the Aztec with the girl at the controls. You can see the Cessna,
with her father flying and coaching her down, just a bit
behind her. There, they've just cleared the end of the
runway and Kate Brandon is about to touch down.
Next you'll see her father land, reverse course, and
come back rather quickly. Those flashing lights you see
are the emergency vehicles."

They watched in silence.

"There's a transition here," Archer said. "One of the
cameramen got in close and he has some excellent
shots of Kate opening the airplane door and coming
out on the wing."

There was no need to comment on the scene of the
fourteen-year-old girl throwing herself into her father's
arms. A series of other shots followed, including the
unconscious pilot being removed on a stretcher.

"Ken Senstad lived, by the way," Archer went on,
"and there were comments to the effect that had the
girl not been able to land as gently as she did, the
pilot would have died. Lights, please."

The lights came on and Harold Archer tapped his
notes. "There is also an excellent recording, should
there be need for it, of the exchange between Kate and
the air traffic center on the ground. Since her father

talked with her by radio on an open frequency, that, too, was recorded on tape. I have a master copy for your use."

Sarah Markham leaned back in her chair, a smile ghosting her lips. "That is excellent material, Mr. Archer. Excellent."

"Thank you, madam." Archer's presentation remained smooth and urbane. "Shall I continue?"

"Please."

Archer adjusted his glasses. "About a year from the time you saw in this film, when Kate was fifteen, Vance Brandon moved his family from Nebraska to Montana. They bought a ranch, which included a rather large airport, near Cut Bank. Their new life would center around a charter airway service. However," and Archer smiled, thinking of Vance Brandon, whom he had come to respect and feel akin to as a by-product of his research on Brandon's daughter, "Mr. Brandon was unable to resist the lure of more dramatic activities. Rather quickly, he bought into a borate bombing group.

"Another term for it would be chemical bombing," Archer explained, "for fighting fires. Forest and field fires, essentially, endangering huge areas that are usually in backcountry. The only way to get to the source of the flames quickly, and with enough fire-fighting punch, is to use airplanes equipped with special tanks or bomb bays filled with such chemicals as borate, and this is dumped on the fire."

He thought for a moment, unconsciously tapping the side of his cheek with a finger. "It is extremely dangerous; it takes steel nerves and great piloting skill. The casualty rate is quite high, I might add."

"I am fascinated."

The speaker was Felicia D'Agostino, a fiery woman who seemed almost to visibly vibrate with life-force. "I am fascinated, I repeat," she said, and for the moment Harold Archer found it difficult to see where this woman fit in with the others. Miss Felicia D'Agostino—in his own research he had learned that the woman would have nothing to do with the title of Ms.—was the only one of the twelve who spoke with something other than impeccable English. There must be a powerhouse of political clout within her reach. As he had done before, Archer doffed a mental hat to the sagacity of Sarah Markham.

"This borate bombing," Miss D'Agostino went on with a tilt of her head, "this is what this child's father, he do?"

Archer controlled the smile that had started to his face when he noted the barely visible annoyance from Susan Bartlett. So all is not entirely cool within the new order, he mused, and then he pushed the thought away.

"Yes, madam," he replied. "In fact, Brandon took over the operation. He flew the lead airplane into any fire, and—"

"That is dangerous?"

Archer nodded. "Someone has to go in first," he said. "The lead pilot checks out the air currents, which can break up an airplane. He finds out about the thermals—all the many factors that must be determined. He also drops the first load of borate. This helps the pilots who follow."

Felicia D'Agostino nodded. She showed a sudden broad smile. "The girl—her father is very special. That is good because part of him is in her, the daughter. Thank you, Archer. I am simpatico with what you say. I had husband once who fight fires. In oil fields," she added, and only the slight shrug that accompanied her last words told Harold Archer what she did not spell out. This woman's husband had died fighting a fire somewhere.

Archer shook his thoughts free. He had some slides made up of photographs of the Brandon facilities in Montana. One of the flying magazines had done a picture spread on what they wrote up as Brandon's Borate Bombers, and there had been photographs of the charter operation as well.

While Vance Brandon heeded the call that took him into the snarling fangs of danger, his wife and daughter attended to the hard business needs of the borate bombing operation and the air taxi and charter flying. Emily found herself the sole manager of the airport as well. Harold Archer emphasized to the women at the conference table that the business acumen imparted to the girl by her mother was an asset she would not and did not forget.

"The girl was growing up, of course. By now she was sixteen and, if I may say so, a very strong attraction for the local swains who flocked to the airport." The slides flashed on and off as Archer spoke. "This is Kate on her sixteenth birthday. She was something less, by the way, than eminently successful in being asked out a second time by many of her dates."

"Why was that, Mr. Archer?" The query came with unexpected sharpness from Helen Greene. Heavyset, crisply tailored, a bit too much with the jewelry, judged Archer. He took his time in responding.

"At sixteen," he said slowly, "Kate was already an extremely strong personality. Young men, at least those who were her peers, were less than enthusiastic about continued dates with a girl who in most instances was their better in athletics, had a scholastic record that placed her in the top five percent of her school, and, as an added fillip, could fly the pants off any of them."

He waited for the smiles and idle comments to pass. "I mentioned,—" he was going to say "ladies" but changed his mind suddenly, "that these pictures were taken of Kate on her sixteenth birthday. There is some motion-picture footage of this occasion, but it might have been too risky to have gained access to it. Certainly it may be available at some future date."

"Was there something special about her sixteenth birthday? Aside from the obvious, I mean." The question this time came from Eleanor Wilson.

"Yes, there was," Archer replied, nodding to the woman. "Vance Brandon celebrated the occasion characteristically. You see, sixteen is the legal age for anyone to fly an airplane solo." Archer gestured to the slide screen. "You can see nine airplanes there. Nine different types—seven single-engine models, and two twin-engine aircraft."

He paused.

"On her sixteenth birthday, Kate Brandon soloed each of those nine airplanes."

6

"Damn it, Kate, there's more to life than just flying!" Vance Brandon gestured angrily, spraying ashes from his cigar onto the living room carpet. His wife only raised her eyes slightly. Now was hardly the time, she reminded herself.

Her daughter sat with crossed legs on the couch, eyeing her father carefully. "Daddy, I don't mean to be unkind, but it's rather strange hearing that from you."

Vance sat up straighter. He stared directly at Kate. "And what am I supposed to infer from that remark?"

"Have you looked in a mirror lately? I mean, just *looked?*" Kate raised both hands in supplication to an unknown force. "You of all people—"

"You mean, this?" Vance touched the heavy bandages along one arm.

"Yes, daddy, I mean that, and the fact that half the hair is burned off one side of your head."

"Kate, I got too low, and—"

"I'm not criticizing, honestly," Kate said with open sincerity. "But this is the first time mother and I have seen you in two months. Two whole months!"

"But—"

"If you hadn't had that accident," his daughter went on, pressing her advantage, "we wouldn't even be seeing you now. The only reason you're home is because you were grounded until your burns healed."

Her father glowered at her. "I don't think I like that, young lady."

Emily glanced up, fighting a smile. "Kate, I think his wounded pride hurts more than those burns."

"Are you two ganging up on me?"

"Oh, dad, I want to *talk* with you."

He fished for a match, fumbling with the bandaged

arm. Kate started to him with a light, but he waved her off. "I can do it myself. You stay put." Clouds of smoke appeared before him. "Go on, go on."

"Well, you were saying there's more to life than flying." Kate smirked at him. "You're hardly a shining example."

"Flying," he growled, "is my business."

"And I want it to be mine."

Was this really his little girl, meeting him head on like this? He shook his head in mild disbelief.

"All right, baby, I understand what you're saying. And I agree. A girl's got as much right to fly as any man, and—"

"Well, *thanks,* dad."

"I didn't mean it the way it sounded." He gave her a crooked grin. "And you know it, too. What I've been trying to say, Kate, is that it's time for you to be interested in something else. There's more to life, you know. Especially for a young lady. You ought to be more interested in, well, you know what I mean, in—"

She sat back, hands in her lap. "No, I don't know what you mean."

"Well, in, uh, you know, the opposite sex, and—" His voice faltered and he tried to swallow his words.

Kate leaned forward suddenly, elbows on her knees, her chin cupped in one hand. "Daddy, I haven't heard a quaint expression like that in, well, I don't know how long."

"Quaint?"

"Quaint. If you get any quainter, I'm going to preserve your body for display in the museum's dinosaur hall." She grinned at him impishly.

"When's the last time I paddled you?" he demanded.

Her laughter hung in the air like music. "You never hit me, daddy. Not once. Not ever. You're a big bear and I love you."

He stared at her. Perhaps, Vance thought, I'm really seeing my own kid for the first time. My God, she's seventeen. That isn't a girl across the room. She is in full bloom as a young woman, and . . .

"All right, baby, what do you want to do?"

Emily rose from her chair. "I'll put on coffee. It's a

reward, dear," she said to her husband. "I thought it would be another hour of snarling and growling until you got around to asking Kate what she thinks about her own life."

"Get, *get!* Make the coffee." He turned back to his daughter. "Let's hear it, honey."

Kate clasped her hands. "I want all the ratings there are to get, dad."

"All?"

"Well, I've certainly got a good start. I'll be eighteen in four more months, and I'll wrap up the commercial and my instrument rating, and my instructor, and I figure I can get the instrument instructor's rating at about the same time, and—"

"Whoa, there." He scratched his chin and dropped more ashes. "Maybe I haven't been paying as much attention as I should have," he admitted. "How many hours do you have? Logged, I mean."

She pursed her lips. "You mean legal time? That I can claim?"

"Uh huh."

"Thirteen hundred hours in the book."

He nodded. "I know you've got twice that much in the air."

"I've been *living* in the air, I think," she said, pleased.

"That is precisely the point I was making before, baby. Now, look, I wasn't being a crusty old bear," he said hastily to ward off any interruption. "It's your welfare I have in mind, and—"

"I know that," she said quietly.

"—and, well, I *did* mean what I said about boys."

"I do date, you know."

"Who?"

"Daddy, you haven't been home long enough to tell one boy from the other!"

He tipped an imaginary hat. "Your point. Let's get back to being a pilot."

"I *am* a pilot."

"Will you back off, honey? I meant what you still want as a pilot."

"Oh." She smiled at him. First time he'd ever seen

canary feathers around *her* lips. My God, turn your back, and your kid becomes a woman before you turn around again.

"I want a jet rating, and—"

"That's all?"

"And my ATR."

He started to reply, to remind her she was just a kid, that an ATR, an Airline Transport Rating, was the highest you went in this business. He wanted to ask her what in the hell she would do with the ATR once she got it.

He said none of it. There was change all around him. He must rid himself of the notion that this was his little girl before him, or he would lose communication with her.

Besides, he remembered ruefully, he himself once had dreams. He was a kid on a farm with hay in his hands and straw in his brain, and he used to dream about a control stick in his hand, whirling through the sky, and—oh, he remembered the hoots and the derisive laughter, and how he grinned under it all, and read the books, every one he could beg or borrow or steal, and it had been a long, long road before he became master of a killer P-51 and met the very best of the Luftwaffe in the high cold arena over Germany, and—

This was his daughter, and why should she accept any less of a dream?

He was about to voice his reply when his wife returned with a tray in her hands. Kate went to help. "It's your favorite coffee cake, dear," Emily told him. He shook his head, wincing from where the still-tender skin chafed against his collar.

"I think I've been had," he said, accepting coffee and cake from his daughter.

She winked at him. "Try it, dad. You'll like it."

"You got your school picked out?"

"I'm glad you're sitting down."

"Wait, wait; let me get this down," he mumbled, "so I don't choke." He swallowed and sipped coffee. "Paris? Berlin, maybe? Or do you have something like Tokyo in mind?"

They laughed. "Nothing like that. It's some way off but still a lot closer to home."

"Spill it."

"Miami."

His eyes went just a bit wider. "All the way down in Florida?"

"Last time I checked it was still there."

"Never mind the sass," he said, trying to catch crumbs on their way to the carpet. "Why Miami? What have they got there that's so special?"

She leaned back on the couch, hands clasped about one knee, smiling at him. "Among other things, boys."

"Boys?" He snorted. "You wouldn't walk around a wing to meet a boy. The way I remember it you let them walk to you."

"Right on, dad. I want to go to two schools, really."

"Two?" He hated himself when he echoed like that.

"The University of Miami. There's a great aeronautical engineering course I can take."

He tried to equate this femininity before him with engineering, and he failed completely. "Of course," he murmured, retreating to his coffee cup. "Don't stop now."

Her eyes seemed to light up. "Well, I'll need the engineering background. I can mix it with some liberal arts I want, and throw in some business courses. Working with mother, running the field, I mean, has taught me there's an awful lot more I need to know."

"Hooray for our side," he said with a nod to his wife. "You said something about another school."

"It's nearby. At Opa-locka. That's Opa-locka Airport, I mean. I can continue my flying there and work on my ratings. I can also get my seaplane ratings. Single and multiengine. The way I've got it figured, daddy, I can handle both schools, get the education I need, *and* I won't lose out on any of the flying."

He held out his cup for a refill. Kate brought the pot to him. My God, she smells like a woman, he thought. "Uh, is that what you've figured out, then?"

"Well, there's more, but it's hardly school. I mean, Miami is a great place for skin diving, and I can learn scuba diving, and there's some really neat water skiing, and I can go to the Keys, and there's the Bahamas, and—"

"Hold it, hold it, you're making me dizzy. A little while ago you said one of the reasons you wanted that university in Miami is because there were boys there. How are you going to meet them? You'll never have time to talk to any of them, let alone go on dates!"

Her smile flashed at him. "I'll manage, somehow."

"I bet you will. Got any ideas about where to live?"

"It's all set, if you say the word. Denise wants to go with me. Her brother operates out of Miami. He's a captain with National Airlines, and he can line us up a super apartment, right off the campus."

"Super, huh?"

"Just super."

He turned to his wife. "What do you think, Emily?"

"It's Kate's life, Vance."

"You aren't going to offer an opinion?"

She set her jaw firmly. "I am not."

"Glory be," he breathed quietly. "That's the first time in nearly twenty years."

"Now, you look here, Vance Brandon, just because—"

Kate stepped in quickly. "Mother, dad. Please?"

He winked at her.

She showed signs of unease. He saw it at once, but he waited for her to speak.

"There's one other thing we haven't talked about, daddy."

Any other time he would have played out the moment, but he just couldn't do it now. Kate was so honest, so open about everything, he wouldn't cat-and-mouse with her.

"I know, baby. You've got it."

There was the slight sound of a gasp. "Daddy! Do you know what all this will cost?"

"Better than you do, Kate. It's my business, remember?"

"And—" Her eyes were wide. "It's all right?"

He nodded. "It's better than all right." He looked from Kate to Emily. After a long pause, he said, "This seems to be a moment for decisions."

Emily held her breath.

"I don't understand," Kate said finally.

"It's this way, honey. You're starting a whole new phase of your life. That's the way it should be. But change isn't just for the young. It's also a way to keep us older folks young." He took a deep breath. "I've been promising your mother for a long time that as soon as the right moment came I'd quit fire bombing."

Their shock was visible.

"Okay, then. Tonight's the night. I quit." He stared at his wife. "Emily, goddamn it, this is no time to start weeping!"

Kate flashed her eyes from one parent to the other. "I think—I think she's just happy. I know *I* am, and—oh, daddy, she worries so much."

Vance lumbered across the room. He pulled his wife from her chair and held her close, and he turned back to his daughter.

"There's one more thing. What I was saying about change. Tomorrow I'm calling Anchorage. Lou Hymoff. I'm buying his outfit." He paused. "And while you're in college, baby, your mom and I are moving."

"To *Alaska?*"

"Last time I looked it was still there."

7

"I am glad the others go to lunch. They go to place where it is important to be seen, no?" Felicia D'Agostino laughed with a show of perfect white teeth, and her hand rested on Harold Archer's arm. Her manner was vibrant and warm and, paradoxically, crisply cool and refreshing.

Felicia flashed a look at Sarah Markham. "It is strange, maybe, but this one, she is so *important,* yes? My friend, ah. For many years." She looked from Sarah Markham back to the Archers. "We are, how you say, strange bedfellows. She know everything that is right, how to do everything right, while all I know is how to be me." A burst of sparkling laughter followed like one musical chord after another.

"You are both remarkable women," observed Harold Archer.

"And you are, yes, you are diplomat." Felicia studied him through narrowed eyes. "You know something else, Archer? You are diplomat, but you also have eye of hunter. Yes, that is it," she announced. "You know what you look for, how to find it. I think, maybe, when you are younger, you can be very dangerous man, no?"

Archer tamped his pipe. "I prefer to think otherwise," he said quietly.

There was no playing games with this woman. When she went quiet Harold Archer knew her thoughts were deep and stirring. The tone of her voice softened, and she was calmer when she spoke again. Not to him, but to his wife.

"You are the quiet one," she said at last, receiving only a gentle smile in response.

Her hand rested easily on that of Evelyn Archer.

"You do not fool me, either. I am woman of, you say maybe, of earth, eh? I feel things. Simpatico. You and Archer, you are like team, like lion and his mate." She threw out both arms expansively. "He roars, frightens everyone. But when you know about lion, you know something else. The lioness is the one who make most of the kill." Her black eyes held steady on them both.

"You are very perceptive, my dear," Evelyn Archer said finally.

Felicia laughed and turned to Sarah Markham. "You hear me, Sarah. Pay close attention to Archer woman. She no speak much. When she do, you listen."

She turned back to Evelyn. "I listen to your man for long time as he tell about this woman, this Kate. You say nothing. But your silence is for meeting. Here, in private room of Sarah, we talk with each other. Friends." Her eyes flicked to Sarah Markham. "You no have bugs in here?"

"Not in *here*," Sarah Markham said sternly, some disapproval patent in her voice.

"You do not shake your tongue to me," came the instant rejoinder. Felicia returned her attention to Evelyn Archer.

"You tell me. Kate, she go to school down in Miami. I know the schools there. Tell me what she is like as student."

Harold Archer was content to let his wife have her say. Among the four of them, at this private luncheon, it would carry considerable weight. The other women had gone off to some fashionable restaurant, as much to be seen and discussed as to dine or sip cocktails. That was part of the business. But this private group had taken him by surprise.

Archer had misjudged Sarah Markham. He had selected Susan Bartlett, with her knife-edged sharpness, as the second strongest in this political conclave. Now he understood that Sarah Markham placed great weight on the instincts and the native intelligence of Felicia D'Agostino.

"She was everything you might have come to expect from what Harold has already told you," Evelyn said. "Her scholastic record was outstanding. She was not a genius in any one area, you understand. But Kate, well, she was excellent in everything she touched. Do you know what I mean? She was a natural leader, and where skill and capability were at issue, you would always find this girl there."

Felicia nodded slowly. "I expect this. All the things your husband say," she shrugged. "If she was not all this, we would not talk about her now. But I am curious about other things. Her flying. Do she do everything she want?"

Evelyn referred the question to her husband.

"Everything she wanted," he confirmed. "How she did it I'll never really understand. She took the full course at Miami, and she did her flying at Opa Locka. They have a very professional and thorough school there and they take pilots right on up to airline. Kate, of course, was well prepared. But no matter how much advantage you give to her previous experience, her achievement was really quite impressive."

Felicia studied him carefully, and he broke out in open laughter. "All right, all right, madam, I'll answer the question for you. You don't need to say it aloud."

"You are good man," the woman said. "Simpatico."

"What Kate Brandon did, when you consider her dual schooling, was nothing less than extraordinary. She obtained every pilot rating the school at Opa Locka had to offer. Seaplanes, helicopter, jets, and her airline pilot qualifications. She also obtained her type rating in—"

"What is that, Archer?"

"To be fully qualified to fly an airplane weighing more than twelve and a half thousand pounds—any large airplane, really—the pilot must be fully qualified, or typed, in that specific machine. It's not enough to know how to fly any large plane. A type rating demands an exhaustive knowledge of the individual aircraft. It's a most difficult undertaking, I assure you."

"And she do all this?"

He nodded. "More than that. She graduated as an aeronautical engineer, as well."

Felicia filled her cup with expresso. "Now, Archer, you answer the question I no ask, right?" Felicia smiled at Sarah Markham, who found this silent exchange faster than she could follow.

"You want to know, madam, if I consider Kate Brandon's accomplishments remarkable for a woman."

"Yes. Your opinion, please."

"It would have been remarkable for anyone, I assure you."

"I think so, too. A man could do this, too?"

"Very few men. Very few, indeed. I personally would not like to have been put to such a test."

"Aha!" The exclamation burst from her with a laugh. "Then I am right to myself. You are pilot, too!"

He nodded.

"Thank you, Archer." Felicia returned her attention to his wife. "Now, I think we get down to what you call nitty-gritty, no?"

Evelyn Archer smiled. "Of course."

"Then you tell me what is really important. This Kate, we all agree is very remarkable girl, and remarkable woman, also. But is danger here, maybe."

Sarah Markham came alert. "How do you mean that, Felicia?"

"You listen, I tell," came the mild rebuke. Felicia patted herself over her heart. "Strong feelings, and I must have answers. Any time woman is strong there can be problem. And problem is, is she real *woman?* How old is Kate now?"

"Thirty-three," Evelyn said quietly.

"That is what I mean. No more young chicken. She very strong, very smart, but does she have affair of heart with man?" Felicia drummed sharp fingernails on the table. "Woman-libber is not what we want, I think. Kate is woman who is pilot. We know she is better than many pilots, many men. She is in what men like to think is their private world. That is bad enough. But if she is woman-libber, many men, and maybe women, too, they turn off. They like their people to be real, to *feel.* They got to be able to be hurt, no?"

"I see what you mean," Evelyn answered after a pause. "But you need have no fears on that matter, my dear."

"You are sure? I ask because she is thirty-three, like

you say, and there is no marriage. Even divorce is all right. But her age and no marriage, this can be strange. Unless," and Felicia's eyes shone, "there is great heartbreak somewhere. I would like this." She laughed. "Then even I feel much closer to her. Other people, too."

Evelyn Archer did not smile. "There was heartbreak, yes."

"You tell, please," Felicia asked, strangely subdued.

"It happened while she was in school. Oh, her life was very full. She went to parties, she dated, there was scuba diving and sailing, and often she would take her friends on weekend or holiday trips with an airplane she flew herself. She was a very popular young woman."

"Then come one man who is special, no?"

Evelyn showed only a half smile. "Yes. His name was Dave Price. He was a student engineer. An architect."

"I will be quiet. You speak."

Two separate worlds threatened to gnaw into her balance and rob her of perspective. They should be compatible, thought Kate. They should be. There isn't a real reason why they *can't* be.

But Dave and I have been at one another like two cats stuffed into a sack. And that's crazy, just plain crazy. Why do two people so much in love have to hack and gouge at each other, when deep underneath what we really want is to be happy *with* one another?

Because, her own voice reminded her, Dave may be a sweetheart, but he can also be a stiff-necked, stubborn, self-centered son of a bitch. She smiled, objective enough to be mildly amused at the tug-of-war within her own mind. She could laugh at herself, find ironic amusement in their angry posturing. At times like these, however, Dave's sense of humor was something akin to a slab of marble.

Dave's imagination soared in cubes and rectangles and blocks and the rigidity of structures. That was fine. *Somebody* had to design buildings. The world lived and worked in the damned things. But when the day ended you went home. You didn't walk around with your slide rule stuck in your ear. *Or somewhere else more appropriate,* her inner voice whispered. She couldn't help it; she giggled.

Dave looked up from the drafting table. "What's so funny?" he asked.

She wondered if the question was an expression of interest or if he were simply annoyed. My God, I'm starting to get paranoid over this, she thought. Dave got to burying himself in that drafting table—right in the middle of his living room!—and if a bird chirped, he scowled.

"Oh, nothing really," she demurred. "My thoughts were wandering."

His pencil went quietly to the table. "If it was that funny, share it with me."

"Dave, I didn't mean to bother you. Really."

"No bother."

"You're patronizing me. Don't." She wasn't happy with herself. Got to watch that temper. But, oh Christ, she'd been sitting here for hours. He was working on some school project, and—

"Kate, why are you so sensitive lately?"

She brushed the carpet with a toe. "Because you're so *in*sensitive."

He leaned back, and she groaned inwardly. You could read Dave's body language. He might as well have worn neon lights. Right arm draped over the back of the chair, the chair itself slid just a short way back from the table. Girding himself. Why did she love this silly ox, anyway? *And I do. That's the craziest part of it all,* she complained to herself.

"Insensitive?" He blinked his eyes rapidly. "All this time I thought I'd been busy."

"Well," she said, forcing lightness, "you're the only one who knows, I guess."

"Don't be a wise-ass, Kate."

"Tell me why not."

"What's that supposed to mean?"

"It means I want you to tell me why I shouldn't be a wise-ass. I mean, you've got to have a reason."

His body tensed just a bit. Good! She was getting through that beautifully tanned skin. Tanned, and well muscled, and, and—oh, hell, he was beautiful and he was really a beautiful person, if only they hadn't molded his character in marble. Maybe there's a genetic link. She tried to stifle the laugh, but it spluttered through the hand she'd brought quickly to her mouth.

His eyebrows arched and, there they were, the furrowed lines on his brow. Before he could speak, she rushed on.

"Dave, let's get out of here. It's Sunday afternoon and we could go to the Keys, or the Bahamas, or, or, *anywhere*. Please, hon? We've been cooped up in here three weekends in a row, and the break would do us a world of good." She smiled at him. "Besides, a girl likes her guy to drag her off to a strange motel now and then."

"I never *dragged* you anywhere."

She examined her big toe. "Try it."

"What the devil do we want with a motel? I've got a beautiful apartment here, and—"

"Oh, hell, forget it."

He started from his chair, thought better of it, and resumed his "arguing position." He shook his head. She loved every movement he made. Even if what came out of his mouth was pure drivel. Damn it, she knew he didn't intend it that way.

"No, Kate, we can't just push it aside. Something's bothering you, and—"

"You noticed."

"Never mind the sarcasm. I—"

"David, for God's sake, all I've got left with you is sarcasm and infinite patience. You don't get off that drafting table until your eyes are so tired you can't see straight. And then you just sort of crawl off to bed and we get laid and—"

"You're complaining about *that?*"

Her jaw tightened. "You're damned right I am. I love you and I want my guy to make love to me. Not just get laid because I happen to be here. The symphony of love has got to be better than your postcoital snoring, David Price."

He was speechless. She'd never seen him that way before. He tried to talk but nothing came through.

"David, David," she pleaded quietly, "don't you understand? I'm going stir crazy in here. I'm ready to climb walls. I know and I understand about your work. But you've got some field trips you wanted to make, haven't you? Why can't we at least do those while we're together? The weekend can be a break, then. I want to share your work with you, David. I know your hopes and dreams. But I can't sit here like wallpaper, for God's sake. I—" Her voice trailed off.

She hadn't wanted to bring it all to a head, but there really wasn't any way out of it. Because she was going mad in this apartment. Work? She worked longer hours than did David, but she knew the wisdom of breaking free from what stared you in the face before it buried you. Perspective was the first thing to go, and, if you lost that, the whole effort became meaningless.

He pushed away from his chair and went through a careful ritual of lighting a cigarette. Hooray for our side, she thought with sudden hope. When he does that he's thinking. Really thinking, not just going through the motions.

He turned slowly. "Maybe you're right. About going somewhere, I mean," he said, measuring every thought and every word.

She wouldn't let a single moment get away. "David, you were telling me about that nuclear power plant. The one up at Buzzard Inlet, just above Jupiter. That's just about a hundred miles from here. We could fly up there, and—"

His eyes blinked as though he'd been stung. "Fly?" he repeated.

"Sure, honey! You said you wanted some aerial views of the reactor. That spherical building, or whatever it is. You were talking about a different angle, seeing it in a way you never could from the ground."

He smiled. "I guess you were listening, after all."

She wanted to throw her shoe at him for that one. It told her loads about the way his square head worked. She listened to him more than he ever knew. She wanted to share his world, and you didn't do that by tuning out when your guy was getting expressive. But she let it pass.

•

"I was," she said simply. "And flying up there would be a perfect way to get those views. I mean, you've got all kinds of cameras. David, you could get still shots and all the movie film you want, all in one flight. I can circle at any height, and you can get the right sun angles, and any oblique view, and, oh Christ, David, *let's do it*."

His hesitation now was simply the need for some assurance that he wasn't being led by the nose. Damn fool, she muttered beneath her breath.

"Maybe it is a good idea at that," he admitted. "Uh, what about an airplane, Kate?"

"They keep a couple of T-34s over at Opa Locka. It's Sunday and they're usually free today. Hang on, I'll check it out." Before he could say another word she'd grabbed the phone and called the school. She hung up with a grin of triumph on her face.

"It's all set. They'll have the airplane ready for us by the time we get to the airport. And, David, we can fly anywhere we want for dinner, because we've got to go out anyway, we haven't even shopped, and we can get back here by ten and you can do whatever work you want to do tonight, and it'll be—"

He held up both hands. "I said *okay,* hon. You get your things ready, and I'll see to the cameras."

She dashed across the room and threw her arms around him. "Ever tell you I'm crazy about you?"

Despite himself he laughed. "Sometimes, the way you crawl all over my back, I'd never know it. You're a pretty tough broad, you know that?"

"Don't forget it, either."

He held her at arm's length. "By the way, I don't mean to sound stupid, but what's a T-34?"

"Oh. It's a Beech. Ex-military trainer. Two seat, tandem, low wing, single engine, and it flies like a dream."

"Uh huh."

She grinned. "Get ready, will you?"

She bubbled all the way to the airport. David had come alive in his own quiet way, she saw. The Camaro took its turns with just a bit of tire squeal, enough to indicate that he was probably just as pleased with respite from the drafting table.

At Opa Locka Airport he took a long look at the
T-34, the wings and fuselage silvered and gleaming.
Some trepidation seemed to crawl back into his manner,
but Kate was all over him, fussing with his seat belt
in the back cockpit, stowing his camera gear, showing
him how to open the canopy during flight so that he
could take pictures, how to hook up the intercom. It
was all pleasure, doubly so because the man with her
was *her* man.

She boomed out of Opa Locka in a smooth curving
climb, heading north, watchful for other planes in the
heavily trafficked area. Then they were at three thousand feet and over the ocean, paralleling the coastline.
The day welcomed them with warm sunshine, scattered clouds, and only mild touches of turbulence. They
drifted past Palm Beach, and the lighthouse at Jupiter
Inlet came into sight, and beyond that she made out
the first signs of the big nuclear power plant, with the
huge sphere and giant smokestack. She thumbed the
transmit button on the intercom.

"There it is, David. Just a few minutes ahead. I'll
start down now. I'll circle at a thousand feet and you
can tell me just what positions you want for your pictures, okay?"

She heard him muttering into his mike. "You all
right back there, David?"

"Huh? Oh, yes, fine. Just trying to get my camera
set up."

"Right. As soon as you're ready I'll slow down to
about ninety and you can bring back the canopy."

It went far better than she'd hoped. David was less
than enthusiastic about the wind screaming past the
open cockpit, and he was downright unhappy with the
airplane banking steeply, but Kate kept the turns gentle, and when he wanted a certain angle she brought
the T-34 through an easy chandelle, hanging on the
nose, banking just below stall speed and letting the airplane slide along invisible rails in the sky.

It was a perfect opportunity for him, and he became
so engrossed in the views that he asked her to descend,
and she took the airplane down to five hundred feet
and went through the gentle turns and banks until he'd

used all his film. She looked back at him through the wide-angle mirror mounted in the front cockpit, and he was all smiles.

"Everything's stowed away, honey," he told her through the intercom. "It worked out beautifully." He screwed up his face. "Home, James," he ordered sternly.

"Yes, *sir*."

"Uh, Kate, this is great like this. Okay if I leave the canopy open on this thing?"

"Great, David. I'm going back to three thousand. We'll stay over the water."

Her heart sang. The flying was magnificent, the airplane as responsive as a swift bird, and David had come absolutely alive. They had finally made it, for the very first time. She'd met him at a party at the close of her second year in college and they'd been dating now for more than a year, but this was the first time they had managed to bring their two worlds together.

She had shared his world, but hers had always been closed to him. Now, she wanted to shout, to sing. She couldn't stop smiling; maybe it was just a happy, lovesick grin, but she couldn't help it, and she felt like music was soaring through her body. The stick was featherlight in her hand and the engine ran so damned smoothly, and the wings trembled with thousands of tiny fingers as they caressed the air, and there was all that incredible sky, and without a moment of conscious thought the stick went forward and the nose dropped and there before her, shimmering in the afternoon sun like liquid gold splashed over glass, was that stunning ocean, and the airplane sped earthward, running faster and faster, and there, it was timed just perfectly, the stick came back and over and the horizon whirled through a beautiful barrel, and they were going down again, but she half-rolled, and that was as neat as anyone could ever ask for, so she let it roll through three more times, racing for the ocean, and she came back with a climb into the vertical, putting the power to the sleek iron bird until it went straight up and their speed fell away.

God, it was marvelous! The nose hauled around to

the side, the edge of the world tilted crazily, and then they were going straight down, and, when she eased into level flight, they were flashing only scant feet along the surf, so low the upsloping beach showed them trees that were higher than their own altitude.

Suddenly, ahead of them, a flock of pelicans. Kate laughed and came back gently on the stick to raise the nose. The big birds always dove when faced with an airplane, they always went under, but for a moment it appeared collision was inevitable. She brought in full power to climb back to fifteen hundred feet, and then she sliced in over the beaches and went for Opa Locka Airport. There wasn't much traffic at the moment, and she brought the silver airplane in like a fighter landing on the deck of an aircraft carrier; they didn't roll five hundred feet when the airplane eased to a stop.

It was a terrible mistake. She had been so wrapped up in exhilaration and freedom and sharing that she remembered that David was with her, but she didn't *think* about it. When she cut the switches, she felt David climbing from the back cockpit. She climbed onto the wing and started down to help him with his camera gear.

She found him standing a few feet back from the airplane, his face white, lips pressed tightly together. He was as cold as ice and the vomit was still wet on his clothes. He turned on his heel and walked away.

8

Alaska lay waiting for Kate. None of her friends, not even Denise, her roommate, could understand her strange attraction to a land that was, to them, the antithesis of everything they found comfortable. Tanned and lithe bodies, swift boats slicing the water, the social whirl; all this was as much enjoyed by Kate as it was by her friends, but, for Kate, enjoyment in this manner, unless it went along with challenge and promise for the future, could never be more than a way-stop on whatever journey she must take.

During her years in Miami she had whetted her appetite with visits to Anchorage—where Brandon Airways had become a thriving success in its own right—and to the far-ranging outer reaches of the northland as well. Her father urged such travel on her, knowing the questing nature of his daughter, and he hoped this part of the world would become her home. He was tired to numbness of plasticity and neon, and he hoped for better for his child. Kate accepted her own penchant for such exploration; she had never denied her compulsion to touch and see and travel where she had never been before. Alaska stirred and excited her, and not simply because of the grandeur of its impressive geography.

A change had taken place in her parents, and Kate began to realize just how deeply their new currents ran. Vance and Emily Brandon had found the place where they wanted to live out the last of their years. The ruggedness, the untamed spirit of the land, the challenge that could leap howling before them at any time of the day or night; all this satisfied the need for contest that had always steered Vance's course in life. For him, as a killer pilot, as a crop duster, and as a

fire fighter, danger had beckoned—life seemed to pall
without its risks of bittersweet consequence—and all
that time Vance had stood helpless before its siren call.

While Emily wept silently through the nights.

Now, to the quiet but fierce delight of his wife, Vance
had "come home." No need to seek danger beyond the
normal ken of everyday. Enormous distances, towering
peaks, the vast nakedness of the land, the savage clawing in a thousand ways of winter; all this, and more,
was the Alaska to which the elder Brandons had swiftly become native, and without conscious effort they
had swept their only child into this warming web.

During Kate's years in Florida, as she moved toward
the completion of her scholastic and flight education
as she had planned, Alaska drew closer. Somewhere
she was aware, although she refused to pursue such
thoughts, that the wounds from her shattered romance
with David had sliced deeper than she cared to admit.
Against this still-fresh scarring of her psyche, Alaska
beckoned as a clean and lively breeze that augured
much for the future.

Alaska was as much a state of mind as it was a vast
carving of territory. In those same years that Kate was
in school in Florida, the land groaned with enormous
change among its people, with inner strife as to how it
would be managed, portioned out, protected for the
future.

Americans—

She stopped her own thoughts more than once,
amused with her use of that description; how quickly
she had accepted the teeming millions who lived in the
contiguous forty-eight states as Americans and those
who dwelt in the northland as a separate breed called
Alaskans. Kate realized almost at first glance that Alaska was only remotely like the land of which she had
heard and read so much. "Those Americans" suffered a
mental picture of their forty-ninth state: Like most pictures when viewed from afar, or through second-person
biases, it contained not merely flaws and imperfections,
but gross distortion.

The year before she graduated, she had flown to

Anchorage to spend several summer weeks with her parents, and Vance seized the opportunity to take his daughter on a splendid flight to the Far North. "You remember Sam Burleyford? We did some flying back in Nebraska." Her father chuckled. "Sam was always the one with the brains. Told me I never had enough sense to get my head out of the cockpit, and I guess he was right."

Kate had a vague memory of a tall, blond man. Broad shoulders, good-looking. Personable as hell, she remembered suddenly, recalling also a young teen-age girl's flush, a warm smile, and deep blue eyes. "I think so," she said.

"Well, Sam's made it big. One of the top airlines in this state is Alaskair, and Sam's the big boy himself. President," her father went on. "They're making a flight in one of their turboprops—"

"They fly Hercules, don't they?"

"Yup. And we're invited to go along. Survey flight, really. Some light cargo to drop off at a few spots, but it's mainly a sight-seeing tour for us. Right up beyond the Arctic Circle. Want to go?"

She hesitated. "Can I get some time on the controls?"

"I'd be disappointed if you hadn't asked that. I'm sure we can swing it, baby."

It was a flight deceptively easy, compared to what air journeying had been not so many years before. The huge turboprop had speed and altitude and range to spare, and they sat in air-conditioned warmth under pressurization while the land seemed to drift magically beneath them. Just north of the invisible line that marked the Arctic Circle, their pilot swung to the right, putting the Hercules into a wide turn. "Down there," he pointed. "Thought you might like to see something special."

She pressed her nose to the cockpit window. There was a river valley and . . . she stared in disbelief and looked up at her father. "It's like someone transplanted Death Valley up here," she said. Well below them, bathed by the sun in slanting golden rays, starkly unreal, spread a desert.

Not an arctic desert of snow and ice or frozen
ground, but *sand,* heaped and tumbled, dunes piled one
atop the other, frozen waves of sand, their upper ridges
ribbed as if they had been gouged by some enormous
rake. It went on for miles. She saw no roads, no sign
of habitation.

"You see sand, you expect to see camels, or at least
horses," the pilot said with an understanding smile.
"Not down there. If we were lower you might see a
grizzly bear. I understand they like the feel of the
place."

Several days after their return, she received a call
from Sam Burleyford. He had been the perfect host on
the northward flight. There was another trip available,
this time in a jetliner on a crew training mission. He
couldn't make it, but there was a jump seat open for
her. She didn't hesitate, and the flight was one more
proof that she could spend years flying this great territory and never fail to be surprised.

When Kate offered to take right seat, and the crew
saw her ratings, Jim Allison, the copilot, went back in
the airplane to sleep. Kate grinned at Tom Stottler to
her left. He grinned back. "You can have it after takeoff. When we climb out, just hold course along the
west side of Cook Inlet."

They were punching up through fifteen thousand
feet, Kate at the controls now, when she became aware
of someone staring at her. She glanced to her left. Jim
Allison was watching her. "I thought you were all
putting me on," he murmured. "How old are you,
kid?"

She kept a straight face. "Twenty-one."

"Twenty-one," he echoed. He pursed his lips. "Uh,
you've got your ticket? Really, I mean?"

"Uh huh."

"Private license?"

"Sure."

"I don't like the way you said that." He rubbed his
cheek, not sure of his ground. "You, uh, got more
than your private?"

"Multi."

"Multi, huh? You working for your commercial?"

"Got it. Airplane commercial. Helicopter commercial."

He blinked. "That's enough, I guess."

"IFR ticket."

"You've got that, too?"

"Instrument ticket," she said, keeping her voice as toneless as possible. "Instructor. Instrument instructor. Seaplane single and multi."

"Good Jesus Christ."

"ATR."

He stared at the pilot. "ATR?" he echoed again. "She's twenty-one years old and she's got her airline rating?" Stottler shrugged. He was enjoying this. He'd been briefed by Sam Burleyford, and he'd already gone through his shock.

Allison turned back to Kate. "I don't think there are any other ratings left, are there?"

"Glider."

"You got that, too?"

"Ground school instructor, tower controller—"

"I don't want to hear any more." Allison's jaw was set.

"Well, you do need type ratings," Kate offered.

"I suppose you're working on them." A statement, not a question, it seemed.

"Well, I'm rated in the DC-3, DC-4, and the DC-6. The C-46. Couple others. Turbine ratings in the Lear, Mooney, Falcon. I'll be taking them soon for the 707, some others."

Allison made one final try. "She's putting us on, isn't she? I mean, this is some sort of gag, isn't it?"

Stottler looked directly at him. "No. It's for real."

Allison stared at them both. "This is a dream. A nightmare. I'm going in the back. I'll forget it all by the time I wake up."

Kate turned back to look at the sky. "Think I should go back and apologize for being female?"

"Wouldn't do any good. You heard him. You're not real. Can't be."

They flew down the Alaska Peninsula to Unimak Island, part of the Aleutian chain. Far below them, immense despite their height, sprawled the caldera known as Aniakchak. It reminded Kate of Crater Lake in Oregon.

Here, too, an entire mountain had once exploded in a monstrous blast that left the crater, or more properly, the caldera, stretching fully six miles from one rim to the other. She gave the controls to Stottler, eager to gaze through her binoculars. From the floor of the huge crater a rounded peak thrust upward, a perfectly shaped volcanic cinder cone reaching nearly a half mile above the crater floor. The water in the caldera was a stunning blue, as if a rich dye had been poured into it. The scene was so intense in its hues it seemed artificial. Set against patches of snow, green forests and fields, etched shorelines that framed the setting, and reddish-brown crater walls, the scene bordered on fantasy.

Vance Brandon was an incurable drunk when it came to looking down on the earth's more dramatic presentations, and Kate had shared her father's enthusiasm. When she was fifteen, they had circled at low altitude the fabled Craters of the Moon. That part of Idaho could easily have been the surface of that world a quarter million miles away.

With an eerie sense of having been here before, she first caught sight of the Valley of Ten Thousand Smokes that made up the Katmai National Monument on the northwestern limb of the Alaska Peninsula. Mount Katmai had erupted in 1912 and the spewing lava had created a long, sloping area of desolation, so stark as to command incredible beauty.

She could never satisfy the urge to discover what her new home held concealed until she paid the price of admission by long flights across the state. On a flight from Anchorage to Fairbanks, she received her first truly clear look at Cathedral Spires, and she was moved almost to tears. Kate flew as copilot, not simply to fill an available seat, but as a working pilot for Brandon Airways. Once they were airborne and at cruising altitude, however, their work was reduced to scanning gauges and holding course. Her eyes were free to drink in the wonders.

And what wonders! Against a descending sun, many miles in the distance, she sighted the ridges of the great mountains. At first the scarps of the upper peaks were only a thin line against that hazy sunlit background, yet the air had become rough, at times even severely turbulent, from the winds howling invisibly off that wall rearing into the sky. Wind and sun and haze brought to the earth an ethereal quality, hiding the ground directly below in a misty veil, lending even greater mass to the mountains drifting slowly closer to them. When Kate looked down she saw the shadows of clouds streaming over the peaks. It seemed she was not looking down through an atmosphere, but through glowing, dormant waters.

The minutes passed slowly in this dreamlike world. A large cloud drifted directly before the sun and, at once, nature painted another brilliant picture in the sky. The cloud rims blazed with fierce light, seemingly afire with white heat. Beyond this were more wisps breaking from the main body of the cloud, transformed by their motion into twisting shapes of steam. Far off to the right, perhaps two hundred miles away, a shadowy mass brooded on the distant horizon.

Then she had eyes only for Cathedral Spires. Hundreds of jagged peaks, an orchestration of granite and stone and ice and snow. A savage wind howling tunelessly.

And beyond Cathedral Spires, in a celestial forest of mighty peaks, reared *Denali,* "Home of the Sun," known to the world as Mount McKinley. Kate knew she would see this granite giant many times in the future.

She felt a pang of remorse when she learned that men and machines would gouge a highway along the flanks of those very mountains so that Anchorage and Fairbanks might be joined by a concrete span. She almost laughed aloud at her instant defense of Alaska, at her own judgment that such a furrow in the earth was wrong. To so many people who lived here, that highway was long past due.

She felt a sense of wonder. She was startled, and pleased, at how quickly she had taken up the cudgel for her new homeland.

Kate sighed. She would soon finish nearly five years of school.

And her education was just beginning.

9

"Are you sure this thing is safe?" Kate hesitated before climbing into the cabin of the gleaming orange and white Bell Jetranger. The long rotor blades trembled in the breeze.

Mike Carew grinned at her, openly affectionate. "Of course it isn't safe. You know that."

"What's that supposed to mean?"

"A helicopter is an optical illusion with sound effects," he retorted. "A bunch of spare parts flying in loose formation. And if it was safe, you'd be bored to tears and I couldn't get you into this thing, right?"

She showed mock fright. "Well, the whole thing *is* held together with only that Jesus nut."

He groaned aloud. "I know, I know," he added quickly. "The whole thing attaches to the rotor blades, and the rotor blades are held onto the drive shaft by a nut, and the reason they call it the Jesus nut is that—"

"If the thing comes off, so does the rotor, and you yell, oh Jesus, and you get an answer, *fast,*" she finished for him.

"So how come you got your commercial rating in choppers?" he demanded.

Her hands went to her hips. "Where'd you find that out?"

"Momma is very proud of you."

"You've been talking to my *mother?*"

"Is there a law against that? I've been at your house often enough, Kate."

The turn in conversation had caught her off-balance. "Well, no, of course not. It's just that I never, well, I hadn't thought—"

"Obviously. Girls seldom do."

"I'm not so sure I like that," she said. Her voice had bite to it.

He had started for the helicopter, stopped, turned slowly. "Look, I don't give a damn what you can fly, how well you can fly, how great a pilot you are. Okay? I've been flying with your old man for three years now. We've gone out on a dozen rescue flights. Sometimes in one of his fixed-wing jobbies, sometimes in a chopper. And on every one of those flights your old man has beaten my ears half off my head bragging about his kid. You. I'm surprised I haven't found any feathers tucked beneath your shoulder blades. I—"

"That's quite a speech." The bite was gone.

"I'm not through. Today we are on a date. You, me. We—"

"You boy, me girl."

He broke up. "Okay, okay, you get the message. Me boy, you girl. Although," he jabbed, "how you can still be sexy with those boots and that parka and everything else is beyond me."

"Sexy?"

"You sound surprised."

"I am." A frown crossed her brow, but Mike couldn't see it beneath the hood of the parka. He was so bloody open that it shook her. It jangled memories she thought were gone. She caught herself with a start, placed her hand on his arm. "Thank you, Mike. You're sweet. Really."

He smiled at her. "I *am* trying, Kate. You're a tough customer."

"I didn't mean to be." She bit her tongue, walked to the passenger door of the Jetranger. She was mildly surprised, but pleased, when he opened the door for her, helped her in, watched her secure her belt. Not until then did he close the door and go around to the pilot's side. She watched him through the curving Plexiglas. A beautiful hunk of man. Mike Carew. Six feet two inches of solid muscle. As lithe as a cougar. Light brown hair, penetrating grey eyes, and a dazzling smile when he offered it.

She liked the way he did his thing. Independent as

a wolverine, with flair and style. Helicopter pilot. Not just a helicopter driver. A rescue specialist. Leader of a pararescue team, also. Mike had more than a thousand jumps, a lot of them in training, a couple hundred as a sky diver, a whole bunch dropping into the wilds, sometimes in vicious storms fit for no man, to save people in downed airplanes.

He strapped in, began to bring the jet helicopter to life. She watched him. Professional, thorough, *knowing*. She made a sudden decision. On this flight she'd be a passenger. Not merely sitting back and watching through narrowed eyes while someone else flew. But strictly and totally going along for the ride. It was marvelous.

"Do I get to know where?" she asked finally. The engine was screaming behind them, the sound muted by heavy insulation. Just above them the rotor blades had become a blur and the machine trembled with increasing power. She glanced at the gauges. No critical look.

Mike looked at her. "Where what?"

"Where we're going."

"I thought you'd never ask." He had a crooked grin on his face. "Dinner."

"I assumed *that*," she said dryly. She gestured. "Fancy way to go to dinner."

"Nothing but the best for my girl."

"For your—" She turned quickly from him, looked straight ahead, waiting.

Mike caught the hesitation. Well, it couldn't be helped. Vance, and Emily as well, had warned him. Something about a busted romance when she was in college. To hell with it. She had to come out of that square corner sooner or later. Well, they *were* together, he reminded himself.

"We're going up to Tyone Village. About 140 miles from here."

She was on safe ground again. "Isn't that by Susitna Lake?"

He nodded. "Right. Friend of mine lives there with his wife and kids. Charlie and Ann Nelson. He busted a leg a couple of weeks back and he's just getting on his feet again. We're bringing in supplies. Ever have moose stew?"

"No."

"You're going to. Today."

"I'm not so sure I'll like it."

"You haven't even tried it and you're knocking it already. Ann's a marvelous cook. Will you shut up and trust your stomach to me?"

"Yes, *sir*." It was getting better all the time. She hadn't had this kind of exchange with a man in so long that— She brought herself up short. She'd never had it like this.

The ground fell away as he brought in power and lifted. He was smooth, oh, he was beautiful the way he handled this thing. No effort, absolutely none, but in a wonderful curving ascent they were at a thousand feet. "We'll drop down as soon as we're out of the city area," he told her. That meant they'd make the flight just above the trees, skimming snow, slicing around hills, rushing through passes. She loved it.

She let the sensations of flight sink in, enjoying the magic carpet ride, surrounded by the protective Plexiglas bubble that concealed the wind and kept away the cold. They were already descending, the last vestiges of greater Anchorage behind them now, snow and hills and white-carpeted forests racing beneath them.

She laughed suddenly, a sound of pure delight.

His smile followed. "I think you sort of like it down here."

"It's *marvelous*. I haven't had a chance to sight-see like this in—in so long I can't remember. I mean I don't have to watch where I'm going, I'm just enjoying it." The chopper eased into a gentle climb. Hills whipped by and they went down again, more now than ever feeling that magical sensation of being suspended above the ground and rushing forward. Or were they standing still and the ground moving beneath and past them? She laughed again.

The horizon snapped over to a sharp angle; for an instant she reacted with hands and feet. Then she forced pilot thoughts from her mind, watched where Mike was pointing. They raced after a sight ever the rarer in Alaska, a full-blown dogsled team, the animals hauling swiftly through powdery snow. Mike slowed the helicopter, held it off to one side, pacing the team. A woman on the sled and a man standing behind on the runners waved to them. They waved back, and Mike slid off to the side, skimming treetops, a whirling-wing butterfly out for a frosty lark.

"That was a nice surprise," Kate said. "You don't see many of them out in the open anymore. All you see are snowmobiles."

As if her words had been prophetic, a dozen of the snarling, fumes-spewing machines raced in and out of a stand of trees. "I could easily get to hate those things," she added. "You know something, Mike? Before I came up here, to live here for good, I mean, wow, the ideas I used to have. To me this was the land of the dogsled. It was the king of the ice, the only way to go. And what do I find? Most dogsleds are kept for races, for the fun of it, in the towns and cities. Out here in the real world?" She gestured and shrugged in the same motion. "Just those stinking snowmobiles."

"There are two sides to the story, Kate," he reminded her.

"*You're* defending those noisy things, Mike?"

"Uh uh. I don't like them. But if you've got to move in the Far North, I mean, where covering distance in the shortest time possible has an effect on how much food you and your family eat, or if they eat at all, then the snowmobile can make sense. The Eskimos are using them more and more, too."

She nodded glumly. "I know, I know, Mike. But I can't help resenting them. The natives here, the Indians and the Eskimos, to me they're the living past. They're *real*, and they make up what Alaska means to me. I—"

He laughed. "Here you are flying in the latest product of technology, using refined petroleum, held in the air by metallurgical, aeronautical, plastic, avionic, and a hundred other sciences and technologies. Even that parka you're wearing is made from a petroleum base.

Half your clothes, the radios we use, just about everything you use to move through this country is an
invasion from the modern world, and you're complaining because the natives don't want to be living
museum pieces."

For several moments she couldn't answer him. Fury,
shock, chagrin; they all swept through her in a turbulent stream. Finally she calmed down. "That was one
hell of a speech, Mike Carew. Would you like me to
climb onto your crucifix all by myself or are you going
to help?"

"Never mind the histrionics, pretty one. Just stick
to reality. Am I wrong?" He kept his eyes on the trees
and hills and snow rushing by them.

She hesitated in order not to stumble over her words.
"No, you're not," she admitted. "Damn it."

"Well, cheer up, Kate. The trick to keeping Alaska
what it is, for as long as possible, is to mix the best of
the old world with the least intrusive or upsetting of
the new. And the dogsled is on its way back. You'll
see. And you know why?"

"I'd like to." If she could just keep this man talking,
she might learn more about Alaska in a few hours,
gain certain levels of insight, than could be accomplished in a year.

"It's because of reality. You can only hide from it
but you can't escape it. And the Eskimos, and many of
the locals who live in the far country—I'm not talking
about the cities now—they need the dogsled and everything it stands for. Need it, not just want it. A long
time ago the flatlanders—"

"The who?"

"The flatlanders, down in the Lower Forty-Eight."

"Oh. I'd never heard that expression before. Sorry;
go on, Mike."

"Well, long ago the flatlanders watched the horse
disappear because of all their stinking cars. I know
they *need* cars. But there's a difference between need-
ing and smothering. That same sort of thing won't happen here, or at least in the far reaches. The snowmobile
made its impact when it hit, but it doesn't work in the

far country where people still live off the land. It runs out of fuel too quick."

She was silent for a while. She had been here permanently now for two years, and all that time she had done everything she could to soak up knowledge and empathy for this land and its people and their ways of living. She had to do this. Kate resisted being absorbed; she wanted to fit into the pattern but in her own way and with her own contribution. But before she could influence even what she would do here, she had to act on something more than a smattering of knowledge.

One of the most difficult aspects for the newcomer to understand about Alaska, although it was easier for her as a pilot, is the altitude. This was a land of height. More than a third of the entire state, an area almost as large as Texas itself, lay at an elevation at least two thousand feet above sea level, and the hills and mountains began their climb upward from there. So she had to think altitude, had to assimilate the startling differences here from everything she had known before.

There existed no single Alaska, and its variety fascinated her. A kaleidoscopic spectrum, vast distances and incredible riches—and lack of life's necessities as well —packaged into an area twice as great as that of Texas. How do you measure astonishment? A single glacier here was as big as the entire state of Rhode Island. The Katmai National Monument alone rivaled in size all of Connecticut. You had to fit into your head new yardsticks and scales and measuring devices. Mount McKinley at 20,320 feet was the largest peak in all of North America, and yet to think of Alaska as a mountain state was *wrong* because Alaska had more coastline than all the Lower Forty-Eight put together, and that included the entire East Coast, the Gulf of Mexico, *and* the West Coast.

It was also one of the most sparsely populated stretches of all the earth's surface. *That* took time to sink in, especially when you looked at the teeming population of greater Anchorage. Yet it was true. The state covered more than a half million square miles, and when she came there to live as a new native, or at least a would-be native, the population was barely over three hundred thousand.

That worked out to just about five people for every ten square miles, and no matter how you slice that population cake it comes out very thin indeed. But, since the four main cities held half of all the people in the state, the statistics squeeze the truth from reality. In this state there were enormous tracts of land where no human moved.

In effect, then, Alaska was a people desert, and you had to adjust your thinking accordingly. The cities, towns, and settlements were actually oases of humanity, with incredible distances and natural desolation in between. For that matter, much of Alaska *was* desert.

Kate had flown many times with her father and other pilots to the northernmost regions of the state. The North Slope, bordering on the Arctic Ocean, in many ways could be likened to the surface of Mars. And if you were to find humans there you had to pinpoint your search.

The North Slope, victim to treacherous weather and numbing cold, lay blocked off from the south by the massive bulwark of the Brooks Range, a sort of Brobdingnagian wall raised by an impetuous Mother Nature. Impetuosity earned its own reward for the living creatures of the land, for the Brooks Range reared its shoulders high as a defense against the savaging winds that bore down from the Arctic, and it held off the mauling of the land farther south.

Kate had always imagined Alaska as grasping eagerly at its brief period of two summer months, during which life was eminently pleasant, and the rest of the year spent warding off the killing cold. Well, if Glasgow in Scotland was to be endured, why should it be worse in Ketchikan, which straddled the same latitude? Greater Anchorage bore much the same weather as the area of the Great Lakes, and in Anchorage the problem was one of population density. Of course, if you were from Florida you had your problems.

Tundra and frozen deserts, vast mountain ranges,

thousands of islands and fjords, forests immense and beautiful and bountiful to where they overwhelmed the eye and taxed the imagination. What else was there? Flatlands and rocky coastlines and glaciers and volcanoes and ice fields and—

Those ice fields. They weren't like anything else Americans could understand. They were distinct geographical features, sprawling across hundreds of square miles. They were, literally, like the surface of some other planet yet unmeasured by man. Kate remembered something she had read of the moons of Jupiter. Or was it Saturn? They were supposed to be made up of sheets of ice that stretched on and on, coming alive sometimes with ice fog.

She didn't know about the great moons of other worlds, but she already knew ice fog. She had landed by a small settlement and even before she could cut her engine and secure the airplane, the world had shifted before her. In a long, swelling moment that seemed timeless, the world faded away. With shocking surrealism, ghostly mist drifted all about her. She could never have seen her wing tip in flight through this treacherous fog of ice; it could have been her end right then and there. Barely safe on the ground, she stared in wonder at phantoms approaching her. Not until they were scant feet away could she recognize human beings moving within their cloaks of fog-shadow.

She learned quickly, under the sharp eye of Vance Brandon, not to confuse ice fields—where she could land on skis—with the waiting talons of glaciers. The glaciers were another breed entirely, frozen mementos of yesterday's snows, compressed into vast ice rivers grinding their way between mountains. The surface of these rivers could be tumbled, crevassed, fissured— enough to tear a landing airplane into glittering wreckage. In ice country, you made your decisions to land with extraordinary care.

On one of her first visits, she and her father were flying at dusk, eight thousand feet above the surface, riding gently on the memory of winds sliding downslope from the Alaska Range—the curving mountain line that began with the volcanic Mount Katmai area.

Where they flew at that moment, just north of Anchorage, the mountains buttressed the sky, guardians to the northland, gentling the sun down from the heavens.

And what a sun! She stared at the spectacular caldron poised above the mountain peaks, its distant fires distorted by the thick atmosphere of the horizon's edge, a great flaming disc that seemed to twist her sense of time. The sun hanging off the edge of the world . . .

Her father's voice had jolted her from a trancelike state. She turned, startled. He laughed at her. "I was asking if you really know what we have here, baby."

"Sorry, dad. It—it just sort of swept me along."

"I know the feeling. *Do* you know what we have here, Kate?"

"I don't understand."

Now he smiled with the wonder he felt within himself. "We have a land where there's a million acres for every day of the year."

His words had never left her. A million acres for every day of the year, and so much of it was beauty. Just as so much of it was strange illusion. A million acres and a million misconceptions.

She had always assumed—ah, the kind of thinking that time and again tripped her up—that Alaska teemed with wildlife. After all, it was famous for its undamaged ecology and for what it supplied for the discriminating palate the world over. Delicious crab, shrimp, salmon, trout; all manner of delectables. Here was the land of the largest carnivore to stalk its prey on the earth's surface, the enormous brown bear. There were also grizzly and black bear, and wolves, and the superbly aggressive wolverine, and caribou and muskoxen and moose and seals and walrus, lemmings and fox and whales and porpoise, dogs and hare, otters and marmots, and an incredible wind-rustling assembly of birds that included everything from the horned puffin to the killer snowy owl and . . .

And yet, nature insisted on stark, almost cruel contrasts. People must eat, but Alaska lived from its petroleum, from its enormous forests, its rich coastal waters, its minerals. It also bore financial fruit from military installations and scientific outposts, and as a way-stop for commercial airliners. It could not grow the food to feed even its miniscule population.

Just as Alaska was tenuous with human form, so animal life was spread far and wide by the inexorable laws of species survival. Beyond the formidable granite peaks that the Eskimos call Arrigetch—a sawtoothed barrier to the extreme northland—sprawled one of the great refuges for wildlife. The very terms—refuge and wildlife—demand visualization of animals in lush profusion. It was true enough, if you thought in nature's terms. But not in the distorted terms of the people so far to the south, beyond Canada. In the Lower Forty-Eight.

To survive north of the gates to the Arctic, to hew to the balance nature has clawed out during thousands of years, a single grizzly must rule a habitat covering a hundred square miles. Anything less overloads the natural balance. The fauna simply will not support more, and so territorial claims here were staked out as much by nature and instinct as by claw and fang.

In this state, half the land endured a coating of permafrost, a carpeting visualized by Kate as so much frozen mush. But in the other half of the land, tundra overlay the permafrost, and each year there came an explosive rush to life, a frantic and dazzling race to burst forth, to display, to drink in warmth and sun before the next great roll of cold thundered down from the top of the world. June in Alaska brought a frenzy of flowers. Millions upon millions of flowers carpeting the forest and grassland in impossible and gaudy hues. Flowers of every color and size and shape, pushing back the earth, emerging from hiding to greet the short-lived summer. It was the single most stirring demonstration of life she had ever seen, and—

"Hey, you still with me?"

She came back to the moment in the helicopter with a start, almost frightened by the intrusion into her thoughts. Her hand touched Mike. "I—I'm sorry, Mike. I was enjoying everything so much I guess I drifted off." She looked forward through the bubble.

"That's the Nelson's place. I've already spoken with

them by radio." He glanced at her. "Didn't you even hear me talking?"

She shook her head. "Uh uh."

He seemed on the edge of exasperation, but it came forth mildly. "Care to tell me where you were?"

She smiled, and the sudden warmth in her face and the glow in her eyes nearly overwhelmed him. "Flowers, Mike. Would you believe it? I was thinking of flowers—the first time I was here in June, and the snow and ice seemed to vanish overnight, and all those millions and zillions of flowers came out shouting with color, and—" She was suddenly self-conscious. "I mean, would you believe it? Really?"

"I believe it," he said quietly.

10

"I couldn't. God, not another bite. No, no, *no*," Kate protested, laughing. "I never believed it could be this great. But if I have one more bite, I'll—" She took a deep breath. "Ann, I'm starting to *feel* like a moose."

Ann brought her a mug of steaming coffee. Kate leaned back, still not believing how much food she'd put away. Bread almost too hot to touch, straight from the oven. Thick, creamy butter. A crab salad that nearly destroyed her.

"Let me help with the dishes," she said, starting from her chair. Ann pushed her back. "You can't even walk," Ann laughed. "Please. Just take it easy. The children will do the rest." She nodded at the expression on Kate's face.

"This is a working family," Ann continued. "Everyone shares. We all pitch in. And we do *not* permit our guests to work."

Mike and his friend had lit up cigars and were sprawled like overfed gladiators on a divan that was covered with bear rugs. "You two look positively indecent," Kate remarked.

Charles belched and grinned at Kate. "Live in the land of the Eskimo," he said loftily, "live like an Eskimo. That, dear young lady, was not a belch. It was merely a gastronomical expression of—of something or other for my wife's wizardry over a hot stove."

Kate nodded. "Well said. At least Mike doesn't—"

They all broke up as Mike followed suit, mixing a groan and a belch and rubbing his stomach. "We'll have to wait for a while," he said finally. "That chopper will never get off the ground with all this food in us."

"Get off the ground, hell," Charles said quickly. "We expect you two to spend the night with us."

Mike blew a long plume of smoke, watched it drift away. "Can't do it, man. I'd love to, but that chopper is scheduled for seven in the morning. Otherwise," he rolled the cigar in his fingers and sighed, "I'd make it a night with the angel with iron wings."

Kate rested her elbows on the table. "I take it you're referring to me."

"None other."

"Iron wings the best you can do?"

"Until you show me more."

"Up—" Kate bit her tongue at the expectant grins on the faces of the children. "I'll attend to you later," she told her date.

Mike nudged Charles with an elbow. "Hear her? Promises, promises."

"More than you deserve," Ann chimed in.

The two women exchanged smiles. Ann went off to the kitchen side of the cabin, and Kate gestured to Charles's crutch. "You did pretty well out in the snow with that thing. I was impressed."

"I did a hell of a lot better," he growled, "before I busted this leg."

"Can I ask how it happened?"

Mike laughed, nudged his friend again. "Want me to tell it, Chuck? I know the memories must be painful."

"Shut up, Mike," Kate said. "Charles?"

"I fell out of a tree."

Kate watched him. He kept a straight face and she realized he was serious. "How on earth did you manage to—"

"A bear chased him up the tree," Mike threw in quickly. "Wasn't a very big bear, either."

Charles glared at him. "Four hundred pounds is a lot of bear, man."

Mike laughed. "Especially when it's trying to get a piece of your tail."

"Mike, let him tell it, please?"

"Nothing much to tell," Charles Nelson told her. "I was coming from town with some supplies. On snowshoes. The stuff was pretty soft and it was sloppy going.

I came over this rise, and there was this four-hundred-pound rug staring at me. I stared back at him. Usually they won't bother you. This one," he shrugged, "was ornery. Don't know why. Maybe a toothache. But he sort of challenged me. Maybe he just wanted to play king of the hill. Whatever he wanted he used a mouthful of teeth to get his point across." Charles Nelson shook his head slowly, still incredulous. "I let the backpack down easy. I had a .44 magnum in a holster and I got that open, quick but without much fuss. I still didn't want to argue, and there was a tree nearby, so I started climbing."

"Even though you had a gun?"

Charles looked at Kate. "I don't like to kill an animal. This is his country as much as mine. If I could get out of his way, sooner or later he'd go home and I'd go my way. I thought he'd be interested in the supplies I'd left on the ground, but I was wrong."

"Chuck started up the tree," Mike added, "and he got going pretty good, and the tree started shaking, so he looked down, and guess what? This fur coat was coming up right after him."

"My God," Kate said quietly.

"That's how I felt," Charles said. "I never had a chance to get settled down. He got in one good swipe, clawed my boot, knocked me clean off-balance. Next thing I knew I was falling."

Ann had joined them again. "He fell right on top of the bear," she said. "That's what knocked the animal from the tree. Charlie fell about fifteen feet and landed smack on that bear."

Charles chuckled. "Don't know who was more surprised at that point. I was winded and the bear was all shook up. But he was also pretty mad. I tried to sort of scramble out of his way, and it felt like someone had jabbed my leg with a hot poker. I saw stars and pinwheels and all sorts of wild colors—"

"And that bear," Mike reminded him unnecessarily.

"Yeah. I saw him. He got in one good swipe with a paw that cut open my parka. He was getting set for a good bite when I got that .44 up. It may be a handgun, but those hollow point slugs will chop down a bear or a water buffalo. Doesn't matter. I emptied the thing into him."

"There's no need to ask if it killed him?" Kate queried.

"Killed him? Shoot, little lady, Mike and I are sitting on him right now."

Kate took her time digesting what she'd heard. She sipped coffee, put her cup down slowly. "Charles, you said before you didn't like to kill an animal—"

"Except for food or to stay alive. Makes good sense to me."

"It does to me, too. How long have you lived here? You and Ann?"

"Eleven years. Came back from Korea. Unfriendly place. Alaska looked marvelous to us. We run a trading post, handle the mail, do some scientific research for a federal agency. Weather patterns, that sort of thing."

"Then I guess I could call you a native?"

"I'd consider that a compliment. Other people might not."

"I don't understand."

He snorted with sudden heat. "Those of us who live off this land, Kate, we're headed for a knock-down, drag-out, head-butting contest with the politicians from the Lower Forty-Eight. To them, native means Indian or Eskimo. They don't care how long a man's lived here with his family, whether or not he lives off the land, or what. All they care about is their stupid ecology. They come up here shouting about conservation. I can't stand the sight or sound of them."

Charles's sudden fury caught Kate off-balance. "I'm surprised. To put it frankly. You don't mind if I speak as bluntly myself?"

He had a half smile. "I wouldn't expect any less from Mike's girl."

"I'm *not*—" She stopped at the smirk Mike showed to her, went back to the subject at hand. "What I started to say, Charles, is that you're the kind of person I thought would *want* to preserve all this."

"Are you crazy?" His voice was almost a shout. "I've been fighting a campaign for years now. I can see the handwriting on the wall. Those damned flatlanders will be coming up here in armies. Preserve things here? Uh uh." He shook his head intensely. "Not just preserve. *Use.* Establish a symbiotic relationship. You can't ignore what nature needs and you can't ignore what people here need to live. The trick, Kate, is to meet the two things in the same bucket."

She was starting to founder. "Isn't that what they, the conservationists, want?"

"Kate, how long you lived here now?"

"Several years. But what's that got to do with—"

"Do you know how to preserve, to utilize this state? I mean, do you have hard, sensible, meaningful answers?"

"No, Charles, I don't. I don't know enough to make decisions like that."

His tone softened. "A gold star for you. You're reflecting honestly what you know or think you don't know. That isn't the case with those sons of bitches from down under. Don't you think our local government is aware of what we need? They're doing everything they can not to repeat the mistakes the flatlanders made—they've turned the rivers into a stink, they've fouled the air, they've—hell, you know what they've done. And the natives—the Indians—what happened to them has been a disgrace the whole world knows about. You know what's going on here right now, Kate? It's quiet on the outside, but in Juneau, and everywhere there are political centers, there's a war going on. Our government, right now, and I'm talking about Alaskan government, insists that we don't repeat the crimes of before. They *insist* that the people here have ancient rights. They *want* to do the right thing by them."

Charles lurched to his feet, supporting his weight on the crutch, too swept up by his own words to remain physically calm. "The difference between us and the flatlanders is that *we know* this land, we live on it, we live from it, we live *with* it. And the key is that symbiotic partnership, not some highfalutin nonsense from people who run up here to stick their nose out in the cold for a few days and run back home!"

He swung up, staring intently at Kate. "They're trying to *order* us how to live our lives—in a way they wouldn't dare tell any foreign power where they pour billions of dollars into the country. They can't do that overseas because the roof would cave in on them, but they're trying to do it here. Their battle cry is conserve. Their flag is ecology, and it's all stupidity because *they don't understand this land*. They come up here in airplanes burning oil and gasoline and kerosene. No more animal skins, they shout, *after* they've decimated whole animal populations and murdered entire species. And why are they coming? Because we're sitting on top of the biggest damned oil fields this country has ever seen, and they want their piece of the action. They'll go with ecology when it serves their purpose. They—"

Charles held out his hand. "Hey, I didn't mean to climb on your back, Kate. I mean that; I'm sorry if I stuck pins in you."

"You didn't. It was fascinating. You're very expressive, Charles."

Mike climbed to his feet and gestured for attention. "Like the lady says, Chuckie boy, it's all very fascinating, but it's dark and it's cold outside and we got to git."

Ann was peering through a window. She turned to the others. "It also looks like some snow out there, Michael."

Mike frowned, went to the door, opened it briefly. "It's light, anyway. I'll cut due south to Glenn Highway and we can make it back following the road."

"You sure, Mike?" Charles Nelson had clumped to his side. "I don't like the idea of you and Kate in that eggbeater with snow."

"No sweat. There's hardly any wind and it's a good bird. Got everything in it we need."

They dressed and went outside. Mike took his time preflighting the Bell, warming it up slowly. They waved their good-byes and Mike lifted easily into the night, snow whipping about from the rotors. He took up a heading that carried them due south.

Kate looked at the darkened world. "It doesn't look very good, Mike."

He nodded slowly. "We'll stay low. If I get altitude we can pick up the omni, but I don't like the idea of climbing in this stuff." He flicked on a landing light. All they could see was a mass of swirling white.

The snow was sticking. Mike had the heaters and defrosters going, but it was gaining on them. He was surprised. There'd been no snow forecast, and only minutes before it had been light, dry stuff. Now it was heavy and wet and building. The gentle winds he'd expected had been replaced by sudden blows that were growing in intensity.

Just a few seconds short of eight minutes after leaving the Nelsons, the turbulence didn't matter much anymore. The engine swallowed a turbine blade and tried to grind itself to pieces, and before they could say a word they were going down in the increasing storm.

11

Kate would never fault Mike Carew for his flying skills. His hands and feet were a blur as he shut down the engine; the fire warning light stabbed at them and there was no choice about what he had to do. Kate didn't need to ask questions. He was trying to get enough downward speed for autorotation so he could flare just before striking the ground. With or without power, they could make a gentle landing. But it didn't work out that way. It was impossible to judge their height properly; the ground beneath them undulated and the altimeter was approximation only. Trying to see—the landing light reflecting wildly from both the blowing snow and their own forward and downward movement—was an eye-twister. Mike was afraid of going into a tree at the wrong angle. Kate felt strangely confident; her first instincts were to go to the controls herself, but the man by her side moved with speed and skill and there wasn't time to talk or even really to think about it and . . .

It all happened at once. The engine was still trying to tear itself to pieces, Mike was fighting for speed and balance, gut-ready for the first bounce of light from whatever might be beneath them, and a shadow reared up on their left. He corrected as fast as was humanly possible, but it wasn't fast enough. The tree jutted up amid swirling snow and spinning light, and she heard the rotor blades smacking into branches, and the world tilted crazily. How Mike ever got that chopper back to some hope of balance was something she would wonder about for a long time, but he did and they didn't slam into the ground at a side angle—which could have spelled the end of everything. They hit with a terrible crunching sound, and the deep snow absorbed a lot of the punishment. Things were still breaking all about them, she couldn't tell if it was metal or wood or what, but Mike was leaning across her and banging her door open.

"Out! Get out!" He studied her only long enough in the light reflecting back from their landing beam to be sure she could move on her own. She looked at him, saw blood on the side of his nose, moved her hand to him, but he had her seat belt off and was shoving. "This goddamned thing may burn, goddamn it, get out *now!*"

She moved. Out of the seat, through the door, she turned to see Mike on the other side reaching behind him and grabbing a heavy package. He had that and a flashlight in one hand and he came around the nose of the crumpled machine, grabbed her arm with his other hand, pulled her away. She moved with him, and they stumbled away from the chopper and dropped behind some trees. She started to her feet and Mike pulled her back down.

"It's leaking fuel like crazy. It's going to——"

The explosion finished his phrase. Instinct brought Kate into Mike's arms, huddled there for safety, when the fuel tanks shattered the darkness. A savage orange glare lighted the snow for hundreds of feet. The concussion wave punched at them. Kate gasped, tried to bury herself in Mike's arms. He sat quietly, holding her. The glare ebbed at once into a deeper glow and she saw the flickering light and heard the sounds of the wreckage being consumed.

"Good Lord——" She pulled herself from him suddenly, reaching for his flashlight. "Your face—you're hurt."

The blood was freezing. He had a deep gash along a cheekbone and down the side of his nose. He pushed her back. "It'll wait. First things first. We've got to have shelter and we can't lose too much time. This storm is picking up. The temperature's going down even faster. With the chill factor——"

Twenty or thirty below could be the equal of anywhere from fifty to a hundred degrees below zero. The chill factor gutted the body of heat. You didn't last

long. Mike turned the flashlight onto his pack, with-
drew a coiled line. "Tie it to your waist," he ordered.
"The other one goes around me. We could get separated damn fast in this stuff." He dug into the pack,
held up a small radio. "ELT. The one in the chopper
was gone." She'd figured that. The Emergency Locator Transmitter. Why turn it on when there was only
wind and snow? Mike would wait until the next day,
until daylight. He climbed to his feet.

"We've got to find some snow."

Kate stared at him. "We're in snow up to our necks,"
she said mildly, then had to repeat herself. The wind
was already a competitor for speech. "I don't—"

"The right kind of snow. Just keep quiet and walk
around with me. I want to hear it squeak."

She kept her own counsel. Mike was the survival expert. She went with him, watching. He stopped suddenly. "Hear that?"

Was everyone mad? All she could hear was the
wind picking up, the rustle of snow, the pounding of
her heart. "Walk slowly, one step at a time," she heard
him say.

This time she did hear it. The snow had a different
sound crunching beneath them. It squeaked. "We're in
luck," Mike told her, "but we haven't any time to lose.
Stay close to me. I'll need your help."

She tugged at his arm, leaned closer to him. "Mike,
I'll do anything you say. But what *are* we doing?"

Even in this crazy situation, bleeding, his cheekbone probably broken, their helicopter exploded and
burned out, he managed that crooked grin of his.
"Home, sweet home. That's what, Kate. An igloo. We
either build one now or we won't see the morning."

He rummaged in the pack, pulled out a long knife,
almost like a machete. "You keep the light on me.
Where I'm working with this thing," he directed her.
"It's the kind of snow we need, Kate. It's layered. You
know, one storm after the other drops layers, and it
compresses. It'll stay in chunks as I work."

He began with a trench, almost two feet deep and
just over three feet wide. "We've got to work fast," he
grunted. "Otherwise we'll get too much drift on us."

Several minutes later he stood within the rectangular pit he had hacked from the firm snow beneath them. The knife never stopped moving. Steadily he accumulated snow blocks, each about six inches thick, twenty inches high, and two feet in length. Moving faster now, he placed the snow blocks in a layered ring around the pit he had dug. As quickly as he had these together in a circle he sheared the long top edges of the snow blocks to create a spiral effect.

He was an artist, snow and wind and cold notwithstanding. Swiftly and with skill, the snow blocks went higher and higher in the spiral, and the knife flashed in the light. Now the blocks were high enough for Mike to start bending them inward, tilting each block as he went along. "When I tell you," he shouted, "start chinking loose snow where the blocks come together. Fill in all the cracks. All of them. We've got to windproof this thing. Not yet, Kate." He raised several more blocks into place. "Okay, start now and keep moving."

Mike was disappearing before her eyes. The dome shape of the structure was almost completed. She jammed snow into the cracks, patting and pushing as the wind tore at her. She'd never known it to come up so fast before, and she realized suddenly how cold she was. Her face felt as if pinpoints were slicing into her skin, and with a dulled awareness she realized this was true. She looked up, breathing hard, recalling a dim warning not to suck in too much air at one time, that you could literally freeze your lungs. She didn't know if the cold had gone that low yet.

But the wind . . . it's tearing at us. I'm freezing. I wonder . . . ice, I feel ice.

She did. Body perspiration from her efforts. Bending, standing, twisting, the wind reaching beneath her hood, around the neck of her parka, freezing her own perspiration. They hadn't really dressed for the flight into this kind of country.

The kind of mistake that kills you.

Mike was gone. She brought her hand to her mouth, moving stiffly. How could he be gone? This was ridiculous. "Mike! Where are you?" She should be panicky, but it was very funny. How could big, wonderful Mike disappear just like that? She giggled. "You big lunk! C'mon back!" The wind blew her words into her teeth.

She stared at the igloo. Light streamed from inside, turning the entire igloo into a glowing fantasy, weird shapes and whorls and patterns. Crazy, hey? Then a door, not really a door, but a space, appeared at the base of the dome. Now there's a neat trick for you. I wonder—

Mike's body wriggled through the opening. He shone a light on Kate's face. She heard him curse, felt her body pulled roughly down. "In there. Get in there, Kate. *Go on*. Get in there." She started crawling, felt his powerful hands push her from behind. She blinked at the light. Standing on a snow block. Warm. It couldn't be. But there wasn't any wind. She could hear it behind her, all around her, but it couldn't touch her anymore. Warm, getting warmer.

Mike spread a piece of canvas on the shelf he'd built when he started the igloo, sat her down gently. "Don't move, Kate. Please. Just stay here by the Primus stove, okay?"

She nodded dumbly. Pain was coming from somewhere. Where the wind had touched her. Mike was doing something with the lines he'd tied around them. Making knots, something. She felt the line going around her leg. "Promise me you'll stay here. Don't touch anything. I'll be right back."

Swift, unreasoning terror. "Don't go—"

"I'll be right back. Snap to it."

"God—of course. I'm sorry, Mike. Fog—like a fog in my head. I—"

"You're coming out of it, Kate, I can't waste any time. Will you stick here and just sit?"

"Y—yes."

He was gone. Everything was still moving slowly for her. She stared at the light. There was more pain, and she knew that was a good sign. She couldn't remember why but she knew it was better. She stared at the light. Wonder where Mike went? Don't move. Promised Mike. Sit.

Mike?

He was there. Dragging stuff behind him. He was

using the knife again, building a windbreak, an elbow bend in a tunnel of snow blocks. She watched him. "I made it back to the wreckage. When she blew, a lot of stuff was scattered around." She saw a seat cushion, a bench seat, curving sheets of metal, a piece of Plexiglas. He was moving things around. "Get up, Kate." She did what he said. He put her back down gently. A seat beneath her. Not so cold.

She dozed. He shook her awake. Warmer, much warmer. The hood of her parka was back. Mike held a cup before her. "Broth. Drink it slowly."

She remembered eating something. Iron rations, she guessed. Some more broth. She fell asleep again. When she came out of it this time she was alert, awake, hating herself. She snarled at Mike, forced him to sit quietly, held the flashlight on him. There were things to do with the first-aid kit. He winced, but made not a sound.

"I think you've got some breaks in your cheekbone, Mike."

"Feels like it. Stop poking, damn it."

"Your nose is broken."

"Guess that's why it feels stuffed."

"Idiot."

He grinned and the facial movement stabbed something inside his cheek. He bit hard on his lip. "Whooee. That was a goody."

"Can't you sit still?"

"I love you."

"You're delirious."

"Is it catching?"

"Michael. Shut up."

"Michael? You never called me that before. Are you in love with me, Kate?"

"Oh, for God's sake."

They slept huddled together, Kate wrapped in his arms, feeling loved in a way she'd never known before. She came awake first, not daring to move, not wanting to disturb him. The delicious moment was brief. He stirred, saw daylight glowing from outside.

"Listen."

She listened. "I don't hear anything."

"That's what I hoped. The wind. *It's gone.*"

He moved quickly, groaned aloud. His body was stiff, his injuries deep stabs. He grabbed the ELT, hit the switch to activate the emergency locator. He bundled up, pushed his way outside, set up brilliant international orange Dayglo marker panels. They could be seen for miles and they were radar reflective. He called from outside the igloo. "Button up and c'mon out, Kate!"

She sealed her clothes as best she could. She remembered to drag the pack with her. Sunglasses, she remembered. In her pocket. When she got outside she saw Mike already had his on. He was pointing to the southwest, in the direction of Anchorage.

"They're looking for us already. That transmitter must be putting out a good signal. Here comes one now."

Mike fired two bright red flares in high looping arcs. The plane banked steeply, rushed at them, passed overhead with a crashing sound. They hugged one another, and Kate saw Mike grinding his teeth against the pain that wouldn't let him go.

It took another twenty-five minutes for the helicopter. Mike tossed a smoke bomb away from them to give the pilot the wind drift in all that white.

One hour and thirty-five minutes later they were at a hospital.

One week later Kate signed herself into a tough, bruising survival school.

Mike Carew was one of her instructors.

12

Each morning the sun rose brilliantly over a life that might have been fashioned from a book of dreams. Rain, heavy snow, thundering winds were only details. Life was full, offering in wide canvas challenge and excitement, and it rewarded the Brandons fully as much as it exacted in effort and skill, as they faced daily the dangers inherent in flying the great northland. They prospered in health, and their joy was in their work.

As close to the earth as they were free in the sky, the Brandons did what they wanted most to do, and what they did was spiced with the risks and the uncertainties that, for them, made life worthwhile.

Kate had made her permanent move to Alaska in 1965, when she was twenty-two years old. For some months, Vance Brandon let her have her own sway, looking, flying, absorbing the wonders, meeting new people, acclimating herself. Through it all, he had his own general plan in mind. If Kate were to make northland flying her vocation, then she would need, in order to survive the inevitable hazards, experience and the benefit of others' experience.

Brandon Airways had proven successful beyond all hopes. They flew everything from single-engine bush planes to four-engined DC-4s; they flew almost everywhere across the state; they flew in most—but not all —weather; and they carried anything that would fit or could be stuffed into the holds and bodies of their machines. They made friends wherever they flew, and no small notoriety accompanied the father-daughter team, for they did much of their flying together. Everything that Vance had hoped for Kate emerged from this period. She grew into a young woman of high spirit and compelling good looks and a pilot of superb skills that were being sharpened with every successive flight.

There was a kicker in Kate's flying, and were it not recognized early, it could be fatal. More than one extraordinary pilot had fallen victim to this flaw. It is one thing to know how to fly under blue sky or stormy weather; it is something else to apply that knowledge under completely unpredictable conditions.

Exposure and experience were essential to her safety, and they could be gained only with time. A flight ticket or a type rating really gives the pilot a license to develop those skills inherent in the valued slip of paper. The vagaries of Alaskan weather were enough to demand a lifetime of experience. No pilot worth his—or her—salt ever forgets that the man who supplies the weather report or the forecast is sitting safely on the ground while the pilot fights for life because everything went to hell in the first stormy handbasket that happened along. Every pilot knows how to operate with the wind blowing from odd angles or gusting unpredictably. How to land in a crosswind is one skill on concrete or macadam and something else again on grass or turf or gravel, or when the surface is slippery or icy. Techniques change from one machine to another, and it is into this enormous caldron of experience that every pilot must reach deeply.

And Kate did learn. Her father accepted nothing less than her striving for perfection. He could never be satisfied. When he saw Kate reach certain plateaus, he would introduce elements of uncertainty. He might wait until she was committed to a landing under instrument conditions, seeing only the gauges before her, the world blocked out beneath snow-blown darkness. Then, at the worst possible time, a match would flare barely an inch from her nose, a match held there by her father. As quickly as it burned out another match would flare, moving slowly from right to left. And another, moving up and down. Through such distractions, through vertigo attacking the last vestiges of her balance or threatening to unhinge body and mind, he demanded flawless performance.

It was a contest in every way and one in which Kate

could only emerge with heightened skills and a level of confidence based on reality rather than on scholastic drill and repetitious paragraphs.

Vance could give Kate what she needed to survive in the unpredictable elements of the northland, where skill was lost without imagination and resourcefulness. Here, school books had to be modified or even rewritten as the moment dictated. Here, a pilot must learn from native and technician alike, for there were signs in the skies, in the animals, in the trees, that told more than the most advanced technological stations.

The Eskimos must never be regarded as simply a tribe living away their lives in remote corners of the great North. "Never forget, baby, that these people are, first and foremost, survivors. They have survived what we could never have endured. Call them a society or a tribe or whatever you wish, but I want you to consider that they have managed to sustain a record of their ancestry, and all the things that have happened to them, since three thousand years before the birth of Christ."

She looked at her father in astonishment.

It was an old Eskimo who brought home a lesson to her that was implicit in what one generation passed to another.

She had landed a long-nosed Cherokee on a rough gravel strip. A short turnaround at the field to drop off two men and some supplies, pick up another man to be brought back to Anchorage. She was uneasy. The weather was nothing like that forecast, and the winds were supposed to be from the northwest and they had wandered.

The old man, whom she knew only as Jack, pointed to distant mountains. "You look, Miss Kate. Look good," he instructed her.

The flowing buttresses seemed to be shimmering, aglow in a strange haze that did tricks to the eye. She had seen haze and glow, she had come to know ice fog, and devastatingly swift whiteouts, and pink snow, but nothing she saw at this moment seemed different or worthy of careful scrutiny.

He smiled tolerantly. "Mountains say wind come from east," he said finally.

She glanced toward the distant peaks, then back to the old man. He nodded. "When mountains have pale fire, wind come from east."

"Thank you." She knew nothing else to say. It might be something to remember for the future. Then she demanded more of herself. Of course—to an Eskimo such knowledge was lifesaving. Along the western and northern shorelines, ice floes would be blown away from the land, with whatever consequences might be involved for men who happened to be on those floes.

And one day, if the electronics systems of her airplane died, being able to tell how the winds would blow could be a factor in her own survival.

That was the point her father and Mike Carew and the veterans of Alaska repeated time and time again. Every scrap and morsel of information fits into place at the right time, and it can save your life.

She recognized early in her professional flying with Brandon Airways that the measure of success, and the survivability of any pilot flying the northland, lay in direct proportion to knowing terrain and weather patterns. Flight after flight, in all kinds of airplanes, her father refused her charts and radio and homing frequencies. Knowing what the ravines and passes were like, how the land lifted or gentled away from higher slopes, where one would find sheltered coves far from any charted harbor; knowing almost by instinct wind and weather patterns; this was the stuff from which successful pilots were made.

Brandon Airways was many things, but the popular picture of an airline it was not. If Kate were to one day take over its management and operation, then she required even more than piloting and office administration skill. Being caught in the far wilds with a balky engine demanded a pilot who knew how to detect what was wrong and how to repair the damage—then and there. She had to be proficient in soothing the people who flew with her, from garrulous old pilots to frightened children. One day she might fly industrial parts, the next a load of moose meat, the day following a family. Because in Alaska so much depended on the airplane, those who did fly were regarded by the natives as possessing virtually all skills and strange powers. If someone were ill, Kate's presence meant enough medical knowledge to put things right. She became expert, both by training and experience, in assisting in childbirth, delivering more children herself than she had ever dreamed would be her lot.

Kate took naturally to these "mercy flights," and slowly her name took strong root among natives and whites alike. In that often demanding, often cruel northland, her ability to fly doctors, medical supplies, and patients over long distances, to squeeze time when it ran swiftly through the hourglass of life, gained her a quiet respect and confidence. She was regarded as uncanny in her ability to find remote gravel strips or small lakes when most pilots considered any operations as suicidal.

An old Indian woman brought her a kinship she might otherwise never have known. In great pain from a broken hip, to be flown by Kate to the hospital in Spenard, south of Anchorage, she looked long at Kate, and then she smiled an enigmatic smile that somehow troubled and pleased Kate. Kate attended to securing the stretcher, tightening the straps. They would be taking off from a lake where the winds were gusting, and it would be a hammering run until they were airborne, and even then it would be rough.

Kate felt as much concern for the old woman's peace of mind as for her physical pain, which these people could bear with a stoicism bordering on the mystic. She leaned closer to the wrinkled face, and the bright, dark eyes looking up at her were startling in their penetrating gaze. "Can I do anything," Kate asked slowly, "to make you more comfortable?"

A long pause, those unblinking eyes, then the barest shake of the old head, and a whispered, "Thank you."

Kate flew as carefully and gently as she had ever flown in her life, feeling every tremble, every gust of wind, with overriding concern for her frail passenger. If she could have lowered the machine to the lakefront by feather; if she could have carried some of the burden of the old woman's pain; but all she could do was to fly with sensitivity and speed.

Tied to the dock, the engine shut down, Kate gingerly unfastened the woman's straps, made sure she was handled with extreme care by the ambulance attendants. The old woman gestured, motioning her to bend closer. Then the leathery old hand reached out, as soft as a whispered breeze, and touched her face. Her voice was barely audible. "We are same." The smile ghosted to her face, lingered. "We . . . same."

Later, Kate's mother explained. "Stand by this mirror, dear." She had seen it all her life but never really noticed. The dark hair, the high cheekbones that gave her such a haunting look, the flowing grace she had always had.

Her mother smiled at her surprise. "Somewhere, Kate, down the family line on your father's side, if we could trace it, we would find Blackfoot Indian."

It filled her with new meaning, made her closer to these people, white or Indian or Eskimo or mixed, all of whom lived under a vast sky and the dominance of winter storms that brought them face to face with the same privations and dangers. Kate was quietly fascinated by what had happened, and to Emily Brandon it seemed that a missing piece had been placed where it belonged. All that her daughter had accomplished, all that she had proved at the controls of machines; all this was simply a gloriously polished exterior. Emily had long wondered if the woman inside her daughter had also come to life. Now she knew. Bless that old Indian woman forever.

13

"In 1972, Kate Brandon lost her parents. They were flying together, and apparently they were caught by a particularly vicious storm. Vance Brandon was, of course, an outstanding pilot, and it would be difficult to surmise what took place. The wreckage of their airplane was found against a mountain. Apparently they were killed instantly."

Harold Archer shifted in his chair. "It was a trying year for her in yet another way. We have already identified Mike Carew as a close friend of her family and, of course, as having a romantic involvement with Kate. Almost within a week of her parents' death, Carew was shot down in Vietnam. He was an army helicopter pilot at the time, and he was missing for almost a month. Somehow he eluded his pursuers and made it back safely to our people."

Susan Bartlett studied long sharp fingernails. "Mr. Archer, is Kate Brandon in love with this man Carew? Is there an intimate relationship?"

Archer smiled. "I'm sorry, Mrs. Bartlett. That is a question I am not qualified to answer."

"Your opinion then, sir."

He shook his head. "That would not be opinion. It would be gossip."

It was the first time he had seen an appreciative response from this woman. "Very good, Mr. Archer. Your words are well taken."

Eleanor Wilson motioned to him. "I assume, from everything we have learned so far, that Kate took over the business?"

Archer turned to face her. "Yes, madam. Everything was left to Kate. With the insurance, and the excellent profits Brandon Airways had been generating, she owned everything free and clear. She—"

"Ladies, if you don't mind. Mr. Archer, excuse the interruption, please." They turned to face an impatient Helen Greene. "I know everything I want to know about this woman—her personal life, how long she has been flying. We know enough. We are wasting time. What I do *not* know is more about these big airplanes. It takes more than what Archer, here, calls a ticket or a rating or whatever. It takes more than she flies nice. Do you all understand me? What I want to know is, is she qualified? I mean really qualified. Where the law, the regulations, the standards, the papers, where all this is concerned. We scarcely need more storytelling, Mr. Archer."

Harold Archer didn't turn his head to receive the nod from Sarah Markham. It appeared the helmsman —he corrected himself, helmswoman—of this group was pleased with the sudden show of impatience. They were about to cut the mustard. Sarah Markham knew her associates well. Everything had moved exactly as she had planned.

"Mrs. Greene," he replied, speaking slowly, "she meets every requirement except one."

"Well, speak up, speak up."

"Kate Brandon is not a man."

"I know that. What I want to know is—" Mrs. Greene stopped herself. "You mean, that's all?"

"It is enough, madam."

Sarah Markham moved to front center. "Then, ladies," she said, her eyes moving to meet those of every woman at the table, "Kate Brandon is going to have her opportunity." She turned back to Harold Archer. "Of course, there is one other question we haven't voiced here—does Kate want to be an airliner pilot?"

Archer smiled. "We did a great deal of talking about that when my wife and I spent time with her on the island. Yes, she wants to be an airline pilot. Not a co-pilot, or a flight engineer. The captain. The person in the left seat. And she wants this quite badly. Brandon Airways can get along well without her. It is being managed by a man named Douglas. He flew for her father and lost a leg in an accident, but he knows the country and the flying as well as any man living. He runs the business end of things for her. There is nothing to prevent her flying for an airlines—except that she is female."

The intensity in the room had begun to crackle. The preliminaries were over; these women could now come to grips with a problem with which they had absolute identification. They transferred from discussion to worrying the subject, gnawing away the outer layers, working toward a solution.

Pauline Reddy stubbed out a cigarette. "Why does she want to be an airline captain, Mr. Archer?"

"I'm not sure I understand your question, madam."

"What compels her, Mr. Archer?"

He almost laughed aloud. "Forgive me, Miss Reddy. Your question went right over my head. Because she wants to, I would imagine."

Pauline Reddy shook her head. "I'm not trying to be difficult." She smiled. "But in all honesty I find myself asking the same question again and again. *Why* does she want to fly an airliner? Especially one that carries passengers. And why would she want all that goes with such an awesome responsibility. I should think that with all the flying she does, she would be more than satisfied."

"Your questions, madam, are valid, if I may say so. I quite understand what you mean," Archer told her. "I may not be able to respond in the way you would like. However, I daresay the answer would be the same if you asked a mountaineer why he must climb a higher mountain. Or why some people must go faster, in cars or boats or airplanes. It's a goal, another plateau, a self-measurement, perhaps. The ultimate test. The proving ground. I don't know how many phrases I could find for it. I would suggest, however, and perhaps I'm presumptuous in speaking for this young woman, that it has nothing to do with flying. It is the whole picture, the granting of such responsibility and its acceptance. Whatever it is, it is what makes skilled, responsible, intelligent people tick."

Now the questions were coming from all sides of the

table. Alice Whittaker sat well back in her chair, a fingernail gliding along the side of her mouth. "Is it woman's equality that drives her? Compels her toward these goals you just described?"

Archer was quick to reject the proposition. "That is the furthest thing from the mind of Kate Brandon. She is a woman, Mrs. Whittaker, and I place emphasis on woman. No, no, Kate Brandon isn't trying to prove anything to anyone. Except, perhaps, to herself. She knows who and what she is."

"Does Kate ever try to be airline pilot before?" Felicia D'Agostino had been unusually quiet, Archer noted. Trust her to slice through it all.

"She has."

"They no let her, right?"

"She was turned down. Quite emphatically, from what I have learned."

"Only because she is woman?" Despite her belief in Harold Archer, the woman found it difficult to accept that *only* gender had blocked a path to Kate Brandon.

"It's not that simple," Archer explained, glancing about the table. "Most pilots might not care who was with them in the cockpit. *Might* not. Some, perhaps many, would object. To be frank, it does offer complications. Crew accommodations. The intimacy of the cockpit. They—the pilots and the airlines themselves —do have their reasons, whether or not the reasoning is justified according to the standards in this room."

Sarah Markham laughed. "You're a born diplomat, Harold. But I do see the point you present. Can these obstacles be overcome?"

"At this moment, madam, as we've noted before, there are at least nineteen women in the United States flying on commercial airliners as copilots or flight engineers. There are many, many more who fly air taxi and charter work, plus many hundreds who are instructors or who run their own flight schools. Every one of them operates from the cockpit of an airliner or some other type of aircraft."

Helen Greene, again. "If she gets her chance it will

be rough on her. I wonder if the girl can stand the pressure."

"I'm convinced she can," Archer said. "At the same time, the opposition can be very difficult. Brutal, in fact. It's a closed circle."

Sarah Markham stood. "There is an old expression. Fish or cut bait. That time is here, ladies. We are all agreed that Kate Brandon is fully qualified, as a pilot and in every other way, to meet our needs. We want her to have her chance to become a captain of a commercial airliner. We will make certain she has that chance."

She looked about the room. "The board of directors of Alaskair, Incorporated will convene at a special meeting, so ordered by the dominant stockholders, who are in this room with me right now. After that meeting, they will announce that Alaskair is hiring four new pilots, to be captains, for the—" She frowned, turned to Archer.

"The airplane is known as the stretched Hercules, madam. It's a four-engined machine built by Lockheed, a civilian version of the military C-130 transport."

"Thank you, Harold. Now, ladies, Alaskair will announce they are opening competition for four new captains, and there will be absolutely no distinction as to sex. Or there will be a new board of directors."

The board of directors meeting did not last long. It was quite to the point. Sarah Markham explained exactly what the airline position would be with respect to hiring the new pilots.

George Robinson, chairman of the board, looked at her with open disbelief. "Mrs. Markham, that's crazy. A woman in the left seat? Ridiculous! You can't tell this board how to—"

"*Mr.* Robinson."

You can't mistake steel. George Robinson sat just a bit straighter in his seat. He waited.

"I will waste no time, sir. It is not crazy, it is not ridiculous, and you are talking to the people who control the majority stock in this line. You will deal with this new hiring with absolute and impeccable impartiality. If we discover anything to the contrary in how you disseminate and practice this new policy, within the hour of our confirming that fact you will no longer retain the title you now hold. Do I make myself clear?"

Robinson glanced at the other directors. No one met his eyes. Somewhere within himself he sighed.

"I understand."

"Absolute and impeccable impartiality. Any and all decisions will be rendered on qualification only."

Sarah Markham pushed back her chair. Seven men rose quickly. Mrs. Markham smiled. "Why, thank you, gentlemen."

Someone noted that long after she was gone her smile seemed to linger in the air.

14

"So you're superwoman. Arms and legs of steel and the eyes of an eagle, I hear. A mighty heart and a computer for a brain. Reaction time faster than light. Know something? You don't look it. From where I sit you look like a very pretty lady." An open grin followed, and a hand thrust forward. "Hello, Kate Brandon. I'm Pete Sizemore, your friendly guide to the secret and inner workings of Alaskair."

Kate Brandon hesitated only a moment, smiled to return the warmth. "I apologize for being completely flabbergasted, Mr. Sizemore. I—"

"Pete will do fine, Ms.—"

"Miss."

His brows started up.

"If it won't compromise your standing with the front office, Pete," she added hurriedly, "Kate would be fine, too."

His eyes sparkled. "I really do believe I'm going to like you."

"I hope so," Kate said, returning to the careful reserve she'd brought to the airlines office. She looked around. "You know, Pete, the last time I applied to Alaskair for a pilot's job, I never even made it this far. In fact, I never had an interview."

He didn't seem to find it amusing. "Mary Mimeograph get you?"

He was utterly disarming—well picked for his front desk seat in personnel. She nodded, a smile forcing itself to her face. "Very good. Mary Mimeograph. I've got to remember that." She flashed between memory and the moment. "Yes, that was about it. I think the letter was printed on offset."

"Oho," he came back quickly. He pursed his lips,

adopting a ridiculously somber expression. "Real style, huh?"

"The rejection was couched in true eloquence, as I recall."

His levity faded slowly. "I don't know, of course, whether you're going to make it this time, Miss B— Kate—but the response to you won't be indifferent. That much I promise you."

She studied him more carefully. He returned her frank gaze, noting how well she had dressed. Feminine but subdued.

"Are you speaking from the airline point of view?" she said.

His answer was immediate. "Both the airline's and my own. And that's still a promise. It may be a bit difficult to accept, especially in light of what happened before, but I assure you that judgment of you as a pilot will be absolutely impartial. I take this job seriously." A smile flashed and was gone as quickly. "But my job requires me to get the best people for this line. So if you turn out to be better than average, to do my job right I've got to do everything I can to get you on our side of the fence."

"It would be wonderful, Pete, if the front office shared your sentiments."

"May I ask you to take that chip off your shoulder until you see otherwise? Give us a shot, lovely lady. You're coming in here with predetermined condemnation. That will reflect in your tests and the competition you're going to go through. You may not be aware of it, but it will tug down on how you score."

Her eyes widened. "I take it that's a reprimand?"

"Not yet, Kate. It's advice. Good advice. *For* you."

"Did you take your master's in psychology, or go all the way to your doctorate?"

"It's the head of the class for you, Miss Brandon. I would consider it a favor if you did not make overly loud sounds over the fact that in the Lower Forty-Eight I was addressed as doctor."

"Cross my heart and hope to die," she said with her own mock severity.

"Now we have a secret to share. So we can go to work. Coffee first?"

"Long session, Pete?"

"Two hours at least," he said. "And to keep nothing from you, this is more than an interview. From this I will prepare a complete psychological profile on you, officially, for the company records. Until this moment nothing said or heard will be placed in that file. But if you're interested, if I were to judge on this introductory period, you come through at the top of the list."

She was easing off with the chip he'd seen so clearly. "I'll take the coffee. Black with sugar, please."

He buzzed for his secretary, who came back almost at once with the coffee. When they were alone again he seemed to shift personality as if he'd turned a switch. "With your permission I'd like to make a tape of this session," he told her. "You may, without prejudice, decline. Before you decide, I'd like to explain that the tape will be for my ears only and will be erased as soon as I play it back one time."

She thought it over. She believed Pete Sizemore. And in this business you had to trust other people. Trust was the glue that held crews together and kept a viable relationship between flight crews and support teams on the ground. She nodded. "You've got it. Go."

"We're on the air," he said disarmingly. "Now, first things first. Your application. You have it with you?"

"All twelve pages." She handed it to him.

"I want to go over it. Not while you sit there quietly. I dislike other people having to fidget. So I'd like to review all the points aloud. That way I'll know you better and we'll both be certain nothing went awry in your answers."

And so it began. So different from that earlier time when she learned that Alaskair had been hiring new pilots. And Saturn Airways *and* Alaska International. Then she had run into a blank wall with all three airlines. She had qualified as flight engineer and as a co-pilot with the lines. She could have pushed the point and made the grade in either one of those two positions, hoping to work or claw her way into the left seat. But the very idea of being walled off from the left seat *only* because of her sex fired her temper, and she'd accepted the rebuff as preferable to the tripe she knew she would have to endure by taking second best.

She had read with open disbelief the recent news from Alaskair. Four new pilots were being hired. There had been notices in the local newspapers and Mike Carew called her at three o'clock one morning to read it to her.

"Mike, it's the same old story," she said sleepily. "Dwarfs and females need not apply."

"Looks different this time, love," he said, ignoring her offhandedness. "Open competition for the left seat. No one's being upgraded from the line. Don't know why, but that's the scoop. There's also a couple of lines in here that say very clearly that the competitive testing will have no bias as to sex, race, or religion, and I guess that includes dwarfs and females."

"I don't believe it."

"For Christ's sake, Kate, at least check it out!"

"It's three in the bloody morning, Michael. Don't shout at me."

"Then stop being so damned negative! The least you—"

She hung up on him. Damn her own impulses. But she was flustered. Being jarred from a deep sleep, the sudden buoyancy at the news he'd brought her, and her own immediate defense against what she had always encountered as a closed corporation. But then— there was all this new stuff about federal laws enforcing impartiality, and—oh hell, what did all that have to do with Mike being on her side? She rang him back. "You're sweet, and thank you, I love you, Mike," and she hung up again before they could get into it.

The next day she chewed it over thoroughly in her head. It did seem to be on the level. But there were all sorts of ways for an airline to act their part, pay lip service, run you through the drill, and shunt you aside without ever really intending to let you break down their walls. She thought of Sam Burleyford. God, he was president of the damned line, and he'd known her father so well, and she knew him better than anyone even suspected, and—

"No way, no way," she murmured aloud to herself. "That would be the worst thing to do." And she was right. If she tried to lean on Sam, even as a friend, she would never know if she really could make the grade completely on her own. Besides, Sam might take umbrage with a move like that. There was only one way to go.

She went to the Alaskair office at Anchorage International Airport and picked up the application papers. The girl behind the desk stared at her with open curiosity. "You really should apply at Saturn Airways," she told Kate.

"You working for the competition?" Kate asked.

The girl shook her head. "No. I'm serious. They hired a woman as copilot only last week, and I understand they're—"

"Thanks, but I'll try my hand at these," Kate broke in, gesturing with the papers.

"Well, good luck, but—" The girl chewed her lip, leaned forward and lowered her voice. "I hope you make it, but this line is stuffed with heroes."

Kate paused at the remark. "You're telling me," she said slowly, "that they've got everything but male chauvinist signs hanging in the back rooms?"

"Honey, these guys are proud to carry male chauvinist pig club cards. And they *do*."

Kate had flown too long and been with too many pilots not to recognize that their hostility had its foundation in something she could recognize. A woman pilot was a direct and overt threat. If the line started hiring women, many more pilots would be applying for the same jobs higher in the line. Ergo, stiffer competition for all. Well, if they couldn't hack the stiffer competition, tough. *She* wasn't asking any favors.

She knew the ropes in this business and she knew them damned well. She'd been flying longer than many of these pilots, she had more ratings than did most of the pilots and copilots with Alaskair, and, as far as she was concerned, she was a damned sight better pilot than most of them.

She told that to Pete Sizemore. He grinned at her intensity when she flatly laid it out before him. "Well, under the heading of self-confidence, I'm going to have to score a triple A for you."

"You'd better believe it."

His gaze was penetrating. "You really believe you're that good, Kate?"

"No. I don't believe anything of the sort. I *know* I'm that good." She leaned forward. "Look, Pete, one of the great things about being a professional pilot is that you can't sustain yourself by empty boasting. You have to *earn* your tickets, your type ratings, and when you've got the big ones, then Big Brother, the FAA, stays on you *all* the time. They've been breathing right down my neck for years, and I've got a record that's cleaner than clean. None of it is an accident. It speaks for itself. That's who's really talking. The record, not me."

He licked his thumb, held it extended before him. "And a gold star for you."

"I'm not sure how to take that," she said defensively.

He nodded. "Better and better. That chip on your shoulder is hardly visible anymore."

"It's tough *not* keeping it there. The questions you ask sometimes—"

"I do my job, Kate," he said, his tone controlled. "Your job is to bear up under pressure, among many other things."

"You got a license for that needle you stick in people?"

"Yes, I do."

"We're even in gold stars."

"Very good, again. Just keep in mind that anyone who sits across this desk from me gets the needle. Don't forget it. It prevents you from making it personal."

She took the coffee mug from the small table by her chair. "You've studied my life history, Pete. You've got copies of all my FAA papers. I had my ATP medical only three weeks ago. You've got enough character references on me to start your own telephone directory. What's next?"

He stacked the paper work neatly on his desk. "You've made it through the first barrier," he said

"And that means?"

"In the category of interview and psychological stability, Kate Brandon, you're a winner."

She didn't answer him immediately. He wasn't probing or testing anymore. "You mean," she said slowly, "we're ready for the next giant step."

"Right on. And it's bigger than you think." He leaned forward. "Look, Kate, I'd like to see you make it. You qualify. From everything I can possibly learn about you, you come through with flying colors. But I'm not a pilot—and you've got to go the course with the flying part of this operation."

"I'll handle it," she said, her face almost grim.

"You've also got to handle the Bull," Pete said, and there was warning implicit in his tone.

She didn't miss the help he was offering. "Would you spell that out for me, Pete?"

"Among the hierarchy of Alaskair," he said, almost sighing, "there is one office, one person, more important—at least where you're concerned—than anyone else. The office is Training and Flight Operations. It has a large staff. But everything centers on one man. He's the king of the whole works, and—"

"You called him the Bull," she interrupted.

Pete nodded. "Bull Atkins. C. B. Atkins is the full name, although no one knows what the initials stand for. I don't even know and I'm supposed to know everything about everybody."

"Why the name?"

"Because he looks like a bull; and he's got the disposition of a water buffalo. He's also the man who makes or breaks new pilots with this line." Pete stood up. "Good luck, Kate."

"You make it sound as if I'll need it."

"Atkins seems to hate women."

"Oh, great."

"Maybe," Pete said, "he's just met his match."

15

First glance told her the man had earned his name. At least six feet four inches tall, with enormous shoulders, Bull Atkins seemed a human-sized edition of a grizzly bear; but there was no mistaking the keen intelligence behind those thick brows. Kate studied him with special care. This man was accustomed to authority, to knowing he would get top performance from anyone who worked for him. Every move he made was an expression of absolute confidence in himself. And he had an inexplicable grace, a fluidity starkly out of place in that bulk.

His hands were calloused but surprisingly supple— like her father's. Working hands, experienced in tearing down engines. Atkins's thick, almost blunt, fingers, she judged, would be superbly gentle in caressing a control yoke.

His leathery face and the crow's-feet creasing his skin at the corners of his eyes spoke their own eloquence of flying in open cockpits. Wind and sun and squinting had left their mark.

Not one to rush into a situation without preparation, Kate had checked out Mr. C. B. Atkins. He was fifty-four years old, had been a pilot in the Second World War, had returned to combat in Korea, *and* had flown for Alaskair as a captain on jet cargo flights contracted with the military for the war in Vietnam. Enough right there, she realized. He was one of those people whose talents extended way beyond those of an ordinary experienced military and commercial pilot. God alone knew how many thousands of hours he had put in at the controls.

When she entered his office, Atkins's first instinct was to stand to greet her. He hadn't moved his hulk two inches from his seat before he changed his mind and let the chair groan under his returned weight. Had she been a visitor, the courtesy would have been proper. But she was just another pilot, and neophytes in the world of Alaskair—and *all* pilots new to the line were fledglings as far as Atkins was concerned—were treated with the same gruffness.

He motioned her, rather offhandedly, to the seat by his desk. For several moments he didn't speak, eyeing her openly, taking her measure. Finally he offered a grunt. That, and no more. Kate wanted to smile. She was furious with herself for being pleased with that animal sound. Oh, she knew it meant he hadn't decided on first impulse to throw her out of his office. She'd actually passed *his* first test. Damn him, he—

"I don't like women in the cockpit."

She looked at him in disbelief. Were those words, or was it a growl with barely sufficient clarity to pass for language? The man sat with the inertia of a Buddha. He had cast forth his wisdom, and he sat waiting.

Kate bit her tongue, but there was no holding back. "Well, goody for you."

As quickly as his eyes widened and the unruly brows began their upward arch, she had her smile ready for him.

"What the devil does that mean?" he demanded.

"It means I'm sure you have your reasons for the statement you made." Damn. She couldn't yield an inch, yet she didn't want to overdo it. But she was convinced this man appreciated strength rather than coy acquiescence.

"You're right," he growled again, but his interest in her was now evident. "You want it straight, or do you want to go through the motions before you find out how I really feel?"

Well, she told herself, try the coy approach this time. It's all part of the business. "How you really feel about what, Mr. Atkins?"

His look was becoming a stare. "About women flying airliners."

"Oh." She paused. "That."

The lace-lined barb snagged him. What the hell was

it with this broad? She should have folded. Or at least flinched. But she sat there as cool as ice and she was taking him at his own game. She knew damned well what he meant! Then why was she—

"I haven't a thing against females who fly airplanes. If they want to—"

"I'm glad to hear you say that."

"Don't interrupt."

She sat motionless but couldn't pass the mental shrug. Maybe this was his juggernaut approach. So much the better; let it all hang out. She didn't answer him. A nod was enough.

"Let women fly their own airplanes and get into aerobatic competition or fly for the hell of it," he went on, his voice somewhere between a growl and a foghorn. "I don't care. I don't care if a woman never flies or if the whole damn country takes to the air in skirts. What they do in *their* airplanes is up to them. I've known some pretty great broads in my time who can hold their own with the best. They flew everything from P-38s to B-17s, and that takes a lot of flying. I've known 'em to fly jet fighters and God knows what else. They're better than good."

He paused to tear the wrapper off a cigar and she seized the moment to study him more carefully. When he began his little speech she had expected nothing less than a tired old tirade about keeping women barefoot and pregnant. She had not expected to hear C. B. Atkins extolling the ability of women to fly. Obviously, she wasn't faced with some chest-beating gorilla, and she had better listen to this man more closely.

Atkins waved his cigar airily as a cloud of choking smoke reached her. My God, did he still buy those things for a nickel apiece? It smelled like burning insulation. "You don't mind, do you?"

She coughed as she shook her head. "It's delightful. Be my guest."

His grin was what she would have expected from a grizzly who's just chewed off the right leg of a hunter. At least he can smile, she groaned to herself. "Would it matter if I objected?" she finally asked.

"Of course not," he told her. "You want to be in this business, Brandon, certain things go with it."

"Like your cigars."

"Like my cigars."

She wanted to keep it going. "You were telling me what wonderful pilots women make."

He twirled the cigar in thick fingers. "Not quite, Brandon, *not* quite. I said that in certain airplanes they do fine: in other places, they just got no business there." Atkins leaned forward, his forearms bulging like cordwood beneath his jacket. "Look, Miss Brandon, I'm trying to be straight with you. I got your papers here from Sizemore. The big dome makes it very clear he not only thinks you're the greatest thing since cream cheese fell off a truck on the turnpike, he also believes you make great material for a pilot for this line."

"Nice to have someone on my side," she said quickly.

"Sizemore's a headshrinker," he said with mild contempt. "He likes to think he can squeeze out the freaks and the meatballs with his fancy palaver. This airline pays him nearly thirty grand a year to do that. But *we* can find out the same thing in ten minutes in the cockpit." He held up both hands to stave off his audience, present and invisible. "Okay, okay, that's what the brass want to do with their money, that's up to them. He just runs interference for flight training anyway. All I'm saying is that he gives you a medal for being what you are. I didn't need him to tell me about you."

He leaned back to create another roiling cloud of burning insulation. "I assume," Kate said, fighting not to gasp for air, "you're saying something positive about me."

He waved aside the smoke. "Hell, your record talks for itself. Your time, your ratings, all your tickets— the works. You didn't get all these by playing Parcheesi."

"Mr. Atkins, I'm a bit confused. You've condemned women in the cockpit, you've told me how great women are in flying, you've said Pete Sizemore is, well, I don't know, but through all this I begin to get the idea that you, ah, appreciate my record."

"What I said, Brandon, was that women don't belong on the flight decks of commercial airliners."

"Is that remark directed at me, Mr. Atkins?"

"I ain't talking to no all-girl band in here, Brandon. You see anyone else besides yourself? Look, I'll lay it out as best I can, and I want you to understand something." He paused, and, when she simply waited him out, he went on.

"Women can do anything they want in flying, but they do not by God belong in a seat driving a commercial job filled with people. Brandon, there are times when the man in the left seat needs physical strength to handle his airplane. Do you understand what I'm saying? When the hydraulic boosts go out or you get in trouble in a thunderbumper or something else like that goes wrong, you need muscle. Muscle. It doesn't happen very often, but when it does it becomes the difference between whether a captain gets his airplane and all his people down in one piece or spreads them all over the countryside. If you got the muscle you make it. If you don't—" He shrugged.

"Do go on, please," she said quietly, feeling her emotions starting to the boil she wanted to avoid.

"I believe implicitly, Brandon, that emotions are a major factor in airline safety. We watch our people like hawks. A pilot gets into a bad snit with his wife, we're on the lookout for it, and we will yank that man from his seat until he calms down. Maybe you think this is overdoing it. You're wrong if you do. I've seen perfectly normal pilots go haywire because of what goes on in their bedrooms or their kitchens. A man who's all screwed up in his head is screwed up in the cockpit; he moves the wrong switches or makes the wrong decisions, he kills people. So we do everything we can to keep this from happening.

"And what happens when we get broads—excuse me, when we get women—in that same seat? What the hell do we do with female problems?"

Female problems? Kate wanted to throw up. She chewed the inside of her cheek and remained silent.

"A woman gets her period, and, bingo, we *know* she's all messed up in her system and in her head. She's strung out, she blows her stack at the first little thing that comes along and upsets her. What are we supposed to do with her? Leave her in the airplane? Uh uh. No way can we do that. So we got to give her time off just when schedules may be tight or some other problem comes along. You know what that means, Brandon? It means crew scheduling starts to come apart. This outfit doesn't fly like the scheduled carriers down in the Lower Forty-Eight where any crew can get together to fly an airplane. Not up here. We put a crew together on a Hercules, we want that crew to *stay* together for at least three to six months. There's no fancy dan flying for this outfit. It's tough and it can be dangerous, and crew efficiency and safety go right up on the chart."

He waved her record folder at her. "We were talking about your records, Brandon. They're great." The folder smacked the desk top. "Well, there's another kind of record. I run the flight operations for this line. A lot of the top commercial carriers in the Lower Forty-Eight are very progressive and all that crap, and you know what? They're bent out of shape. Where the dollars are concerned they're about to take the big tumble, the last dive. Not this outfit, Brandon. Alaskair is in the black. My job is to keep it there. And women do not belong in the front seats of our airplanes."

A dozen retorts leaped to her lips and a dozen times she shut off the words. The worst thing she could do now was to come back at this man with heat or anger. He *believed* what he'd said to her. He was being honest with her, and that was the best any man could do, even if his convictions were way over on the pigheaded side. So there wasn't any purpose in rattling the cage of C. B. Atkins. It wouldn't do any good. Counterpoint or logic didn't belong here. Atkins was, from his own point of view, absolutely logical. So she'd have to go with what she had on her side.

"I was unaware," she said slowly, making sure each word was cool and calm, "that a requirement for flying for this airline involved arm wrestling or placing unsullied Tampax on your desk."

That was all she'd give him, and she knew it was

more than enough. As he absorbed her words, his face
seemed to go dark. He studied her through narrowed
eyes.

"That's it, huh?"

"No, that's not it, Mr. Atkins. You have my application. You may turn me down, sir, but to respond in
kind, you will by God do it on the basis of open competition, skill, and performance, and for no other reason."

"You're *telling* me all that?" She'd yanked his string,
all right. It couldn't have been more obvious.

"Yes, sir."

He started to reply, hesitated, all but chewed his
cigar in two. A thick finger tapped her papers. "All
right, Brandon. They got all these fancy new federal
laws about no discrimination as to sex, color, religion.
Maybe they've even excluded common sense."

She ignored the remark.

"You report back here tomorrow morning, lady. Sev-
en o'clock sharp. See John Baxter in crew training. You
go through a medical first, and then we see what makes
you tick, right?"

"You have my Class One medical in my folder, Mr.
Atkins."

"So what?" he said.

16

Bull Atkins dropped his heavy flight boots on the edge of Sam Burleyford's desk. Sam winced. No one did that to the desk of the company president, but Atkins wasn't aware of anything out of the ordinary. He did the same thing everywhere. His bachelor apartment had all the evidence of a constant bruising scrimmage.

"I've just had my meeting with the Brandon dame."

Sam Burleyford nodded. "I imagine it was interesting."

"What the hell kind of remark is that?"

"Noncommittal, C.B."

Atkins looked at him long and hard. "I don't like the smell of what you're saying, Sam."

Burleyford leaned back in his chair and studied the heavy gold ring on his hand. "Spell it out, C.B."

"What's there to spell? How do you want me to get rid of her?"

"Get rid of—" Burleyford cut himself off. "It's not that easy anymore."

"She's a dame! She doesn't belong in a captain's seat. Not on this line, anyway. All I want from you is how you want me to handle it, for Christ's sake."

Sam smiled, and the tolerant look on his face didn't amuse Atkins. "Like I said," Burleyford continued, "it's not that easy anymore. This line deals in government contracts, C.B. That makes us a party to certain federal regulations, one of which is that we will not discriminate in our hiring policy as to the sex of anyone who applies to this line."

"You sound like a goddamned fag."

"Get off my ass, Atkins." The sudden sharpness caught the flight director by surprise. "You come in here breaking everything in sight, and you forget we have no choice but to comply with those regulations. I don't necessarily like them, but I have to live with them, and you'd better start learning, and *fast,* that you've got to do the same thing. How long do you think Alaskair would stay in business without those government contracts for running supplies up to Prudhoe Bay or supporting the radar sites? Even the oil companies couldn't deal with us if the government established that we weren't hewing toe-and-foot to their standards of civil rights. It's a new world, C.B., and you'd better get on it with the rest of us."

Atkins drew his feet beneath him slowly, planted his weight solidly. "What'd you do, Sam, sell out to the limp wrists and the libbers?"

"Bull, you're not that dumb. What are you chewing on?"

"Women don't belong in our cockpits!"

"I've checked out Kate Brandon's papers. She qualifies in every way as an applicant for captain."

"Except that she's—"

"Being a *she* doesn't count anymore."

"It counts in *my* book!"

"Then you'd better tear out the pages and write some new ones." Burleyford climbed from his chair and came around to sit on the edge of his desk. "Listen to me, old friend. It *is* a new ball game, and we've got to play by the new rules, and that's all there is to it. You think I like the way we're buried in paper work this far up the line? You just bet your sweet ass I don't, C.B. But Alaskair has grown, and we want to grow some more, and there's a people's mandate or whatever the hell you want to call it. If we want the cash flow from the Lower Forty-Eight, then we have to abide by their numbers. Otherwise, we can kiss off forty to fifty percent of all the dollars we earn. You want to try to talk the board of directors into doing things *your* way?"

Atkins glared. "Sam, goddamn it, all I did was come in here with some crap about a broad and you've just read me the Constitution and the budget for next year. I want—"

"What *you* want is no longer enough."

"That's moose crap. You can talk to me day and night about contracts and budgets, Mr. President, but it still boils down to the fact that we're operating in the black because of the way I run flight operations for this outfit. Any argument on that?"

"None."

"Then listen to me, damn your soul. I'm not playing any games with you, Sam. I'll save us a lot of back-and-forth. On paper this Brandon girl has it all going for her. She's got more than enough time, she's got all the ratings, and she's got more experience than I believed she could handle."

"So what's the kick, C.B.?"

"It is one goddamned thing to be able to fly an airplane," Atkins said, his voice rising to a pleasant bellow, "even to be checked out in the heavy equipment; and it is a hell of something else to fly by the numbers. You of all people should know that! Our pilots have got to anvil their schedules, stay on top of them all the time, be ready day or night in any kind of crap to get out there and fly."

Atkins exploded from his chair, pacing the office. Sam Burleyford noticed his water pitcher and glasses tinkling with every pounding stride. "You know what our pilots got to do? They got to be able to handle their crews. They've got to ramrod through on shitty schedules. The crew has to be willing, even eager, to follow their orders. We're not flying the cocktail run to Las Vegas! We handle everything in the world." He stabbed a finger at Burleyford. "What the hell does a woman pilot do with a drunken passenger? Some beefy guy who's half out of his skull on rotgut and wants to tear up the airplane? Does she order the man in the right seat to handle things? Hell, whoever rides left seat is the *captain,* and you don't pass the buck in that job. How does a woman react to a hundred different things that are tough enough for the people we got right now?

"Maybe—just *maybe*—she can handle the controls as well as a man. That I doubt. But even if she can, she sure as hell ain't going to fly no better than the people on the line now. All we end up with, Sam, is a minus, no matter how good she may be. Don't any of you dummies up here in the front office understand all this?"

Burleyford returned to his seat and leaned back. Several times he started his answer, then shook his head. Atkins looked at him with impatience. "You forget how to talk?"

"No, C.B. It's just that I'm trying to find the easiest way I know to lay it on you."

"You never played pussycat before."

Burleyford came straight up in his chair. "Okay, C.B., I'll lay it out. The cards face up on the table, all right?" His own finger stabbed at the bigger man. "Short and sweet, here it is. You better start remembering something. I take orders from topside. You got that, C.B.? *I take my orders from on top.* I run this outfit, but I do not make company policy. There's a group of people called the majority stockholders, and they've made up a tight little bloc all their own, and they have passed on the word.

"And the word is, you will judge Kate Brandon, or any other woman who qualifies for a position with this line, strictly on her merits, and by no other qualification. Those are the *orders* I've been given."

Atkins stood rooted to the floor. "I don't believe it," he said, and his voice was deceptively quiet.

"Start believing; because that's straight."

"No one is going to tell me how to run my operation, Sam."

"Quit."

An electric pause, then: *"What?"*

"I said, quit. Put it in writing. I'll accept it the moment it's on my desk."

"By glory, you're *serious.*"

"No choice, C.B."

They let the silence hang between them like a shroud until they'd both collected their thoughts. Burleyford recognized that Atkins really didn't know what to say. "Look, C.B., you really believe a woman can't hack the left seat?"

"You're damned right I believe it."

"Then what the hell are you so hot and bothered for? Play it through, man. *But keep it aboveboard.*

You know how to handle something like this. Play it straight. Absolute fairness. But there's nothing in all this that says you can't put the woman through the meat grinder, is there?"

Atkins scraped heavily on chin stubble. "No, there isn't."

"Then do it by the numbers, C.B. Just don't do anything that will give anyone the opportunity to crack down on this office by claiming you're being unfair."

Atkins came to his decision. "By thunder, I'll play it just that way. But I don't think she'll last that long."

Burleyford nodded. "What's the average time for our pilots, C.B.?"

"About seven thousand hours." He hadn't expected the query. "Why?"

"Kate Brandon has more than nine thousand. She's got over three grand in the heavy equipment, *and* all the ratings."

"You on her side, Sam?"

Burleyford shook his head. "Uh uh. Neat and clean, C.B., neat and clean." He grinned. "But it's going to be interesting. *Very* interesting."

"What the hell does that mean?"

"C.B., you knew Vance Brandon, didn't you? He owned Brandon Airways. Old Mustang driver, just about everything else in the book. I think you mentioned once you'd flown with him a couple of times. What kind of pilot was he?"

"The best."

Sam Burleyford chuckled. "I told you it was going to be interesting. This girl is Vance's kid." The chuckle grew into a laugh. "You know something, C.B.? You may have more here than you can handle. Who knows? She might even show *you* a few new tricks. That ought to be pretty funny."

C. B. Atkins didn't think it was one goddamn bit funny.

There was always the chance she'd fall flat on her face in the company physical. The FAA medicals for a Class One were tough. Alaskair was tougher because of their specific needs for operating in the Far North:

you had to be thirty percent superman. C. B. Atkins thought about that a lot, and the more he dwelled on the subject the more he was pleased with the possibilities. He fidgeted through the days, while Kate Brandon went through the torture mill in the medical labs, and then he stomped down to the office of Dr. Louis Stevens.

"How does the Brandon broad shape up?" Atkins demanded.

"She's beautiful," the doctor said, admiration all over his face. Atkins wanted to smear it on permanently. "A lovely young woman, and—"

"That's not what I meant and you know it," Atkins rumbled. "Pilot talk, doc. How does she stack up?"

"She—never mind." Dr. Stevens took a deep breath. Atkins's feelings on female pilots were hardly a secret. "In terms of physiological standards, the woman is close to perfect. She—"

"Pilot talk, goddamn it!"

"That is precisely what you are getting, Mr. Atkins, if you'll keep quiet long enough to listen." The doctor took a quick breath. If he and Atkins hadn't been friends almost as many years as stretched behind them he knew he'd be sliding through those glass doors by now. But he knew the Bull; he plunged on. "Kate Brandon, C.B., is just a shade better in physiological condition, depth perception, reaction time, vision, and, well, anything you want or care to name, than any pilot now flying for this company."

"I don't believe you."

"Get another doctor. But I'm the best in this whole state and you know it."

"There's nothing wrong?"

"You have the report of Dr. Sizemore in terms of the psychological profile. He—"

"Who?"

"Dr. Peter Sizemore."

"He's a goddamned ribbon salesman."

"He's a Ph.D. No one will contest his findings. He rates her about as perfect as you can be in terms of stability and reliability. *I* rate her the same way physically. C.B., I wish *I* was that healthy."

Atkins began to grope. "What about the spin chair? You know, how she reacted to vertigo."

"She has the reflexes of a cat."

"Are you telling me there's *nothing* about her that—"

"Knock it off, C.B. Look, we've spent four days testing this woman. In every way possible. We have put her through the wringer. No one has ever taken tougher tests, and no one, but no one, has ever scored higher. What the devil do you want me to do? Make up problems? I won't do that, and—"

"Nobody asked you to. Okay, doc. Thanks." As he slammed through the doors he looked back for a moment. "Thanks for nothing," he added.

Atkins found Nick Wayne in his office down in Training. Nick ran the simulators—electronic and mechanical marvels, perfect duplicates of an airliner cockpit down to the last nut and bolt. Run by computers, they simulated any condition of flight the director wanted to program—from a leaky faucet to exploding engines and violent storms. Special tapes, films through the cockpit windows that imitated to remarkable believability what a pilot would see were he in a real plane, crew members who went along with the whole show. Pilots had found the simulators so real that they had become ill or panicked. If anyone could catch Kate Brandon napping, or find a flaw in that smooth-assed armor, it would be Nick Wayne.

Wayne knew his boss well enough to know what he sought. "I'm sorry to disappoint you, C.B."

"Yeah?"

"Out of a possible one hundred, the lady gets better than ninety-eight."

Atkins glared at him, not trusting himself to speak.

"The line average for the same tests runs approximately ninety-two, C.B. I only know of three pilots who have ever done better in the simulator."

"That's wonderful," Atkins snarled. "She got the works?"

Wayne sighed. "Everything. The four pilots who are under consideration got the same treatment. We even put her into a spin in a 737. She knew more than any of the others about coming out of it within limits."

"Did you birdbrains ever think about checking her out with hydraulic boost loss?" Atkins remembered his speech about pilot strength when control boost went out in a big airplane. He crossed mental fingers.

"She couldn't handle full control at the high Mach numbers, of course," Nick Wayne explained. "She—"

"Well, goddamn, finally we got something."

"*You* couldn't handle the controls at high Mach, C.B."

Atkins shook his head slowly. "Never mind me, damn it. What happened?"

"She went through it all. Power reduction as pretty as you please. She got the fans unspooled, worked on the trim, found it was inoperative, ordered her copilot on the yoke with her, their feet on the dash, and started a steady pull. At one point they lowered the gear and—"

Atkins's eyes lit up. "What happened?"

"The doors went at once, and the gear started coming apart right after."

"That's it, then. She screwed up, and—"

"Under the conditions simulated, her procedures were correct. Recommended by the manufacturer. A deliberate move to suffer some structural separation as a trade-off for reduced velocity."

C. B. Atkins looked as if he'd been poleaxed. "There's nothing else?"

"Uh uh, boss. She's one of the greatest pilots I've ever had in here, and—"

"Shut up. I don't want your opinions." Atkins rubbed his face, shaking his head slowly. "I guess there's no way out of it, then. Schedule her for flying. Day after tomorrow."

Nick Wayne nodded. "Who's her check pilot, C.B.?"

"Who the hell did you think?"

17

When Kate Brandon arrived at C. B. Atkins's office before sunup for the opening bid in the flight competition, the other three hopefuls were there. C. B. Atkins met them with a face any self-respecting mother would have rejected out of hand. His words were as blunt as the visage staring at them.

"We'll get right to it. You've all made the grade. Brandon leads the pack. But from here on we're through making chicken scratches on paper. We fly. I don't know how familiar you people really are with the policy of this line, but you're a hell of a long sight from earning the left seat of *any* airplane we operate. And before you can fly for us you've got to be fully qualified in each and every piece of equipment we have."

Kate chewed on his words while Atkins paused to inhale a long slug of steaming black coffee. Everything she had heard so far pleased her. Alaskair, which flew every conceivable type of cargo, wasn't much different from her own Brandon Airways, except that it operated on a much larger scale and with some much heavier and more demanding equipment.

So the pilots had to be rated in each airplane? Kate kept her smile to herself. She was already type rated in every single one of the dozen or so types of airplanes flown by Alaskair. Her real test wouldn't be flying.

The big man shifted his weight. "I'm going to test you, push you, needle you. And, judge you. Understand that. I'm also going to throw the four of you against one another. Not nice, huh? But if you want to make it through you'll have to learn how to cut throats. When you're flying on regular runs you're *always* judging the people with you. So," and he added with a

demonic smile, "you will rate one another, and give
me your findings. All right. The iron bird is waiting by
flight operations. Six Two Tango. Sikes, you'll lead off.
Catlin, you're right seat today. Get out there and preflight."

Del Sikes nodded, but his movements were hesitant.
"Ah, Mr. Atkins, you didn't say what type aircraft."

"No, I didn't, did I?" Atkins impaled the pilot with a
look of contempt. "Sikes, just how many goddamned
airplanes do you think you'll find at operations with
the same number?"

Well, that's one on the debit side for Del Sikes, noted
Kate. She didn't fault Atkins for the move. Sikes wasn't
thinking. Maybe he was under Atkins's thumb so badly
he couldn't hack it. The three men left in a sudden
rush, leaving Kate in the same cage with Atkins. He
stared at her for several moments, and the belligerence
in the office seemed to fade. He motioned to the table
across his office. "Pour yourself some coffee, Brandon."

She didn't know where the truce had come from, but
she enjoyed it. This was the first time she'd seen Atkins
as a man instead of an antagonist. And despite the rack
on which he tried to put all potential pilots for the line,
Kate admired the skills that had placed him where he
was.

"This coffee," she said with a mild gasp, "would
burn the fur off a grizzly."

He cocked one eyebrow. "You don't make my coffee, you don't knock it."

"It wasn't a knock, C.B. My father made it the same
way. We could almost use it for diesel fuel."

"Yeah."

That was all. Just a verbal sound. She sipped again,
looking at him across her cup. "You remind me of him
in many ways."

He showed a flicker of interest. "Who?"

"My father. He was a great deal like you." She
laughed. "Nicer, though."

This time he returned her gaze without comment.

"You knew him, didn't you?"

The leonine head nodded. "A good man."

"Did you ever fly together?"

"Lodestar. We did some backcountry flying. He used to take that thing in and out of places that were impossible." Atkins's eyes took on a brighter tone. "Why did you ask?"

She shrugged. "Tying pieces together, I suppose." She studied the powerful man across his desk. "Did you know you two are a lot alike?"

Atkins snorted. "You're taking a long shot in saying that, Brandon."

"Not really." Her smile was genuine. "Look, could we talk off the record for a moment?" She had almost resisted those words, but the mood between her and Atkins had reached an unexpected level.

"Shoot, kid."

"Like I said, off the record. I was thinking—I was wondering if you really think your trying to browbeat me is going to do any good. I know how you handle your pilots, run them through the mill, I mean, and I'm not criticizing. This is just personal. But my father used to put me through the mill every day, one week after the other. I really believe he was rougher on me than you ever could be. When I flew for him, Mr. Atkins, I didn't have to be good."

Thick eyebrows raised at her last line.

"I had to be about as close to perfect as you could get," Kate went on slowly. "If I screwed up I was on the griddle and I stayed on it. He yelled a lot, too, and I don't think you're one ounce nastier than he was," she took a deep breath as the words came faster, "and I loved my dad very much."

Bull Atkins leaned back in his chair. He was off-balance suddenly. Through whatever damned magic she had, this young woman had changed things. He saw her as though she'd walked into his range of vision for the first time. A woman who was tawny and fascinating and smarter than hell; and she was talking to him on an equal basis as a pilot. The mixed realizations were disconcerting to Atkins, and he held onto his own gruffness for defense.

"Yeah, well that's all great, Brandon, but I'm not your daddy, and when you screw up with me there's more to it than standing in the corner. When I—"

"C. B., I am looking forward very much to the flying we are going to do. The hard nut, as you would call it. The *flying*."

"You seem damned eager to end this nonsense."

She showed strong white teeth in a humorless smile. "Just so there will be no mistake about it, Mr. Atkins, I can, and I will, fly the ass off any pilot you have in this operation, man *or* woman."

"We don't have any damned women on this line," he growled.

"Past tense, Mr. Atkins. Past tense."

Flying an airplane is the easiest part of being a pilot. The statement is, of course, a contradiction; but not to someone who flies. All airplanes work in basically the same manner. They are mechanical objects reacting to mechanical forces, and the differences in handling are mostly a matter of detail.

The secret—aside from inherent and achieved skills —in knowing an airplane is in knowing its systems, understanding well ahead of time its procedures and how it will act under unusual circumstances. Handling an airplane on the ground is often much more demanding, and precarious, than simply flying the thing, even when the skies are unfriendly and the clouds filled with reefs and rocks.

C. B. Atkins started the flight-test program not in a modern jetliner, or even in one of the high-performance turboprops, but in the old twin-engined Douglas DC-3, an airliner that had been around since its first commercial flight in 1936. Atkins's move made good sense. Heavy jet equipment often disguised many of a pilot's traits; the power-boosted controls and the excess energy could frequently make up for human foibles.

The Gooney Bird—as the DC-3 was known to thousands of pilots who had flown it to war, glory, and hell—also lacked the comfortable landing-gear system of the newer planes. No nosewheel for this machine; it sat on two main gear legs and a tail wheel. It was demanding in crosswind landings and takeoffs. It responded willingly, almost eagerly, to the caprice of the wind, and it insisted on full attention from the pilot at all times during ground maneuvering. It liked to swerve and bob and weave if conditions were less than optimum.

It was the kind of airplane that behaved beautifully as long as you remained one step ahead of its pilot-stomping characteristics. If you didn't, you could "lose" the airplane faster than you realized. On a modern jet-liner with four great spools hurling back energy, a pilot could lose an engine and with no more than a raised eyebrow fly his machine across an ocean. Losing an engine during the critical takeoff roll also lay within the bounds of very reasonable safety with jet equipment.

Lose an engine on takeoff in a loaded Gooney Bird and you were in sheep-dip up to your neck—that fast. You were pilot, magician, and priest, with three legs and four hands moving in a blur just to keep the airplane working.

For Kate, flying the DC-3 under the scrutiny of C. B. Atkins was a joy. She had flown this type of airplane for years with her father and then on her own as the chief pilot of Brandon Airways. She climbed into the left seat and wore the Gooney Bird as if it were an old shoe. Her drill work was as close to perfection as any pilot, including Atkins, might demand—takeoffs and landings under a wide variety of conditions, stalls, unnatural attitudes, single-engine flying, instrument flying, handling the airplane like a roughneck when the moment demanded, and flying it with razor precision when that touch was called for.

They went from the Gooney Bird to several single-engine aircraft, from wheels to floats, from floats to skis, and from airplanes to helicopters. For nearly three weeks they flew, day and night, in fair weather and murky. They flew airport patterns and they ran the drill through down-to-the-second scheduled flights. They went into mountain strips and operated from runways two miles long—the pressure mounting all the time.

And C. B. Atkins knew how to squeeze—but in a way Kate had never expected.

The man who could hold his thumb up, or turn it down, never climbed into an airplane with her. Oh, he still carried the name of C. B. Atkins, he still had that same craggy face and iron-jawed scowl to present to them, but the man she had known in the airlines office was gone.

She could hardly believe it. The great bull moose had vanished. Bellicose roar and overwhelming brawn and abrasive presence—they all disappeared the moment Atkins strapped himself into an airplane. It was a transformation no louder than two snowflakes clashing in an arctic sky.

It was unnerving. Atkins never raised his voice. The deep growl became a pleasant bass. The hammering gestures flowed into gentle motions. It was as if the sky had no need for the man he was on the ground. In the air, he soared in spirit as well as body.

But you kept waiting for the damned shoe to drop because you knew Atkins had a very heavy boot.

He kept you waiting. His touch was velvet. He was as good as any pilot Kate had ever known, perhaps even the best.

And he never invited comparison between his touch and the pilots he flew with. Yet he was relentless with his squeeze because they all knew he missed nothing, forgot nothing. Quietly, almost hushed.

Until Kate and Atkins were out one day in the four-engined DC-4, the same friendly cow type of airplane she flew on her own line.

In which she had her first head-to-head clash—violently—with Atkins.

18

"We'll clear with Elmendorf Control and go direct to Skwentna. On the deck all the way, Brandon. When we get there we land at Fox Hill. You set it all up. I play dummy until we make the field. You got one hour before wheels up. And I want it right on that schedule. Questions?"

She paused. Sometimes C.B. could be a sneaky son of a bitch. Skwentna, to the northwest, beyond the last curve of Cook Inlet, was on the charts. Fox Hill was also on the charts but as a private airstrip. If she didn't call in ahead for prior permission to use the field, he would use the lapse against her.

First things first. She found Craig Wilcox, flight engineer for the DC-4, in the snack bar. She rousted him from a bull session and sent him to the aircraft to attend to fuel loading, weight and balance sheets, and the other paper work. She made a direct-line call to the air force controllers at Elmendorf and set up their clearance, effective just before takeoff.

Twenty minutes later she was doing her own detailed preflight, checking the squawk sheets for discrepancies that needed attention before another flight, going through an elaborate checklist. She was strapped into the left seat when Atkins came aboard. He picked up his clipboard. "I'll ride as copilot," he announced, and with those words he passed full command of the four-engined plane to Kate.

It went with the same professional skill she had demonstrated from the first. Atkins played his role as first officer with full support to the pilot in the left seat; he saw no woman there. And from the way the engines were started, the manner in which the pilot ran through the lists, rolled to the active, and thundered

down the runway, there was no way to tell whether man
or woman eased the big airplane from the ground.

Kate signaled for gear up, went through the checklist
on flaps, eased off on power, set the engines for so much
manifold pressure, so many revolutions per minute, ran
a cross-check with her copilot and flight engineer on
fuel flow, fuel pressure, oil pressure and temperature,
cylinder head temperature; all of it neat and quick and
right on the money.

The DC-4 went through its pleasant wallowing in the
light, choppy air as they crossed the upper arm of Cook
Inlet, flew overland, and then passed over the Susitna
River. She kept the Yentna River just off her right
wing, flew a thousand feet above the ground, adjusting
for height as distant hills came closer. The signal from
Skwentna grew stronger and then she was within direct
range.

"Skwentna Tower from Six Eight Eight Juliett. Two
zero miles southeast. Over." She waited for the ac-
knowledgment.

"Ah, Skwentna, we have permission to use Fox Hill
for some pattern work." She listened again, then:
"Roger that, Skwentna. Six Eight Eight Juliett is a
Delta Charlie Four. Right, we'll monitor your fre-
quency and call you before we leave. Six Eight Eight
Juliett out."

There must have been some weather rolling down
from the hills. In the short time it took to fly from the
Anchorage area to Fox Hill, the surface winds had
picked up by fifteen to thirty knots, perhaps more.
Sometimes the hills formed a trough down which the
winds howled as if driven through a flue. Kate didn't
like the feel of it. She studied their side drift over the
ground. She frowned, called Skwentna again and asked
for their surface winds.

A mere eight miles between Skwentna and Fox Hill
was all the difference in the world. Skwentna reported
winds from the north at eighteen knots with gusts to
twenty-five. It could have been a hundred miles away,
Kate thought, because if she was any judge, the winds
where they were now—at Fox Hill—were at least forty
knots and no telling how strong they were gusting.

And Fox Hill was an airport in name only; it had never been intended for use by anything except small airplanes. You could bring in the DC-4, provided the wind was strong and right down the runway. As she circled the field, her feelings intensified. Damn, they had a direct crosswind. That meant *no* head wind component, and they'd be going like a bat out of hell as they came down on final. Too fast, she judged. She would have to keep in an exaggerated crab, a wing kept low with crossed controls, to compensate for the wind, and even then it would be very, very sticky. It appeared as if the various combinations were starting to gang up on them. Fox Hill might not be for them this day.

The field itself consisted of patchy combinations of grass and gravel. It looked like lousy braking action. Once you started those main tires skidding on gravel, the airplane had ideas of its own about where to end up, and you could let it get out from under you in a hurry. The field was short and it was rough and the approaches were miserable. Trees on both ends of the field. Some trees on the upwind side, which meant tumbling wind action. The more she saw of it the more her danger signals were flying. The only way to land a DC-4 into that stinker was to make a clean approach into a dead-on wind and set down properly. Any flight distractions or unusual forces would immediately change a normal cliff-hanger approach to one of red-flagged danger.

Well, you couldn't get hurt in shooting the approach. She set up the airplane, called out power settings, flaps, gear; she put everything where it belonged. The downwind leg was ridiculous; the wind changed almost constantly. Her corrections were immediate and effective, but their passage over the ground was more a drunken waltz than a smooth path. She fed in power to compensate for the wind as they rolled into base leg, descending steadily, and then they were on final, the airplane acting as if it were going down a stairway.

Atkins sat quietly, offering no criticism because none was deserved. The DC-4 flew like a drunken sailor, but Kate was holding everything within limits, compensating constantly. The trees kept expanding before them, seeming to wobble and dance from the cockpit view. Lower, holding extra speed because of the chop, until they were almost ready to commit.

Kate aborted the landing. No warning calls to the crew, the decision was made instantly. She judged everything that was happening, could happen. She was almost there, the yoke jerking and shaking beneath her left hand. At the last moment, with everything still within her complete control, she snapped out the order.

"Abort!" In the same breath her right hand went full forward on the four throttles. The engines picked up their thunder with a great cry and the DC-4 surged forward.

"Gear up," she ordered. "Flaps to takeoff position."

C. B. Atkins stared at her. For the moment, he had forgotten the cardinal rule. Kate Brandon in the left seat *was* the captain and he was copilot; she was fully qualified in the DC-4 and her orders were to be followed instantly and to the letter.

But so great was his astonishment that all he could do was gape. Finally he caught his wits. "I told you to take it in!" It was also the first time the man she knew so well on the ground had climbed into the airplane. His voice was a half shout, a command.

The transport lurched from the winds tumbling across the trees. Kate held it with exquisite care. The wind condition was worse than she'd expected, and she hadn't made her decision a moment too soon.

Her hand whipped from the throttles across the quadrant to the landing-gear lever, slammed it into the Up position. With full power now and the gear retracting, cleaning up the airplane, she brought in more back pressure to the yoke. The runway raced beneath them, the trees perilously close.

"Takeoff position flaps!" she said, her voice as flat and cracking as a whip. *"That's an order, Mr. Atkins!"*

He gritted his teeth, moved his hand to the flap controls, brought them into the takeoff position detent.

Kate's voice was icy, sharp. "Gear?"

"Three red," Atkins said after a momentary pause, confirming three red lights. The gear was up and in the wells, the airplane cleaner, with less drag than before.

They were past the trees, airspeed building. She brought back the throttles to climb power. "Flaps up," she ordered.

It would have been impossible to measure the anger in that flight deck. Atkins turned in his seat. They were climbing out smoothly and he didn't have to wait any longer.

"Brandon, I told you to—"

"*Mister* Atkins." Her cheek muscles worked furiously and she fought to keep her voice level. "I am the captain of this aircraft. Remember that. Whatever you have to say will wait until we are on the ground. You may now direct me to land at Skwentna or return to Anchorage."

Great fists clenched quietly. "Take it back. Anchorage."

The only words passing between them for the rest of the flight were those between captain and first officer. Kate landed and went through the shutdown checklist. When everything was secure, Atkins climbed from his seat and left the airplane.

In his office, Atkins sat heavily in his chair, swung around to face Kate as she came through the doorway. He set his jaw and pointed a finger in her direction. He never got to say a word.

The door slammed behind her with a crash that rattled glass up and down the hall. She had never before felt such rage as diffused hotly through her body at this moment. She threw her flight bag to the floor and moved purposefully to his desk, her eyes almost flashing. She leaned across the desk, the palms of her hands flat on its surface.

"Before you open your mouth, Atkins, you listen to me. And I mean listen, you overbearing, stubborn fool. You were wrong out there today, Atkins. You were wrong on your decision to go into that field, but most of all, and it was insufferable, you were wrong in not following, at once, the orders of your pilot. Do you understand me? You violated every safety rule in the book!"

She stood up, taking a deep breath for better self-control. "As the captain of that airplane, as the pilot in command, Mr. Atkins, my judgment was clear. We were over the legal crosswind component. The situation was aggravated by a poor approach and by turbulent conditions that made a gust stall likely. We had too much speed, and we needed it, to land safely on such a short strip.

"I gave you a direct order as the copilot in that airplane. You failed to obey that order. Because of the special circumstances of a training flight I am willing to let the whole thing slide."

Her finger stabbed at him. "But if you would care to make an issue of today, Mr. Atkins, let me tell you loud and clear that I would be delighted to appear before any FAA board of review you have in mind.

"Where," she added with what was by now an icy calm, "I will press charges against you for insubordination on the flight deck."

The door crashed again as she stalked out.

"Mike, I'm so glad you were home." Kate leaned back on the couch. A fire crackled in the stone fireplace of Mike's cabin.

Mike held her tighter. "It's the right place to be."

Kate sighed. She had thought of nothing except those final moments of explosive temper. Not until she left his office had she realized that Atkins had never spoken a word.

She shook her head slowly, staring at flames leaping around a log. "I'm beginning to wonder if it's really worth it."

Mike laughed. "It's all over the line, honey."

She looked up at him. "What do you mean?"

"Kate, they heard you up and down the hall. They all heard you. The story's around half the state by now. Everyone's been in hysterics."

She studied him, her eyes wide. "You're serious."

"I am. I think it's beautiful." He kissed her forehead. "You're beautiful."

"I do not think it's hysterical, Mike. It's hardly a laughing matter. And I'm sure Atkins doesn't find it a bit funny. It could cost me everything."

Mike pushed her to a sitting position, looking straight at her. "Could you have landed that iron bird? Into Fox Hill, I mean?"

She shrugged. "Maybe."

"Maybe? What kind of answer is that, Kate? You've got to do better than that."

"It was chancy, Mike. Very chancy."

"And you were in the left seat. Okay. You did the only right thing there was to do. You said yourself you were way over the specified component for the crosswind, right? The numbers are very plain. If you *had* gone in you would be at fault." He gripped her arms. "Kate, don't you realize that if you had gone ahead and landed, *then* Atkins had every right to bust you out of the program?"

"Oh, I've thought of that too, but—"

"But, hell. How would you justify, without an emergency situation, flying deliberately into something that could have pranged the bird and killed some people? By aborting, you exercised command prerogative, common sense, and—well, you did what you should have done."

Kate had a whimsical smile on her face. "I wonder if Atkins knows all that."

"He does *now*. He's got to know. He hasn't busted you. And if you were wrong he'd have lowered the boom on you so fast your head would ache for a year."

"Well, maybe—"

"Maybe, hell."

"Mike?"

"What, honey?"

"Shut up, will you, please?" She held out her arms to him.

19

Sam Burleyford was forty-two years old and stood six feet two inches tall. He carried his 185 pounds on a neat, lean frame. A thick shock of blond hair with impudent touches of white, set over piercing blue eyes, accented a wide, strong smile. Sam Burleyford had what people liked to call an *aura*. Some people called it leadership quality; but whatever it was, Sam carried it through his personal and professional life. He knew he had an effect on people, and his sense of it allowed him to use it just a bit. Charisma was the kind of asset that Sam Burleyford checked off in his personal ledger. It made rung climbing that much easier in the business world, and, since he had begun to court certain political powers, he was fully aware of how vital his own personality could be.

Unknown to even his closest friends, the tug of politics beckoned so greatly that Sam had begun to determine his chances for success. Sam wanted what success in the political arena could bring him. The concept of wielding power was one kind of magnet, and he was drawn to it. Despite these aspirations, Sam Burleyford also judged high political office as a position from which to serve. It was not power for power's sake. He believed honestly that he would be an excellent and perhaps even a great leader.

Giving form to these desires involved planning, arranging, working, and dealing. And recognizing the media through which you had to work. That's where Sam Burleyford knew he had an intrinsic advantage. Most men had their personalities bleached and sucked dry by television cameras. Sam seemed to be bigger than life on the restricted surface of the TV screen.

He knew he must be better than good, and he must

waste nothing available to him—including the electronic media which showed him so advantageously. Every move he made in his personal and professional world could edge him that much closer to the desired political niche. Sam's niche was very big indeed—the governor's chair of the state of Alaska.

Sam exuded the air of a "man who gets things done." He ran Alaskair with verve and energy and professional skill. Alaskair operated in the black. Its growth was constant, its reputation gleaming, its future star-bright. What probably identified the man more than anything else was the plaque on his desk that read: *"If you want something done, give it to a busy man. That's me."*

Sam's best-kept secret was that he hated flying.

Not from a fear of being aloft, not from any terror of winged forms. In these respects, his fears were those of any competent pilot—sensibility emerging from caution.

Sam Burleyford simply did not like to fly. He found no joy in watching a horizon spinning madly. He liked even less the tedium, the discipline so necessary for precision in instrument flight when no part of the outside world was visible. Not that Sam couldn't hack it; he had *done* it.

It was one thing, the way Sam looked at it, to comprehend and even become proficient in the new and exquisite techniques of flight—where electronics were almost more important than flying itself. It was quite something else to be slavish to those techniques. There was no escape, of course, if you were going to operate as a pilot in the business of scheduled commercial flying, because without those new systems you had no place in the air.

Sam knew how to operate a system that functioned under these new rules and requirements—but he swore to himself he'd never again do it from the flight deck.

Besides, an airline has hundreds of pilots, but only one president.

Not even Sam's closest friends ever suspected his rejection of the thinner regions of the stratosphere. No one would even consider such heresy. Sam Burleyford was the public relations ideal for an airline president. And he was a proven pilot. No one had ever bothered to find out how *much* of a pilot he was. It simply didn't matter.

He was more than the president of Alaskair; he was a howling success at the job.

Only one man had ever cracked his shell. A long time ago. Vance Brandon, a man who never climbed into an airplane so he might fly—he simply strapped the damn thing to his back and soared into the blue. They had been good and true friends. Vance was the warmly garrulous type of which aviation lore is written. Sam had flown with and for Vance Brandon, and there had finally come that inevitable bad moment in the air. Sam was in the left seat of a creaking old DC-3, fighting through storm turbulence to a short strip between high hills.

During that metal-straining descent, Sam's stomach had turned traitor, and his balance teetered precariously. Sweat poured from him and he feared for his life. He knew that the man to his right, with only a gesture or a short phrase, would have taken the controls and brought them down with ease and precision. But Sam fought and struggled with himself, the DC-3, and the elements, and more than once they hung on the edge of disaster. It was a rough landing and a wild swerving down the rain-hammered runway, but Sam brought the machine to a halt. He sat quietly, utterly exhausted, drenched in sweat.

Later, in the paneled office, among mementos of ancient flight and the smell of leather jackets and strong coffee, Vance put it to him straight: "Quit."

Sam took his coffee slowly. "Why?"

A thin smile appeared on the weatherworn face. "Because you don't know how to make love to metal," Vance told him. "You can dominate a woman, Sam. You can't dominate an airplane. No way. You meet her halfway and you embrace. If you don't, then in the end she'll kill you." Vance sighed. "If you want to stay alive, get out of the cockpit."

Well, okay. Sam Burleyford had made it all the way through the pain of qualifying in umpteen different types of airplanes. He didn't need the damn things. Vance's words did him more good than the man would ever know because with those words Vance liberated him, freed Sam forever of any nagging questions that he was a quitter. Okay, okay; this just wasn't his ball game. He had played it and fought through.

Now, goddamn it, he'd go after bigger game. It had corporate stickers all over its hide.

In the following years, he took pains to assure, as he climbed the corporate ladder, that he never lost sight of what lay beyond. Alaska was still a frontier. Sam learned the ins and outs, the whys and wherefores, the lore and history, and the now and the future of the state. Once he was an expert on Alaska, he could relate with telling impact the role of his airline to the needs of the state and its people. He developed a technique into a compelling art.

Everything he did hewed religiously to his goal, covert for a long time, of opening his chances to be governor. There were ways to command public attention, and, in Alaska, mercy flights were among the best. He looked for such moments and when they came he milked everything possible from the news media. The press were always on hand because he always gave them good copy and a red-carpet ride all the way.

He had truly come to understand the unique characteristics of the forty-ninth state. He was an incredible salesman for Alaska, and he knew how to pitch for its needs. For all its size, its splendors, its mineral and other wealth, the state still had a total road network, paved and potholed dirt, of less than eight thousand miles. That was barely a scratch. The railroads were even more sparse: trackage was limited in scope and distance—less than six hundred miles. Moreover, the greatest portion of what roads and trackage did exist was confined to the east and served barely a tenth of the entire state.

In Alaska, people lived on the land, but they moved through the skies. The airline was perfectly named— *Alaskair.* You did not, you could not, live in this land and not be somehow linked to the winged machines that overflew the awesome barriers of surface travel. There were more private and business aircraft in Alaska, per capita, than in any other state. Most were single-engine airplanes, and, when you considered the rugged mountain ranges, the distances, the paucity of facilities, the vicious weather that took the thermometer down to minus seventy degrees, the fact that these people took to the sky was a human miracle unto itself.

Behind all this stood Alaskair, and Sam Burleyford ran it all, and he ran it with a touch for his people that was more sure-fingered than his feel for machinery. He liked to believe, and he was right, that flying comprised the arteries of Alaska, and his team was its lifeblood.

Sam, once bearish on the gridiron, knew the value of a slab stomach. He knew how well a proper cut of figure could pay its dividends from both a male and female audience. Alaskair maintained a strong policy of physical fitness for its flight and ground crews. Operating as they did in the great northland, the men and women employees, and certainly their families, had precious little available to them in the way of athletics. When Sam moved to the front office, he established full recreational facilities at every main base—from basketball courts to swimming pools to gymnasiums. Sam was a wildcat at handball, and he was proud of winning the company play-offs for three years running.

Sam never relinquished his focus on the all-important imagery he knew he must cultivate if his long-planned goal was to be realized. For long years, Alaska had suffered a communications hodgepodge, but the last vestiges of isolation were disappearing. The communications satellite now made it possible to reach across the state—in living color—into any area where there was electrical power—even if it came from batteries, solar cells, or gasoline-driven generators.

Sam was impatient. He wanted to make his play for the 1980 elections. Yet he knew the pitfalls of premature commitment. He knew the many pieces hadn't yet been placed in their best possible positions. He was almost ready, but in this business "almost" could be fatal. He vacillated between caution and commitment, knowing the wrong move now could cripple him. It was a hell of a thing to endure. He felt that time was outrunning him.

Then, suddenly, the pieces started coming together. The decision could very well be taken from his hands. The change came, actually, in the form of two visitors. A team of two young women unlike any he knew. Smartly dressed, turned out crisply and perfectly, they had an air—irrespective of sex—of perfect self-confidence. They were professionals. But at what?

"We represent a certain party, Mr. Burleyford. That party has made a most thorough study of your plans, your hopes, and most especially your qualifications and your chances for becoming governor. You will not make it on your own, sir. You will not make it with the party interests to whom you have broached the matter. You have the proper background, the image, the charisma. You also lack the necessary funding, the contacts in the right places, the appropriate sway."

Finally, he broke his own silence. "And?"

"The party we represent can fill the missing pieces, Mr. Burleyford."

My God, did they even know how he *thought?* "There's a price, of course," he said carefully.

"Out of our jurisdiction, sir. Our purpose here, if you are interested, is to arrange a meeting."

Three days later he went to a small airport in the Anchorage area where a Gulfstream jet was waiting. It had numbers only, no names or company identification. There were two pilots, and one was a woman.

They landed on a long private airstrip in the Canadian wilds. He saw two more business jets, people clustered by a lodge. He was led to a large, plush office, and the door closed quietly behind him. One look at the woman standing behind a desk told him that these people would be able to deliver anything they promised.

Sarah Markham. One of the most powerful women in the country. She controlled majority stockholder shares in half a dozen industries. She was brilliant, and the avenues of the political world she—Good Lord, thought Sam Burleyford, her husband is Senator Benjamin Markham! He alone could sway . . .

As if reading his thoughts, she disallowed further contemplation. "I represent myself and a private group," she told him without preamble. "My husband plays no role in this. Indeed, and this is to remain in this room, he is very much against what we are doing. We are a coalition, Mr. Burleyford. Twelve women with the strength and the means to swim against the tide. We are not interested so much in overthrowing as we are in equalizing."

Still standing, he matched her penetrating gaze. "You want a woman as vice-president of the country." He said it simply. It didn't need elaboration.

She nodded. "Please be seated." She swept right on. "The presidency lies beyond our means. Now. For some time to come. But you are, of course, correct. It is the second office we want. And—" She hesitated, and he knew in that moment that she would cross the line.

He smiled. "I'm very interested, Mrs. Markham."

"Good. Let me make it clear that what we offer is not exactly simple. It is, however, straightforward. Even," and she frowned, "if it carries its own complications."

She laid it out with breathtaking clarity and an insight into his own plans and hopes that startled him. Everything he had done had been scrutinized and evaluated.

"You have made powerful friends in the right places. Truly extraordinary for a man who is still a political amateur. No offense, Mr. Burleyford, but, despite everything else, you face a powerful opponent in Michael Stark. Frank Bothwell will not be running for reelection, but Stark is lieutenant governor. He lacks full incumbency, but petroleum interests support him heavily. He is strong and he has already established his fences and he is tough to beat. Alone, you have no real chance."

Sam made a steeple of his fingers and waited. The American Congress Party had certain plans to complete before they could make their move for the office of vice-president going to a woman. Sarah Markham told Sam Burleyford what she had discussed so many times and in such detail with Harold and Evelyn Archer and her secret group of eleven other women. When she was through with her essential presentation, she went to case points.

"We want, we need, *now,* a woman as captain of a commercial airliner."

Sam's eyebrows lifted with her last remark. Things were beginning to fit, and swiftly. "I agree with everything you have said, Mrs. Markham. May I offer an observation?"

"Please."

"There are pitfalls in your plans. If right now you were to take a poll of women—not men, but women—and ask them as passengers if they want their pilot of a two- or three-hundred-ton airliner to be a woman, at least ninety-five percent would say, 'Absolutely not.' "

She surprised him with a level of agreement. "I might feel the same way myself without some very detailed knowledge of the woman," she admitted. "And that is precisely why you are here, Mr. Burleyford. Your airline is a supplemental carrier. You haul cargo and people together, and—"

"Much more."

"So much the better, then. There are already many women flying as copilots and flight engineers of scheduled carriers in this country. More will be hired this year. I find it, well, tantalizing that thirty-two women fly as captains with the main Russian airline, Aeroflot."

"The *only* Russian airline, madam."

"But not one captain in this country is a woman. Breaking the barrier with a scheduled carrier will take too much time. A supplemental carrier is our choice."

Sam was already well ahead of her, but he kept silent. This was her ball game.

"We want a woman to be a captain with Alaskair."

He smiled. "That's all?"

"No. There's more." His smile vanished. "But that," she said, "is the first condition. Tell me frankly. Can a woman qualify?"

"No question of it."

"Will you do it?"

She was taking it in leaps and bounds. "Everything depends on the rest of this conversation, Mrs Markham."

"I fear I must interrupt my own plan for the moment, Mr. Burleyford. There *is* another consideration we learned of only yesterday. A secret agreement even now being negotiated between the American and Soviet governments. It will involve Alaska enormously. It will require the full approval of the Civil Aeronautics Board. Or," she shrugged, "if the CAB fails to go along, they will simply be overruled."

He had heard rumors. Damn, if—

"Are you familiar with the Russian city of Yakutsk? It lies in eastern Siberia at approximately 130° east longitude and 63° north latitude—"

"Almost precisely the same latitude as Anchorage."

"Quite so. The agreement is being worked out for a flight between Anchorage and Yakutsk, which lies just below the Verkhoyansk Mountains, on the Lena River. Two times a week a Russian airliner will fly from Yakutsk to Anchorage. A reciprocal flight will be made by an American airliner. There will be no continuation of the flights except through change of aircraft. That is part of the agreement. The Russians want very much to bring attention to Yakutsk and eastern Siberia as a major terminus with the United States. It will make the Chinese unhappy," she said as an afterthought, "but I'm sure no one will be concerned about that."

He was interested in everything except the goddamned Chinese.

"We have no objections to assuring that your own line receives the contract." She smiled. "Besides, you will have nothing to do with it if the rest of this conversation proceeds according to plan. Ours—*and* yours."

"One thing has been left out so far."

"Ah. You've seen it, then."

"I believe so. If we wish a woman as an Alaskair

captain, then that woman is also a prime candidate to fly the route to—what was that city again? Yes, of course. To Yakutsk."

"Precisely. She will be lionized. The Russian press, Mr. Burleyford, the *Russian* press alone would be worth it. Ours could do no less than to follow in case. We're talking about an international flight, some of the worst weather in the world, and—"

"I have the complete picture."

"Good. You must sell your Alaskair stock, Mr. Burleyford. Immediately. There can be no compromises on any point. Your reward is the governor's chair. Everything must be clean. If Alaskair gets the contract, as I am certain it will, you must accrue no personal gain."

He frowned. "You'll forgive me, but I don't appreciate your reference to my 'reward.' We're talking about something more than tossing a bone into the political pot."

"You have my apology." God, he thought, but she's smooth. "Shall we talk about it?" she added.

"I'm fascinated."

They promised all the right things. The finances to back his campaign. All of it aboveboard. And behind the scenes, the right pressure to the right people in the right party. Unless something wholly and completely beyond their comprehension came to pass—and he agreed with her—the governorship would be his.

"How far does the debt carry?" he inquired.

"An excellent question. It doesn't. Once we have what we want, and you have what you want, the slate is clean. There are no debts, Mr. Burleyford."

His laughter was soft. "There's no use in acting, then. Do we shake hands, or what, Mrs. Markham?"

"Your word in this room will be sufficient. I want you to understand I appreciate your immediate grasp of the situation and your immediate response. I cannot abide a dillydallying fool."

His eyebrows went up a notch. "Which I would have been if I hadn't accepted, and as quickly?"

"Answer it yourself."

"Your point," he yielded. He rubbed his cheek. "Another question seems necessary. Do you have someone in mind?"

She seemed to be struggling to hold back a knowing smile. "Yes, we do."

"There may be a joke here, Mrs. Markham. Its subtlety escapes me."

She sighed. "This is the touchy part of all this, Mr. Burleyford. Are you ready to give up sleeping with Kate Brandon?"

20

The whole thing was sticky, and if he didn't handle it well it could blow up in his face. His affection for Kate was honest, although they didn't see much of one another. Their lives were far apart, despite their both living and working in the Anchorage area. But every now and then . . .

During the flight from Canada back to Anchorage his thoughts swirled through his head. How the hell was he going to handle all this? Had Sarah Markham known that Alaskair was going to open bids for new pilots and that for the first time they didn't dare reject a woman on the basis of sex? Had she known about it? Goddamn it, she and her group must *control* Alaskair! That memo he had received from the chairman of the board. All about impartiality and the rest of that nonsense. But they were dead serious about it. The issue of government contracts had been raised high enough for even a blind man to see.

The pieces came together like a jigsaw puzzle impelled by its own fitting. Sure, all this time Sarah Markham and her team were setting it up. They'd never bothered with Sam Burleyford because up to this point they didn't need him. More than that, they didn't want him involved. They knew about him and Kate Brandon, and, obviously, they'd had her in mind all this time.

So he needn't make any moves with Kate yet. Lay low; that was the answer. Let her go her own way.

There was the matter of C. B. Atkins. But Sam knew that Atkins would go through the motions and come to him before he'd dump Kate. Atkins was totally dedicated to Alaskair, and he understood the necessity of front office politics.

Sam could do some maneuvering on his own. Wait out both Kate *and* C. B. Atkins. And then put on his own crunch. Although no one would know there was any involvement save the new federal demands. He would—he would have to—make sure that Atkins played it absolutely straight. He'd sympathize with C. B., but behind the scenes he would maintain an iron grip on what was happening.

Again, the best thing to do was to keep hands off. Kate Brandon was better than good. Jesus, he'd just about watched her growing up in the cockpit. For now, he would let Kate's own strength carry her.

What would happen if Atkins played the martyr? If he insisted no one could tell him what to do with "his" airline? Sam didn't dare squeeze Atkins except on the basis of official company policy. That was the toughest nut to crack. He and Atkins were old friends; he knew the Bull better than anyone else in this world.

Well, if it came down to the wire, he would simply have to throw Atkins to the wolves, draw him into a showdown where Atkins's pride would become his own worst enemy. Either Atkins would quit, or Sam, acting on orders from the board of directors, would demand his resignation. He hoped it wouldn't come to that because it was slippery as hell.

Sam sighed; he was fast learning the business. When you wanted something bad enough, and he damn well wanted that governor's chair, you faced having to dump your own friends. Shit.

For the next few days he couldn't shake thoughts of Kate from his mind. She'd tackle a grizzly bare-handed to get captain's stripes on her shoulders. Getting past C. B. Atkins amounted to almost the same thing.

Sam spent a long time trying to judge just what Kate's chances were. Forgetting the rumbles she would pick up from Atkins, he was convinced she could make it, where the flying was concerned, anyway. He had her records sent to his office. Jesus, she had more going for her than he'd ever dreamed. If everything went fair and square, she had that left seat nailed.

He wondered why she hadn't come to him. Almost

as quickly he dismissed the thought. Kate was too proud, too professional to play the game that way. She wouldn't lean on anyone. In fact, when they were together she'd hardly talked about her flying. But then she *owned* Brandon Airways. It was a going, successful operation. Why talk shop when there are other things to do?

Several times after Vance and Emily were killed, he had crossed paths with Kate. It struck him that the child was an attractive, compelling woman. How long had that been going on? *She's still in her twenties,* he'd reminded himself.

They'd had dinner. Once he had a trip arranged for San Francisco and invited her along. She was a dazzling companion and, it turned out, left nothing wanting in their hotel suite. It became an open and warm relationship in which sex remained low key and was an expression between them.

But there was one danger, mused Sam. Their feelings had grown with time. If Sam had made the effort he knew there was every chance it could become permanent. He couldn't have that. Absolutely *not.* He had to be sure he didn't back himself into any corners, and . . .

Wait. There was someone else. Mike Carew—that rescue specialist who flew every now and then with Alaskair. Of course; he was under contract as a survival instructor. A big, husky man, warm, and—Sam remembered now. He was absolutely ape over Kate. He breathed a mental sigh of relief. He wouldn't trip himself up.

Okay. Back to his more pressing problem. To make certain Kate had every chance to work her way into the left seat. There wasn't any use—he reminded himself for the hundredth time—of laying his needs on the line with Atkins. The old bastard wouldn't compromise with God or the devil.

But if Kate was as good as Sam believed her to be, he wouldn't have to put on the crunch with Atkins. Just make sure C. B. didn't bounce the girl only because she was the wrong sex.

If Sam played it that tight and careful, he could let Sarah Markham believe he was riding herd on the pilot selection program, that he was—invisibly, to be sure—guiding Kate through the maze into the cockpit.

So he had to play a waiting game, juggle all the pieces on the board. He was betting on Kate Brandon all the way.

But there was still that little matter of their personal relationship. He must see Kate alone. He timed his call to her, waiting for a stretch of bad weather so she wouldn't be flying. He picked her up and they drove to a lodge at Mount Alyeska where they could have a long dinner and plenty of time to talk. It might be his only opportunity to break the relationship gently, easily, without Kate's knowledge of the complex machinations behind the scenes.

There was always the truth, even if it was only a half-truth and bent the hell away from what was real. That evening he was a paragon of virtue. With some small self-sacrifice thrown in. That always helped.

"I'm not going to be able to see you for a while," he told her at dinner. "There's no easy way to say this, and—"

Her smile stopped his words. "Someone else, Sam?"

He looked at the beautiful woman across the table. Had he never really seen her before? He shook his head. "No, honey. It isn't that. If there was a woman, you'd be the first one I would tell."

"I think I know."

He held his breath. She reached out to place her hand on his. "I want that left seat, Sam. I want it just about more than I want anything else in the world. But I want it fair and square. And if people know we're seeing one another, it could get sticky, couldn't it?"

He could hardly believe it.

"Damn it, Kate, I didn't want you to, I mean, seeing you is more important to me than—"

She squeezed his hand. "Don't be silly, Sam. We're hardly lovers. Not really. It's not as if we were planning a gingerbread house." She held up her left hand. "There's no ring there, Sam. I hate to agree with you, but you're right. I don't want anything to interfere with my chances."

He leaned back in his seat. "I think you'll be wearing those four stripes before you're through."

She studied him, her eyes intent. "You're not putting on the squeeze, are you, Sam? For me, I mean."

"No. No, I'm not. I feel that maybe I—"

Her strength was unmistakable. *"Don't."*

"The same old independence. I recognize it from a long way back, Kate."

She nodded.

"Well, have no fears. Answer the question yourself. Can you imagine anyone putting the pressure on that old water buffalo?"

"I'm glad, Sam. Because that's the way it's got to be." She looked around. "Hey, this may be our last night for a long time to come. Why don't you ask the lady to dance?"

21

C. B. Atkins came into his office the next morning, his face a mask. He'd never quite known the strange sense of loss pervading him. It was incredible the way stories moved through this goddamned office. The rumor mill must have its own hot line. No one said anything. That was the key. They said *nothing*. How the hell did they learn so fast? He walked heavily along the corridors, dumped himself into his chair. Vicki brought his coffee and he stared at the mug, barely seeing it. What in hell was this leaden feeling in his arms and legs? He . . .

Sam Burleyford came into his office unannounced. If he got past Vicki without her being able to buzz, well, either he'd come through on the run or told her to stay put. Whatever it was, Sam's grimace was almost menacing. He stood across the desk from Atkins, his arms at his sides, his face pale.

Atkins sat like a rock. He didn't need this kind of shit. Not now. If Sam . . .

"All right, goddamn it. Tell me what happened," Sam ordered.

Atkins nodded slowly, turned his chair to face the company president directly. "She blew it, Sam."

"What the goddamned hell happened!"

Atkins's face hardened. President or not, if he hadn't known that Sam was under some kind of pressure, he would have thrown him through the glass door of the office without bothering to open it. Instead, Atkins checked his own temper, deciding to tell it just like it happened.

"We were making instrument approaches. Not practice. The real thing. The weather was light rain, patchy fog. The approach lights were on. You know, the flashers—"

Atkins tried to tell it slowly and carefully. Those approach lights had undone more than one pilot. They were dazzling flashes that rippled swiftly away from an approaching pilot to the touchdown point of a runway. They were known to inflict wild illusions on pilots. Maybe Brandon was tired. Maybe she had a headache. Maybe an inner ear infection that toppled her balance or at least brought it to a precarious level. Maybe anything. But it was a killer effect.

The pilot comes in, speed held carefully or decreasing, altitude coming down steadily. Then those lights get brighter and larger and more dazzling. They create an illusion of real motion where there is none. The illusion is of greater speed and height than the pilot actually has. The rain, the patchy fog, the lessened visibility because of a wet windshield. Whatever. It all comes together.

In that DC-4, it should have been a piece of cake for Kate. But she was snared by the glittering web of flashing lights and apparent motion. There is a way out, of course. Don't believe what you see until you're past those lights. *Don't believe it.* You fly the airspeed and the heading and the rate of descent and the changing altitude and the slope indicators, all the things by which a pilot flies and trusts absolutely; and when your consciousness is absolutely locked onto that part of you that's cerebral instead of emotional, *then* you can look through those front windows.

Kate didn't do it. She committed the awful error of judging with her eyes only, looking outside the airplane. The impression is overwhelming, real beyond all else that's real, and it's a trap— the flashing movement of lights and the reflections deceived her.

They began to lose airspeed, and they weren't going to make it. Atkins told that to Sam Burleyford, who listened without a word.

"We were going to be short. It was obvious," Atkins said. "All right. I was flying as first officer. That job is to call out whatever's off margin to the pilot. I called it out, told her we were low on speed, we were much too low to make the threshold."

Atkins stared at Burleyford. "She didn't respond. I went for the throttles myself. Full bore, Sam. I had to take over. We made it. Barely. We were hanging on the edge of the stall. If I'd have let her be, we would have put the gear short of the runway."

A long silence followed.

"You ever make that mistake, C. B.?"

"A lot of us have made it at one time or another."

"Then why the hell did you bounce Kate Brandon!"

Atkins stood up slowly. "I don't know what you're trying to prove, Sam, but—"

"Just answer me, damn you."

Atkins held his breath. "Easy, Sam. Very easy." He made sure there was a long pause between those words and his next ones. "If the girl were flying alone, if there were no competition, she'd have another chance. But there are three other pilots in this, and the line is hiring only two out of the four. Because of what happened, Kate Brandon is no longer one of those two. That's all there is to it."

Sam stared at him, swung around violently, and started from the office. He stopped, jerked about heavily. "No it isn't, by God. It sure as hell has more to it than that." Then he was gone, his fury still smoldering in his absence.

Atkins was now completely baffled. Sam's performance in his office didn't fit anything. He—oh, hell, Atkins himself had reached the point where he judged the best pilot to be Brandon. He had made an honest decision. He was convinced that Kate would never again commit the same error, for one mistake like that gets burned pretty well into your system, and you're ever alert for the problem. But she had blown the landing, and he had taken over, and this was a competitive selection, and the other people by those two simple acts were simply making better brownie points. If the line opened up more positions, then Kate Brandon had every right to apply once more, and she'd be so far ahead of the game that likely she'd walk right into the job.

But not now.

It wasn't all that complicated. It was in the open and honest and it was fair, so why the hell was Burleyford going bananas? Atkins struggled to bring it all together. He hated playing host to the rumor mill, but maybe the answer lay there—the old-fashioned straight poop right from the latrine.

There'd been talk about some sort of plum going to one of the airlines operating in Alaska. An exchange route between Anchorage and a Russian city. So what? What the hell did that have to do with Sam half mad over what had happened? And throwing all his anger at his flight operations chief?

22

"One whole, blessed month. It's been a reprieve, Mike. A touch of——"

"Self?" Mike Carew finished her thought.

She rested her hand on his arm, nestled her head on his shoulder. "You have the right words, the right thoughts, Michael."

"You only call me Michael when you're emotional."

A shudder went through her. "Equilibrium hasn't exactly been my cup of tea." A long sigh followed. "But thanks to generous portions of tender loving care——"

"Most especially the loving."

"Most especially." She hugged him. "I never thought I would have nightmares. When you were with me, it wasn't so bad." Her eyes seemed to film over. "But when they came, and you were gone——" She left it unsaid.

"They're gone now?"

She brightened. "Gone. Oh, I still see those bloody awful lights in my sleep sometimes. But they're not horrors anymore." She turned to him. "You know, it's strange, Mike. They used to frighten me. Then the fear began to ebb, thanks mainly to you, I suppose, and when I dreamed of them again I began to study them. Do you understand? Since I no longer had to fear them, there was no need to run away."

"Then you've beaten it, love."

She tapped the side of her head. "In here, anyway. But I don't know about making that approach. Maybe it will all happen again."

At least she no longer dreaded the possibility. Her spirit of competition had too long been subdued. She was looking forward to flying that same devilish approach again and again, as many times as it took to convince herself that she would no longer fall unbalanced as its victim.

She had spent this past month in Mike's cabin. Fishing, walking, thinking, loving when he was there with her. Until it had all worked free and she understood that common mistake she had made, how the brilliant lights had robbed her of her own intelligence.

She climbed to her feet and pointed to the end of the wooden dock. A fishing pole bent sharply. "You've got a bite," she sang out, "and I've got a stew on the stove."

From the kitchen window she saw Mike netting a beauty of a trout. She laughed to herself; breakfast for the morning was in hand. She busied herself in the kitchen. This place had been a haven, but once again she understood that it was past time to face reality. She had been angry, disappointed, harsh with herself, feeling overwhelmingly stupid. She was grateful that she hadn't tried to blame C. B. Atkins for anything. He had been so scrupulously honest in everything he'd done with her.

It was simple. Four pilots had been in competition for two positions. Kate Brandon was in the lead. She'd made a ghastly error, common enough, and blown her chances. A tremulous sigh made her shiver. Thank God she had never gone through the poor-little-old-me routine.

She went to the cabin door to call Mike, but the sound of an engine pounded overhead. She stepped outside and looked up. Super Cub, on floats. No mistaking that garish yellow paint job. Bill Anders had come for a visit. She watched the wings bank, float down to the lake, and taxi to the dock.

"Got a hungry man here!" Mike shouted.

Before Kate went inside to put on another plate, she paused long enough for a rib-squeezing hug and a kiss from Bill. He'd been like an uncle to her for years. When they were at the table she broached the reason for his unexpected visit.

"I never talk with my mouth full," he mumbled, sopping up stew with thick chunks of bread. They laughed at his contradiction, but through the meal Kate wondered why Bill had chosen to fly this far out of his way.

Not until he was settled in a comfortable chair with his second cup of coffee, his pipe well-lighted, did Bill Anders emerge from his silence. "I got a couple pieces of news for you," he told Kate. "You ready?"

"You sound positively threatening," she said.

"How long I know you, Katie?"

"Why, just about all my life, I guess. I mean, well, what I mean is that I don't understand the question."

"What *I* mean," he harrumphed, "is that I've known you since you weren't much bigger than a field mouse. That," he said with what seemed like premature triumph, "sort of gives me the right to speak blunt with you, don't it?"

"You asking or telling her?" Mike threw in.

Bill Anders winked at him. "Stay out of this."

"Yes, *sir*." He looked at Kate and shrugged.

"What is it, Bill?" she asked.

He leaned forward and pointed his pipestem at her. "Your old man would roll over in his grave and throw up if he knew you were a quitter."

Kate gaped with open mouth at Anders. "What," she said to the old man, "the hell are you talking about?"

He peered at her through narrowed eyes. "Bless me if I think you don't even know."

"Know *what?*" She wished she weren't so exasperated, but this—

"Alaskair announced it three days ago. They've got new contracts to support the Prudoe oil fields." He looked from Kate to Mike and back again. "They're increasing their fleet. Four new Hercules. The long-body jobs. *And* they're bringing in more pilots. Some promotions within the line. Two, maybe three new pilots from outside."

He grew visibly impatient with every moment of silence. "What the hell's the matter with you, Katie? Aren't you even going to say something? Aren't you going to give it another shot?" He peered at her owlishly. "The Brandon girl *I* knew would have been halfway out that door by now!"

"Not so fast," she cautioned him. "This is the first I've heard of anything about Alaskair for a month."

"You've been in hiding, hey?"

"Yes," she said defiantly.

"Hurt your thumb much with all that sucking?"

"Bill! That's—uncalled for."

"Ahh, you poor, poor dear."

She looked at Mike. "I'm sorry we fed him. It just made him nasty."

"You haven't been hiding, Katie. You've been sulking."

"I have *not*, damn it!"

"Then why haven't you put in again with Alaskair?"

"I just heard about it! From you!"

"Then you are going to try it again."

She was flustered. "I guess, I mean—I don't know," she said finally.

"It's flying, Katie. What in thunder is there to wonder about?"

"You know what happened. I—"

"You made a mistake. The saints will all do pirouettes along the shadow of the moon because no one ever made a mistake before, right?"

"I have no idea if they'll consider me again," she said stubbornly.

"You have no ideas at all, period," he snapped. "Confound it, I'm talking about *flying*, not anything else, and flying is what your old man taught you to do, and you're terrific at it, and you were leading the field until you made your little boo-boo and—"

"Boo-boo?" That came from Mike.

"Call it what the blazes you want, you rotary-headed nincompoop. You both know what I mean. She had it in the bag. She dropped the bag. Now it's time for her to pick it up again."

Kate shook her head slowly. "I really don't know, Bill. I got to the point of being so very tired of it—and the hassle, that constant, unending hassle, that was the worst of—"

"When was it ever easy?" he shouted at her. "When was it ever *supposed* to be easy!"

Mike stood, stared through the window for a long moment, turned slowly. "Wait a minute, Bill. Something doesn't fit here. I've known you for years. You're a friendly, mild-mannered man. You've always been that way. Now you show up here like a leprechaun with a thorn stuck up his backside." He gave Anders a crooked smile. "Come on, you old bastard, why don't you level with us?"

Anders's face was dark and grim, but he couldn't hold back any longer, and he chuckled badly enough to send him into a coughing spasm. A smile spread across his leathered face. "Okay, you've found me out," he told them. "But it'll cost you another cup of coffee before I'll tell you what I've been saving for you. For Katie, really."

He relit his pipe and sipped his coffee. "Did you know," he asked, "that me and Bull Atkins were cadets together in the old Army Air Corps? You know how far back that goes? Katie, here, wasn't even born yet, and you," he gestured to Mike, "were still feeding at your momma's breast."

"Thank you, Methuselah," Mike quipped.

"Mind your manners or I'll drag you outside and beat you to a pulp," Anders threatened. Mike put up both hands in mock horror. They exchanged grins.

"Get on with it," Kate pushed.

"The Bull washed out of cadets." He savored the moment, the stunned expression on Kate's face. "That's right," Anders went on. "They washed him out. Flunked him. Kicked his ass right out of flight training."

Anders took a deep breath, settling down to his story. "You've got to understand there was nothing ever wrong with his flying. Bull was a natural. A genius. But the poor son of a bitch was always getting airsick. He couldn't help it, of course. He just plain threw up. Every damn time. My God, that man vomited day and night. It got so bad he even threw up blood. He hung in there and he fought it out, but there was a war on and there wasn't time to waste on pilots who were always spilling their cookies all over the cockpit."

"You mean," Mike said slowly, "they forced him out of the program? Completely?"

Anders nodded. "They busted him out of flight cadets."

Kate seemed to be sharing a pain from long ago. "What happened to him, Bill?"

"Well, the first thing he did, and I guess it was the toughest thing a man like him could do, was to swallow his pride. He volunteered for gunnery school. He was still sick but since he didn't always have to concentrate on flying he could spend more time on beating his gut. It began to go away little by little. After a while he was only sick half the time he flew." Anders shook his head. "I'd have hated to have been Atkins. It was an absolute bitch."

He looked up at them. "You know what? He was a hell of a gunner. He flew eighty missions as a gunner, and he earned his stripes as a flight engineer in a B-17. He shot down a couple of fighters and rotated back to the States." Anders grinned and it kept getting wider. "He applied for flight training again and they told him no, but he raised all kinds of mortal hell and said he'd earned his shot at it again. He was such a pain in the ass they just wanted to get rid of him. I mean, he came home with the Silver Star and a couple of Purple Hearts—"

"He was wounded?" Kate broke in.

"Would you believe four times? He had a bunch of other medals, but he never paid much attention to them. All he wanted to do was fly, and he got that shot he was screaming for. Would you also believe he *still* threw up? Not as much as before, and he managed to get his instructor to keep his mouth shut, and he went all the way through cadets and he earned his wings. In the last few months of the war, Atkins went to the Pacific in a Lightning and he shot down six Japanese planes."

Anders studied his pipe. "Now all that was one hell of a tough row to hoe."

"Yes, it was," Kate said quietly.

Anders stood up and slipped the pipe into his pocket.

"I said what I came here to say. Atkins had it a lot rougher than you will ever know, Kate. He fought his way back the hardest way there is." He pointed at her. "And if *you* don't take your shot again, Miss Brandon, you're a quitter."

She lay awake a long time that night. She'd made sweet love with Mike and he slept deeply, his body against hers. There wasn't any question but that she'd try again. She was thinking with her mind again instead of with her emotions.

She kept wondering about Sam. He'd been absolutely impossible when Atkins washed her out. He'd shouted and pleaded for her to get back into the competition. They would be hiring more pilots soon, they were expanding; she *had* to make the attempt. Even Atkins had been so damned solicitous it made her sick. She was being squeezed from one side and then the other. She had needed time and peace and quiet and understanding love, and Mike had all that to give to her.

Well, first thing in the morning she would go back to Anchorage and walk straight into Atkins's office and sign up like any pilot trying to crack the whip the first time around. She no longer would flinch at any drill they might throw at her. She knew that Atkins would run her through a crash course of all the things they'd done and passed so well before. Where she'd screwed up, he'd apply the hammer until she might feel as if she was on the bottom side of an anvil. Okay, that's the way the game had to be played.

The error was in her past. She no longer feared it.

Now she understood *why* C. B. Atkins had squeezed so hard, why the crunch was always there. Not because he was simply a crusty old bastard—*he* had had it so much rougher than anyone had ever known and he'd made it through.

But first he'd failed.

So had she. And for much the same kind of reason. It was the same kind of pressure that had broken Atkins out of cadets. It simply came in a different package.

For the first time she believed absolutely that no matter what he thought about women in the cockpit, if she met his standards she would earn that left seat.

Fair enough.

Her fury was as carefully controlled as the woman herself. Sarah Markham looked across the dinner table at Sam Burleyford. For a while he had felt as if this were his last meal. No matter the protocol and the pleasantries, the woman wore velvet gloves over steel fists.

"Let me understand this all very clearly," she said, seeming to ignore him, studying the deep red wine reflecting light in her goblet. "The girl *is* back in the program?"

He nodded slowly. "She is. Not at the bottom of the ladder. Atkins has been the sore point, Mrs. Markham. He likes to run his railroad his own way, and—"

"Mr. Burleyford, I do not care one whit about how your Mr. Atkins runs his railroad or anything else." Her eyes locked rigidly on his. "I do not wish to be bothered with explanations or inside knowledge. Excuses are for losers. Now dismiss this fellow from your conversation and tell me what is happening with Kate Brandon."

Sam took a deep breath. "We put her back in flight competition just where she had been before. That means the weeks that were spent in initial training and testing are behind us. She's flying with Atkins right now. He still makes the final decisions about hiring new pilots, and—"

"If he gets in our way once more, rid us of him."

He had a blank look on his face. "It could cause problems."

"Do you wish to be a governor or a janitor?"

Her words stung. "All right, Mrs. Markham."

"We're running short of time, Sam." She could switch from her official line to a personal relationship with a speed that unbalanced him. "We can never get back what we lose. Kate Brandon must make captain. The word is *must*."

She didn't have to say anything else. If Kate didn't

make it then Sam Burleyford wasn't going anywhere. And he'd find he wasn't wanted at Alaskair, either.

That was the problem with having a tigress scratching your back. Even the slightest pressure could cut deeply.

23

Fairyland.

Impossible and beautiful beyond description. A billion motes of gleaming white and another billion of pale blue and some of pink and yellow and white, billions of shapeless stars streaming swiftly at them, sweeping to the sides and over them and beneath them and everywhere, an endless celestial migration that . . .

The nose landing light winked out, and instantly they were hurtled back into the reality of instruments and controls and voices. For a while they'd flown through the snowstorm with the forward landing light turned on, and its brilliant arc transformed night flight in snow to an enchantment that only a pilot can ever know. A brief moment snatched from the training syllabus. Night flight, instrument conditions, but with a ceiling of at least two thousand feet so they weren't pushing too harshly into conditions that might snare them.

In the left seat of the Boeing 737, a thick-bellied small giant with two powerful jet engines, Kate flew with grace and precision through the snow, her world of instruments and avionics and procedures as comfortable to her as if the sun shone brightly in a blue sky outside their cockpit windows. No rumbling vibration, no pistons flailing and propellers whirling madly. The Boeing was a symphony of great violins and bass drums, and it didn't need the harsh cacophony to which the older piston-engine planes were host.

She guided the sweptwing jet along its electronic pathway through the snow-filled night, hewing to the course and changes required of their safe passage through the sky as determined by men who were sitting in darkened rooms studying dull scopes that glowed with moving objects.

The invisible web in which was woven the safe and expeditious movement of great giants in the night. Through this web, singled out from the other machines, Kate slipped earthward again and again, dropping from the abyss within the night storm to a world whose roof measured two thousand feet above the ground. Earthlights, neoned and glowing spots in the snow, waiting for her, to be ignored. Far ahead of them, advertised by blue-white flashes, the approach lights and the runway. C. B. Atkins was with her in the cockpit, comfortable, watching, monitoring, but obeying every command in the copilot role he played.

Again and again, they rushed toward the same dazzling lights that had speared her vision and tumbled her balance and made a mockery of experience and intelligence. No trouble now, none since that time in the DC-4. Now they slipped earthward along the exacting rails of electronic descent. The 737 was a delight, a dream and a wonder, and it obeyed her every whim. This was the sixth time around the pattern tonight, and there had been no flaws, not even whimsies. Kate was back in the groove, again an eagle with night vision and electronic sensing and all the rest she needed. She had set up the last landing for the night, the end of this phase of her testing, and she was relaxed, the yoke starting back on the flare and . . .

"You've lost your right engine. There's a truck on the runway before you. You can't go over him and land in the runway remaining."

Atkins said it quickly, with emphasis, but quietly and clearly, simulating the kind of emergency on a snow-blowing night that pilots hated, but that might be all too commonplace in Alaskan winter flying. Her hands flew through the motions to the controls and levers, and she snapped out the instructions to the crew in the flight deck with her; she was talking with the tower, requesting to stay in a low, wide pattern and the hell out of the stuff above them—exactly as she would have done had this been an actual emergency.

She had everything under control when he threw another wrench into the situation. The instrument panel lights went out: electrical system failure. With the flight engineer they went to standby systems and were right back in business.

Atkins told her they were finished. "Take it on home, kid." They were coming around on base leg, setting up for the long final. He was cute; he set up a gear-system failure. Moving with skill, she went through the emergency system. They sailed down through the snow, glided across the fantasy of approach lights in the blowing white, and eased onto the runway. She played it carefully, ready for incipient skidding under the poor runway conditions. She parked the airplane and he climbed from his seat. "Tom, you shut her down with Brandon," he ordered the flight engineer. He turned back to her. "Meet me in my office in thirty minutes."

She brought the coffee, and he motioned her to take the comfortable chair across the room. Few people were around. His was the only office along the executive corridor with lights still burning. It was a moment of peace. Sounds drifted to them from the maintenance shops, and the mournful howl of a jet brought them to glance up instinctively, then return their attention to each other.

Atkins rubbed his eyes and scratched chin stubble. She laughed at him. "You look like a bear settling down for his winter hibernation," she teased.

He had a bleary look, and he spoke with a growl, but there was no mistaking something she had seen so rarely in him—an obvious feeling of warmth. "Brandon, you're wearing me out."

A brief smile met his words. "I thought you were the one who was trying to grind me down."

He nodded. "Damn right I am. Only,—" she saw open admiration and was nearly stunned, "you're holding up a hell of a lot better than I thought you could. Half the pilots I know would have folded by now."

Her amazement grew. "Watch it, Atkins. You're saying nice things about a woman."

"Yeah. It stinks. I must have a bug or something."

"You almost make it sound like an endurance contest."

"It *is* an endurance contest." He shifted his bulk and

his chair groaned. "Endurance can be the name of the game in this business. It's the best thing you've got going for you when the ball of wax starts coming apart and you know it's going to be a mess for a long time to come." He leaned back, the steaming coffee held in two hands. He started to speak, looked up at her, looked away again.

"Look, kid, I got some things to say. They may not come out very nice." He watched for her reaction. The sudden impulsive laughter she'd shown, that flash of white teeth, her mannerisms—all things he might never have noticed had she not carried her own weight in the cockpit. But he was at ease with Kate now, the rawboned competition was behind them. They were two pros—or almost two pros, anyway—relaxing in the same arena. The last of the gladiators for the day. And she was giving him a sense of delight he'd never really known before. If this girl was his own kid he'd be popping buttons off his shirt with pride.

"C. B., I've never known you to be anything except blunt. Brutally so at times. But that's you, and I accepted it a long time ago. Is this all off the record?"

"Yeah. It is." He moved with sudden discomfort. "It's about the left seat."

"I didn't think it was anything else."

The words almost blurted from him. "Look, Kate, the captain's seat involves a hell of a lot more than flying. The feel—hell, you've got all that going for you, so I'm not kicking anything you do with the airplane. It's something else."

She held her coffee mug, waiting.

"It's politics. Stuff inside the line, I mean." Now he waited. He watched the coffee mug come down slowly, her eyes widening slightly.

"This may be off the record, C. B., but just what are you talking about?" she demanded.

"Goddamn it, this ain't easy. I've been trying to understand a lot of things for the past couple of weeks. Longer than that, really. I'm trying not to use the wrong words here, Brandon, you understand?"

"Go ahead, C. B."

"Okay, okay. I want to be sure you understand this

hasn't anything to do with your flying or how or if or when you qualify for the left seat in this outfit. But there are some fine points I have got to work out. Clean up the place, so to speak. You following all this, Brandon?"

"No."

He sighed. "All right, all right. Retract those claws, kid. This is all behind closed doors. This conversation has never happened. It stays right here with you and me. It has no effect on anything else. You may not like all of it, but can I get you to accept my word it's honest?"

"I don't like all of you to begin with, Atkins, but I've never questioned your being honest. Stubborn, pig-headed—"

"That don't count right now. This isn't about me." He paused just long enough for her to hang on his words. "It's about Sam Burleyford."

Whoo-ee, he thought. *That did get her attention. . . .* But Kate didn't offer any response. Just a long, unblinking look. She sat straighter in her chair. An inch away from ramrod, in fact, he noticed.

"You're shacking up with him. But that's not—"

"We *were* shacking up, as you so crudely put it," she snapped, her voice dripping ice. "But there are two things I'm going to tell you right off. First, we haven't been together for a long time, and second, it's none of your goddamned business."

He shook his head and motioned wildly for her to stop. "Back off, back off," he said in a rush. "It doesn't matter. It never did. All it tells me is that the man's got taste." He saw her stare; he didn't know if it was disbelief, or what, and he didn't have time to play guessing games.

"There's more to it than just that. Damn it, somehow —I don't know how—you're part and parcel to some big master plan Sam has put together. He's got some deal set up with a woman by the name of Sarah Markham. She—do you know her?"

Kate shook her head.

"Well, she's power all the way. Money, business, politics. Her husband is Mr. Big himself in Washington.

The whole thing's snarled up like a kitten in a ball of yarn. You don't know where it starts and where it stops, or how much old man Markham is tied in, or even *if* he's tied in."

"And I am?" she said, as cold as before.

"Little girl, the point I want to make to you is that Sam Burleyford has promised to deliver Kate Brandon —to *deliver* you—all tied up in a pretty pink ribbon, to Sarah Markham."

"C. B., that's the most ridiculous thing I ever—"

"Shut up, Brandon. He's doing a whole string of things that would flip you out if you knew about them. First, this delivery deal with you. Then, well, did you know Sam's already sold all the stock he owns in Alaskair? It's a strange thing for the company president to do, but he's done it. It's a smart move on his part, or else he's been given orders to sell."

He let her digest what she'd heard. She was listening intently.

He let the pause hang for several more moments, then hammered on. "He's got the Markhams, or at least the old girl, supporting his bid for governor. A whirlwind campaign, right? The full electronic razzle-dazzle. Now, what happens, Brandon, if he gets what he wants and *you* get into the left seat? He can crow then and he can crow loud. And sure as hell that old biddy and her American Congress Party will be beating the drums about how you're the greatest thing since polar bear ice cream—"

Kate shook her head, frustrated, anger growing in her, forcing her way into his stream of words. "C.B., let off for a moment. Let me ask you something, will you? I've got to know—"

But he was relentless. It was all spilling from him, spoken for the first time, and he didn't want to let go. "No, hold it, Kate. Listen to me, damn it. If Sam makes it, where you're concerned, anyway—now try to follow me here—if you make captain and Markham guarantees him the office of the governor, then—"

He cut off his own words, his face suddenly coming alive. "Sure! He gets that, and Sarah Markham's interests—and they are damned big—*they* tie up that route into the Russian city." He jumped up from his chair, the floor pounding beneath his feet, then turned abruptly to glare at her. "Want to bet, little lady, that they're grooming *you* to be one of the lead pilots for that run to Yakutsk?"

She refused to believe it. The whole thing was insane! She was competing like any other pilot, and competing on her qualifications only. This—this was ridiculous. But if her head whirled from what she'd heard so far, the crusher was yet to come. Atkins pounded his way along.

"And when everything is set up, then Sam announces his upcoming marriage to you." Striding heavily back and forth, he failed to see the blood drain from Kate's face. "Sure, sure," he said, his voice gravelly, growing louder all the time, "it's the prince and the princess routine. And there's Cinderella, wending her winged way over the Siberian cold beneath the northern lights. A thousand Eskimos playing violins or lutes or whatever the hell it is they play. Jesus Khee-*rist,* what a package—"

"*Will—you—shut—up!*"

She screamed into his abrupt silence. Shaking himself free of his own introspective fog, Atkins looked, really looked, and saw the white-faced girl.

"What—" She sucked in air, as deeply as she could, fighting for control, "What in the name of hell are you talking about? *What* marriage!"

Atkins studied her with animal wariness. "You mean you don't know?"

She forced her words through gritted teeth. "I swear I will kill you with my own two hands, big and ugly as you are." She shook her head abruptly. "C.B., you've been living with me day and night in those goddamned airplanes. You've been closer to me than any other human being. You'd know in a second if I were lying, or playing some stupid game, or—"

He waved away the rest of her words. The tension flowed from him. "I get the message, kid. You're not lying. I know that. But—but how the hell could you not know about—" His voice trailed away and when he spoke again it was with a crooked grin on his face. A lopsided face, leathery and cragged, but friendly. "How does it feel to be a pawn on a chessboard, kid?" An ironic laugh rumbled from deep within his huge chest. "Sure, I got it now. You've been so busy day and night, like you say, out of contact with just about everything, that—I mean, if they're talking only in their own circles, they—"

"C.B., for God's sake, please—"

He gestured for her to be patient. "Sam's been spreading the word, I guess in a very tight little circle, that after all the pressure is off with training and politics, you two are going to tie the knot."

"The hell we are," she snapped.

In the silence following her remark, Atkins chewed on a lip, then spoke again. "Yeah, but I don't figure it, Brandon. The way I'd looked at it, I mean, what the hell, Mike Carew is one hell of a guy, and I thought—" He shrugged. "Ah, Christ."

"C.B., I want you to understand that Sam Burleyford has never spoken one word to me about this. Not one hint, not a sound. Nothing. Absolutely nothing. I—"

"It sounds like the idea doesn't rev up your engine none too much, either."

She seemed startled by the remark. "I don't know what ideas Sam has ever had, but *I've* never entertained them. Oh, sure, it's easy to judge otherwise."

He didn't know if there was sarcasm or bitterness in her voice. "C.B., if I were to say we were lovers it would be vastly overstating the truth. So we've gone to bed. So what? My God, am I supposed to be a virgin to get this stinking job of yours?"

His response was a welcome sound of loud laughter, honest mirth that fairly exploded from him. "Score a touchdown for your side, kid." He scratched the sandpaper that passed for chin stubble on his face, and as swiftly his mood changed and he was back to the subject of Sam Burleyford. "Then why is Sam playing bastard about all this?"

"A game?" she offered.

He shook his head. "Outside of this room, with anyone else but you, Brandon, I wouldn't say this." He took a deep breath and plunged. "It stinks, kid. There's something hidden in yonder woodpile and I think I'd better try to find out just what."

He made a sudden decision. "Kate, knock off the flying for a couple of days. Nobody going through what's happening to you right now is in any condition to be pushing throttles."

She flared. "I don't want any goddamn favors from you or—"

"That's an order, Brandon. Without prejudice. The way you are now, one sticky decision could take you apart at the seams, and you can't afford that anymore. Understand? If you were a man the order would be the same. Three days off the treadmill, and that's strictly from me to you. Got it?"

24

Kate stretched like a cat on the bear rug in front of the fireplace. She rolled over. "I've got a message for you, Mike. Tomorrow morning it's back to the grindstone. C.B. was right. I needed this."

He moved suddenly and gave her a sharp-sounding whack across her rear. "You needed *me*."

"Have it your own way." She frowned suddenly. "You know, Mike, there's one thing I don't understand."

"Only one? You're lucky."

"Oh, shut up and pay attention. I'm serious. It's about Atkins. For the life of me I can't figure why he's still keeping me on the anvil. Don't get me wrong. He's as fair as anyone can be. It's just that he's dragging his feet."

"Do you think he's waiting for just one event, one move, to push him over the line to decide about you?"

"That's it, Mike!"

"The question is," Mike said dryly, "which way over the line?"

"I wish I knew," she said wistfully.

Mike sat up, snapped his fingers. "Wait a minute. You've just given me one hell of an idea. Atkins is begging off only because he doesn't want—what I mean, love, is that if Atkins accepts you now, he's afraid it may look as if he yielded to pressure from higher up, right?"

"It could," she said doubtfully.

"So we need to give him something that will tip him one way or the other."

"Thanks for the confidence, Michael."

"Watch it. You're getting emotional again. Damn it, Kate, if C.B. needs something to prod him, then we—

you—have just what the doctor ordered. And," Mike said with obvious glee, "it's right in his own ball park." He rubbed his hands and laughed. "God, I'd give anything to see his face when he—"

"Mike, stop it. I haven't the faintest idea what you're talking about."

"Look," he said, his excitement growing, "he's still got you on the grill, right? He's always testing you. Okay, okay, hon, that's the name of the game. But you've passed everything he's thrown at you. Why don't you turn it around? The trick, baby, is for you to put *him* on the grill."

She shook her head. He stared at the firelight shining through her hair, forced himself back to their conversation. "You're crazy," she was saying. "How would I do a thing like that? He's Mr. Aviation himself."

Mike tapped her on the nose. "Crazy, am I? Listen, is that old iron crate still up at Crazy Falls? That old airport?"

"Yes, but I don't see—"

"Katie, my sweet, why don't you take him up there and invite *him* to fly the thing? No checklist, no help from you. Let's see just how big Mr. Big really is."

Her smile seemed as warm as the fire. "Oh, my," she said quietly, relishing the thoughts he had conjured for her.

"Do it."

"I just might. It would—" She giggled. "Can I ask you a question?"

"Anything."

"Do you like girls?"

"C.B., I want you to fly with me to Crazy Falls."

He swung around in his chair. "What the hell for?"

Her smile had feathers along the sides of her mouth. "Oh, well, we could consider it a final test."

"A *what?*"

"We've run your drills until our fingernails are worn down. You're hedging about me."

"I don't like the way you say that, Brandon. Besides, *I* decide what tests are—"

"Are you afraid, Mr. Atkins?"

"Brandon, something's broken loose inside your skull and it's rattling around making strange noises." His pause was almost a snort. The kind you expect to hear from a very big moose. "Afraid, huh? What the hell would I be afraid of?"

"That you, uh, might not be able to handle the situation I have in mind."

"Woman, you're mad. And you talk in riddles. You—"

She sat on the straight chair by his desk, hands folded primly in her lap. All she needed was an old-fashioned skirt to complete the picture of a young schoolteacher. He studied her with open suspicion.

She went on carefully. "Just the two of us, C.B. There's an airplane up at Crazy Falls. I suggest we go there to fly it. You," she smiled quickly, "and, me. If I don't fly you straight into the ground with that airplane, C.B., you can close the book on me, if that's what you want. Wash me right out of your hair." She couldn't resist the twist. "What's left of it, that is."

He had a beautiful habit of shrugging off barbs. "What kind of airplane?" he growled.

Kate shrugged. "What difference does that make? I've heard so *many* times that you can fly anything, and—"

His voice rumbled at her. "I damned well can."

"Then you can also wait to find out until we get there, right?"

"You trying to box me into something, Brandon?"

She rolled her eyes in purity and innocence. "Heaven forbid."

"Do you realize what you just said? You're giving me carte blanche to pack you in, kid."

"If you come out on top."

He shrugged. "You're nuts. Okay. Deal."

She held up her hand. "Not so fast. I don't intend to lose. What happens then?"

"You really believe—" He was incredulous. "You really believe you're going to outfly me?"

"I do, I can, and I will. You haven't answered my question."

He rose slowly to his feet, a small mountain of brawn and muscle looking down on her. "You get left seat."

"Your word."

"Don't you damned dumb women know when it's been given to you?"

Eighty miles to the northwest of Anchorage, they looked down on Crazy Falls from their single-engine Beaver. The airport was appropriately named. On one end of the airstrip a small waterfall splashed down through a rock tumble, so there was really only one way to get in and out. You landed toward the waterfall; and you took off with the tail of your plane as close to the misty air as possible. Kate slipped in easily, the Beaver right at home on the rough field of grass and stones. It really wasn't an airstrip, just an area bull-dozed long ago by someone who wanted to jump in and out with a small plane.

Kate eased the Beaver off the strip onto a level area to one side. They climbed to the ground and Atkins stood with his fists on his hips, staring toward the falls end of the airport. He shook his head slowly, with a mixture of actual and mock disbelief.

"I don't believe it, Brandon. I just don't believe it."

"It's a beauty, isn't it?" she said, grinning.

"I haven't even *seen* one of those things for more than twenty years. I didn't think there were any left in the whole bloody world!"

They walked along the strip. The "thing" sat heavily at the extreme end of the airport like some monstrous creature trying to lay an egg that would probably weigh several tons.

Seemingly welded to the earth, it presented a ponderous air. It was a giant, slab-sided, box-shaped airplane, to beggar the term, with three great metal propellers stuck onto three equally great radial engines. It rested on a massive-framed fixed landing gear supported by two huge tires. The body, as well as the wings and tail, was corrugated. The entire affair sloped back to a distant tail wheel which, naturally, appeared low on air and sagged entirely of its own accord. The cockpit, two stories above the ground, seemed to have been hammered from heavy iron and then shoved rudely together so that it resembled a greenhouse fashioned by an idiot. Square, ungainly, grotesque, impossible.

It was a Junkers Ju-52/3m, a German trimotored transport that, since 1934, had served as seaplane, bomber, military attack transport—just about every possible role one might conjure for a machine spawned by ill-mannered elves in some black forest of Bavaria.

Atkins stood beneath the nose engine, looking at the bends and knocks, at the skin rash, peeling paint, streaks of oil, splotches of grease, and other assorted signs of mayhem inflicted on the machine for forty years. He glanced briefly at Kate. On this monstrosity, the huge ailerons that usually formed the trailing edge of the wing, as did the flaps, formed separate trailing wings of their own, hooked onto the main wing. It was insane.

"My God," Atkins said finally. "Does it fly?"

"It flies."

"Brandon, how long is this strip? Two thousand feet?"

"Seventeen hundred."

He looked down the runway and made a rude sound. "How'd you get this ironworks in here? With a mule team?"

"I flew it in, Mr. Atkins."

"Who?"

"Me."

"*You* flew—"

"Yes, sir. Little old me. And now we're going to see just how well *you* do in Iron Annie."

The great Junkers waited menacingly. Atkins followed Kate around, on, and through the airplane, opened doors, climbed out onto the wings to check fuel and oil levels, unscrewed panels, twisted handles. Two black sharklike fins jutted up from the wing engine nacelles. "Are those things fuel gauges?" he asked, shaking his head.

"Uh huh. But they're unreliable. You check the fuel with a dipstick." He watched her probing into the tank. "Good enough," she said, replacing the stick and sealing the cap.

"How much does she hold?"

"Three hundred fifty in the right wing and three hundred gallons in the left. Twenty gallons of oil for each engine. Then there's the hydraulic fluid. See that handhold, C.B.? Grab it, then put your foot into that step, and climb out by the engine. It's a bit tricky. You'll have to hold on with one hand while you open the hydraulic fluid filler cap and check the level."

"Brandon, you gotta be an acrobat to—"

"I do it all the time, C.B. *You* do it now."

The wind nearly blew him off the precarious surface. He made it back to the right wing and they climbed into the cabin.

"You'd better unchock the tires and untie the ropes," she directed him. "We're the only crew. We'll have to dispense with the outside fire bottles during starting. When you come back in, close the cabin door. Number one engine will just about blow it off its hinges if we leave it open."

He stood stock-still, staring at her, his face devoid of expression. He went past her to the door and onto the ground, pulled the chocks, and nearly broke his fingers undoing the tie-down ropes. Finally he was back in the cockpit. Kate sat in the copilot seat and motioned him to the left.

He faced—even for his experience—a bewildering system of dials, gauges, knobs, switches, levers, wheels, buttons, and other strange apparatus. He could determine a fair amount of the equipment—but much of it baffled him. He stared at the identification plates. "What the hell is this?" he demanded. "I can't read those things."

"They're in German, Norwegian, and Spanish," she said.

"Where's the flight manual?"

She handed him a thick book. He went through the first few pages, looked at her. Ah, a touch of anger, she thought with delight.

"This goddamned thing is in Spanish," he growled.

"Yes."

"But this is a German airplane."

"Uh huh."

He looked around him. "And this cockpit is like a Chinese boiler room."

She clapped her hands. "Wonderful! That's the best description I've heard."

He tossed the flight manual onto the floor behind them. "All right, Brandon, gimme the goddamned checklist."

"No one ever made one up."

"Then how the hell do we—" He stopped short, eyed her suspiciously. "You *do* know the sequences?"

"By heart."

"All right, how do you start this animal?"

Her smile was pure concentrated sugar. "Mr. Atkins, you have flown with me as check pilot in a dozen different types of airplanes. Not once did you ever lift a finger, except to respond to a printed sequence of items as directed by me, to start one of those machines. You are the man who can fly anything. You're the man who needs no help. I suggest, sir, that you reach deep into your bag of tricks and see if you can start *this* son of a bitch the same way."

She smirked; he glared. "Half the goddamned instruments are in three different languages! This thing isn't old—it's ancient!" He banged a fist on a small twist lever. "Take this thing. What the hell *is* it?"

"Spark advance."

"Spark advance?"

"Yes."

"I thought this was—what are we in? A Model T?"

She shrugged. "Don't complain to me. I—"

"And the fuel system is like the Chicago reservoir!"

"C. B. Atkins can fly anything. I have been given this word as gospel."

"Goddamn it, Brandon, I said *fly*. To get this thing under way you'd have to be a—"

"Start it."

"You know I can't without—"

"Temper, temper. Are you giving up the left seat?"

He took a long look around the cockpit. He gritted

his teeth and he fumed. His face grew red, but he knew when he'd come a cropper. He nodded.

"Switch," she announced.

They changed seats. The starting procedure for the ancient Ju-52 was a hysterical, almost religious, ritual. Kate pointed to a row of switches behind Atkins's head. "Numbers three and five. Move them down to On."

"Down?" It was the opposite of all other switches.

"Down. All right, that row of breakers to your right. Number four; press in." He jabbed it in.

He watched her move the fuel selector to Center Feed, pull the quadrant master up to On; move all three spark advance levers to full On, the supercharger control to below nine thousand feet; bring the number three engine ignition switch to Up; move another lever to both mags; remove a safety cover over an inertia starter T-handle; pull the fuel flow selector on number three to Start. She motioned to a long handle with a sphere at the end. "Grab that, start pumping. This thing hasn't run for a while. You may need a hundred strokes or more."

"What the hell is it?"

"Wobble pump."

"Use the electric pump, damn it."

"This is an airplane, Mr. Atkins. It takes a strong hand to start it. You're a big boy. There aren't any electric pumps." He started pumping. It was ludicrous. "Faster," she urged.

His arm began to kill him. "When," he gasped, "do you know it's ready?"

"Look out your window. When you see fuel running from the engine to the ground, sing out."

Twenty seconds later he called out. "Keep pumping," she ordered. She pressed down on the number three starter, holding down the T-handle. She gave it a count of fifteen. They heard the starter winding up. "It won't start the first one or two times around," she told him. "Got to get the fuel through, loosen up the oil, and—"

"I know how engines start, damn it!"

She pulled up on the handle, keeping in the pressure. The big propeller jerked around, screeching and whining. It dragged to a stop. Down with the inertia starter. "Pump, damn it!" she shouted. This time the engine caught. Smoke belched out in a huge cloud. "That kicks in the generator!" she called above the roar. "Number two gives us hydraulic pressure." She glanced at the gauge, pumped the brakes.

"You forgot to set the parking brake!" he bellowed.

"There isn't any!" she yelled back, delighted. "The fuel's got a long way to go to get to that nose engine. Keep pumping!"

He thought his elbow was going to break. At the same time he watched her. She seemed to have three hands. He'd never seen an airplane with so many things to do just to bring it to life. The number two engine hammered and belched smoke and clattered. "Okay!" she shouted above the din, "now for number three. That gives us the vacuum system! *Keep pumping!*"

All the time she was staying on top of it—fuel pressure, fuel flow, oil temperature and pressure, RPM, manifold pressure, hydraulic pressure, cylinder head temperature, carburetor controls, oil cooler controls, ammeter, voltmeter—the works. Finally, all three engines were running, and she kept a rotating check of the gauges. Alongside her seat was a huge wheel. She turned it for a long time, watching a dial on the side of the cockpit to her left. Then she pulled up on a knob in the center of the wheel and kept turning. "Integrated trim and flap system," she called. She pointed above her. "Release that catch and slide back the overhead hatch. I want you to give me a visual check on tail control movement." He did as she directed, stood up, the wind from the nose prop banging him in the face. The elevators moved and the rudder moved and he dropped back into his seat.

"Okay, okay," he shouted.

The yoke in her hands was a wooden monster. He would have sworn they'd salvaged it from the *Titanic*. She checked the ignition system. "Okay," she shouted. "We're all set to go!"

The airplane vibrated and roared and swayed as if they were in an earthquake.

"Are you ready, Mr. Atkins!"

"Do it!"

She laughed.

The trees only seventeen hundred feet away seemed ominously close. Atkins glanced at her. "Are you sure this thing can—"

Before he could complete his question, she was off the brakes. At the first lurch forward she shoved on the yoke, and the tail was up, the airplane level with the ground before it moved a dozen feet.

Six hundred feet from where they'd started, the huge old airplane floated into the sky. It was not a takeoff. The machine fell gently into the air. Atkins couldn't help the thrill that went through him. Good God, this was a time machine, turning back the clock forty years.

Kate came around in a high approach. "Just a damn minute, Brandon. You're too high, you'll never make it in from here on that short a strip."

She grinned at him and he went silent. Pilots don't slide such big airplanes sideways through the air. Slips are made for smaller machines. But Kate did it now. The Junkers fell out of the sky at a crazy angle, one wing pointed dangerously to the ground. Atkins watched the approach speed lock right onto eighty miles an hour. As the trees slipped beneath them she straightened out, killed the power, let the plane settle on the main gear with the first tremble of the oncoming stall. She brought down the tail, went to the brakes. They came to a dead stop less than nine hundred feet from the end of the field.

They sat for several moments, the big engines ticking with a satisfying rumble. "Mr. Atkins, you may fly this airplane as well as I just did. I expect that. But in no way will you ever fly it better."

He stared straight ahead, then looked around. Finally he nodded. "All right. You've done it."

She didn't dare to breathe.

"What the hell's the matter with you, Brandon?"

"I'm not sure if I want to shout or to cry."

"Woman, you've just made captain. I don't like—" He stopped and glared at her. "Never mind. You've earned it. I'll send somebody after the Beaver. Take us home. In this thing. I want everybody to see what a flying dinosaur looks like."

She motioned to the yoke. "You want it?"

"Uh uh. Enjoy the trip, Brandon. Tomorrow you start C-130 school. Sixty days. And nights. Then you have two months in the right seat like any other peon. Then you get another check ride, from me, and *then* you've got that left seat. That's four months from now. And you know what? I'm going to be on your back every day of those four months. Now let's get the hell out of here."

She made the second takeoff in five hundred feet flat.

25

The driver eased the black car to the side of the road. They were at the end of a runway at Anchorage International Airport. In the back seat were Sarah Markham and Felicia D'Agostino.

"Watch closely," Sarah Markham urged the other women. "She's doing what they call short-field work. Getting off the ground as quickly as possible."

The nose of the thick-bellied machine rushing toward them lifted from the ground, and the Lockheed Hercules arrowed into the sky at a frightening angle. It seemed that at any moment it must fall, its high wings askew, but it held its grip on the air, began to curve away, and passed directly over the car with a sound of great authority.

Sarah Markham gestured to the woman in the right front seat. "Helen, watch what she's doing with that airplane. She lives in it. This is the best time to get the footage and still photography we want, both of the girl and the airplane. Also, you can set up your people in Alaskair's offices and shops. The photography must be candid."

Helen Sherman nodded. "Except for the pictures that will be taken openly—airplanes, shops, hangars, that sort of thing—Ms. Brandon will never know a camera's been pointed in her direction. We have the contract to shoot film of the Hercules—a company deal—so our presence will be quite normal."

Sarah Markham ordered the driver to take them to the opposite end of the runway. "I want to see her land. I'm not sure I understand this, but they have been talking about some controlled crash landings."

Felicia D'Agostino looked at her with wide eyes. "Crash? What kind crazy is this?"

"I'm not at all certain myself. Controlled crash is what I was told. I don't mean that the airplane actually crashes, only that it seems to."

D'Agostino shook her head. "Is crazy."

"We'll see."

When they were in position to watch, and the huge airplane fell from the sky, the women in the car were convinced that all their months of preparation had come to a sudden and inglorious end. A controlled crash landing in a Hercules is an explosive and frightening spectacle. The blur of movement, the sudden roars, the complaining slam of rubber and metal, and the extraordinary flexing of the airplane all add up to a *crash*. For the eyewitness, that is. For the pilot, it's a combination of precise timing, great skill at the controls, and the most incredible airplane of its kind that has ever flown.

At the first explosion, everyone in the car gripped someone or something, freezing heart and lungs in shock and fear.

Still in the air, but on the precise line she wanted, Kate had reversed the giant thick-bladed propellers. The effect was a thundering roar, the sound from the prop blades, and it seemed as if the airplane had flown into a sandpit, so effective and visible was its rate of deceleration.

Seconds later, the nose came up and the Hercules slammed onto the very lip of the runway on its main gear. The nose wheel went to the ground; the airplane dipped like a kneeling camel; the long wings flexed madly, flapping like an albatross; and the entire tail, reaching high above the ground, twisted and slewed crazily.

The airplane was coming apart before their eyes. They braced themselves for the screech of tortured metal, waiting for brilliant flames to shoot out in all directions, and . . .

Sarah Markham prodded Felicia, who had her eyes closed and was gripping the heavy gold cross on her neck and praying fervently. "Felicia, open your eyes, for God's sake, and *look*."

Disbelief refused to leave them, even as they watched

the huge transport lunge forward, again to claw into the air at its steep, ridiculous angle.

"It is *our* Kate who is doing this thing?" Felicia's astonishment could hardly be disguised.

Sarah Markham laughed. "That's wonderful. *Our* Kate. Yes, yes, it is."

Helen Sherman turned to them. "She's been doing this six hours a day. Here; at small airports; on snow and ice; on dirt fields. She—"

"Just get those films. And," Sarah Markham stressed, "get her in the cockpit, somehow, where she works, where she lives. And I want them to be absolutely natural; and get them as quickly as possible."

Helen Sherman nodded. "One question, please." Markham gestured for her to go ahead. "Her personal, well, her personal life with Michael Carew is going to be a bit more difficult."

Markham smiled. "You're being paid very well to do the difficult. Do it."

For two months Kate went through nearly nonstop sessions as a captain-to-be, albeit a student, in the Lockheed. Punishing, demanding, mentally exhausting work in the classroom, the hangars, the maintenance and overhaul shops. An Alaskair captain had to know the systems of the airplane inside and out; she had to be able to effect emergency repairs, live off and from the airplane. They often encountered situations where the only power source was the airplane itself. Not simply the engines, but their auxiliary power unit as well. In the great northland the Hercules had to be a self-sustaining unit of total energy and performance.

Kate often flew operational missions to radar sites and oil field construction sites. When she made such trips, it was never as senior captain, for a check pilot went along, watching and evaluating. In every other respect, however, Kate Brandon was flying as captain. Traversing the huge Alaskan territory came to her easily, but the training was backbreaking. And often mind-bending, for there was no letup in her own determination to be the very best of the new pilots with the line.

At night, or whenever she was free from the cockpit and the books, she fled to be with Mike Carew. Her muscles yielded willingly to his strong hands as they worked oil into her back and legs.

Tired as she was, and overwhelmingly preoccupied, she paid no heed to the many photographers who seemed to be hanging around Alaskair operations. There was a contract with a commercial photo company covering supply flights supporting maintenance of the Alaska pipeline. Lockheed had their own people to record every facet of Hercules operations, and the oil companies were around with their public relations flacks. She had no reason to wonder at their presence and dismissed them from her mind.

Which was perfect for the needs of Helen Sherman. The library of still pictures, many of them made with telephoto lenses, and of films, grew steadily. Sarah Markham was satisfied. The films and pictures would not be used until the moment for greatest effect was at hand. In the meantime the American Congress Party continued preparations to nominate a woman for vice-president. Kate Brandon, if all continued to go well, to help their V.P. candidate, would make up the "best of all possible backgrounds" for their promotion campaign.

And all continued to go very well, indeed.

He shuffled forward, still awkward about the whole affair, uncomfortable beneath the barrage of lights and flashbulbs, the smiles and grins on the faces of so many people. He had wanted this to be a quiet event, with some personal dignity to it, but Sam Burleyford had pulled out all the stops on the publicity. Well, to hell with them all. As far as C. B. Atkins was concerned, this was strictly between himself and the trim woman in the Alaskair captain's uniform.

He stood before her. "I suppose, since I'm old enough to be your father, all this is up to me." He reached out to pin captain's wings to the uniform tunic of Kate Brandon.

He didn't know what the hell to do after that, so he stuck out his hand, burying hers in his huge paw.

"Congratulations, Brandon." He hesitated. "I still don't believe in girls flying big—"

"I'm a woman, C.B., not a girl." But she said it with a kind smile.

"I don't give a damn. But I'll tell you something. You earned those wings."

Impulsively, she leaned forward to kiss him on the cheek. "Thanks, boss."

"Watch it, kid. You're on candid camera. About a hundred of them, from the looks of it. Sam's got a press conference set up for you."

"I know." Her expression was doubtful. "I wish he hadn't done that."

"It's his railroad. Chin up and all that sort of stuff. When it's over, come see me in my office." He glanced at the mob of press and dignitaries. "And no drinks. You're on duty."

It took two hours. And it was a mess. They were all over her. Posing her for pictures, asking the same tired questions again and again. Idiots who didn't know one end of an airplane from another. Sam Burleyford was everywhere, running the show.

Well, she *was* the first woman to become captain for a commercial airline. She couldn't blame Sam, even if she remained cool to him. She'd never gotten that private talk with Atkins from her mind.

Finally, she dragged Sam to a corner. "I have *got* to get out of here," she insisted.

"Kate, look at that crowd. We're getting the best coverage this line has ever had! You can't just leave now. Listen—"

"Sam, I'm flying tomorrow. I'm on duty, to quote the boss. And I'm ordered to report to him, *and now*." She patted his arm. "Don't worry, Mr. President. I'm sure you'll be able to dazzle them with that great big smile of yours."

He flashed her a sharp look. Anger? Suspicion? She didn't know, she didn't care. She just wanted out of the zoo. She made quick good-byes, slipped through a side door, and walked quickly to Atkins's office.

At least *he* didn't waste any time. "You start first thing in the morning, Brandon. You already know the run. You're a milk train. You fly everything there is to fly. Whatever people need and want and wherever they think they want it. You'll try to stay on the basic schedule we've set up, but don't count on it. You'll get pulled off to any job that comes up."

"I understand."

"It's the toughest run we've got, Brandon."

"I know that, too." She smiled at him. "You have anything to do with that?"

"I had everything to do with it. And you know damned well that if I didn't think you could hack it you wouldn't be going."

"I guess that's a compliment."

"Guess anything you want." He paused, drummed thick fingers on his desk. "One more thing. Private conversation. Has Sam or anyone else spoken to you about that Russian run?"

She shook her head. "Not a word."

"Well, it's in the works. There's a lot of pressure—it's official now—from the front office for me to recommend you for it. They're really not playing games. It's big money, big political clout."

"What am I supposed to say?" she parried.

"Not one word to you yet?"

"You're it, C.B. No one else."

"Good. Damn them all, it *is* good politics and good business. It's getting so you've got to be a wizard to run flight operations. Ah, well, let it lie quiet, Brandon. In the meantime, get the hell out of here. There's some overgrown boy scout waiting for you outside, and—"

"Mike?" Her face lit up, and she ran for the door.

"Be here at 6:30 A.M. sharp!" he bellowed after her.

In the hall she threw herself into Mike's arms. Tight against his shoulder she whispered, "For God's sake, let me be a woman tonight. Because tomorrow—"

26

Twenty-five thousand feet.

It's marvelous up here, a singular universe. All those shifting moods and scenes I love. We devour distance without seeming to move.

It doesn't seem possible we're flying through this air at 355 miles an hour. I can't see that river of air through which we're pushing. At seventy miles an hour, its great current sweeping toward us, and we're snagged in its syrupy content. So we move northward with a true speed over the ground of only 285 miles an hour. How easily we say "only" 285 miles an hour! Dogsleds and the Hercules, all in one breath. I suppose I'm an incurable romantic. But what the hell, so was my father and many like him.

Kate Brandon shook herself from her reverie. Around the Hercules, five miles above the ground, was a strange cloud condition, and they ghosted their way through it bound from Anchorage to Prudhoe Bay. It might be called a cirrus fog—clouds with changing shapes impossible for eye or mind to grasp.

In brief minutes, they also moved from fading day into night. It came swiftly this far north. The darkness swelled the feeling of spaciousness on the flight deck of the Hercules, for it was all enhanced by skillful selection of lights and colors, of equipment and panel shapes—a triumph of anthropometric engineering. Science and technology had tailored the area for comfort, convenience, and efficiency. The flight crews made no bones about their feelings; the Hercules was a winner, and its freedom in the cockpit—unlike the pressing confines of other, even larger, transports—was a constant wonder to its crews.

For the most part, things were bathed in red light. The human eye can be saturated in red, can resolve instruments and controls and figures, and lose not at all the vital capacity for night vision. The instruments swam in redness, and there were isolated pools of blue white, tiny sparkles of green and sometimes amber. Occasionally there came a soundless mushrooming of greater redness. This was a red beam in the hands of Jim Phillips, providing additional illumination for the scrutiny of a dial or control.

Most commercial aircraft don't have navigator spaces, but the unique world of the northland dictated that the Lockheed L-100-30 models flown by Alaskair have this capability. Art Mankowitz played a dual role: full-time flight engineer, and navigator when necessary. From their constantly changing position, the magic wand of electronics at his fingertips, he was free to connect the Hercules to the outside world with the aid of compass and protractor, pencil and slide rule, computers and charts, and an elaborate sextant. From the pattern of the celestial vaults, he could extract the mathematical bits and pieces needed to arrive at their longitude and latitude coordinates. Fortunately, there were long-distance navigational aids that swept the skies with their own electronic needles; the navigator aboard the Hercules was simply an essential part of northland "backup life."

Kate slid back into her seat and strapped in. A thorough scan of the panel and a brief word with the crew assured her that everything proceeded exactly as planned. The mechanical world once again in order, she returned her gaze to the outside world. Clouds still rode the convoluted earth far below. Now, as the guardians of the dark, they growled their presence and bristled angrily at the Hercules above them, warning of their fierce energies. Jagged tongues flashed freely from their battlements; lightning gleamed and reflected weirdly in the bottomless gloom.

Were the human souls in the winged form children subjected to the sudden appearance of flickering goblins that cast a spectral glow in the sky? How deep, truly, was the abyss falling away beneath them?

On this night, the air was crystalline above the murkiness of lower atmosphere. Thin and bitterly cold outside the glass enclosure of the Hercules, the air gained unbelievable clarity. Kate felt she might have been in a spacecraft drifting between worlds, and for long minutes she gave herself to the siren call of her imagination.

They were suspended in the midst of some incomprehensible bowl of stars that was blazing in such profusion that belief in the reality of the sight was almost impossible. The strange nature of the earth's atmospheric horizon—a band of darkness lying just above the curvature of the planet—created an effect eerie and misleading. The stars spilled down to the horizon, vanished, and reappeared again beneath the blackness at the edge of the world. If you were not careful, and remained unaware of this strange behavior on the celestial stage, all conception of up or down could vanish. The stars looked for all the world like lights on a distant shore.

Unseen fingers of turbulence snaked up from the clouds below to touch the Hercules, which responded with mild trembling to the invisible caress, flexing its wings slightly. No one paid any heed; it was a normal signature of flight.

Abruptly, Kate was back on the flight deck of the Hercules, with a different preoccupation. Kate understood she would make or break her place as captain depending on how well she and the men who flew this machine with her formed a deep partnership.

Her first meeting with her crew had the quality of a pack of dogs quietly circling one another.

Jim Phillips, who was to be her copilot, hesitated, then offered his hand. He made a feeble attempt to be lighthearted. "I don't know," he said, smiling weakly, "if I should call you sir or ma'am."

Kate shook his hand firmly and squared her gaze on him. "Captain will do fine, Mr. Phillips. Shall we get to the point at hand?"

Had she been brawny and heavily bodied he might have been able to cope with her controlled aggressiveness. But he faced an extremely attractive woman who spoke crisply and with unquestioned confidence. "Oh, well, of course, uh, captain," he blurted from his unbalanced position.

She hesitated a long moment. She had been ready and willing to expect everything up to and including outright hostility; but she wasn't going to leave any doubts about her own capabilities and absolutely no questions about her strength of command. She had learned certain lessons long ago; she didn't much care how her crew felt so long as they operated their equipment and functioned as a team. It spelled support of her position as captain. She understood that Phillips most likely held no grudge against her personally; he seemed decent enough, in fact. Likely it was that old bugaboo that top airline slots were tough to come by, and qualified women who had the jobs made it that much tougher for qualified men.

But that was the kind of reasoning that chewed on its own entrails, and she wasn't having a bit of it. She offered no sympathy. After they'd talked for a while she put it on the line. "All you have to do, Jim Phillips, is to outfly me, match the time I've logged. Get a few thousand more hours under your belt, in the equipment I've flown, and *then* go to the front office and tell them you deserve this seat more than Kate Brandon does. And until you do all that, and you convince the brass you're right, you will bloody well do everything your job calls for you to do. That's right, isn't it?"

His stammered reply pleased her even less. "Of—of course I will, but—"

"But me no buts, mister. Because if you can't hack that right seat you'll be out of this airplane so fast you'll think C. B. Atkins is just a big pussycat and I'm the real baddie in this outfit."

Where there had been a wariness and a potential for conflict with Jim Phillips, she found an instant bond with Art Mankowitz, her flight engineer. Art had spent most of his life in the Far North. His skills were matched with his knowledge of Alaska, the Aleutians, and Canada, and from his extensive experience had come a hard-nosed attitude toward anyone in his crew. Nothing mattered to him but ability, skill, and courage.

He had seen too many men die because of great pride and inability thrown together in the same pot. It did not take him long to cast his measure of Kate Brandon. To Art Mankowitz, the captain of this airplane was a professional in every sense. She knew what she was doing, and he had yet to meet more than half a dozen pilots who could match her artistry with the powerful Hercules.

As far as Mankowitz was concerned, the real test of the pilot came on snow, wet grass, and gravel. They were what separated the men from the boys. He chuckled at his own use of the phrase, but his intent was unmistakable. There are those who have the touch, and there are those who are competent but lack that instinct.

"And this broad has it," he told the other flight crews. "She's got more damned talent in one finger than half the guys on this line have in their whole bodies. You ought to see her working on ice when it's all power and no brakes worth a polar bear's ass. The damn airplane acts like she's talking to it and it knows how to answer." He shook his head and grinned. "I've been flying with her for three months now. She's the best."

The usual retort wasn't long in coming. "You sound like you're getting a case, Art. Couldn't be something like you'd like to climb into a crew bunk with her, could it?"

Art Mankowitz was known up and down the line as probably the gentlest man in all of Alaskair. So it was totally unexpected, and greeted with open-mouthed shock, when Art quietly left his seat and just as quietly slammed a very large fist into the nose of the man who'd just made the remark.

Characteristically, Art also helped the man to his feet and produced a handkerchief to stem the flow of blood. "You were talking about *my* pilot. Don't do it again."

Kate learned of the incident. "Art, you can't go around defending me like that. I appreciate it, but good God, you'll need an application for the Golden Gloves. I—"

"Captain, you fly the old girl, okay? That's your job. I'll take care of my crew. And," he added, "any others that need attending to."

She squeezed his arm.

What she valued most of all in Mankowitz was his incredible feel for the northland. He had been a flight engineer in the air force and one of the best survival specialists in the business. He'd been there when the DEW radar systems were first set up; when research teams drifted for months on ice floes, when men parachuted into remote country to test with their lives the equipment they'd designed and built themselves. He'd flown and operated in Antarctica as well, and he was an expert in keeping machinery functioning in temperatures down to fifty and sixty degrees below zero. She could not have had a better man in her crew.

She learned quickly that just as invaluable to her was Paul Grayson, the only black member of the crew. Another air force veteran, a former master sergeant, he had flown as crew chief and cargo master of the C-130 —the military version of the Hercules—where he fulfilled the same tasks. When he left his blue suit hanging in a closet, Alaskair had snatched him up for his priceless expertise in working the great slab-bodied turboprop transports.

How did Paul Grayson feel about his captain being a woman? He didn't much give a damn. He hadn't cared for officers when he wore his blue suit, and the people who sat up front in the Hercules were the same as officers. They wore different suits, but they still came out the same. Period.

27

"Jesus, if the moon had air it would have to look like this," Art Mankowitz said, as Kate drilled the Hercules toward the frozen landing strip at Prudhoe Bay along the northern coast of Alaska. There were actually several airfields in the area, set up by the various oil companies and by the state government, but the Hercules needed none of them: all that was required could be produced with markers on a frozen surface. Markers for depth perception, lights for landing at night or in gloom, a homing station because the damned weather could close in at any moment. And, what every pilot wanted, a GCA radar unit. Ground-Controlled Approach was sometimes the only way one of the big airplanes could land. When a whiteout or ice fog or a sudden snowstorm rolled in, the ground became utterly invisible, and only a man on the ground, literally talking the pilot down, could bring in the Hercules, its wheels touching even before the pilots could see beyond the nose of the machine.

Now, dawn was breaking as Kate eased the Hercules toward the icy strip. The sun seemed to have weakened, and it cast long but strangely indistinct shadows—structures and towers in stark isolation against an otherwise featureless surface.

The main tires crunched on ice overlaid with snow, and snow swirled about, surrounding them as the great propellers chewed air in enormous gulps. The Hercules rolled slowly to the unloading area. Brilliant arc lamps cast their own eerie illumination.

The outside temperature was minus forty, and the wind made the chill factor low enough to keep any sensible man under cover as long as possible. In the cockpit they were warm, even snug, and they had to

remind themselves that only the thin separation of glass
and metal kept out the savage temperatures.

"I was right," Mankowitz said, as much to himself
as to the others. "If we put up a base on the moon, it
would have to be like this. Even the BP building, the
way it's shaped." He studied the BP Alaska structure
with its flowing aerodynamic contours. "Nah, change
that," Mankowitz added with sudden life. "Screw the
moon. It's more like Mars here. We got winds, it's
colder'n a polar bear's butt, and every goddamned
thing you use, from toilet paper to screws and ham-
burgers, has to be flown in. And when you get here,
you're here for a long time to come." He snorted in
contempt of ever being stuck in a place like this again.

The main building that housed people, supplies,
power facilities, eating and living areas, communications, just about everything, stood on pilings so it
wouldn't start down into the permafrost of the nakedly
barren area of Prudhoe Bay. It had been designed and
built somewhere else, taken apart, shipped here, and
put together again. It was an oasis where men girded
themselves for a winter about as savage as they might
expect on the desert world of Mars.

Just south of where they had landed was a gravel
runway at Deadhorse. Weather permitting, Boeing
737 jets slid into Deadhorse on a scheduled run that
would have required a Siberian route to match its isolation. Sometimes, even when you got in, leaving the
airplane was a vicious risk. When the temperature went
down to 60 or 70 below, as it did all too often, and
the winds screamed down from the polar region, the
chill factor plummeted to 150 degrees below zero. In
thirty seconds unprotected skin is frozen to dead tis-
sue, and in not too much longer even metal becomes as
brittle as dry twigs.

The Hercules's cargo was palletized. Everything was
sealed in pallets which were ready for winging out of
the airplane through the yawning rear hatch, on rollers.
The Hercules could land, park, and twenty minutes
later be empty of all its cargo—and ready to get the
hell out of Prudhoe. Delays occurred when there was

cargo to load, engines in need of repair, people returning south—anything.

This was one of their faster trips—dump the load and get out before a blowing storm enveloped the Prudhoe area and locked them onto the surface. Her crew took care of the details while Kate went into BP Alaska flight operations to get the latest check on weather and see if any messages had come in through the land telephone link to Anchorage or by satellite.

There were none.

In Anchorage, at Moose Lodge, on a winding side road just north of Fort Richardson, Sam Burleyford had joined Sarah Markham and three members of the ACP steering committee. Sarah Markham was quietly but deeply excited.

"We've cracked the first wall," she announced to Sam. "The run to Yakutsk."

"You mean it's set?" He was openly surprised. "I don't understand how they could have gone through with it. Every carrier here in Alaska is keeping the others informed of what—"

"Forgive me," Sarah Markham broke in. "I didn't mean to say the negotiations were a matter of fact. They're not. What has been agreed upon, between the White House and the Kremlin, is a test run. A proving flight."

Sam saw the picture as quickly as he'd heard her words. "Makes sense," he said. "That way, if difficulties arise, neither we nor the Russians will be faced with an entire program coming apart. It's just one more test of détente—or whatever they want to call it."

"Exactly, Sam. But it can be so much more for us," Markham added quickly. "I want Kate Brandon to have that run." Her face grew intent. "Very, *very* frankly, what are her chances? Without our putting on undue pressure, I mean. We want to avoid, at all costs, any action that would seem to reflect our maneuvering. If that happens it could suppress all the positive results."

Sam leaned back in his chair. He was a great deal

less apprehensive than if the question had been put to him several months ago. "Would you believe," he asked, a smile crossing his face, "that she qualifies in every way? I mean that," he stressed. "I'm not bending anything or making any attempt to enlarge on Kate Brandon's record as a captain with Alaskair. Her performance has been as close to perfect as we could ever ask for—consistently on the same level as our most experienced captains. For her time with the line, that is extraordinary. She *does* qualify. She can handle the run as well as any other pilot we have and likely better than most."

Sam Burleyford had already anticipated Sarah Markham's next question. "We know you'll approve Kate Brandon, then."

"Totally on the basis of her qualifications."

"The problem is Atkins?"

"I never said there was a problem, Mrs. Markham."

Her smile was fleeting. "No, you did not. *Is* Mr. Atkins a problem?"

Sam thought for several moments, then shrugged. "I don't think so. Kate Brandon passed every test on her own—as a potential employee, as a copilot in training, as well as going through a probationary period of several months additional. C. B. Atkins approved everything she did every foot of the way. He pinned on her wings himself. For the last several months her performance has been excellent. There is no reason why Atkins would object to Kate Brandon making the Russian flight. To him, it's just one more run."

"You say," Pauline Reddy responded, "that this man Atkins won't object. But, Mr. Burleyford, will he *approve?*"

"He hasn't been asked, Ms. Reddy."

"But—and it is a very large *but*—will we get his recommendation?"

"You can't pin me down like that," Sam objected, disliking the repeated questioning. "You can't do it because you're asking me to state to you, unequivocally, what Atkins will say or won't say. I told you no reason exists for him to object, on the basis of Kate

Brandon's performance and record. I can only answer your question *after* I talk with Atkins."

Sarah Markham stepped quickly into the exchange. Sam was right, of course, and Pauline was demanding guarantees that no person could promise. "Sam, how much effect will your recommendation have on the issue?"

"A great deal. Atkins may come to any decision he wants to on the basis of pilot performance. But that isn't enough in any airline. If the greatest pilot in the world walked through an airplane picking his nose in front of the passengers, he wouldn't last very long, obviously. So I may make a selection based on all factors. I will recommend and I will push for Kate Brandon. Anything beyond that point would be foolish."

"You will call me the moment you talk with Atkins?"

Sam nodded. "Day or night, Mrs. Markham."

"Thank you. Because we are ready with a very powerful promotion campaign, and the instant we hear from you in the affirmative we will roll with that program." She smiled self-consciously. "Forgive me if I appear to be adopting the language of mass publicity. My thoughts have been preoccupied in that direction." Again the smile was gone and the power stood in its place. "Suffice it to say it will cover all branches of the media and go well beyond that. We have had several meetings with members of the Russian group, and they are prepared to join our effort. They anticipate gaining as much from all this as do we. They, of course, are somewhat more limited in their freedom of expression and their goals."

Sam wasn't interested in that kind of bait. "Of course," he murmured. He straightened in his chair. "I believe we ought to coordinate *both* of our campaigns," he said.

Sarah Markham waited out any further comment, received none, slipped smoothly into the new subject. "The timing would be advantageous all the way around. All right, Sam, it's no secret you have aspirations for the governorship. Nothing official yet, of course. When Kate Brandon returns from her initial round-trip flight to Russia, we'll commit you fully to the campaign. We'll arrange an indefinite leave of absence from Alaskair."

Goddamn it, she's done it again. Boxed me in neatly. I'm to commit my ass to this whole thing, and everything's in order. Except that with that one line she's locked me in again. If Kate blows this trip then I'm dead. I'll not only kiss the governor's seat good-bye, but this woman will make sure I'll never see the end of the year from my office in the company . . .

Everyone in the world seemed to know about their selection for the run to Yakutsk before they'd ever heard a word. The announcement was made only minutes after their takeoff from Prudhoe Bay for the return flight to Anchorage. It was Sam Burleyford's intention to inform Kate and her crew while they were still airborne. By the time they landed, the small army of press controlled by Sarah Markham would be ready and waiting.

They didn't make Anchorage on that flight. Their electrical system shorted out while they were in the air, about to cross the Brooks Range. They had four engines operating perfectly, and the odds were overwhelmingly in their favor for continuing on to Anchorage. But in Alaska you never throw away *any* options. When your equipment starts coming unglued . . . well, Kate was a fervent believer in Murphy's Three Laws of physics.

The First Law stated that what can go wrong, will go wrong. That had already happened. The Second Law affirmed that what is already wrong is bound to get worse. That could easily happen because of additional failures or suddenly worsening weather. And the Third Law made it clear that if the first two laws have already been enacted, *then Jesus Christ, it's time to panic*.

With their electrical systems on the edge of becoming spaghetti, Kate elected to land at the first available field. They put into a high mountain airstrip at Anak-tuvuk Pass, along the northern lip of the Endicott Mountains. They managed to get word to Anchorage that they were safe and effecting repairs. Two days later they took off for their home field—and a storm of publicity that caught them by surprise.

Tired and worn from their flight, they had no problems in begging off. Kate did her best to reach Sam Burleyford, but Atkins told her he was in Washington, D.C., sifting out details of the trip to Yakutsk. "I'll take you to your apartment," Atkins offered. Alaskair kept living quarters in town for crews when needed. Kate sat quietly in the car until Atkins felt he'd waited a decent interval.

"Lady pilot, would you mind if I sound a bit nasty? Well, maybe just unfriendly," he added.

"Who bit your ankle?" she asked.

He laughed, a sound of gravel falling down a pipe. "I said I'd *sound* unfriendly."

"Nothing would surprise me right now," she told him.

"You sound pretty unfriendly yourself."

"Unfriendly, tired, and angry," she said. "C.B., I haven't been off that airplane two hours, and there are movies of me on television, there are spreads in newspapers and magazines, there are—" She scowled. "Where did they *get* all that stuff? I never gave any permission for it. I was never *asked* about it! Where'd they have their cameras? Who's doing all this?"

Atkins stared straight ahead, taking the traffic slowly. Finally he sighed. "Brandon, I take it back."

"Take what back?" she snapped.

"My being unfriendly or nasty. It's the other way around. You've answered all the questions I was going to ask."

She turned to him in astonishment. "C.B., you can go straight to hell with the rest of them. Are you telling me you didn't know about any of this?"

He glanced at her. "Kid, I didn't know. That's on the level."

"Then who handled all this?" Her voice was rising.

He shrugged. "You get three guesses and the same name comes up all three times. Who else is on top of the heap in this outfit?"

Her face showed fury. "That son of a—"

"Look, forget all this. Just keep on trusting me. You stay out of it."

"I'm in it up to my neck, C.B."

"Only on the boob tube and in the columns."

"That's all, huh? Thanks a lot."

"Forget it, Kate. You've got three days to get ready for your big ride to the land of the commissars. You get your rest tonight because tomorrow you start going through the mill. Among other things, you're going to fly a complete run to Yakutsk in the simulator."

"You've got to be kidding."

"Nope. Government orders. It's the only way to handle it. You'll have actual films of the whole run."

"How—how could that be?"

"We have some very sophisticated equipment that little girls like you know nothing about. Blackbirds."

"Blackbirds?"

"Advanced reconnaissance. They've made the run from over 100,000. The special cameras show the flight as if they were at 25,000. We've got the film adjusted to Hercules speed and altitude."

He pulled up before the apartment building. "Get that sleep tonight. A whole special crew is going along as backup to yours. You'll meet them all tomorrow."

She nodded, overwhelmed with weariness.

"And Brandon, leave the Sherlock Holmes stuff to me."

Leave it to him? She was too tired to care. "Good night, C.B. Thanks for the ride."

28

It was all set up with military precision. The preparations were staggering, and there were so many bodies wandering around it felt as if they were in the midst of a casual invasion. The press, of course, replete; public relations groups; the State Department; representatives from Lockheed; every official from Alaskair who could horn into the act; state representatives, congressmen, and senators. Kate was certain the place was also swarming with secret agents. Too many bland-faced men in dark suits who paid no attention to anything but missed nothing.

She had to force discipline on herself. For a while people came crowding into the flight deck, but she put a firm halt to that. She told Jim Phillips to get into the cockpit and to stay in it.

C. B. was standing behind her on the flight deck when she reached her limit. She picked up the microphone.

"Your attention, please." She waited a few moments, knowing it took a while for jaws to stop moving. "Your attention, please," she repeated, and went directly on. "This is the captain. We are now ready to preflight this aircraft. Guests are required to leave. If we are to maintain the schedule for this flight, you must leave immediately." She paused to let it sink in, her thumb off the transmit button. She pressed the button again. "As of now, the flight deck of this aircraft is off limits except to those personnel who have been assigned to cockpit duties."

She looked up as Sam Burleyford came up the ladder and started into the crew compartment. "Sam, that goes for you as well," she told him.

He stopped with an astonishment he couldn't disguise. "I need to talk with you for a few moments, Kate. It won't—"

"This aircraft is in preflight, Mr. Burleyford. Be good enough to leave this flight deck until your presence is not a factor of interference."

He stared at her, caught the eye of Atkins, whose expression matched granite. For a long moment, indecision stirred within Sam. Finally he nodded. "Whenever you're free, then," he said, disappearing down the ladder.

"This is the captain again," she said into the mike. "Those of you who are passengers aboard this aircraft will be directed to your seats by Mr. Grayson. He has your positions assigned. Please be good enough to follow his instructions. If there are any difficulties, he will make last-minute changes. Mr. Grayson is crew chief of this aircraft and his decisions will be followed. Anyone who finds this to their dissatisfaction will be invited to leave the aircraft at once." She hesitated. "That is all."

Atkins looked at her and she held his gaze, defiant. His cheek muscles twitched, but after a short while not even his own iron discipline could keep his craggy features from breaking into a huge grin. "I couldn't have done it better myself, captain." He had his own barb to throw. "Anyplace in particular you want *me* to be?"

"What's your position on this flight, Mr. Atkins?"

"You know what it—"

"Do *you* know?"

"Hell, yes. What's the matter with you, Brandon? You know I'm riding the jump seat right behind you!"

"Then if you know, why waste my time with silly questions?"

She looked into the cargo hold. Good, Sam was helping Paul Grayson clear the plane. Sam directed a ground crew into the machine to clean the odd debris scattered by the visitors.

"Mankowitz?"

He stuck his head around from his flight engineer's panel. "What's up, captain?"

"We've had a herd of cattle going through this airplane. Would you do a visual, please?"

It took the better part of an hour to get ready. Paul Grayson had some unpleasant words with a TV crew that insisted on loading their equipment in their own way, and Paul went to the point of telling them they had sixty seconds to straighten out their asses or he'd throw them off the plane. Kate heard the whole thing while she was doing her own visual inspection of the cargo-passenger hold. Sam Burleyford came up to her. "Kate, you'd better cool down your boy. That's an important TV group. They—"

Kate turned on him in anger, but managed to calm herself. "Mr. Grayson is the crew chief and cargo master of this airplane, Sam. You of all people know he handles this machine by the book. If he decides to throw them out he has my full support. And there will be no arguments."

Grayson didn't miss the exchange. Art Mankowitz was quietly jubilant. Paul Grayson had just promoted Kate Brandon *out* of officer country.

When Kate returned to the flight deck, ready to start firing up the Hercules, C. B. Atkins was waiting with a face as grim as a stone mask on Easter Island. He handed her a folded note. She took it, looked up at him, her defiance rising swiftly. She started to ask what the hell was going on *now*. Instead, she climbed into her seat before unfolding the paper.

"You're way ahead. Don't quit now. C.B."

She was afraid that if she turned around to say anything, she'd never get past the lump in her throat.

"Well, we've got four burning and four turning and the soup's ready in the kettle." Art Mankowitz had his own quaint expressions: everything in the Hercules was ready.

Kate made the last-minute check in her mind. She sat in left seat, Jim Phillips in the right, Art Mankowitz at the flight engineer panel, Paul Grayson in position back in the cabin. But there were others. C.B. was there to ride as an observer on the new run and to offer any help when and if that need came. His presence was reassuring to Kate.

Directly between the two pilot seats and just behind them was the seat usually occupied by an observer or check pilot. This time an air force colonel in civilian clothes occupied the chair. He would observe everything that went on. He knew every Arctic station, every radio system, every communications and electronics facility not only of the United States, but of the Russian system as well. He also spoke fluent Russian, and he had more than fourteen thousand hours logged, of which three thousand had been accumulated in the military Hercules.

Another seat had been jury rigged on the flight deck. A radio operator, also fluent in Russian, who would back up the pilots with any Russian aircraft or ground-control facilities.

There was an additional presence: a *very* special computer-operated global guidance system that told the crew their position—at any altitude or speed, no matter where they were in the world—accurate within three-quarters of a mile, *at any time* during the flight. By punching certain buttons in appropriate sequences, a pilot could also determine his speed over the ground, his estimated time between any checkpoints he chose, and, well, it did everything but make chicken soup.

And if anyone but Colonel John ("Dog") Dougherty tried to operate the system without tapping out buttons in prearranged code, it would quickly turn itself into a pile of melted slag. Kate was quite willing to let Dog Dougherty have his own way with his expensive and beautiful toy.

The damn trip was almost anticlimactic. Everything operated as if the flight schedule had been written by the chamber of commerce. Kate had made this part of the flight dozens of times before to different airports within the Seward Peninsula or the land north of Kotzebue Sound. This time they were simply to keep right on flying.

Nome passed to their south, the Bering Strait—and Russian territory—lay directly ahead.

Colonel Dougherty turned to study his electronic watchdog. A light blinked on. "Welcome to the land of vodka and caviar," he said quietly. "You have crossed into Russia, and we are also north of the Arctic Circle." He lit a cigar. Kate had the distinct impression he'd been here many times before on flights no one would ever admit had ever taken place.

They were following the earth's curvature. So much farther along their flight they would cut back down to the Arctic Circle and fly south of that line.

They didn't see much of the Chukchi Peninsula that made up the easternmost landmass of the U.S.S.R. Clouds covered most of what was, even for Siberia, a wintered desert of savage cold and stark isolation. Not until they reached the Kolyma Lowlands did the clouds break.

The Hercules bounced gently in waves of cold air that streamed down from the Arctic. "You can just make out that range ahead of us," Colonel Dougherty observed. "That's the eastern flank of the Cherskiy Range."

Kate motioned him forward, tapped her chart. "These rivers, colonel. The Moma and the Indigirka. If we're following our planned course, we should—"

"You're smack on, Captain Brandon," Dougherty broke in. "You're expected to cross over the confluence of those two rivers. That also happens to be where we cut back across the Arctic Circle."

Kate nodded. "You sound as if I have your approval, colonel."

He twirled his cigar. "You do. But more to the point, the Oracle says so also."

She looked past him to the electronic navigation system. "It's too bad we can't have those on our aircraft as a regular item."

Dougherty laughed. "Captain, this little goody costs more than every airplane owned by Alaskair, and probably Saturn and Alaska International thrown in." He shook his head. "I hate to say no to a pretty lady, but—" He shrugged.

"Colonel, for a member of the military industrial complex you are a very warm human being," Kate told him. "Were you cast in the wrong role by accident or by design?"

"Don't jump to conclusions, Miss Brandon. Every midnight I turn into a werewolf." He sobered. "I'll not be leaving this aircraft when we land, by the way."

She gave him a sharp look. "I thought this was going to be an aboveboard flight, colonel. None of the usual nonsense that—"

"Relax, please," he broke in quietly. "Our governments have agreed to three of us remaining on the airplane. They have a couple of goodies of their own, and they'll be using them on their flight to Anchorage. Same details, same arrangement, all nice and friendly."

"I'll bet," Kate retorted. But there was no use pushing that subject. They flew on autopilot; Jim Phillips and Art Mankowitz monitored all systems; and the electronic oracle and its human companion, Dougherty, dutifully tagged their position—past, present, and future—throughout the flight.

Far below, a contour map laid out miles before them, she saw the joining of the Moma and Indigirka rivers. Within minutes the Cherskiy Range was sliding beneath the nose of the Hercules. The world below was gaining in variety—all of it hugging the bottom of that invisible demarcation line called the Arctic Circle. Strange, she thought, how I can easily accept the idea of the Arctic winter as long as it's in Alaska. Here in Russia, it assumes infamous dimensions that make it seem almost unbearable.

Before them reared a range of respectable, even mighty proportions. She was more alert now, for this was the last high barrier between them and their destination. The Verkhoyansk Range ran almost diagonally across their flight path. As the peaks eased beneath the nose of the airplane, Kate came back easily on power. Their flight plan called for a steady descent from this point on. They headed for a wide bend in the Lena River, where waited the city of Yakutsk and whatever reception committee had been set up by the Russians.

Their company showed up without warning. Off her

left wing Kate watched two great swing-wing jet fighters easing into escort position. Colonel Dougherty watched them with what appeared to be mild interest. "Mig–27 fighters. Some of their best. Right on schedule, I see."

"How fast can those things fly?" Kate asked.

"Seventeen hundred miles an hour flat-out," he said casually. "And they can top a hundred thousand feet."

Jim Phillips shook his head. "My God, we haven't got anything like that."

Dougherty shot him a look of surprise. "Don't be so sure." He said no more and Phillips didn't pursue the matter.

"Company to our right," he announced, and they turned to see a Russian turboprop holding formation with them. Antonov, Kate guessed, and correctly. The crew waved with obvious enthusiasm. The passenger windows were filled with faces, and cameras pointed in their direction.

"I don't know," Phillips observed, "if they're a welcoming committee or an escort."

"They're friendly," Dougherty said with a straight face. "Those fighters to our left were above and behind us at about 65,000 ever since we crossed into Russian territory. The transport was sent out to make friendly motions."

"The fighters aren't friendly?" Kate inquired.

"They are now," Dougherty replied. "They're out for their portraits."

Even as he spoke, the big Mig fighters eased in closer. One slipped beneath the Hercules and reappeared suddenly on their right wing, and then the Russian jets eased in tight until their wing tips were near to touching those of the Hercules. Kate tensed and her hand went to the yoke.

Atkins touched her shoulder gently. "Play it easy, Brandon," he advised. "I know formation flying isn't in your contract, but this is a show, not an airline operation. Those boys are very good. There's no danger. Just keep right on flying your original course."

"Thanks a heap," Kate said dryly, but she took his

advice. Obviously the Russians were getting some great footage of the Hercules being toyed with by the killer jets.

"They're just funning," Dougherty said in his bland tone. "It's also important to them."

"How?" Kate asked.

"Nobody does anything in this country," Dougherty said with obvious sincerity, "without having to answer to someone. So, maybe some people in Red Square object to an American airliner flying over remote Russian country. It's stupid, from their point of view. Who knows what nefarious schemes we might be hatching? So they bring in some of their bullyboys for films, and the people who've set this up can prove that everything's under control. It's all a part of their system, Captain Brandon. From their viewpoint, a necessary part. This way nobody gets hung on a hook."

"That's ridiculous," Kate retorted. "We wouldn't—"

"Ah, ah," Dougherty said to stop her. "We would and we do. We're playing by the same rules. And why not? They're not interfering with us. Like I say, they're—"

"I know," she broke in, "just funning."

"That's right," Dougherty said, a strange smile on his face.

She told herself to forget the playacting and concentrate on going downstairs. "Jim, dial in the frequency they gave us for Yakutsk approach control."

He turned the communications knobs. "You want our interpreter to handle it?" he asked.

"I'll give it a shot first. Be interesting to get a Russian accent." She depressed the transmit button. "Yakutsk Control, this is Hercules Six Six Four, Alaskair. Identification code Tango Tango Whiskey. Do you read, please?"

To their surprise a voice answered immediately in flawless English. Their interpreter looked somewhat put out. Just like that, he was surplus cargo. "Ah, hello, Tango Tango Whiskey. We hope you had an excellent flight. You are coming in very loud and clear. We have radar confirmation, your transponder is sharp, and we paint you at six zero miles to the northeast, at two five thousand feet. How do you read Yakutsk, please? Over."

Kate shook her head. Surprises never ended. "Yakutsk Control from Tango Tango Whiskey, I read you five by five. Do you wish us to begin our descent at this time? Over."

"Ah, excellent, Hercules. Welcome to the Soviet Union, Captain Brandon. Please initiate descent at this time, as you say. When you reach the airport, continue your descent in a wide circling pattern to the left. At five thousand feet our tower will continue your instructions on this same frequency. Is that satisfactory? Over."

Kate glanced at Jim Phillips. "Everything but flowers and candy," she remarked.

Behind her, Dougherty chuckled. "You'll get plenty of that on the ground. Go ahead with your descent, captain."

She came back on power and the Hercules slid smoothly from the sky. They saw the wide curve of the Lena River, and the city of Yakutsk clear and sharp just beyond the waterway. The airport lay on the edge of the city and even from their distance the long runways were unmistakable. They came over the field at seven thousand and Kate slid into a wide descending pattern. She glanced to her left; the fighter was gone. So was the one on the right, but the big Russian turboprop was out there, a comfortable distance away, still getting its pictures.

Atkins studied the field with binoculars. "That's one hell of a welcoming committee they've got down there. Looks like a brass band and all the works with it."

Kate ignored the conversation in the cockpit. She had an airplane to fly. She contacted the Yakutsk tower and was greeted with the same crisp, friendly response. They gave her a left downwind to runway 23 and she went to work with her crew on the checklist. When she swung around on her long final approach the Hercules was in the groove. She knew she was being watched by hundreds of people and God knew how many cameras, but to hell with them all. She brought the Hercules down as if it were riding an invisible rail in the sky, and she stopped the airplane in less than a thousand feet, everyone in the cargo compartment hanging on for dear life. It felt damned good to do that.

"Welcome to Yakutsk, captain," came the tower. "A vehicle will lead you in, please."

Dougherty chuckled quietly. "We're in isolated country. They must have ordered the whole town out for the occasion. I can see it all now. 'Huge mobs greet American airplane.' It's going to look great on TV all over the world."

When they embarked, they faced a long red carpet, soldiers in dress uniform as an honor guard, a small mob of dignitaries, women in peasant clothes bearing flowers, and lines of officials dressed up like furry penguins. Motion-picture cameras, flashbulbs, microphones; it was Anchorage all over again, but now the Russians held center stage. They went through greeting ceremonies, Kate posed for a hundred pictures, and then limousines whisked them to a modern hotel where everything was laid out with sumptuous detail.

In her room, Kate shook her head in dismay. The first cocktail party began in exactly one hour.

She studied herself in the mirror, indecision gnawing at her over what to wear to the official reception. Finally, compromise seemed the answer. She let her hair fall long, and she went just a bit easier with jewelry than discretion might have called for. Damn discretion; there wasn't any precedent here. She ended up with a very feminine pantsuit outfit, indelibly marked with her status as an airline captain, yet free of the insignia and hardware she wore in the cockpit. It was perfect.

She hoped.

Atkins—God bless him—picked her up at her room. He wore a tuxedo, very severe, very black, and he looked absolutely enormous and fearsome, all the more so when compared to the trim woman who linked her arm with his.

"You look like my bodyguard," she told him as they walked toward the reception room.

He patted her hand. "I feel like your bodyguard."

She didn't like his demeanor. More serious than it should have been. "What's wrong, C.B.?"

"Oh." Her question startled him. "Nothing dangerous, if that's what you mean. We're better protected here from just about anything than we would be anywhere else."

"Then what is it?" she demanded.

He stopped in the hall. "Hang onto my arm, Brandon. They're going to try to cut you out of our pack like cowboys working a steer for branding."

"I don't—"

"Lady, they've got fourteen Aeroflot captains waiting for you in that reception room."

"Well, of course they would. I mean, that's their national airline and—"

"All fourteen are women."

"Oh, Jesus."

He grinned crookedly at her. "Something, ain't it."

"Why the hell didn't Sam tell me what was going on?"

"Cool it, lady pilot. What difference would it have made? Probably the Russians never said a word to anyone about it. They like to spring surprises like this." He turned to study her face more closely. "You scared, Brandon?"

She glared at him. "The hell I am."

"Then, m'lady, let us go slay the dragons."

"Why, C.B., you're positively *gallant*."

"I taught Clark Gable everything he knew."

It was a good thing she'd been warned. Fourteen women in a special group and every blessed one of them was a bona fide Aeroflot captain with years of experience flying everything from helicopters to huge jetliners. That wouldn't have been so bad, but several of those same women looked tougher than C. B. Atkins.

And they were. Olga Ivanov, who was well into her fifties, weighed in at about 190 pounds, a stocky, powerful woman who brought on Kate's instant distrust but won her over completely after several minutes. Olga Ivanov radiated a deep strength that Kate felt almost as a physical presence. Flustered at first by the power she felt, Kate was cautious, almost defensive. Until Olga smiled. Every last touch of wariness fell away from Kate. Olga had extended her hand; Kate ignored it and embraced the older woman. The smile turned positively radiant. Olga spoke little English, Kate knew no Russian, but their communication was complete.

Later, Kate's feeling of warmth turned to awe. Olga Ivanov had commanded an air regiment of the Soviet Air Force in the Second World War. That grandmotherly woman—and she *was* a grandmother, with four children and nine grandchildren—had flown several hundred combat missions as a bomber pilot and had been decorated with the Hero of the Soviet Union medal.

Which, explained their interpreter, was the equivalent of the Congressional Medal of Honor.

"What," Kate asked, almost breathless, "does she do now?"

"She is the captain of an Ilyushin IL–62." The IL–62 was something on the order of the biggest international model of the Boeing 707.

Kate transcended the barriers of language and strangeness as she was introduced to the different Russian women pilots. Their warmth was genuine. They shared a bond Kate had never known with other women.

Natasha was the first woman Kate saw who was not in uniform. A beautiful, long-tressed blonde with high cheekbones and a regal carriage, she wore a long gown, a choker necklace, a simple ring, and—well, the woman was stunning. There was something different about Natasha Vasilyev that Kate must wait to define. Natasha spoke English surprisingly well, and she was the first woman there whom Kate could converse with easily.

When dinner was announced, they left Natasha with Sam Burleyford (no small wonder there, Kate murmured to herself) to enter the dining hall. "What did you think of her?" Atkins asked.

"The words are easy. Beautiful, but *really* beautiful. That facial structure—"

"Asiatic-European," Atkins offered.

"But so much more. She's—so totally herself. Is the word self-confidence? That can't be it, not alone, I mean, because all those women are so strong."

"What," Atkins asked casually, "would you guess she does?"

"Obviously, the wife of someone very high up in government," Kate said, her answer conclusive.

Atkins chuckled, and Kate demanded to know what she had said to provide amusement. Atkins stopped, held Kate at arm's length. "I hate to do this to you, kid, but then again, you'll probably be happy to know it."

"I hate mysteries, C.B."

Atkins sighed. "Natasha Vasilyev is one of the best test pilots in the Soviet Union," he said slowly.

Kate gaped at him.

"Not only that, but in jet fighters and experimental aircraft as well," C.B. continued. "And, anytime she wants it, she's got a seat in one of their Soyuz spacecraft."

"My God." Kate took a deep breath. "You know something, boss man? It's a good thing I'm flying tomorrow morning."

Atkins was puzzled. "Why especially?"

"Because I can't drink tonight, and if I could," she said grimly, "I would get stoned drunk out of my mind."

"You mean—meeting all their women pilots?"

"No, C.B. Because *you've* met them and haven't gone into a corner to sulk."

They were up early the next morning, stuffed with a rousing breakfast and coffee that would have scalded the nape right off a wolf, and in the air by ten o'clock. Kate was both glad and sorry to be leaving so quickly. She'd had enough of the questions and the press conference the night before, but she regretted not being able to know better those incredible women she had met. Perhaps there would be more time in the future.

The relations with the Russians had gone beautifully, and Sam Burleyford waxed enthusiastic about the regular run that could be opened between Anchorage and Yakutsk. Kate pushed it all from her mind. They had weather on the way home and were solid on the gauges in rain for nearly two hours.

Anchorage was another of those floodlight-studded nightmares. Fortunately, she'd reached her limit of permissible flying hours, and after the minimum time necessary at the press conference she flatly told Sam she'd had it and she was leaving.

Burleyford looked at her, saw the fatigue, and nodded. "All right, Kate, slip out of here."

Kate shifted her thoughts. "No, not yet, Sam." She gestured to take in the milling throng of newsmen and officials and hangers-on. "I want to talk to you first. Alone," she stressed, "about all this. I want some answers, Sam."

"All right, honey. My office. It'll take me about ten minutes to close this up."

"I'll be waiting."

29

She leaned back in the lounge chair across from Sam's desk, her head against the soft cushion, trying to let her body relax. She was cramped—pulled muscles and tight nerves and the whole damn bunch of it. She thought of Mike's hands kneading her body, and she closed her eyes.

Kate was just beginning to realize the pressure she'd kept on herself. She was desperate for peace of mind. She opened her eyes and held out her arm. She watched her fingers tremble. My God, was she really that close to coming apart? She felt strangely disembodied—as if she were able to stand aside and watch all the warning signs. What she needed most was to recognize what the devil was causing it all.

Not the flying. She flew prescribed times and hours, and after so many hours in a month she just didn't fly the Hercules until minimum time passed. Besides, that was a crew job and she had a great crew. It wasn't flight time and it wasn't . . .

Her life wasn't her own. She was jostled, crowded, prodded—there was too much insidious maneuvering. She saw it more clearly with each passing minute. She hadn't been able to make a move without some reporter or writer badgering her. The press, or whoever they were, were like a great flock of phantom gulls, wheeling and turning about her from all sides, and she never knew when a phantom shape would materialize and come straight at her with raucous questions, garish floodlights, and the sinuous stab of a microphone.

She understood the needs of Alaskair where promotion was concerned. Kate was fully cognizant of her unique status, but Jesus, there was a limit. She'd been hired as a pilot, not as a public relations stunt.

She was plain damned embarrassed by what was going on, this heralding of her as some champion or other for the acceptance of women in key positions in American life. She'd heard stories that she would be influential in upcoming political campaigns. She'd thought that was crazy, but so much was being spoken and written about her that she finally recognized that a campaign using—*using* her—was actually under way. And disturbing questions were being raised among too many people as to whether she'd actually earned that left seat or had been set up for the deal.

Who was doing all this? Who had authorized the films, the pictures, the stories? Who was bankrolling all of it? There was money here, power, organization. Confronting Sam directly was easier said than done, but they were back now from Yakutsk, and she was here, and so was he, and his office at night, away from the pressing, clamoring people out there . . .

She'd heard stories about Sam talking about her. Oh, nothing derogatory; just the opposite, in fact. She mused over the conversation she'd had with Atkins. That nonsense about Sam slipping the word to people about a marriage coming up between Kate Brandon and Sam Burleyford. That was so much crap, she thought bitterly. Direct confrontation, straight questions, straight answers; it was the only way.

She had built up a heavy head of steam when the door opened and Sam came in. Tired, but all smiles. A winner.

"What is it, Kate?" Sam sat behind his desk, leaning his elbows on the polished wood, looking at her with what seemed to be honest concern.

Kate had planned to go into it slowly, but she was too worn out. She knew the words would stumble from her mouth, but she didn't care. Nor did she much give a damn anymore about ladylike elegance.

"Sam, what the hell is this crap about you and me getting married?"

Sam took a deep breath. He didn't answer right away. She saw the stall. The shuffling of mental gears. "What have you heard, Kate?"

"I asked you a question, Sam. You're giving me

questions for answers. What the hell is this, asking *me* what I've heard? Will you answer me? What have you been telling people? And why, for God's sake?"

"It's not what you think."

She didn't believe what she was hearing. "Sam, you sound like a sneak." She couldn't help the contempt stealing into her voice. "You're involved with someone named Sarah Markham. Somehow, in some way, you've been using me—my name—with her. You want to be governor. That's great. But when did you ever get a license to start *using* me for your benefit?"

"Just take it easy, Kate. No one's using you. Not the way you're saying it. You make it sound dirty or—"

"It *is* dirty," she flared. "And you still haven't answered my first question. This marriage thing. Which," she said icily, "never was, and never will be."

He rubbed his finger along the desk. "It was possible once," he said.

"Will you answer the goddamned question!"

Sam didn't. His office door opened. They turned to see Atkins, his face like stone, looking at them both.

"I've been listening to this happy little conversation," Atkins said. "Oh, not eavesdropping. Fortunately, no one is working in this area tonight because you can be heard up and down the hall."

Sam came alive unexpectedly. His face was screwed up in anger and his words came out in a snarl. "Get out of here, Atkins. This doesn't concern you."

Atkins came into the room slowly; neither Sam's sudden anger nor his words appeared to bother him. Moving with deliberation, he pulled a chair from the side of the office; turned it backwards; sat down carefully, resting his forearms on the seat back. He seemed to ignore the presence of Kate Brandon.

"I want you to understand something, Sam. I've always known you were scared shitless of flying."

Sam's face narrowed into a mask. His words came through clenched teeth. "You don't know what the hell you're talking about."

Kate stared at them.

"Stop it, Sam," Atkins said easily, waving off Sam's

feeble protest. "Remember who I am. I need to fly only once with a man and I can tell you his history all the way back to his cutting teeth. And you—"

Sam was half out of his chair. "Are you calling me a coward?" he shouted.

"No."

Sam froze, nonplussed with the tight answer. "Then —then what the hell is this all about?"

Kate motioned to Atkins. "C.B., you're confusing me, too. I—"

"Just listen." Atkins turned back to the other man. "It's *why* you're gun-shy that interests me. No, you're not a coward, not when it comes to airplanes, anyway. Because when it was rough you kept going back—and I know how rough it was."

Sam's words were strangling in his throat. *"You* know how rough it was? How rough *it is?"* A guttural laugh followed his acid tone. "What the hell do *you* know! You're made of stone. You don't know anything, you old bastard! You—"

Atkins was like a bulldozer. "I know how rough it would be on any man to remember, every day and every night, that he was the pilot who—"

"Shut up!" Sam's scream edged on the primordial.

Still, it didn't affect Atkins. "If Kate weren't involved, I wouldn't say a word," he told Sam, almost sadly. He pressed his lips together before speaking again. "But she is involved and there's no other choice, Sam."

Kate looked at Atkins, bewildered. The old pilot turned to her, took a deep breath, and let it all out.

"Kate, Sam is married."

She felt the blood draining from her face.

"It's true." Atkins was relentless. "It needn't go any further than this room. That's up to you, to him. But you deserve to know and you deserve to know all of it. Maybe it will explain a couple of things." Sam sat with slumped shoulders, staring vacantly at him.

"He was married a long time ago. He fell in love with a girl, and one day he took her flying. He—"

"C.B." Kate reached out with her hand, pleading.

Whatever pain tore through Sam Burleyford was reaching her also. "Maybe you shouldn't. Please?"

Atkins shook her off. "He took her flying one day," he said, his voice grinding on. "And when he came in to land he made a mistake. They crashed. Sam was hurt. Not badly. But Carol was torn up. She was burned. None of this is very nice, but it can't be helped now. For a long time they didn't think she would make it. Sam had pulled her from the burning wreckage. He saved her life. But I suppose he'll hear her screaming for every day he lives."

"But—but why are you saying all this *now?* His wife—it's his own affair about what happened—"

"She wasn't his wife *then,* Kate. Carol couldn't take the crash and the fire and the pain afterward. She retreated within herself. Not all at once. It was slow and it was, well, I guess for Sam it must have been brutal. The doctors said she needed something, desperately needed something to hang onto, something that might stop her from sliding backwards."

"You mean—" Kate stared from Atkins to Sam, whose face was now ashen.

"That's right. That's when Sam married her."

She went to the desk before Sam. "But—why have you kept this a secret? *Why,* Sam? Anyone can make a mistake, crash. You've done nothing to be ashamed of! All these years—" She felt dizzy. "Oh, my God, when I think—" She cut off her own words, shook her head fiercely. "Why didn't—"

"Carol's in a sanatorium." Sam's voice was hollow. "She's—completely insane. Gone. She's a child again, has been for years. A child." He looked up. "How much of a chance do you think I would have had to make it as president of this company if the word was out that I'd screwed up as a pilot and burned and maimed and tortured that woman into insanity so she could escape being grotesque and in pain and—" He sucked in air with shuddering breaths. "And if people found out *now?* Where the hell do you think I'd be! I could kiss good-bye any chance I had to make it as governor and—"

"Sam, Sam," she implored, "you make it sound as if she were a leper."

"As far as the public is concerned, that's just what she would be! *Because I put her where she is!*"

"But it was *an accident!* C.B. just said so, and—"

"What good would it do parading her before the world!" His voice scarcely concealed his feeling of hopeless rage. "Isn't it enough that *I* have to live with it, for Christ's sake? What the hell do you two want? A three-ring circus? You think maybe she'd look great on television?"

He stood suddenly, legs apart, quivering. "What the hell do you two *want* from me!"

He stumbled from behind his desk and he was gone.

Atkins saw the shock on Kate's face. Her eyes seemed unable to focus. "Come on, Brandon. I'll buy the drinks."

They went to a small bar at the airport, secluded themselves in a booth well in the back. Kate downed three quick drinks, and all they did was to make her numb.

"I'm sorry, kid," Atkins said, "but now Sam won't be talking about marriage with Kate Brandon."

She had her voice under control. "The whole thing makes me sick to my stomach. I've known that man since I was a child. It's not—it's not that Sam's married, or what happened, but the way he hides from it. There's all the difference in the world between doing what he's done to marry that woman, and—and hiding from it as if any knowledge of her existence makes *him* unclean." She shook her head sadly. "At the same time, C.B., who am I to judge? Sam married a woman who he knew would be a burden the rest of his life. It took a *man* to do that."

"It did," Atkins rumbled. "No one's asked you to judge him, Kate. But I've done what had to be done. I couldn't stand by and see your name dragged about because someone wanted to be a political hero."

"What do you think he'll do?"

Atkins shrugged. "Don't know. And I don't really care. The way I look at it, one thing doesn't always balance another. Whatever he did with Carol is his own affair. What he did, what he does with you, isn't."

She found she could smile at that. "None of this one good deed offsets a bad?"

"Hell, no. That's like the mother who raises her child until he's twenty-one or so. She loves him so much that the thought of his being exposed to the horrors of life is too much for her to contemplate. So, in full demonstration of that love, to save him from all the baddies out in the world, she poisons him."

"You do go for drastic analogies, don't you."

Another shrug. "Brandon, three thousand perfect landings don't compensate for the first time you fly into a mountain."

"No contest," she admitted. She looked up. "I hope Sam runs. I mean, stays in the race. With all his faults he'd make a very good governor."

"You forgive quickly."

"One of my faults, I guess."

"A good one. But it's all up to Sam. He's got to wrestle with his own conscience. What about you, Brandon?"

She sighed. "You want it straight?"

"Is there any other way?"

"I'm sick of it all, C.B. I think I'm ready to pack it in. It's not worth it."

Disbelief stamped his face. "You mean *quit?*"

She nodded.

"Crap."

"Believe what you want. You asked, I answered. Damn it, C.B., I got into all this to *fly*. The rough stuff has all been outside of the airplane."

"So what?"

"So I'm bushed. I'm worn out, inside and out." She sighed. "I've got a week coming to me. I'm damned well going to take it. Away from here."

"Mike?"

"Uh huh. His cabin. Way out in the woods."

"Best idea I've heard yet." He eyed her warily. "You're not serious about quitting, are you?"

"You can have my resignation right now."

"And you can stick it—" He sat straighter. "No deal, Brandon."

There was no humor to her smile. "You can't stop me."

He stood up, looming over her. "No. Maybe. I don't know."

"I bet you'd try, too."

"Damned right I would. I'll make a deal with you. Take your week, then come back and talk to me. Maybe that big buck of yours will get some sense into your head."

30

Snow sprayed out in a great misty cloud as Mike Carew eased the helicopter down. Kate opened her door, let the cold, clean air wash over her, looked at the thick forest beyond the clearing. She reached for Mike's hand. "I need this, Michael. I need you."

He hesitated. "I'm glad you're here." Enough to say.

They spent part of the day walking, fishing through the ice in a nearby stream. "I'll cook," he told her. "You look like your batteries aren't connected."

"That bad?" She had a wan smile on her face.

"Whatever went on back there must have been rough."

"It was."

"Want to talk about it, hon?"

"I want to forget it."

"Okay."

Bless him.

They talked that night, resting on thick rugs, hot rum warming them. "I told C.B. I was thinking of quitting."

"That's talking. Is it real?"

She leaned her head against his shoulder, watching flames curling around logs. "Too real, maybe."

"Maybe you've proved what you wanted, Katie."

"I never did it to prove anything. I didn't need proof."

"Then what is it?"

"They won't leave me alone. To fly, I mean."

"Then get the hell out." He sensed her sudden tension. "I mean it, Kate. In the best way. When it gets to be too much, it's time to pack it in. There are better ways to live than gutting yourself."

She clung to him. "You make it sound easy."

He kissed her gently on the forehead. "Katie, there's an old saying about human beings. We're so hard to kill and so easy to die."

"What does that mean?"

"Build. Create. Live well, laugh often, love much. It needn't be a fight all the time."

She was quiet for a while. "Did you ever hear of Rene Carpenter, Mike?"

"No. Should I?"

She smiled up at him. "Yes. She was Scott Carpenter's wife. You know, one of the astronauts who flew one of those Mercury capsules into orbit."

He nodded. "Okay. I know who you mean. But what—"

She placed a finger against his lips. "She was speaking to some women about being the wife of a test pilot and an astronaut, how her whole life had been conditioned by a man's world and the challenges men like her husband had to face. Or wanted to face, anyway. She talked about sweating through flight training, about being lonely and afraid when Scott was flying off carriers and was gone for months at a time. It all taught her to face life on her own when what she wanted most of all was to be with her man. She had to toughen herself, she said."

He shifted to hold her tighter. "Go on, hon."

"Well, she learned a lot. Her fear gave her strength because she came to recognize what Scott, and other men like him, were really like. She said that they were rare and wonderful creatures; they had what she called a questing spirit."

"Jesus, don't stop now."

Her laughter was warm. "All right. There's more. I wish I had memorized it. Things like a man wasn't necessarily made to be chained to a home, that there was more to love and marriage than schedules and procreating. To her, our society is overburdened by a search for security. She said that any woman who truly loves her man must always be ready to risk everything to send him where he needs most to go. In the sky, up there, wherever. She must have known what she was talking about, Mike. She watched her husband ride a rocket away from this planet."

'Mike's arm cradled her. "If I didn't know better, Katie, I'd say you were proposing to me."

"I—" Was that what she *was* saying?

"You started to say something."

She snuggled closer. "No."

Gently, firmly, he sat her up and faced her. "Kate, I love you. I want you to be my wife."

She cried for longer than she knew, and then she fell asleep in his arms.

When she woke he was still awake. She brushed her lips against his. "Yes," she whispered.

On the morning of the third day, the radiophone in the cabin rang shrilly. In that state between heavy slumber and instant alertness, their minds responded to what they both knew spelled emergency.

"Why the hell don't they leave us alone?" Mike said with unexpected anger.

"Mike, we've got to, I mean, they'd use it only if there was—"

"I know. It means trouble. Maybe if we ignore it the damned thing will go away."

She sat up in bed, her arms around her knees. "Answer it, Michael. We have to."

He padded across the room, cursing, reached for the set. He established contact, identified himself, then listened for a long time. Kate knew all the signs. She had the coffee on while he was still on the radiophone. He hung up slowly, came to the table where the coffee waited. He took a long swallow before he spoke.

"It's bad."

"Who's down?"

"It's a full-blown flap, Katie."

"Michael. Spell it out."

He took another long swallow. "They don't have that much yet. Just enough to know it's a rough one. A Boeing 747SP. Government flight. American *and* Russian officials aboard. All in all, forty-two passengers made up of adults and children, plus the crew of eight."

The soft woman, his lover, was gone. In her place was a professional, tough, thinking pilot. "Where?" she asked.

"En route from Moscow to Washington. Air force job. They're not sure where it went down. All they know is that it must be somewhere in Alaska. At least," he amended, "they hope so."

"Polar crossing?"

"Uh huh. Diverted from course. Tough storm pushed it to the south."

"That could help. That *will* help," she noted.

"Best bet is that it's somewhere in central Alaska."

"You said government flight," she reviewed slowly. "Air Force, right?"

"Yes. The American ambassador to Russia and his entire family. That was for starters. High Russian officials as well."

"That means they'll pull out all the stops. The search is under way?"

"What they can do right now, love. The storm covers the whole area where they think it went in. Low ceilings, high winds, heavy snow."

"What about temperatures?"

"Bad." Mike finished his coffee, went across the cabin and started dressing. "I'll get the heater going for the chopper. You pack our things, hon."

She looked at him. "Short honeymoon, Michael."

He glanced up from pulling on his boots. "I've waited a long time, Kate. We'll have our honeymoon." He glanced through the window at the sea of white snow showing everywhere. "In Hawaii, damn it."

They were in the air an hour later, flying direct to the Alaskair complex at Anchorage airport. They snatched a kiss and Mike went off to the search team headquarters. Kate went straight to flight operations. Everyone who had heard the news was there, including Atkins and Burleyford. There was no trace of what had happened between them. All that went by the boards when a plane was down.

Frustration, endless cups of coffee, weather reports, contacting stations out in the field. All the satellite photos showed was a dense cloud cover. What they hoped for was a trend that could show them when they might get into the air. The military was grounded. Everyone was grounded except aircraft that could fly high enough to pass over the storm. They had several of those out, and the crews had spectacular views of clouds.

Twenty-four hours went by with maddening slowness. Most of the pilots and crews were sleeping in emergency crew quarters or on cots rushed to the Alaskair offices. Some men slept in their planes, willing to rough it so they might fly the first moment they had the chance. In this part of the world, and especially in winter, every hour added onto being lost was another drop in the chance of survival. If that 747SP had gotten down without tearing itself apart, its occupants had a chance. That chance got slimmer as time dragged on.

The storm abated slowly, the thick clouds drifted across the great northland. Kate and the other pilots kept moving from flight operations to the weather office, calling the military fields, trying to get any scrap of information. They simply had to get into the air and begin their grid pattern of search.

Kate ran into Atkins in the weather office. "Still no signals?" she queried.

He shook his head. "Nothing yet. And they had every damned thing known to science on that airplane. Including military comsat and navsat monitoring. It's a big fat silence, Brandon."

"Maybe not," she reflected. "Even if they're transmitting a signal, they could be somewhere so that it's blocked."

"If the rabbit hadn't stopped to crap, the hound would never have caught him. If, if, *if*."

"We could fly tonight," Kate noted. "It'll clear enough for that, C.B."

"Mountain search missions at night? I know the time is rough, but there's no use losing airplanes."

"Mankowitz thinks otherwise."

Atkins started a sharp retort, held his words. If Art Mankowitz wanted to go out at night, well, he was the best. "Why?" Atkins prodded.

"Art says we're in the middle of a severe solar storm. It screws up the kind of signal any emergency transmitter sends out. Especially if the lost airplane is in a valley somewhere. Hills or mountains, combined with that solar storm messing up the electrical atmosphere—"

"I know the program," Atkins said.

"We might get a shot at flares, or even a fire, if they hear engines," Kate added.

"If they're alive. No, Art's right, and so are you. We aren't doing anyone any good sitting on our hands. Where's Art now?"

They found him in the main hangar, propped up against the nosewheel of the Hercules. "Brandon says you want to give it a go. Night mission. She told me what you said about the transmitter problems."

Mankowitz nodded. "We can't find anybody in *here*," he said, gesturing to take in the huge hangar.

"Never mind the philosophy. You sound like me now," Atkins told him. "What are their chances, Art?"

"They stink." He shrugged. "It depends on things we don't know about. It could be twenty above or twenty below where they went down. They could have been torn to pieces, or they might have put that thing down in good shape. It all hangs on where they went down, and how, and what they were like when they stopped. If they can move, they can make some sort of shelter. If they can do that, they can live off their survival gear for a while. If they can do that, they can build fires from all the fuel that thing holds in the tanks—if the tanks haven't been torn open. What the hell do you want me to tell you, C.B.? You know this game as well as I do."

"No, I don't, or I wouldn't be asking."

"All right," Mankowitz said. He climbed slowly to his feet. "The whole thing is, they're running out of time. This snow could be burying them, and if this storm doesn't do it, the next one coming down from the pole will. This kind of snow's a bitch. It could cover any signs of where they went down. So even if they did make it down okay—"

"We'll give it a couple of hours," Atkins decided. "Stand by to spool up the minute you get the word."

Mankowitz nodded slowly. "You think I'm out here not ready to go?"

Mike had joined Kate for coffee in the crew mess when the first break came. Sam Burleyford gave them the word. "The blue-suit people have been flying a high-altitude grid pattern. An electronic sweep. They've picked up a signal."

"Thank Christ for that," Atkins said.

"It's not much," Sam continued, "but it could be everything. The signal was weak. Normally it would be suspect. You know the kind of electrical interference we've been getting from that solar storm. But the signal was also coded, and they're just about positive it's from the 747SP." Stubble showed on his face and his eyes were red. "Some other good news. The front's rolling by in a hurry. Everybody gets into the air four hours from now. You'll have good visibility."

"How long will it last?" Kate queried.

"Maybe two days. Another front's already building and moving this way."

End of briefing. Find that downed airplane in the next forty-eight hours, or there won't be any need to rush.

Kate and her crew grabbed the chance to sleep. When they started firing up the Hercules, they were all in heavy arctic gear, and the airplane was loaded with special equipment, all aimed at keeping people alive. At the last minute, Kate ordered additional gear, sent Mankowitz to attend to it personally.

They were in the air an hour later. Everything that could fly was off the ground. Search missions are stinkers. This one was no different. They had a grid pattern marked on their charts, they were assigned a specific area to comb, and they spent the entire day and much of the hours of darkness flying back and forth along those lines that stretched across their charts.

Below them was a world of blinding white broken

by trees and steep slopes that showed gray or black against the white mantle. Again and again, they crossed the Yukon River that ran through Yukon Flats.

They heard nothing on their radios, saw nothing. They'd hoped the darkened skies might help in case of flares or a signal fire.

Nature played its own cruel, beautiful trick on them. Any other time they would have held the heavens in awe. The aurora splashed the northern heavens with an incredible display of ghostly streamers and bands of colored light parading magically in the high air above the planet. Eerie light pulsated and beat hypnotically, shimmering like the rustling folds of great luminescent draperies.

They strained their eyes. Could that have been a flare below, knifing into the sky? They turned and sped toward what might be. No flares. Ribbons of light, instead, moving through the sky like soft and limitless searchlight beams.

They knew they had to quit. Kate called Anchorage, told them they were landing at Fairbanks, closer to their search area. They'd get some rest, be out again with the first indication of daylight. On the way in, the aurora haunted them, arching across the sky, moving steadily to the south so that they seemed to be flying beneath an enormous cathedral dome. The spectacle was maddening, frustrating, and undeniably beautiful —kaleidoscopic pageantry of pastel green, pink, red, purple, and yellowish tinge rustled by some ethereal wind of space.

They could easily have hated it. They tried not to waste futile anger on God's handiwork.

They found Atkins, Burleyford, and their top airline team at Fairbanks waiting for the search crews with hot meals. They had to force themselves to eat. They were worn to a thin edge, and they could hardly wait to get back into the air.

Atkins joined the crew in the dining room. He asked questions, absorbed what they had to say, cursing quietly. "When you finish eating, get some rest. I hope to hell we do better tomorrow. Even if Coleman put that plane down in—"

A bell rang sharply in Kate's head. She didn't notice her fork clattering to her plate. "Wait, wait a minute," she said quickly. "That name. Who did you say?"

"Coleman. Why?"

"Was he the pilot of the 747? The air force pilot?"

"Yeah. Colonel Robert Coleman. Handpicked. You know him?"

"Yes, yes. He was a good friend—he and my father flew together. I remember—I flew with them both one time. A hunting trip, and—" She lapsed into silence.

"Brandon, what the hell's on your mind?" Atkins demanded.

She pushed back her chair suddenly, her meal forgotten. Something was clicking in her head. Something she remembered hearing from that same man, from Bob Coleman. "The operations room," she said aloud. "I've got to look at some charts."

31

They spread out the charts. Directly north of Fairbanks sprawled low mountains, and beyond that the Yukon River formed a frozen path along the center of Yukon Flats. Just to the north of the river were scattered mountains. Kate's finger slid along the chart to the northwest of Fairbanks, stopped by the line marking the Koyukuk River set in its own smaller valley.

"We've gone over the planned route again and again," Kate insisted, referring to their grid pattern. "I'm convinced we're off the track. Look, we've got the wind reports at the time the Boeing went down." Her finger returned to the charts, tapping insistently. "I'll never forget what Bob Coleman once told me. Once? They drilled it into my skull. We were just crossing a range, and he kept pointing out emergency landing areas to me. He said that if ever I had to go down in just this sort of country, then no matter what else I did I should always head for a river. That would almost always point me toward a valley. The winds would be easier to predict that way, and the lay of the land. He said a lot more, but—"

"Damn it, Brandon," Atkins butted in, "everybody up here who flies knows that!"

"Yes, they know it, but Bob Coleman *lived* by it, and he flew by it, and we've gone over the other areas, and so have the other aircraft, and," she took a deep breath and stabbed at the charts, "if those people are alive they've *got* to be in this valley." Once again the Koyukuk River area had come under her finger.

Atkins looked at her. He almost seemed to sniff suspiciously. "That sounds as if there's a hell of a lot of woman's intuition in those conclusions."

"Then come up with something better," she snapped.

"Back off," Atkins shot back at her. "This isn't a contest."

She nodded. "But we're spinning wheels, C.B.! We're going by the book and the pages are empty. It's—it's just that I'm so damned *sure* we ought to get down low, I mean real low where we can eyeball what's down there, and—" She shook her head and stared again at the charts.

Atkins mulled over her words, her attitude, judging all the many pieces. Kate didn't know it, but those feelings of hers were just the sort of thing that sometimes could make the difference between failure and success.

"What's your plan, Brandon?"

"I want our ship to be released from the grid pattern tomorrow."

"To do what?"

"Let us concentrate on the valley along the Koyukuk. Sweep it up and down, as low as we can fly and still get some good coverage." She placed her hand on his arm. *"Please,* C.B. I know it sounds crazy, but I swear it's their best chance, and Coleman would have taken it."

Atkins nodded slowly, rubbing his face. "Hell, so would I or any pilot with smarts. I'd have done just what you've been talking about." He held off. It wasn't that easy a decision. The grid pattern assigned to Brandon's airplane still had to be covered. Well, he'd work it out somehow. Pilot's intuition was something he had never ignored, and now wasn't the time to start. If they had a couple dozen extra helicopters or small aircraft, they could cover the area Kate clung to with such intensity. But they didn't, and time was fleeing, and . . .

"Okay. You've got it," he said suddenly.

Her breath nearly exploded from the tension. "I'll need some special gear. Just in case I—"

"Don't stand there talking, Brandon."

She tossed a wave at him and left for the hangar.

She'd get together with her crew; they'd give the orders to the maintenance teams; and the crew could get some sleep in the precious hours before takeoff.

Kate drank coffee with her crew. They were almost ready. She went thoroughly over her conversation with Atkins and explained the circumstances. She went over the charts in detail. "I don't want to give you any false impressions." Phillips, Mankowitz, and Grayson seemed to stiffen with that remark. "Everything I feel could be completely wrong. But I'm betting that Boeing is down somewhere along the south slopes of the Endicott Mountains. Everything points to Bob Coleman trying to get his crippled airplane to Fairbanks.

"But if he couldn't make it all the way to Fairbanks, well, what would any sensible pilot do? Get below the Endicott Mountains and use them as a bulwark against winds coming down from the pole. Look at the charts—"

"Don't have to," Art Mankowitz broke in. "The whole area along the Koyukuk River is loaded with airfields. Coleman had to figure that if he couldn't make a field, then having that many planes around there would help in any search effort. Hell, look here." His finger banged the chart.

Kate could feel the crew moving along with her.

Jim Phillips bent closer to the chart. "Three places look best for our search," he said, his excitement growing. "Here, along North Fork Koyukuk, here along the Wild River, and, over here, along the John Trail."

Art Mankowitz traced a fingernail line on the chart. "Captain, why not in this area? The whole of Kanuti Flats? It's open country compared to what we've been looking at."

"He could have come down anywhere in that area," Kate agreed. "But don't forget it's been searched again and again and no one's come up with so much as a whisper. He *could* have gone down in a hundred places, but I've been over every detail of the scheduled course, the weather and the winds and the *time* they gave their last position report. I know I'm repeating myself, but above all I know the pilot. I know how Bob Coleman thinks."

"If we just knew he had control going down," Phillips said intently.

"If, if. It's all *ifs*," Kate came back. "I'll ask you the same question I asked Atkins. Has anybody in this crew got any better ideas?"

There was silence for several moments. Paul Grayson was the first to speak. "People, I'm with the lady. She's got it nailed."

Art Mankowitz banged a fist against Grayson's shoulder. "Then what the hell are we standing here for?"

"Let's fly," Jim Phillips added.

The horizon was almost a cruel joke as they thundered into cold, leaden skies. Kate stayed low, flying north from Fairbanks. They crossed over Prospect Creek. It was here that the coldest temperatures ever officially recorded in Alaska had been reached. Eighty degrees below zero *without* considering the wind for the chill factor.

Light snow flurries made them curse as they entered their search area. Kate eased the big Hercules as low as she dared, working out the angles of wind, peaks rising steeply, suddenly, from the long finger valleys slicing into the mountains. They flew so that every pair of eyes in the airplane had the best of all possible chances to study the terrain for any sign of life. Or wreckage.

Minutes dragged, hours sped by, the Hercules riding the weather as if it were doing everything it could to aid its human crew. A dreary grayness seemed to suck the spirit from their souls. Eyes began to strain, heads to ache. They hammered on.

They had only five and a half hours of light during which they could search the ground below. They scanned ravines, slopes, trees, white slanted hills.

A world below them without visible life.

Snow and ice and rising winds and darkening skies. Mankowitz cursed behind the two pilots.

Nothing. He'd seen something down there. It was a shadow, or a blur in his own vision.

Nothing.

Kate sat back in the pilot's seat. Jim Phillips was flying, had been for the last hour, spelling her at the controls. "I'll take it, Jim," Kate said, unable to disguise the disappointment in her voice. "We've got time for one more run. We won't be able to see anything after that."

She brought the big airplane around to start their final run from south to north along the wide valley of Wild River. The light was low on the horizon; shadows stretched over the frozen world.

Something caught her attention. She slammed the Hercules into a steep left bank. Don't lose it! her thoughts shouted to her.

It was . . . a shadow, maybe. No, *a shadow effect*. "Look! There—see it?" The crew strained to follow her lead. "Like a furrow in that snow. Deep snow. As if something plowed a path through there and the snow that was falling covered most of it. But not all—"

You could see what appeared to be a long trough in the snow, a depression of some sort. But the light was gone. Darkness crashed down on them and she had to climb. There was no choice. She didn't dare risk flying down among those peaks in the dark, the downdrafts clawing and unpredictable. It was a sure way to prang their own iron bird.

But it was maddening because they had something they *must* study further. Phillips marked the chart carefully as Kate boomed the turboprop to safe altitude for night flight. She went on the intercom to her crew. "We're coming back with the first available light. *Something* made that furrow."

Mankowitz leaned forward from the observer's seat. "It could have been the wind, captain."

"And it could have been Santa Claus, too," she snapped. "We take off in the dark, we get up here with first light, and we go down there, damn it, and we look until our eyes are ready to fall out."

"I'm with you, captain."

32

A crowd of pilots and crew members had collected around them. Atkins and Burleyford stood before the big table charts with Kate and her own crew. Everything they said was a repeat of their arguments in the Hercules cockpit.

"*Something* made that furrow," Kate insisted. "Sure, it could have been the wind, or drifting snow, but I don't believe it. Not the way it cut across the ground. It was along a line to the north, which is how Coleman would have tried to come down into the wind."

Art Mankowitz shouldered closer. He spread out a detailed chart and aerial photographs of the area. "I think the captain is right," he told the others. "Look at these photos. They were taken when the ground was clean. No snow, so you can see the lay of the land." They bent closer, and he waited several moments.

"See what I mean?" Mankowitz went on. "Look at the ground patterns. There's nothing there to let the snow drift that way, I mean, the kind of trough we saw. But if something as big as that 747 went down here, if it bellied in, it would have cut a wide swath, and there was almost enough snow after they went down to cover their path. *Almost*. But not quite." He stood up from leaning on the table and looked directly at Atkins, then Burleyford. "Surer than hell it's the only lead we've had so far."

Atkins and Burleyford exchanged glances. Sam let out a long breath. "I agree it's the best shot."

"Then we'll hit it first thing," Kate told the others. "We'll have at least five hours to search, and—"

"No you won't," Sam interrupted.

"Why—"

"It's the weather," Sam went on. "That second front is working its way down faster than anyone expected."

"We'll have *some* time! Thirty minutes, maybe even an hour. That's all we may need," Kate insisted.

Atkins shook his head. "That's stretching it mighty thin," he said slowly. "But we've got to go along with you. If those people *are* up there and anyone is still alive, any kind of chance is worth it. All right, Brandon. You and your crew get some food and sleep, then you fly before the weather blots you out."

He turned to Burleyford. "Sam, I'm sending out every other plane we can get into that area."

"I'll take care of it," Sam said, and he left for the dispatching office.

Kate and her crew were in the mess, grateful for a decent meal, when Mike Carew came in. He greeted Kate with a quick strong hug and joined them at the table. "Atkins gave me the story," he said. "I sure hope you're right." She saw the misgivings in his eyes. "I hope that front doesn't knock you out before you get up there."

She rested her hand on his. "Can you fly with us tomorrow, Michael? You'd be a help."

He shook his head. "Wish I could. But we're taking two of the big choppers to an area just east of Twenty-two Mile Village. Some Indians reported a plane down. We don't know if it's an old wreck or what. The report was sketchy." Mike stifled a yawn; he'd been out in those choppers for long hours. "But we've got to follow it through. Low pattern, one chopper covering the other. That sort of thing."

She nodded. She wanted to spend time with Michael, talk to him, be held by him, but. . . . He rose to his feet, showing his weariness. "Got to sleep." He brushed her forehead with his lips, and he left.

They sat for several moments in silence. "Captain, he looks like the man," Paul Grayson said finally.

Kate's eyes met his. "He's the man," she answered.

"You got yourself a winner, lady captain," her crew chief told her. Phillips and Mankowitz just grinned.

"Oh, Christ, you all look like a bunch of school-boys," she chided them. "Go to bed."

"Yes, teacher," they chorused.

It was their only lighthearted moment.

In the morning you could hardly tell black from gray. But it was daytime and they could see and that was all they asked. No sky was visible above them, only threatening clouds and wide patches of snow like phantom fog in the air.

They boomed out, silent and uneasy, their nerves plucked raw, feeling that time was running out on them. Their chances were better than before, however. They had something hard to look for. Two other Hercules would work the areas adjacent to their nar-rowed site.

They hadn't been in the air fifteen minutes when they heard one of the other Hercules call in a May-day. "Niner Three Five Tango is returning to Fair-banks. We've had a fire in number two and we're losing pressure in number four."

One other search plane besides their own. Wild River appeared before them, and Kate started down. There wasn't that much room between the lowering clouds and the rough ground.

The other Hercules had to quit. Heavy snow howled down the finger valley it was searching, and the pilots went for altitude. Snow thickened the sky about their own plane.

"We've run out, captain." Jim Phillips's shoulders slumped and his eyes had a haunted look. "We've run out of sky and we've run out of—"

"I see them!"

Mankowitz's voice nearly tore out their ears. The intercom rattled under his bellow. "Up there! I saw the tail fin! Come right, captain—the tail, it's in deep snow, but I saw it!"

She hauled the airplane over to one side, looking. She didn't know . . . the area was flat, a wide trough in a rough valley. But there was that same strange furrow along the ground.

Frozen ground. The words stuck in her mind.

Her eyes ached. Too much snow in the air about them. She couldn't see any details. They'd have to be so low they would just about be landing.

"Goddamn it, we were so close!"

Kate ignored Phillips's agonized cry. "Art, are you really certain you saw——"

"I *saw* the tail of that plane," he came back instantly.

Kate clenched her teeth. "Landing checklist," she ordered Phillips.

His disbelief was stark. "Down *there*? In this stuff? You're mad—you can't——"

"Checklist, damn it! We've got skis, we can land. If they're down there we can save them. If they're not we'll just wait out this storm on the ground. Get with it!"

She didn't wait for him. "Art, get a message back to Fairbanks. Use the comsat frequency. Do it fast. We're going down."

Phillips was calling out the checklist, lowering the skis to full landing position, bringing down flaps. Kate stayed in a low, sweeping circle. The snow was blinding. It would be rough as hell and they'd only have one chance. Maybe not even that. She couldn't land completely blind.

"Art, Paul. Strap in. It's going to be rough. Art, how about that radio call?"

"It's off," Mankowitz answered.

At least Fairbanks would know what was happening. She came back on power, rolling into the wind, sliding down, bouncing and slamming from side to side with the fierce gusts close to the surface. Under the best of circumstances it would be hazardous. Right now it was insane. But Kate thought of anyone still alive down there. This was what it was all about. All the years coming to this focal point.

The wind screamed down the slopes, shrieked and twisted out of the finger valley.

Shortly after they had left the runway, a private jet landed at Fairbanks, taxied quickly to the terminal. The tower called Sam Burleyford and he hurried to the gate. It was one time he had no pleasure in seeing Sarah Markham. Inside the terminal, they managed to find a lounge where they could talk privately.

"Sam, what the hell is going on up here?" she demanded.

He sucked on a cigarette. "What the hell do you think?" He knew he was bitter about what he considered an intrusion, and suddenly he didn't give a damn whether she liked it or not. "You know a plane's down. We've been searching for—"

"I know all that. But there's a wild storm north of here. *We* just made it in, according to my pilot. What I'm talking about is Kate Brandon. Is she really out there? In this kind of insane weather?"

Sam nodded. "That she is."

Sarah Markham was incredulous. "Sam, it's a killer storm, they're saying. How on earth could you let a woman fly in—"

She sucked in her breath.

Sam had an acid smile on his face. "Your walls just came tumbling down, Sarah," he said slowly. "Just in case you hadn't noticed."

She was shaken. "So they have," she murmured. "I am, well, more than surprised. I had thought that kind of thinking left me a long time ago."

"Obviously it hasn't."

"No," she admitted. "But I *am* worried, Sam."

"You've got good reason to be," he told her with unexpected abruptness. "It wouldn't matter *who* was flying that airplane, though. It's a bitch out there."

He got to his feet, lighting another cigarette. He'd been chain-smoking for three days now. He turned to face the woman who held his political career in her hands. "Sarah, when this is over, I'm withdrawing from the race. To hell with being governor. I've lost something of myself from all this. I'm sitting here and that girl is out there and, oh hell, it isn't worth it."

Sarah Markham was back on familiar ground. She was cool again. "I don't buy it, Sam. You're not telling it all."

He was surprisingly calm. "No, I'm not. There is more. It's not pleasant."

"Try me."

He told it all to her. That there had been an accident long ago, that he was married, that he felt he was selling his soul for a political office, that . . .

"Sam, don't you think we've known about that accident, about Carol, your wife, about everything you've said and still haven't said?"

"You know?"

"We've known from the very beginning. We've known how you stood by that woman, what you tried to do for her. You poor, damned fool, Sam. Everything that's been tearing you apart is the strongest thing you've had going for you! Why do you think we gambled so much on you? What you're ashamed of, Sam, is what you should be most proud of. It's your greatest asset with us. We never said a word to you because we felt it was entirely your own affair and it had no place in politics or anywhere else. But every woman on my committee has known all the time, your entire story, and if there's anything you've ever received from us, with or without your knowing, it's been our *respect*. You can't quit because of what you—"

She looked up as a pilot dashed into the room. "Sam, we just got a comsat signal. From Brandon. They're in the edges of the storm but they spotted something and—" He took a deep breath. "They're going down. They're landing."

Sam couldn't believe it. "Landing? *In that stuff?* In that goddamned storm? Jesus Christ—that's suicide!"

He ran from the office, heading for operations. Sarah Markham trailed behind. One word clamored like an alarm bell in her head. *Suicide*. But even more than the word had been the stricken look on the face of Sam Burleyford.

Kate flew as she'd never flown before, grinding the complaining Hercules down the invisible approach rail in the wind-lashed sky, fighting the constant sledgehammers of turbulence, struggling to see. Mankowitz and Grayson were in the flight deck with them, straining to catch sight of any sudden obstruction, a crag, a clump of trees, anything that could snap them around crazily in a great spouting plume of flames and tearing wreckage. Lower, lower, Kate fighting the wind, trying to grope for the ground gingerly in a huge airplane. Where the hell did sky end and ground begin? She had to watch her speed, keep it where it belonged. But they were wallowing drunkenly. They pitched downward; she came back on the yoke to stop the sharp descent, to hold them off . . .

"Too slow!" Phillips barked. "Give her power!"

Her hand was on the throttles, slamming them forward. The Hercules seemed to stumble as it fought clear of the downdraft.

"The ground! I've got it—we're almost—" Mankowitz didn't finish his cry of warning.

Kate had seen the piled snow at almost the same instant. It was this moment or never. She chopped power, held the Hercules level, brought up the nose just a hair.

They felt the trembling vibration of skis against packed snow, then the slamming controlled crash as the thick belly roared into the ground. Kate had flown the furrow, that trough they'd followed as if it were a magnet. It was their only chance, for any obstructions would have already been ground down or pushed aside by the huge Boeing that had crashed along this very same path. Their vision blurred with the pounding they were taking, and Kate had full reverse power, the propellers screaming.

They banged wildly to a stop, unbelieving, their landing lights stabbing into a howling blizzard.

33

"I don't believe we made it." Jim Phillips let out his breath in a long shuddering sigh. His body trembled. There wasn't anything worse for a pilot than to sit, poised, fingers ready, but not quite touching the controls. "I just don't believe it," he repeated.

"Amen," came the remark from a very shaken Art Mankowitz. He tapped Kate on the shoulder. "Anytime you'd like a free lifetime supply of jockstraps, captain, call on me."

Their banter lasted only long enough to release the tension that had flailed their nerves. Mankowitz turned to Paul Grayson, who was unfastening his seat belt and shoulder harness.

Grayson quipped, "Captain Kate's twisted my whole family tree right around." He looked at Kate. "Scared me right *out* of whatever color I had left." He sobered as he looked at the snow smashing against the Plexiglas. "I've never even heard of getting through a landing like this. You some kind of witch?"

For the moment Kate adopted their tone. "All right, troops, knock it off." They waited for her orders. "Art, crank out another radio signal through the comsat frequency. Don't know if they'll get it, but we've got to give it a shot."

She turned to Paul Grayson. "We're sure they're somewhere up ahead of us, Paul. But we don't know how far, and we've got to get this airplane closer to them." She paused, knowing his own thoughts were racing ahead of hers. "Do you think you can handle it?"

Grayson understood. So did the others. Someone had to get out into that frozen, screaming hell, to walk the giant airplane forward into the teeth of the storm. To taxi into a tree or a boulder now would be beyond all insanity.

"I can handle it. I'll use the helmet with the visor. Good communications that way." Even as Grayson agreed, a screaming blast of wind pounded against the enormous airplane, rocked it sharply. The winds were toying with them.

"You'll need a lifeline," Phillips broke in. "You could get lost out there in seconds. Fifty feet away from these engines you'd never see or hear a thing unless you were tied to the nose somehow."

Grayson nodded. "I'll use the parachute harness. Unclip the pack and—"

"And nothing," Mankowitz came into it, turning away from his radios. "What the hell are you going to see from one side of this iron horse to the other? You're crazy." He turned to Kate. "One man can't hack it. You need two people out there, one ahead of each wing tip, all the time talking to you in here."

"You're right." That's all Kate had to say. Why mess around with false heroics? Mankowitz knew what to do better than anyone else. "Both of you. Helmets, parachute harness, all the clothes you can get on. The chill factor is going to be critical."

Grayson was already on his way out of the flight deck. "Let's go, man," he told Mankowitz.

They helped one another into survival clothing, linked their bodies with long, thin lines. With the lines went intercom systems that kept them in communication with one another and also with both pilots in the cockpit.

"I've got the flares," Mankowitz told Grayson. "They're the easy-pull type. You can ignite them by just twisting the end and pulling. They won't be any trouble even with these mittens. Stick a couple extra in your leg pocket."

"Got 'em," Grayson acknowledged.

"When we get outside through that bottom hatch, *stay against the skin of the airplane*. You understand?" Mankowitz stressed. "You move so much as a foot from there, the wind can suck you into that inside prop before you know what happened. And then I'll have to fill out a form and you know how I hate to do that."

"Shee-yit, who'd do the writing for you?"

Mankowitz threw him a quick grin. "When we get outside, go back until you reach the gear housing. Then work your way to the wing tip. Light your flare before you move away from the fuselage. I'll do the same on the other side. And don't go forward until you're at that wing tip. Those props can—"

"You talk too much. Let's move out."

Outside, even in their survival clothing, even with the jet helmets and face visors, the wind-driven cold and the snow lashed viciously at them, squeezed and tugged and poked at their bodies. Underfoot was deep snow, a stationary plume that had been hurled to the sides by the Hercules as it smashed through the snow. Grayson twisted his flare into life. It would burn for thirty minutes. He waited until he saw Mankowitz's flare explode. The flares turned their immediate world into a crazy quilt nightmare: dazzling points of light, two rosy glows casting outward in all directions, for the most part disembodied from the hands holding them.

The two men struggled to their positions.

"Paul, Art. We've got good eyeball on both of you," Kate called on the intercom. "Are you reading me?"

"Got you, captain," Grayson called back.

"Five by," Mankowitz acknowledged.

"Start moving forward," Kate directed. "We'll try to let you get ahead, then pace you. Keep each other in sight at all times. If you've got to stop for any reason, including igniting a second flare, call me first."

"You ready, Paul?" Mankowitz called.

"Building up steam," Grayson shot back, starting forward.

It was slow, crawling, almost agonizing, Kate and Jim Phillips in the cockpit inching the great airplane along, watching the flares to either side to keep the depth perception they needed, using the propeller thrust to slide them along on the skis. They watched for any sudden swinging of the flares, hung on every sound for a warning call from the two men.

They inched, slid forward, Mankowitz and Grayson leaning into the killer wind, fighting for each step in snow that was often waist-deep. The Hercules dragged itself on, responding to the touch of Kate's hands on the throttles, dipping and swaying on the uneven ground.

"Captain, there's no question," Mankowitz's voice came to her, "something's come through here and it wasn't that long ago. The ground's been scoured beneath me. Rocks, furrows, that sort of thing."

Kate glanced at Phillips. "Keep it going, Art."

"Roger."

Another ten minutes went by, the Hercules rocking as it moved. The flares every now and then faded almost from sight because of heavy snow, and ...

"Hold it!" Phillips shouted at her from the right seat. "Art—he's signaling!"

But you didn't just stop that big damned airplane. They were on skis and they were on a slippery surface, and what you did was to pull power and let her grind to a stop from that slow crawl. If you wanted braking action you eased in some reverse thrust. They weren't moving that fast. Kate came to zero thrust on the propellers. There was enough wind to bring them to a halt within several feet.

"Captain!" They couldn't miss the different tone in Mankowitz's voice. "It's up ahead! The Boeing—I can just make out some form of wreckage—I'm cutting loose, going up there."

"Art!" She was shouting into her microphone. "Wait—I don't want anyone going alone. I—"

Mankowitz had disconnected. Kate cursed, started undoing her seat harness. "Where the hell are you going?" Phillips demanded. "Out there," she said curtly. "I'm taking the VHF radio in the helmet so I can talk to you. I—"

"Jesus, Captain, you stay here and let me—"

"I'm going out," she broke in. "Shut down two, three, and four, but keep number one running."

"Damn it, I should be the one who goes out!"

"Do as you're told," Kate snapped at him. She busied herself with her equipment.

Phillips talked to Grayson, told him what was happening. "Got it," Grayson came back. "No use my staying out here by the wing. Can the captain hear me?"

"Not yet. I'll relay."

"Have her bring some of that long line we got. We'll hook up and follow Mankowitz together. He's crazy, going up there without that safety line. No use in all of us being nuts."

Phillips passed the word to Kate, who nodded.

"You stand by 121.5," she directed.

"Got it."

She had started from the flight deck, stopped for a moment. "Did Art ever get confirmation on our message?"

"Nothing. Not even a laser beam would cut through this storm, I guess."

Kate shrugged. "All right, Jim. Mind the store."

She ignored his troubled look. Down the ladder, clumsy in her gear. In the cargo hold she picked out the long lifeline, secured it to her body, pushed open the crew hatch. She could hardly believe the howling storm. The wind hammered her back against the fuselage. The props were still turning, and she hugged metal as she worked her way forward until she was clear. Grayson had just lit another flare and she saw it bobbing in the snow as he came closer. Her lungs felt as if fiery needles were being poured into them. Suck in a lungful of this stuff and it could kill you.

Grayson took her lifeline, secured it to the parachute harness on his own body. He stopped for a moment, handed her his flare, bent to secure one end of the line to the nose gear of the airplane. He motioned forward.

They started out together, staying close. They couldn't see fifty feet before them. The world disappeared into that swirling light. In almost no time the sound of the powerful number one engine was whisked away. The wind dominated everything. Leaning forward, breathing ever so carefully. One step after another. Sometimes the drifting snow covered only their ankles; a few steps on, the snow might reach almost to their waists.

Then they saw the great mass of wreckage, the

wings crumpled at crazy angles. The fuselage seemed buckled but not broken in half as they had feared. The great tail—the tail that Mankowitz had seen—jutted upward in the snow.

They worked their way along the wreckage toward the nose. Art must be inside. Kate stopped for a moment. The VHF radio. "Jim, can you read me?"

"Go ahead, go ahead," she heard in her helmet headset.

"We're by the wreckage. About to go inside. Art must be in there. We'll let you know what we find as soon as we can. See if you can get a message through. Use the satellite links."

"I'll give it a try," Phillips acknowledged.

She motioned to Grayson for them to continue. They went under the wing. The huge engines were gone, torn metal in their place. Grayson pointed to the nose of the airplane, and Kate felt cold deep inside.

The entire nose had been smashed in. The cockpit area was crumpled and crushed. There wasn't a hope in the world that the crew had lived through that impact. If anyone was still alive, it was because Bob Coleman and the others up front had done their job just long enough.

They found a cargo door, banged on the surface. Almost at once the door moved aside. Art Mankowitz offered his hand to help them in. With the door closed behind them the screaming wind subsided. But it was still bitterly cold. A flashlight showed in the distance. Art pointed to a ladder leading up from the cargo hold to the passenger compartment. Two men stood by the ladder, looking at them with vacant eyes, half-frozen. Shock, Kate judged. Possible injuries.

"They hit what they think was a rock wall," Art said in clipped tones, trying to get all the vital information to Kate. "The whole crew was killed. Seven other people were killed on impact. There are thirty-six people still alive in this thing. They're in the upper deck."

"How bad?"

"At least a dozen who have broken bones or other

injuries, who can't move by themselves. They've stayed alive with the emergency equipment. A doctor lived and he's pulled off a couple of small miracles. But we've got to get them out of here. The cold is killing them."

They climbed the ladder into the main passenger cabin. It was orderly chaos, bodies lying on the floor, others in seats. Children were huddled together or held by adults. Kate had an instant impression of hopelessness. That was the worst sign of all.

She pulled the helmet, with its VHF radio, from her head. No use trying to reach Phillips from inside the wrecked Boeing. "Paul, take this," she told her cargo master. "Give me your helmet."

"Art, how many able-bodied men do we have in here?"

"A dozen."

"Get them here. Bundled up as best they can. I want them to go back to the Hercules with Paul. They're to bring back as much line as they can carry, and some stretchers. Tell them that number one engine is running and to stay on the right side of the airplane. Use those hatches. Get them back here as fast as you can with everything we need."

She looked along the cabin; the people stared at her. "We've got to get everyone into our airplane as quickly as possible. We've got heat and rations. Move them out and *now*."

A heavyset man came forward, offering his hand, trying a feeble smile. "Anatoly Korkeshkin," he said. His face was discolored, one cheek badly swollen. "Second ambassador from Moscow. We are grateful." Pain moved his swollen features. "Hope—we had given up. I still do not know how—" He let it hang. "I heard what you said. We will do everything we can."

Kate nodded. "We don't have much time. Can you get your people started down into the cargo hold? It doesn't look like the escape chutes are working."

"We will do what is needed."

"There's no time to waste," she stressed again. "If we're to have any chance of getting out of here, every minute counts."

Korkeshkin and the others who had moved forward behind him stared at her in disbelief. "Your pilot—he is going to try to take off *in this weather?* It is impossible!"

Kate's patience was fleeing as if the wind itself drove it from her. "You will forgive me, ambassador. I don't have time to talk or to argue. But this storm is bad now and it's getting worse all the time. If we don't get out of here now, we could be here for weeks. Weeks, do you understand? None of us might be alive then. Get your people moving, *please.*"

"But it would be suicide!" Murmurs from behind showed the agreement of the others. "I insist on talking to your pilot!" Korkeshkin said with open incredulity.

Kate took a deep breath, forced herself to consider what these people had been through. "Sir," she said carefully, "you *are* talking to the pilot, and I say we will take off as soon as we move everybody from here to my airplane. As captain, I have no choice but to *order* you and everyone else to help, and at once. Now, please, Mr. Korkeshkin, will you—"

The Russian stared at her. "In my country I would believe this. Our women, well—" He studied her as if seeing her for the first time. "Of course! Yakutsk—" A brief smile again. "Yes, captain, we will all do as you say, and at once."

It took nearly three hours to transfer the survivors to the Hercules. Some of the injured had to be carried, some tied to the stretchers and lowered with agonizing care to the outside surface. Others were dragged and helped, hobbling, limping, nearly frozen, following the guidelines. Inside the great cabin of the Hercules, where Phillips had the heaters going full blast, they felt their first warmth in days. Most of them were dazed and in shock and little more than numb. For another hour the crew and the able-bodied survivors spent every minute tending to the more helpless, feeding them, providing emergency medical treatment, securing them to the available seats and the floor. Jim Phillips had all four engines going for the power they needed.

By the time the hour passed, the storm had worsened in its fury. Kate had her crew assemble in the flight deck, Korkeshkin with them.

"We've simply got to get out of here," Kate said. "We can stay on the ground with one engine running for heat and power, but our fuel would never last as long as this storm would keep us on the ground. The auxiliary power systems won't put out enough juice for what we need."

Phillips shook his head. "You're talking about a blind takeoff, captain."

"To hell with that," Mankowitz broke in. "The big problem is getting room for the run." He paused as they looked at him. "We haven't got the room to take off straight ahead. And we can't turn around. We can't see, we don't know what's under that snow. If we're going to make it into the air we've got to go along the ground exactly where we landed. That's our only chance."

Korkeshkin looked from one crewman to the other. "Could you not just turn around and take off that way?"

"Not in this wind," Kate replied. "It's doing at least fifty miles an hour now, maybe more. Without knowing how long a run we have, well," she shook her head, *"that* would be suicide."

She looked at her crew. "There's only one way. We've got to go to reverse thrust and back up along the path we made when we landed." She turned to Mankowitz and Grayson. "You think you could stand it out there again?"

They nodded. "You name it."

"We'll need some extra bodies out there with you. You've got to get behind us with some flares and the intercoms and walk us back along the landing roll. And we've got to go *exactly* where those skis made their marks. Paul, I've changed my mind. I want you in the airplane. You crack that rear cargo ramp down about a foot or so. No more than that. Get a good grip back there and work that position as lookout. Art and some others will do the walking, and you keep talking to me from the ramp. You've got to direct us from there. One false move as we go back and the curtain comes down."

"Got it," Grayson said.

Mankowitz picked the three strongest men, clothed them in arctic gear, tied lifelines to them, equipped everyone with flares, and climbed from the airplane. Grayson cracked the downward loading ramp about two feet, anchored himself in place. Clouds of snow blew past him into the cavernous cargo space.

The survivors from the 747 just stared as thunder resounded all about them and the world began to shake and jostle beneath them.

Mankowitz and the others were walking slowly, the flares giving Grayson the depth perception he needed. "All right, captain, keep her moving just the way you are. That's it, nice and easy. We're doing great."

Inch by inch, foot by foot, the first hundred feet behind them, then two hundred feet, the great heaters howling warmth into the hold, the open space snatching it greedily and sucking it from the airplane.

Kate glanced at Jim Phillips, who nodded to her. "Like the man says, we're doing just great. One step at a time."

"The only way to go sometimes," she said, her lips pressed tight.

The great airplane backed its way slowly through the deep drifts.

The last gray slivers of the day slipped into darkness.

Night, a screaming wind, and a blizzard.

Kate kept her thoughts to herself. Anatoly Korkeshkin sat in Mankowitz's seat, watching her.

Kate never dared let him know of her fears. Their odds for getting out of this storm alive were lousy. They'd have one chance—brief, dangerous.

About the best you could say was that it was better than waiting to freeze to death.

34

Art Mankowitz stumbled and fell into a deep drift. His face felt frozen. He had been perspiring heavily and now he felt icy fingers within his clothes. A few more minutes and the freezing sweat would mean huge chunks of his flesh coming off later. The storm was whipping him and the others to death. They stumbled along like walking corpses. Foot by foot they kept moving, crawling their way to the point where they might have that slim chance of living through the take-off yet to come.

Within the airplane the roar of engines and the flailing scream of propellers mixed with the rush of the wind, the groan of metal, the sounds of rocking impact, the shuddering of the huge structure. It was a demonic symphony, a fitting orchestration to the madness of where they were and what they were trying to do.

Finally there was no more room. "Paul—" Art Mankowitz could barely talk. His facial muscles felt frozen to slabs. "No more. Can't move. Snow's piled up. Packed. Too tight. Now—now or never."

"Captain, that's all she wrote," Grayson called to Kate on the intercom. "Art says it's packed in behind us. Those people outside are half-dead. Hold everything where it is. I'm lowering the ramp to bring them in."

The great clamshell of the lower half of the airplane's aft fuselage went down into the snow. Wind thundered and snow slammed into the cargo hold. The Boeing survivors huddled together, bewildered and frightened. Paul Grayson half dragged in the four men.

"Coming up with the ramp now," he told the pilots. "Okay, okay, come on, you mother," he implored the ramp, grinding slowly in the savage cold. "Green light!" he shouted. "We're closed!"

"Great work, Paul. Can Art make it up here?"

"I'll bring him. He's like an icicle."

Mankowitz was half carried and half pushed up the ladder into the flight deck. Snow fell from his clothes. Ice had formed on his face from his breath. Korkeshkin moved to him, cleared away the snow and ice. Mankowitz's teeth chattered uncontrollably.

"Art—can you hang in for a while?" Kate was shocked by his appearance.

"I've been cold before," Mankowitz ground through clenched teeth. He stumbled to his seat at the flight engineer's panel. "For God's sake, Kate, get this thing off the ground or we'll be here forever."

Kate thumbed the intercom. "Paul, are you secure back there?"

"They're tied down or hanging on, captain."

"Keep it like that." She turned back to Mankowitz. "We may be too short of room out there. Our only chance is to use the rocket bottles. The skis are starting to freeze to the ground."

Art moved numbed fingers along his panel. He hit several switches. "Okay, okay," he murmured. "They're hot." A professional tone slipped back into his voice. "Confirm JATO active."

"Confirm JATO," Phillips sang out. "We have a green on the rockets," he said to Kate. "You're go."

"Stay with me on the controls."

"I'm on. Let's do it, boss lady."

She tried a quick smile. She wished she had brakes to hold them back, to let those propellers bite into the air, to give them maximum thrust before they started rolling. Not on skis, though. No way. She fed power slowly at first, then moved the throttles forward in a steady motion. The Hercules strained.

"We're freezing to the surface," Phillips said.

Kate went to full power. The airplane trembled madly. The great propellers whirled with all their energy. The shaking became wilder. They felt the skis break free, and then they were moving forward.

The Hercules bolted free, clawing frantically for

speed. Kate kept trying to get the nose ski out of the surface, where it was acting like a blunt plow that was killing their forward motion. They couldn't punch forward.

"JATO!" she snapped.

Behind her Art Mankowitz hit the master switch. Beneath the airplane, to its sides, eight powerful bottles with solid rocket fuel exploded into life with a shattering roar. Garish orange flames lighted the windwhipped snow. The airplane shot ahead. Enough power to bring that nose ski up some more, get the hell out of that morass.

They were frantic for speed. The rockets boomed through the airplane, a great roar of doomsday. Nothing was more precious now than shaping the flow of air over the wings, changing the pressure out there, creating that magic of lift.

The moment of truth arrived with shocking suddenness, dictated by the fact that the takeoff space was gone, swallowed up in the Hercules's elephantine rush through the brooding night.

She didn't know if she had enough speed. "Come on, sweetheart," she murmured, and Phillips came back on the yoke with her, and they prayed for that blazing rocket thrust to do the job for them.

There was no refined rotating upward of the nose. No smooth coordination between speed and angle of climb. They had to punch into the air, give the wings enough speed to bend air into lift that counted, go fast enough and climb fast enough to clear the ridges that were consumed in snow and darkness all around them. They were squeezing, praying, pulling. They didn't dare bank, didn't dare rob those wings of precious lift. The airspeed indicator crawled around.

They just had flying speed when they felt the sudden lurch, the loss of thrust as the rocket bottles burned out.

Mankowitz hit the jettison switches instantly to rid the airplane of weight and drag. "Confirm JATO jettison," he sang out.

Instantly Kate went forward on the yoke to hold their speed. Moments later she was coming back on the pressure again. The ridge—higher to their right. She eased into a left bank, away from the waiting killer peaks. The rocket power had been their slingshot.

If they could make that left turn . . .

They watched the compass swinging steadily. Seventy more degrees would do it. She wanted to bank steeper, to swing the turn faster. She didn't dare. Thirty degrees to go. A sudden shock turned them white. It could have been turbulence. Ten degrees . . . Kate rolled out, came back on the yoke. The wings were level, the lift stronger, they were climbing, and the invisible sky before them had no more rocks to snatch them to ultimate destruction.

"Thank God," Phillips said.

Anatoly Korkeshkin nodded.

Art Mankowitz tried to grin. The pain lanced through his face. He didn't give a damn. "I guess we lied our way out of that one," he said.

They had 240 miles to go to reach Fairbanks. Jim Phillips got out a radio call ten minutes after they were off the ground. They were high enough now for their VHF radios to reach the first station down the line. The word was flashed at once to Fairbanks.

Pandemonium swept the airport. It was snowing there, but they had an acceptable ceiling and the visibility was infinitely better than down in that finger valley.

Every crash truck and ambulance and dozens of other vehicles waited with headlights on and beacons rotating. Half the damned town was there. Standing by a helicopter, watching the lights of the Hercules easing from the sky, was Mike Carew.

C. B. Atkins stood by his side, and the two watched the airplane come to a stop by a hangar. A tug moved to tow it inside so the doors could be closed and the survivors kept warm as they were carried from the Hercules.

Mike glanced at Atkins. He had started for the hangar, but he stopped as he looked at the older man. Tears were freezing on Atkins's cheeks.

He glared as Mike grinned at him. "Well, what do you know," Mike said quietly.

"Ah, shut up," Atkins said with that gravelly rumble that was his voice. "I always said she was the best, didn't I?"

ABOUT THE AUTHOR

MARTIN CAIDIN, a prolific and versatile writer with more than eighty books to his credit, is also a commercial and military pilot, a stunt flyer, parachutist and a recognized authority in the field of aviation and astronautics. From 1950 to 1954 Martin Caidin served as nuclear warfare specialist for the state of New York. He analyzed the effects of nuclear and other weapons on potential targets in the United States. As a commercial multi-engine pilot, Mr. Caidin flies his own plane all over the country. He has flown two-engine and four-engine bombers to Europe. For a time he flew his own World War II Messerschmitt in Europe and the United States. Martin Caidin's first novel, *Marooned*, a thrilling account of a space rescue, became a major motion picture, and *Devil Take All*, *No Man's World* and *Almost Midnight* were all bought for films. *Cyborg*, published in 1972, is now the highly popular ABC-TV series "The Six Million Dollar Man." Mr. Caidin is the author of an impressive list of authoritative books on military air history. Many of them, including *Samurai!*, *Zero!* and *The Ragged, Rugged Warriors*, are considered classics in their field. Martin Caidin is a charter member of the Aviation Hall of Fame, a Fellow of the British Interplanetary Society and a founder of the American Astronautical Society. Although he and his wife, Isobel, live within sight of the launching towers at the Kennedy Space Center at Cape Canaveral, Martin Caidin is giving much of his attention these days to the problems we have fashioned for ourselves with nuclear weapons.

A Special Preview of
the exciting opening section of

~~~~~~~~~~~~~~~~~~~~~~~~~~~~~~~~

Aquarius
Mission

by
Martin Caidin

~~~~~~~~~~~~~~~~~~~~~~~~~~~~~~~~

author of
WINGBORN

Copyright © 1978 by Martin Caidin

4

~~~~~~~~~~

The pilot kept his toes on the brakes, a ridiculously puny action in comparison with the effect his gentle toe pressure had on the shaped metal pads. Just that slight nudge, boosted by electrical and hydraulic systems, was enough to keep the C-14 cargo transport locked solidly to concrete as the copilot spooled up the great engines. Seven hundred tons of airplane vibrated and trembled, the enormous swept wings flexing as power strained to break free. Behind the two men in the cockpit high above the ground, the flight engineer satisfied himself with the readings of multiple rows of gauges. He nodded and spoke into his lip mike.

"It's time to fly, boss. She's all in the green."

The pilot's nod was barely perceptible, but he rotated his feet to remove the pressure against the brake pedals, dropping his heels to the metal floorboard. With the groan of an imprisoned dinosaur shaking free from confinement, the huge machine accelerated. It seemed too big to move fast enough to fly, but the engines hurled back screaming air and sped the giant faster and faster down the long runway. The flight crew worked quietly, expertly, gnats riding in the brain cavity of a winged mammoth. The copilot called out the critical numbers: the point beyond which they could no longer stop on the runway remaining; the next point at which they reached safe speed should an engine fail; and the final quiet word, as much a command as if someone had screamed *Fire!*

"Rotate," the copilot said calmly, and the yoke in the pilot's hand came back steadily until the nose of the giant was lifted precisely seven degrees above the horizon. For suspended seconds the great airplane continued, riding its main gear only, the changed angle of the wings modifying the flow over the upper surfaces until the lift generated by the airfoil exceeded the weight of the aircraft. Tugged by forces invisible to the eye yet unchanged from the moment when the Wright brothers lurched into the air ninety-six years before, the great birdlike monster lifted magically away from the hard concrete. With every passing instant, lift increased and thrust increased, and what had been a shaped mountain of inert metal only moments before was now a winged wonder slicing upward into the lower stratosphere.

The miracle of what took place was an everyday occurrence to these men, and the flight crew went through the motions of hands and eyes and ears and minds with practiced skill, with as much reflexive action as conscious attention. As the C-14 thundered into thinner and less resistant air, Lieutenant Colonel John Hughes in the pilot's seat studied the computer autopilot system, tapped in numbers that had been determined well before he left the flight operations office, and turned control of the plane over to the black boxes that were buried in the machine's nose section. The computer, working with accelerometers and other gyroscopic and inertial systems, would now fly the aircraft with robotic precision; the crew was content to sit back and drink coffee in their pressurized windowed world, keeping alert for any malfunctions that might arise. The robots that guided them, although aspiring to great electronic heights, were still subject to glitches that tweaked the aircraft's movement. At subsonic speeds, even a small tweak can produce an instant and gut-clenching pucker factor, but at the moment, tranquillity and performance matched, so the crew could relax.

However, their cargo made them uncomfortable, caused some physical squirming and also some mental gymnastics. Hughes sipped his coffee and glanced at his copilot. Major William Bagwell nodded. The question had been with both of them from the very moment they entered their airplane and saw their Q-Secret cargo.

"I've heard of them all, but this one is a record."

Hughes held his cup gingerly for a moment during a gentle roll through mild turbulence. "Well—there's a first time for everything."

Their flight engineer leaned forward. "Sure, sure, but who'd believe a submarine in this thing at fifty thousand feet?"

Hughes turned in his seat, looked back through the open hatchway into the cavernous hold. "To hell with the tin can—you people get a close look at the bunch *with* that underwater lizzie?"

Bagwell shuddered. He was a wiry, intense man who'd been in the thick of nuclear hell only five years before. "Jesus, yes," he said after a long pause, "they're killers. Every one of them."

He was right. They were killers, and they looked up, a hundred feet distant, and stared unblinking at the flight crew studying them through the small hatchway. They sat or stood around the long slim submarine that was chained and cabled securely to the cargo deck of the C-14. Twelve men. Four of them crew of that sinister *Swimmer IV* killer sub, and eight security guards, every one of them holding rapid-fire submachine guns. Which the pilots of the C-14 knew, because they had been told, were loaded and ready to fire.

Their orders had been blunt. Take your cargo to your appointed airport. Don't try to get near the sub. Don't ask any questions of the naval personnel aboard. Mind your business. Fly your airplane, and then leave, and mention to no one what you've carried.

Bagwell heard a chime and studied the gauges. "Fifty thousand," he said quietly, a human confirmation of computer-controlled flight. "We're on our way."

Hughes nodded, not speaking. The feeling in the small of his back, the sight of those hand-held machine guns, all of it unnerved him. All he wanted to do was to get that bunch the hell out of his airplane. The computer blinked its digital message; they had a tail wind. Hughes was grateful for the small favor. The flight would go that much quicker.

Secretary of the Navy Frank Cartwright leaned back in his leather chair in New Washington—sixty miles straight-line distance from the radioactive rubble that had once been the nation's capital—studying the videophone display on his desk. His office was situated four hundred feet beneath the earth's surface, and the space in between was filled with thick percentages of steel and reinforced concrete and permeated throughout with all manner of sensors and detectors and filters and traps. Despite the weight overhead, Cartwright felt no oppressiveness, and claustrophobia was not counted among his problems. He gave his unique positioning only a fleeting thought as he concentrated on the face and voice that came to him through the electronics equipment on his desk.

On his screen, Cartwright saw the man whose title was Commander, Pacific Ocean. Vice Admiral Timothy Haig was an old friend, and his face showed the need for this direct contact that had been initiated by a call with a coded scrambler priority. They exchanged personal amenities, and then Cartwright, never one to waste time with so few years remaining in his life, went straight to the issue of the call.

"That's an incredible report from Chadwick," he said, opening easily.

In Pearl Harbor, above the surface, Tim Haig nodded, enjoying a breeze gliding through his office. He didn't answer at once, still studying Cartwright's features on his own screen. The navy secretary had been wounded grievously in at least two wars, and the cumulative effects of his personal agonies were stamped on his scarred features. Frank Cartwright in his prime had been a muscular hulk of a man; he still carried his great frame, but now he was like an old and wounded buffalo, moving stiffly and with effort but with all the commanding presence he had known in younger days.

"Yes, sir, it is," Haig said after the pause. "So incredible we can't discount it, as much as I'd like to dismiss the entire affair as so much nonsense."

"I take it you've equated your judgment with action."

Timothy Haig almost laughed at the other man's words. "Yes, sir, I have. I dispatched *Swimmer IV* by air to Amchitka. They'll be in the water about twelve hours from now. Their orders are to duplicate as much as possible Chadwick's mission profile, to try to instigate whatever happened to Chadwick."

"After that point, Tim?"

"They're to keep right on going, sir. All the way to the bottom."

"I've read the full report, Tim." Cartwright paused for only a moment, weighing his words, keeping it taut. "Do you really believe the Chinese are involved?"

He watched Haig roll an unlit cigar from one side of his mouth to the other. Cartwright detected a shrug that meant "no commitment."

"Sir, their boat was attacked," Haig replied carefully. "I don't know by what or how, really, but there's no way to ignore the event itself."

"Of course not," Cartwright said with a nod. "Sending out the boat was the only thing to do."

"Thank you, sir."

Cartwright leaned forward, an instinctive move bringing him closer to the videophone, as if this might lessen the physical distance between himself and Haig. "Tim, your feelings are important here. Disassociate yourself from your office. I'd like to know your gut reactions. Can you give me any further evaluation of Chadwick's report on the whales?"

Haig shook his head, his expression unhappy. "I wish I could, Frank. But we lack data—and what we do have is, well, it's self-contradictory. Too much conflict involved. We've never known sperms to dive to six thousand feet, and moving in a herd simply is not the same as moving in formation. If I want to be hard-nosed about it, and I have to, then all I *know* is that the minisub was attacked by what Chadwick insists were sperm whales, moving in concert, using audible signals of aggressiveness or attack, and deliberately ramming the boat with Chadwick and Templeton in it. I can't go beyond that. Too many ands, ifs, or buts are involved."

There was nothing else to say, really. Haig had it all in hand. Cartwright was unhappy about their inability to pin down any leads that might involve the Chinese, but precious little could be done about that at this time. "All right, Tim," he said to wrap it up, "keep me informed."

"Yes, sir. If it turns out to be the Chinese instead of the whales—"

"Of course," Cartwright said quickly. "No matter what time of day or night, or where I am. Break in."

"Yes, sir." Haig watched the screen dissolve into the random pattern of the disassociating scrambler code.

The great transport sliced through a thin cirrus cloud deck, the shrill whine of the jet engines at reduced power sounding unusually loud within the aircraft. Clouds flashed by in eye-blinking wisps as the plane descended, and the earth's surface showed through in momentary glimpses. They rocked gently in turbulence and suddenly the world above became the long flat bottom of the cloud deck, creating the impression of an enormous amphitheater below. Water, stretches of islands, mixed sunlight and shadow, and a subdued exclamation, an intake of breath, from Major Bagwell in the copilot seat.

"Jesus Almighty—"

They looked down through the cockpit glass at what had been an island, part of a chain, on which there had once been a large city and a military reservation. *Had* been. Now it was nothing more than a huge crater. Just a large island made up of a high-rimmed creater that contained radioactive glass.

"No one survived that," the navigator said quietly.

"What the hell was there to survive?" Bagwell demanded. "It wasn't even an accurate strike. The goddamned warhead came out of a missile that went wild, and—"

Hughes didn't like the conversation—or the mood it created. The triple-damned war was far behind them, and he preferred to keep it that way. "Get your heads back in the cockpit," the pilot told his men with just enough sharpness to bring them around. "Amchitka's coming up."

Several moments later Bagwell turned to him. He'd been talking with the people on the ground. "We're locked in and number one to land. Straight-in approach."

"Good," Hughes said. "Let's get to work. Start the checklist."

They went in by the numbers, steadily descending toward the expanding concrete ribbon, flaps coming down, gear extending, leading-edge flaps boosting lift, spoilers playing gently out on the wings; they drilled her back to earth as though she were filled with helium, nice and easy and gentle. When they were on the ground they discovered that they were intruders on a naval facility and the navy was running the show. Vehicles with turreted 20-mm cannon rode on either side of them, another was behind, and the familiar Follow Me truck carried a rapid-fire cannon aimed unerringly at their cockpit. Ground control taxied them to a parking site by a dock ramp, and a voice came over their headsets.

"Thank you, gentlemen. Keep your engines running and all your crew at stations. If you'll open those nose hatch we'll unload, and you can be on your way."

They looked at one another and shrugged. Their orders had been explicit. Do *exactly* as they were instructed by Amchitka Control. The nose latches were freed, the great nose cone lifted up and away. They felt the airplane shaking as the submarine and its protective crew vacated the cargo hold.

By the time they were ordered to close the loading hatchway and they could see ahead of them once more, the ramp was deserted—submarine and all.

"It stinks," Captain Sam Duncan, USN, muttered to himself. "It stinks all the way." He stood on the

bridge of his catamaran and watched the submarine
—he knew it was a submarine because his crew had
told him so; you couldn't see anything beneath that
canvas covering—being winched to the grapples between his knife-edged hulls. He didn't like the se-
crecy—not because of the security, but because *he*
was the captain of this vessel, and he didn't know
what the hell was going on or who was coming
aboard. He watched a security crew, armed to the
teeth, surrounding four men in strange dark clothing and woolen skullcaps. Definitely not uniforms.
Once their sub was secured between the cat hulls,
the security team moved back and set up a heavy-
fire cordon so that no one else could approach the
catamaran. Sam Duncan didn't like that either.

He studied the four men who obviously made up
the crew of the long boat that was hugging the
catamaran. Three white, one black, all tough, confident, almost contemptuous of everyone around
them. They wore name tags on their chests, and
he'd already learned their names, as if that told him
anything. He had the curious idea that the names
might not even be real. The one named Ritter
seemed to be the leader, or commanding officer, but
Duncan didn't know that for a fact because they
wore no other insignia or markings. The other two
whites were Tobias and Young, and the black was
Sanford. He confirmed Ritter as the leader when
his communication came alive.

"A Mr. Ritter to see the captain," his exec told
him.

Duncan's eyes narrowed. *Mr.* Ritter?

Several moments later they faced one another,
and Duncan was as much put out as before. Ritter
was a tough no-nonsense man who spoke in
phrases as tightly clipped as his dark beard. He
saluted Duncan, who returned the salute in an off-
handed manner that betrayed his bristliness.

Duncan watched for some clue, anything that might break this strange fog of anonymity. Ritter forced the issue by standing in silence.

"I hope you can tell me what this is all about," Duncan said finally.

The man before him betrayed no expression, showed no discourtesy, but remained beyond his reach. He slipped a folded envelope from a back pants pocket, unfolded it, and presented it to Duncan.

"Your orders, sir," he said.

Duncan held the sealed envelope in one hand and tapped it on his other palm. His eyes narrowed. "That's it? Just this envelope?"

Ritter's face remained a mask. Steel-polite, Duncan would have called it. "My orders were to come aboard this vessel and personally hand you this envelope," Ritter told him.

Duncan showed a flush of anger that he tried immediately to repress. "What's your rank, Ritter? You're no 'mister.' "

"Sir, it's all in that envelope." A split-second hesitation, a decision that was made on the spot: "Captain, I suggest we go to your cabin and you read what's in that envelope."

Duncan's eyes went wide. "You suggest that I—"

The steel was out in the open now. "Sir."

Duncan paused at Ritter's word.

Ritter went on. "I could make it an order."

Duncan swallowed it. He knew when to quit. "Come with me," he said, and he walked off. Ritter followed, still expressionless.

They were well at sea, the catamaran prows slicing like knife blades through the water, moving under full speed toward that specific but unmarked site in the ocean where Chadwick and Templeton had been lowered into the depths. Ritter stood slightly behind and to the side of Duncan as both men watched the swiftly darkening sky. Duncan's air was proper but stiff—that of a man who'd been upstaged in a manner he couldn't yet understand. Ritter's voice came to him quietly.

"How much longer?"

Duncan didn't turn. "I estimate zero two hundred."

"Good. We'll have a low moon."

They stood together in silence, and then Ritter left to meet with his crew. When he returned to the bridge, the cat was hove to, rocking gently on a sea that was unusually calm for the Aleutians. The moonlight seemed to cast a baleful glow across the ocean surface. Between the twin hulls, men were working with the submarine. An officer came to the bridge and spoke to Duncan. Curiosity had replaced the captain's pique. He hoped Ritter would let him know something about what was going on.

"Your men report that they're ready," Duncan told Ritter.

"Thank you." That was all he got as Ritter left the bridge to go below.

Duncan followed, leaving his exec in command on the bridge. He watched the men enter the narrow hatchway into the *Swimmer IV*. Tobias was the last in, and his swarthy face broke into a grin as he turned and tossed a salute to the catamaran crew. The hatch clanged shut behind him.

At a signal from the deck officer, the crew winched the sub into the sea, water swirling easily over its rounded flanks. The winches continued releasing cable for another minute, then the cables went slack. Duncan stared at nothingness. They were gone.

Ritter looked up through his port at the shimmering moonlight. The catamaran hulls were distorted pylons seen through moonstruck water, and the sight faded slowly as they fell. Ritter brought in the power gently, feeling her out as he always did when initiating a dive, and the four men went through their drill with practiced, soft-spoken competence. A powerful thrumming grew from far behind them in the bowels of the sub, the shrouded hydrojets increasing their thrust as the throttle beneath Ritter's hand moved forward. The dive angle steepened. The beginning of the dive followed the track of Chadwick and Templeton in their minisub, but this time the scenario played to a different act. *Swimmer IV* had fangs.

Ritter went through the litany they all knew so well. "Commence combat alert. Confirm."

Tobias's voice came back at once, a gentle chanting sound. "Propulsion, electrical grid, all maneuvering thrusters status red."

"Sonar, masers, communications, navigation, autocomputer standby, everything's green." That from Young.

Sanford's voice had the hint of a chuckle. It always did, thought Ritter as he heard the black man join them. "We're hot with fire in the belly, Ritter Baby." It was the sound of a man who had a light but lethal touch, a swift-finger deftness with weaponry.

They went down steadily, four men in two rows of tandem seats, Ritter left front, Tobias to his right, Young behind Ritter, and Sanford, with more space and a wider control panel than the others behind Tobias. They were all in their late twenties and early thirties, tough and trim, combat veterans of a war short-lived, but not that many years back, that had left its impression indelibly in their psyches. Sanford's fingers played lightly across his weapons console like a musician fingering an organ.

"Search torps are in the gate," he said quietly. "Seek-and-destroy fish are stage-three arm."

Sanford grinned as Ritter turned to look at him. "It might be interesting, you know," Sanford said.

"Finding some of those Chinese whales. Know what I mean?"

"Chinese whales." Ritter let the words hang for a moment, glanced at the other men. "Any of you troops believe the sperms really go down six thousand feet?"

"That's a thousand fathoms of fairy tales," Sanford chuckled.

"Made in Peking," added Tobias.

Young hesitated. "I wouldn't be so sure. Old man Chadwick is tops in his business. He doesn't make mistakes."

Sanford's laugh was almost velvety. "He's a civilian. Loves peace above all else. Logic, reality, rationale—none of it counts. Peace at any cost—even if the price is smearing what life is all about. He thinks the world is so flat everything's laid out like the dinner table." The laugh came again and his fingers brushed the deadly keys and buttons beneath his hands. "Man or beast," he added, "it don't matter to what we got."

Ritter's gaze took them all in, one by one, an unblinking meeting of eyes. "I don't want anyone going off half-cocked. This job is more than going downstairs to beat the pulp out of something—whatever that something may be." They laughed lightly at his own hesitant admission. "No matter what any of us thinks here and now, we're guessing. Got it? Just guessing. Chadwick and his assistant may be civilians—sucking lollipops for all we know —but they're good at their job and they were here. So we play it cool, we give out our invitation by our presence, and we try to find out what it was that beat that little sub about the head and shoulders. And we bring the story home. All of you understand me?"

He paused and leveled his gaze at Sanford. "And you, Killer, keep off the trigger-happy crap."

Sanford showed a white smile, then screwed up

his face in mock insult. "Team, we got us a nervous turkey for boss-man tonight."

Tobias was ignoring the exchange. Ritter's tone, and his demeanor, had told Tobias something. He turned to the lead man. "You know something we don't, skipper?"

Ritter nodded. "Uh huh. Before we left, after I had my little conversation with the admiral, I went down to S2 and spent some time with friends."

"It pays to have friends in Intelligence," noted Young.

"And?" Tobias pressed.

"There's not a trace of any Chinese boats working the Aleutian Trench," Ritter told them.

Young shrugged. "So maybe they're Russian."

"And maybe," Ritter threw back at him, "Chadwick really knew what he was talking about."

Sanford was openly scornful. "Come off it, man. You're starting with those whales again like—"

A pinging chime interrupted him. Silence clamped a hold on the tight cabin. Silence, except for the background hum of machinery they had long before ignored, broken only by the chime and the increasingly louder pinging sounds. Young bent intently over his scanning displays. He didn't bother to look up.

"Targets bearing two six zero. Range eight hundred yards and they're closing fast."

While investigating the mysterious disappearance of two nuclear submarines, the U.S.S. Sea Trench discovers a vast uncharted land and civilization. Now read the complete Bantam Book, available wherever paperbacks are sold.

RELAX!
SIT DOWN
and Catch Up On Your Reading!

☐	11877	**HOLOCAUST** by Gerald Green	$2.25
☐	12836	**THE CHANCELLOR MANUSCRIPT**	$2.75
		by Robert Ludlum	
☐	10077	**TRINITY** by Leon Uris	$2.75
☐	2300	**THE MONEYCHANGERS** by Arthur Hailey	$1.95
☐	12550	**THE MEDITERRANEAN CAPER**	$2.25
		by Clive Cussler	
☐	11469	**AN EXCHANGE OF EAGLES** by Owen Sela	$2.25
☐	2600	**RAGTIME** by E. L. Doctorow	$2.25
☐	11428	**FAIRYTALES** by Cynthia Freeman	$2.25
☐	11966	**THE ODESSA FILE** by Frederick Forsyth	$2.25
☐	11557	**BLOOD RED ROSES** by Elizabeth B. Coker	$2.25
☐	11708	**JAWS 2** by Hank Searls	$2.25
☐	12490	**TINKER, TAILOR, SOLDIER, SPY**	$2.50
		by John Le Carre	
☐	11929	**THE DOGS OF WAR** by Frederick Forsyth	$2.25
☐	10526	**INDIA ALLEN** by Elizabeth B. Coker	$1.95
☐	12489	**THE HARRAD EXPERIMENT**	$2.25
		by Robert Rimmer	
☐	11767	**IMPERIAL 109** by Richard Doyle	$2.50
☐	10500	**DOLORES** by Jacqueline Susann	$1.95
☐	11601	**THE LOVE MACHINE** by Jacqueline Susann	$2.25
☐	11886	**PROFESSOR OF DESIRE** by Philip Roth	$2.50
☐	12433	**THE DAY OF THE JACKAL**	$2.50
		by Frederick Forsyth	
☐	11952	**DRAGONARD** by Rupert Gilchrist	$1.95
☐	11331	**THE HAIGERLOCH PROJECT** by Ib Melchior	$2.25
☐	11330	**THE BEGGARS ARE COMING** by Mary Loos	$1.95

Buy them at your local bookstore or use this handy coupon for ordering:

Bantam Books, Inc., Dept. FBB, 414 East Golf Road, Des Plaines, Ill. 60016

Please send me the books I have checked above. I am enclosing $_____
(please add 75¢ to cover postage and handling). Send check or money order
—no cash or C.O.D.'s please.

Mr/Mrs/Miss _____

Address _____

City _____ State/Zip _____

FBB—2/79
Please allow four weeks for delivery. This offer expires 8/79.

MS READ-a-thon— a simple way to start youngsters reading.

Boys and girls between 6 and 14 can join the MS READ-a-thon and help find a cure for Multiple Sclerosis by reading books. And they get two rewards — the enjoyment of reading, and the great feeling that comes from helping others.

Parents and educators: For complete information call your local MS chapter, or call toll-free (800) 243-6000. Or mail the coupon below.

Kids can help, too!

Mail to:
National Multiple Sclerosis Society
205 East 42nd Street
New York, N.Y. 10017

I would like more information about the MS READ-a-thon and how it can work in my area.

MS
Mystery Sleuth

Name_____
(please print)
Address_____
City_____ State_____ Zip_____
Organization_____

BA—10/77